Travel beyond the limits of our world and enter a realm of dreams.

Year's
Best
Fantasy
5

Edited by David G. Hartwell

Edited by David G. Hartwell & Kathryn Cramer

YEAR'S BEST FANTASY

5

EDITED BY DAVID G. HARTWELL
AND KATHRYN CRAMER

An Imprint of HarperCollinsPublishers

To Carl Caputo,
for last-minute help and good cheer,
and to Elizabeth Constance Cramer Hartwell,
in the hope that you will sleep better.

Additional copyright information begins on p. 501.

EOS
An Imprint of HarperCollins*Publishers*
10 East 53rd Street
New York, New York 10022-5299

Copyright © 2005 by David G. Hartwell and Kathryn Cramer
ISBN: 0-06-077605-6
www.eosbooks.com

First Eos paperback printing: July 2005

HarperCollins® and Eos® are trademarks of HarperCollins Publishers Inc.

Printed in the U. S. A.

10 9 8 7 6 5 4 3 2 1

Contents

Introduction

〜〜〜〜〜

If we consider the fantastic in literature as a geographic section of the world of literature, it is about the size of North America, very large and diverse, and with widespread influence. And included in that geography is the fantasy genre (about the size of French Canada), where things are done a bit differently, language used a bit differently, and large amounts of territory are not yet inhabited, though it has a long history and intimate connections to the larger geography and history of the continent and the world. The whole world can honor and respect prominent citizens of the genre territory, but generally ignores the rest, and doesn't include much of their news on the News unless there is a notable death or grand disaster there. Yet if you visit, you will find a flourishing culture, grand cities, and beautiful landscapes.

We found that the good fantasy short fiction this year is notably international. Although all of the writers in this book write in English, some of them live and work outside the United States—in Canada, Australia, the British Isles. Australia is still full of genre energy, as evidenced by the founding of a new Clarion workshop in Brisbane in 2004, and Australian fantasy novelists are continuing to break out worldwide, at least in the English language. Canadian SF is still thriving, and Canada is still introducing world-class fantasy writers to the world stage each year. *The Third Alternative* has grown into one of the leading fantasy magazines, and this year purchased *Interzone*, which will henceforth publish mostly SF. *Realms of Fantasy* and *F&SF* are its peers.

So welcome to the fifth volume of the *Year's Best Fantasy*, representing the best of 2004. Like the earlier volumes in this series, this book provides some insight into the fantasy field now—who is writing some of the best short fiction published as fantasy, and where. But it is fundamentally a collection of excellent stories for your reading pleasure. We follow one general principle for selection: this book is full of fantasy—every story in the book is clearly that and not primarily something else. We (Kathryn Cramer and David G. Hartwell) edit the *Year's Best Science Fiction* in paperback from Eos as a companion volume to this one—look for it if you enjoy short science fiction too.

The year 2004 was notable for magazines, both large and small. The SF and fantasy magazines that were widely distributed are *Analog, Asimov's, F&SF,* and *Realms of Fantasy.* And the electronic publishers kept publishing, sometimes fiction of high quality, though none of them made money at it. We are grateful for the hard work and editorial acumen of the better electronic fiction sites, such as SciFiction, Strange Horizons, and Infinite Matrix, and hope they survive.

The very small press zines, strongly reminiscent of the fine literary little magazines of the 1970s, and led in this fantasy generation by Gavin Grant and Kelly Link's *Lady Churchill's Rosebud Wristlet,* have been a growing force for several years, and this year were particularly prominent. Excellent zines include *Say . . . , Flytrap, Electric Velocipede,* and *Full Unit Hookup,* but there are many others. We have a strong short fiction field today because the genre small presses and semiprofessional magazines (such as *Alchemy, Talebones, Weird Tales,* and *Orb*) are printing and circulating a majority of the high-quality short stories published in fantasy, science fiction, and horror.

In early 2005, as we write, professional fantasy and science fiction publishing as we have always known it is still concentrated in ten mass market and hardcover publishing lines (Ace, Bantam, Baen, DAW, Del Rey, Eos, Pocket, which distributes Ibooks, Roc, Tor, and Warner), and those lines are publishing fewer titles in paperback. But they do publish a significant number of hardcovers and trade paperbacks, and all the established name writers, at least, appear in hardcover first. The Print-on-Demand field is beginning to sort itself out, and Wildside Press (and its many imprints, such as Prime) is clearly the umbrella for many of the better publications, including original novels and story collections.

The small press has been since the 1980s a force of growing strength and importance in the field, in part due to the availability of computers within reach of the average fannish budget and in part due to the new economies of instant print, now prevalent in the U.S. A perceptible increase in the number and quality of small press publications helped to create the impression that the fantasy fiction field is growing.

And in 2004 the small press was the most significant publisher of anthologies, though the two best original anthologies of fantasy—*The Faery Reel*, edited by Ellen Datlow and Terry Windling, and *Flights*, edited by Al Sarrantonio—came from big publishers. Those two, and a slew of ok books originating from the tekno-books packaging operation by various editors and publishers, accounted for a majority of the production of the trade publishers. The small press, however, originated dozens of good anthologies—for example, *McSweeney's Astonishing Tales*, edited by Michael Chabon, and *All Star Zeppelin Stories*, edited by Jay Lake and David Moles.

The continuing small press trend, evident in, for instance, *Polyphony #4*, edited by Deborah Layne, and *Leviathan 4*, edited by Jeff VanderMeer, among others, was toward nongenre, or genre-bending, or slipstream fantastic fiction. This is not a commercial trend, but a literary one. And it is an ironic counterpart to the trend evident in *McSweeney's*, of established literary writers breaking into genre. The economics are indistinguishable (the pay is low). There are a lot of promising signs, though, and talented new writers in unexpected places. Now that we have finished our fifth annual volume, we remain confident of the quality of future books. Now we invite you to visit the flourishing culture, grand cities, and beautiful landscapes in *Year's Best Fantasy 5*.

David G. Hartwell & Kathryn E. Cramer
Pleasantville, NY

The Dragons of Summer Gulch

~~~~~~~~~~

Robert Reed

Robert Reed (tribute site: www.starbaseandromeda.com/ reed.html) lives in Lincoln, Nebraska, where he turns out story after high-quality story, seeming inexhaustible. His first collection was The Dragons of Springplace *(1999); a new collection,* The Cuckoo's Boys, *is out in 2005. He has published a steady stream of novels since 1987, the most recent of which is* Sister Alice *(2003), and his new book in 2005 is* The Well of Stars, *a sequel to his most famous novel,* Marrow *(2000). This year he appears in both our* Year's Best Fantasy *and our* Year's Best SF *volumes, and he had several stories in consideration for each. There is substantial evidence for calling him one of the five or six best writers of fantasy short fiction today.*

"The Dragons of Summer Gulch" appeared in SciFiction (and so this is its first appearance in print). Here Reed explores the gray area between myth and science. It is set in a plausible land that might be many places—the American West, Australian aboriginal lands, China, giving an impression of once-mighty peoples now past decadence and hungry for better times. He begins with an intriguing premise: remains of ancient dragons can be found buried in the ground. There is treasure there with them. But more importantly to the characters, some of the buried dragons have viable eggs.

I

A hard winter can lift rocks as well as old bones, shoving all that is loose up through the most stubborn earth. Then snowmelt and flash floods will sweep across the ground, wiping away the gravel and clay. And later, when a man with good vision and exceptional luck rides past, all of the world might suddenly change.

"Would you look at that," the man said to himself in a firm, deep voice. "A claw, isn't it? From a mature dragon, isn't it? Good Lord, Mr. Barrow. And there's two more claws set beside that treasure!"

Barrow was a giant fellow with a narrow face and a heavy cap of black hair that grew from his scalp and the back of his neck and between the blades of his strong shoulders. Born on one of the Northern Isles, he had left his homeland as a young man to escape one war, coming to this new country just in time to be thrown into a massive and prolonged civil conflict. Ten thousand miseries had abused him over the next years. But he survived the fighting, and upon his discharge from the Army of the Center, a grateful nation had given him both his citizenship and a bonus of gold coins. Barrow purchased a one-way ticket on the Western railroad, aiming to find his fortune in the wilderness. His journey ended in one of the new prairie towns—a place famous for hyrax herds and dragon bones. There he had purchased a pair of quality camels, ample supplies for six months of solitude, and with shovels enough to move a hillside, he had set out into the washlands.

Sliding off the lead camel, he said, "Hold."

The beast gave a low snort, adjusting its hooves to find the most comfortable pose.

Barrow knelt, carefully touching the dragon's middle

2

claw. Ancient as this artifact was, he knew from painful experience that even the most weathered claw was sharp enough to slash. Just as the fossil teeth could puncture the thickest leather gloves, and the edges of the great scales were nastier than any saw blade sharpened on the hardest whetstone.

The claw was a vivid deep purple color—a sure sign of good preservation. With his favorite little pick, Barrow worked loose the mudstone beneath it, exposing its full length and the place where it joined into the front paw. He wasn't an educated man, but Barrow knew his trade: this had been a flying dragon, one of the monsters who once patrolled the skies above a vanished seacoast. The giant paw was meant for gripping. Presumably the dragons used their four feet much as a coon-rascal does, holding their prey and for other simple manipulations. These finger claws were always valuable, but the thick thumb claw—the Claw of God—would be worth even more to buyers. As night fell, Barrow dug by the smoky light of a little fire, picking away at the mudstone until the paw was revealed—a palm-down hand large enough to stand upon and, after ages of being entombed, still displaying the dull red color made by the interlocking scales.

The man didn't sleep ten blinks. Then with first light he followed a hunch, walking half a dozen long strides up the gully and thrusting a shovel into what looked like a mound of ordinary clay.

The shovel was good steel, but a dull *thunk* announced that something beneath was harder by a long ways.

Barrow used the shovel and a big pickax, working fast and sloppy, investing the morning to uncover a long piece of the dragon's back—several daggerlike spines rising from perhaps thirty big plates of ruddy armor.

Exhaustion forced him to take a break, eating his fill and drinking the last of his water. Then, because they were hungry and a little thirsty, he led both of his loyal camels down the gully, finding a flat plain where sagebrush grew and seepage too foul for a man to drink stood in a shallow alkaline pond.

The happy camels drank and grazed, wandering as far as their long leashes allowed.

Barrow returned to his treasure. Twice he dug into fresh ground, and twice he guessed wrong, finding nothing. The monster's head was almost surely missing. Heads almost always were. But he tried a third time, and his luck held. Not only was the skull entombed along with the rest of the carcass, it was still attached to the body, the long muscular neck having twisted hard to the left as the creature passed from the living.

It had been a quick death, he was certain.

There were larger specimens, but the head was magnificent. What Barrow could see was as long as he was tall, narrow and elegant, a little reminiscent of a pelican's head, but prettier, the giant mouth bristling with a forest of teeth, each tooth bigger than his thumb. The giant dragon eyes had vanished, but the large sockets remained, filled with mudstone and aimed forward like a hawk's eyes. And behind the eyes lay a braincase several times bigger than any man's.

"How did you die?" he asked his new friend.

Back in town, an educated fellow had explained to Barrow what science knew today and what it was guessing. Sometimes the dragons had been buried in mud, on land or underwater, and the mud protected the corpse from its hungry cousins and gnawing rats. If there were no oxygen, then there couldn't be any rot. And that was the best of circumstances. Without rot, and buried inside a stable deep grave, an entire dragon could be kept intact, waiting for the blessed man to ride by on his happy camel.

Barrow was thirsty enough to moan, but he couldn't afford to stop now.

Following the advice of other prospectors, he found the base of the dragon's twin wings—the wings still sporting the leathery flesh strung between the long, long finger bones—and he fashioned a charge with dynamite, setting it against the armored plates of the back and covering his work with a pile of tamped earth to help force the blast downward. Then, with a long fuse, he set off the charge.

There was a dull thud followed by a steady rain of dirt and pulverized stone, and he ran to look at what he had accomplished, pulling back the shattered plates—each worth half a good camel when intact—and then using a heavy pick to pull free the shattered insides of the great beast.

If another dragon had made this corpse, attacking this treasure from below, there would be nothing left to find. Many millions of years ago, the precious guts would have been eaten, and lost.

"But still," Barrow told himself. "These claws and scales are enough to pay for my year. If it comes to that."

But it didn't have to come to that.

Inside the fossil lay the reason for all of his suffering and boredom: behind the stone-infected heart was an intricate organ as long as he was tall—a spongelike thing set above the peculiar dragon lungs. The organ was composed of gold and lustrous platinum wrapped around countless voids. In an instant, Barrow had become as wealthy as his dreams had promised he would be. He let out an enormous yell, dancing back and forth across the back of the dead dragon. Then he collapsed beside his treasure, crying out of joy, and when he wiped back the tears one final time, he saw something else.

Eons ago, a fine black mud had infiltrated the dead body, filling the cavities while keeping away the free oxygen.

Without oxygen, there was almost no decay.

Floating in the old mudstone were at least three round bodies, each as large as the largest naval cannon balls. They were not organs, but they belonged inside the dragon. Barrow had heard stories about such things, and the educated man in town had even shown him a shard of something similar. But where the shard was dirty gray, these three balls were white as bone. That was their color in life, he realized, and this was their color now.

With a trembling hand, Barrow touched the nearest egg, and he held his palm against it for a very long while, leaving it a little bit warm.

∼ II

At one point, the whore asked, "Where did you learn all this crap?"

Manmark laughed quietly for a moment. Then he closed the big book and said, "My credentials. Is that what you wish to have?"

"After your money, sure. Your credentials. Yes."

"As a boy, I had tutors. As a young man, I attended several universities. I studied all the sciences and enjoyed the brilliance of a dozen great minds. And then my father died, and I took my inheritance, deciding to apply my wealth and genius in the pursuit of great things."

She was the prettiest woman of her sort in this town, and she was not stupid. Manmark could tell just by staring at her eyes that she had a good, strong mind. But she was just an aboriginal girl, tiny like all of the members of her race, sold by her father for opium or liquor. Her history had to be impoverished and painful. Which was why it didn't bother him too much when she laughed at him, remarking, "With most men, listening is easier than screwing. But with you, I think it's the other way around."

Manmark opened the book again, ignoring any implied insult.

Quietly, he asked the woman, "Can you read?"

"I know which coin is which," she replied. "And my name, when I see it. If it's written out with a simple hand."

"Look at this picture," he told her. "What does it show you?"

"A dragon," she said matter-of-factly.

"Which species of dragon?" Manmark pressed.

She looked at the drawing, blowing air into her cheeks. Then she exhaled, admitting, "I don't know. Is it the flying kind?"

"Hardly."

"Yeah, I guess it isn't. I don't see wings."

He nodded, explaining, "This is a small early dragon. One of the six-legged precursor species, as it happens. It was unearthed on this continent, resting inside some of the oldest rocks from the Age of Dragons." Manmark was a handsome fellow with dreamy golden eyes that stared off into one of the walls of the room. "If you believe in natural selection and in the great depths of time," he continued, "then this might well be the ancestor to the hundred species that we know about, and the thousands we have yet to uncover."

She said, "Huh," and sat back against the piled-up pillows. "Can I look at the book?" she asked.

"Carefully," he warned, as if speaking to a moody child. "I don't have another copy with me, and it is the best available guide—"

"Just hand it over," she interrupted. "I promise. I won't be rough."

Slowly, and then quickly, the woman flipped through the pages. Meanwhile her client continued to speak about things she could never understand: on this very land, there once stood dragons the size of great buildings—placid and heavily armored vegetarians that consumed entire trees, judging by the fossilized meals discovered in their cavernous bellies. Plus there had been smaller beasts roaming in sprawling herds, much as the black hyraxes grazed on the High Plains. The predatory dragons came in two basic types—the quadrupeds with their saber teeth and the Claws of God on their mighty hands; and later, the winged giants with the same teeth and Claws but also grasping limbs and a brain that might well have been equal to a woman's.

If the girl noticed his insult, she knew better than show it, her face down and nodding while the pages turned. At the back of the book were new kinds of bones and odd sketches. "What is this tiny creature?" she inquired.

Manmark asked, "What does it resemble?"

"Some kind of fowl," she admitted.

"But with teeth," he pointed out. "And where are its wings?"

She looked up, almost smiling. "Didn't it have wings? Or haven't you found them yet?"

"I never work with these little creatures," Manmark reported with a prickly tone. "But no, it and its kind never grew particularly large, and they were never genuinely important. Some in my profession believe they became today's birds. But when their bones were first uncovered, the creatures were mistakenly thought to be a variety of running lizard. Which is why those early fossil hunters dubbed them 'monstrous lizards' . . ."

She turned the page, paused, and then smiled at a particular drawing. "I know this creature," she said, pushing the book across the rumpled sheets. "I've seen a few shrews in my day."

The tiny mammal huddled beneath a fern frond. Manmark tapped the image with his finger, agreeing, "It does resemble our shrew. As it should, since this long-dead midget is the precursor to them and to us and to every furbearing animal in between."

"Really?" she said.

"Without question."

"Without question," she repeated, nodding as if she understood the oceans of time and the slow, remorseless pressures of natural selection.

"Our ancestors, like the ancestors of every bird, were exceptionally tiny," Manmark continued. "The dragons ruled the land and seas, and then they ruled the skies too, while these little creatures scurried about in the shadows, waiting patiently for their turn."

"Their turn?" She closed the book with authority, as if she would never need it again. Then, with a distant gaze, she said, "Now and again, I have wondered. Why did the dragons vanish from this world?"

Manmark reminded himself that this was an aboriginal girl. Every primitive culture had its stories. Who knew what wild legends and foolish myths she had heard since birth?

"Nobody knows what happened to them," was his first, best answer.

Then, taking back the book, he added, "But we can surmise there was some sort of cataclysm. An abrupt change in climate, a catastrophe from the sky. Something enormous made every large animal extinct, emptying the world for the likes of you and me."

She seemed impressed by the glimpse of the apocalypse. Smiling at him, she set her mouth to say a word or two, perhaps inviting him back over to her side of the great down-filled bed. But then a sudden hard knock shook the room's only door.

Manmark called out, "Who is it?"

"Name's Barrow," said a rough male voice.

Barrow? Did he know that name?

"We spoke some weeks back," the stranger reported, speaking through the heavy oak. "I told you I was going out into the wash country, and you told me to be on the lookout—"

"Yes."

"For something special."

Half-dressed and nearly panicked, Manmark leaped up, unlocking the door while muttering, "Quiet, quiet."

Barrow stood in the hallway, a tall man who hadn't bathed in weeks or perhaps years. He was grimy and tired and poorly fed and mildly embarrassed when he saw the nearly naked woman sitting calmly on the edge of another man's bed. But then he seemed to recall what had brought him here. "You mentioned money," he said to Manmark. "A great deal of money, if a hunter found for you—"

"Yes."

"One or more of them—"

"Quiet," Manmark snapped.

"Eggs," whispered the unwashed fossil hunter.

And with that, Manmark pulled the dullard into the room, clamping a hand over his mouth before he could utter another careless word.

⌐ III

Once again, the world was dying.

Zephyr enjoyed that bleak thought while strolling beside the railroad station, passing downwind from the tall stacks of rancid hyrax skins. The skins were waiting for empty cars heading east—the remains of thousands of beasts killed by hunters and then cleaned with a sloppy professional haste. It was a brutal business, and doomed. In just this one year, the nearby herds had been decimated, and soon the northern and southern herds would feel the onslaught of long rifles and malevolent greed. The waste was appalling, what with most of the meat being left behind for the bear-dogs or to rot in the brutal summer sun. But like all great wastes, it would re-make the world again. Into this emptiness, new creatures and peoples would come, filling the country overnight, and that new order would persist for a day or a million years before it too would collapse into ruin and despair.

Such were the lessons taught by history.

And science, in its own graceful fashion, reiterated those grand truths.

"Master Zephyr?"

An assistant had emerged from the railroad station, bearing important papers and an expression of weary tension. "Is it arranged?" Zephyr asked. Then, before the man could respond, he added, "I require a suitable car. For a shipment of this importance, my treasures deserve better than to be shoved beneath these bloody skins."

"I have done my best," the assistant promised.

"What is your best?"

"It will arrive in three days," the man replied, pulling a new paper to the top of the stack. "An armored car used to move payroll coins to the Westlands. As you requested, there's room for guards and your dragon scales, and your private car will ride behind it."

"And the dragons' teeth," Zephyr added. "And several dozen Claws of God."

"Yes, sir."

"And four dragon spleens."

"Of course, sir. Yes."

Each of those metallic organs was worth a fortune, even though none were in good condition. Each had already been purchased. Two were owned by important concerns in the Eastlands. The other two were bound for the Great Continent, purchased by wealthy men who lived along the

Dragon River: the same crowded green country where, sixty years ago, Zephyr began his life.

The spleens were full of magic, some professed. Others looked on the relics as oddities, beautiful and precious. But a growing number considered them to be worthy of scientific study—which was why one of the Eastland universities was paying Zephyr a considerable sum for a half-crushed spleen, wanting their chance to study its metabolic purpose and its possible uses in the modern world.

Like his father and his grandfather, Zephyr was a trader who dealt exclusively in the remains of dragons. For generations, perhaps since the beginning of civilized life, the occasional scale and rare claws were much in demand, both as objects of veneration as well as tools of war. Even today, modern munitions couldn't punch their way through a quality scale pulled from the back of a large dragon. In the recent wars, soldiers were given suits built of dragon armor—fantastically expensive uniforms intended only for the most elite units—while their enemies had used dragon teeth and claws fired by special guns, trying to kill the dragon men who were marching across the wastelands toward them.

Modern armies were much wealthier than the ancient civilizations. As a consequence, this humble son of a simple trader, by selling to both sides during the long civil war, had made himself into a financial force.

The fighting was finished, at least for today. But every government in the world continued to dream of war, and their stockpiles continued to grow, and as young scientists learned more about these lost times, the intrigue surrounding these beasts could only increase.

"This is good enough," Zephyr told his assistant, handing back the railroad's contract.

"I'll confirm the other details," the man promised, backing away in a pose of total submission. "By telegraph, I'll check on the car's progress, and I will interview the local men, looking for worthy guards."

And Zephyr would do the same. But surreptitiously, just to reassure an old man that every detail was seen to.

Because a successful enterprise had details at its heart, the old man reminded himself. Just as different details, if left unnoticed, would surely bring defeat to the sloppy and the unfortunate.

Zephyr occupied a spacious house built on the edge of the workers' camp—the finest home in this exceptionally young town but relegated to this less desirable ground because, much as everyone who lived in the camp, its owner belonged to a questionable race. Passing through the front door, the white-haired gentleman paused a moment to enjoy the door's etched glass, and in particular the ornate dragons captured in the midst of life, all sporting wings and fanciful breaths of fire. With a light touch, the trader felt the whitish eye of one dragon. Then, with a tense, disapproving voice, the waiting manservant announced, "Sir, you have a visitor."

Zephyr glanced into the parlor, seeing no one.

"I made her wait in the root cellar," the servant replied. "I didn't know where else to place her."

"Who is she?" the old man inquired. And when he heard the name, he said, "Bring her to me. Now."

"A woman like that?" the man muttered in disbelief.

"As your last duty to me, yes. Bring her to the parlor, collect two more weeks of wages, and then pack your belongings and leave my company." With an angry finger, he added, "Your morals should have been left packed and out of sight. Consider this fair warning should you ever find employment again."

Zephyr could sound frightfully angry, if it suited him.

He walked into the parlor, sat on an overstuffed chair, and waited. A few moments later, the young aboriginal woman strolled into the parlor, investing a moment to look at the furnishings and ivory statues. Then she said, "I learned something."

"I assumed as much."

"Like you guessed, it's the barbarian with all the money."

She smiled, perhaps thinking of the money. "He's promised huge payoffs to the dragon hunters, and maybe that's why this one hunter brought him word of a big discovery."

"Where is this discovery? Did you hear?"

"No."

"Does this hunter have a name?"

"Barrow."

Unless Barrow was an idiot or a genius, he would have already applied for dig rights, and they would be included in any public record. It would be a simple matter to bribe the clerk—

"There's eggs," she blurted.

Zephyr was not a man easily startled. But it took him a moment to repeat the word, "Eggs." Then he asked, "More than one egg, you mean?"

"Three, and maybe more."

"What sort of dragon is it?"

"Winged."

"A Sky-Demon?" he said with considerable hope.

"From what they said in front of me, I'm sure of it. He has uncovered the complete body of a Sky-Demon, and she died in the final stages of pregnancy." The girl smiled as she spoke, pleased with everything that had happened. "He didn't realize I understood the importance of things, or even that I was listening. That Manmark fellow . . . he is such a boring, self-important prick—"

"One last question," Zephyr interrupted. "What color were these eggs? Was that mentioned?"

The girl nodded and looked about the room again. Then, picking up a game cube carved from the whitest hyrax ivory, she said, "Like this, they were. They are. Perfectly, perfectly preserved."

∽ *IV*

Manmark was an endless talker, and most of his talk was senseless noise. Barrow treated the noise as just another kind of wind, taking no pleasure from it, nor feeling any insult. To be mannerly, he would nod on occasion and make some tiny comment that could mean anything, and, bolstered by this gesture, Manmark would press on, explaining how it was to grow up wealthy in the Old World, or why bear-dogs were the most foul creatures, or why the world danced around the sun, or how it felt to be a genius on that same world—a grand, deep, wondrous mind surrounded by millions of fools.

It was amazing what a man would endure, particularly if he had been promised a heavy pile of platinum coins.

There were five other men working with them. Four were youngsters—students of some type brought along to do the delicate digging. While the fifth fellow served as their protector, armed with a sleek modern rifle and enough ammunition to kill a thousand men. Some months ago, before he left for the wilderness, Manmark had hired the man to be their protector, keeping him on salary for a day such as this. He was said to be some species of professional killer, which was a bit of a surprise. A few times in conversation, Barrow had wormed honest answers out of the fellow. His credentials were less spectacular than he made them out to be, and even more alarming, the man was extraordinarily scared of things that would never present a problem. Bear-dogs were a source of much consternation, even though Barrow never had trouble with the beasts. And then there were the aborigines; those normally peaceful people brought nightmares of their own. "What if they come on us while we sleep?" the protector would ask, his voice low and haunted. "I am just one person. I have to sleep. What if I wake to find one of those miserable bastards slicing open my throat?"

"They wouldn't," Barrow assured him. Then he laughed, adding, "They'll cut into your chest first, since they'll want to eat your heart."

That was a pure fiction—a grotesque rumor made real by a thousand cheap novels. But their protector seemed to know nothing about this country, his experience born from the novels and small-minded tales told in the slums and high-class restaurants left behind on the distant, unreachable coast.

In his own fashion, Manmark was just as innocent and naïve. But there were moments when what he knew proved to be not only interesting but also quite valuable.

During their second night camped beside the dragon, Manmark topped off his tall glass of fancy pink liquor, and then he glanced at the exposed head of the great beast, remarking, "Life was so different in those old times."

There was nothing interesting in that. But Barrow nodded, as expected, muttering a few bland agreements.

"The dragons were nothing like us," the man continued.

What could be more obvious? Barrow thought to himself.

"The biology of these monsters," said Manmark. Then he looked at Barrow, a wide grin flashing. "Do you know how they breathed?"

It was just the two of them sitting before the fire. The students, exhausted by their day's work, were tucked into their bedrolls, while the camp protector stood on a nearby ridge, scared of every darkness. "I know their lungs were peculiar affairs," Barrow allowed. "Just like their hearts, and their spleens—"

"Not just peculiar," Manmark interrupted. "Unique."

Barrow leaned closer.

"Like us, yes, they had a backbone. But it was not our backbone. There are important differences between the architectures—profound and telling differences. It is as if two separate spines had evolved along two separate but nearly parallel lineages."

The words made sense, to a point.

"North of here," said Manmark. "I have colleagues who have found ancient fossils set within a bed of fine black shale. Unlike most beds of that kind, the soft parts of the dead have been preserved along with their hard shells and teeth. Have you heard of this place? No? Well, its creatures expired long before the first dragon was born. The world was almost new, it was so long ago . . . and inside that beautiful black shale is a tiny wormlike creature that has the barest beginnings of a notochord. A spine. The first vertebrate, say some."

"Like us," Barrow realized.

"And lying beside that specimen is another. Very much the same, in its fashion. Wormlike and obscure. But in other ways, it is full of subtle, very beautiful differences."

"Different how?"

"Well, for instance . . . there is a minuscule speck of metal located in the center of its simple body."

"Like a dragon's spleen?"

"But simpler, and made of ordinary metals. Iron and copper and such." Manmark finished his drink and gazed into the fire. "This dragon's lungs were very different, of course. Instead of sucking in a breath and then exhaling it out the same way, she took the air through her nostrils, into the lungs and out through a rectal orifice. We don't know enough to be certain yet. But it seems reasonable to assume that our dragon did a much better job of wringing the oxygen out of her endless deep breath."

Barrow nodded, very much interested now.

"And then there's the famous spleen," Manmark continued. "Have you ever wondered why these beasts needed to collect precious metals? What possible advantage could they have lent to the beasts?"

"I've thought about it some," he confessed.

"Gold and platinum and sometimes silver," said Manmark. "They are precious to us because they are rare, yes. But also because they barely rust in the presence of oxygen, which is why they retain their lovely sheen. And for the newest industries of our world, these elements are increasingly valuable. Were you aware? They can serve as enzymatic surfaces for all kinds of impressive chemical reactions. Perhaps our lady dragon would mix her breath and blood inside the spleen's cavities, producing all kinds of spectacular products. Even fire, perhaps."

Barrow nodded as if he understood every word.

"One day, we'll decipher what happened inside these

creatures. And I suspect that knowledge, when it arrives, will revolutionize our world."

"Someday, maybe," Barrow conceded.

"In the distant future, you think?" Manmark grinned and took a long drink from his mostly drained glass. "But not in our lives, surely. Is that what you are thinking?"

"Isn't that the truth?"

"The truth." The self-described genius stared into the campfire, his gold eyes full of greed and a wild hope. "This isn't well known. Outside of scientific circles, that is. But a few years ago, an immature egg was dug from the belly of a giant tree-eating dragon. Dead for perhaps a hundred million years, yet its color was still white. The oxygen that had fueled its parent had been kept away from the egg in death, and some kind of deep coma state had been achieved. Which is not too surprising. We know dragon eggs are exceptionally durable. It's perhaps a relic trait from those days when their ancestors laid their eggs in sloppy piles and buried them under dirt and then left the nest, sometimes for decades, waiting for the proper conditions. Since these creatures had a very different biochemistry from ours . . . a much superior physiology . . . they could afford to do such things—"

"What are you saying?" Barrow interrupted. "I'm sorry, I don't understand half your words."

"I'm saying that the dragons were exceptionally durable."

The dragon hunter glanced at the long, lovely skull and its cavernous eye sockets. "I have never heard this before. Is there some chance that those eggs over there . . . in that ground, after all of these years . . . ?"

"Remember the immature egg that I mentioned?" Manmark was whispering, his voice a little sloppy and terribly pleased. "The egg from the tree-eater? Well, I have read the paper written about its dissection. A hundred times, I have read it. Diamond blades were used to cut through the shell, and despite everything that common and uncommon sense would tell you . . . yes, there was still fluid inside the egg, and a six-legged embryo that was dead but intact . . . dead, but that looked as if it had died only yesterday, its burial lasting just a little too long . . ."

⌐ V

Three eggs became four, and then five, and quite suddenly there were seven of the treasures set on a bed of clean straw, enjoying the temporary shade of a brown canvas tarp. It was a sight that dwarfed Manmark's great dreams, marvelous and lovely as they had been. Each egg was perfectly round, and each was the same size, their diameter equal to his forearm and extended hand. They were heavier than any bird egg would be, if a bird could lay such an enormous egg. But that was reasonable, since the thick white shell was woven partly from metal and strange compounds that were barely understood today—ceramics and odd proteins laid out in a painfully delicate pattern. The shell material itself contained enough mystery to make a great man famous. But Manmark could always imagine greater honors and even wilder successes, as he did now, touching the warm surface of the nearest egg, whispering to it, "Hello, you."

The students were standing together, waiting for orders. And behind them stood a freight wagon, its team of heavy camels ready to pull their precious cargo to town and the railhead.

Barrow was perched on the wagon's front end, leather reins held tight in both hands.

Manmark took notice of him, and for a moment he wondered why the man was staring off into the distance. What did he see from that vantage point? Looking in the same general direction, Manmark saw nothing. There was a slope of gray clay punctuated with a few clusters of yucca, and the crest of the little ridge formed a neat line dividing the rain-washed earth from the intense blue of the sky.

The dragon hunter was staring at nothing.

How peculiar.

Manmark felt a little uneasy, but for no clear reason. He turned to the students now, ready to order the wagon loaded. And then, too late by a long ways, he remembered that their very expensive security man had been walking that barren ridge, his long gun cradled in both arms, haunted eyes watching for trouble.

So where is my protector? Manmark asked himself.

An instant later, the clean crack of a bullet cut through the air, and one of the large camels decided to drop its head and then its massive body, settling with a strange urgency onto the hard pan of clay.

Manmark knelt down between the great eggs. Otherwise, he was too startled to react.

The students dropped low and stared at the sky.

Barrow remained on the wagon, yanking at the reins and braking with his left foot, telling the surviving three camels, "Hold. Stay. Hold now. Stay."

Something about that voice steadied Manmark. Something in the man's calmness allowed him to look up, shouting to Barrow, "What is this? What is happening?"

Next came the sound of hooves striking dirt—many hooves in common motion—and he turned the other way, seeing six . . . no, eight camels calmly walking down the long draw, each built to race, each wearing a small saddle as well as a man dressed in shapeless clothes and heavy masks.

Manmark's first thought was to deny that this was happening. Hadn't he taken a thousand precautions? Nobody should know the significance of this dig, which meant that this had to be some random bit of awful luck. These were raiders of some kind—simple thieves easily tricked. A few coins of debased gold would probably satisfy them. He started to calculate the proper figure, filling his head with nonsense until that moment when the lead rider lowered his fat rifle and fired.

A fountain of pulverized earth slapped Manmark in the face.

He backed away, stumbled and dropped onto his rump. Then in his panic, he began digging into his pockets, searching for the tiny pistol that he had carried from the Old World and never fired once.

"Don't," said a strong, calming voice.

Barrow's voice.

"Give them what they want," said the dragon hunter, speaking to him as he would to a nervous camel.

"I won't," Manmark sputtered. "They are mine!"

"No," Barrow said from high on the wagon. "They aren't yours anymore, if they ever were . . ."

The riders didn't speak, save to wave their weapons in the air, ordering him to back away from the eggs. Then each claimed a single white sphere, dismounting long enough to secure their prize inside a silk sling apparently woven for this single task.

The final pair of riders was dressed as the others, yet they were different. One was small in build, while the other moved like a healthy but definitely older man. Manmark stared at both of them, and with an expertise garnered from years of imagining flesh upon ancient bone, he made two good guesses about who was beneath all those clothes.

"Zephyr," he muttered.

How many candidates were there? In one little town, or even at this end of the territory, how many other men were there who could possibly appreciate the significance of this find?

"And you," he said to the whore, his voice tight and injured.

She hesitated, if only for a moment.

Through the slits about the eyes, Zephyr stared at his opponent, and then he made some decision, lifting a hand and glancing back at the lead rider. For what purpose? To order him shot, perhaps?

The next blast of a gun startled everyone. The riders. Zephyr. And Manmark too. The concussion cut through the air, and while the roar was still ringing in their ears, Barrow said, "If we want to start killing, I'll start with you. Whoever you are. Understand me, old man? Before they aim my way, I'll hit your head and then your heart."

Barrow was standing on the back of the wagon now, holding his own rifle against his shoulder.

"Hear me, stranger? The eggs are yours. Take them. And I'll give you your life in the deal. Is that good enough?"

"It is adequate," said the accented voice.

Under his breath, Manmark muttered grim curses. But he stood motionless while Zephyr claimed the last of his eggs, and he swallowed his rage while the riders turned and started back up the long draw, the final man riding backward in his saddle, ready to fire at anyone with a breath of courage.

Manmark had none.

When the thieves vanished, he collapsed, panting and sobbing in a shameless display.

Barrow leaped off the wagon and walked toward him.

The students were standing again, chattering among themselves. One and then another asked no one in particular, "Will we still get paid?"

All was lost, Manmark believed.

Then the dragon hunter knelt beside him, and with an almost amused voice, he said, "All right. Let's discuss my terms."

"Your what?"

"Terms," he repeated. Then he outright laughed, adding, "When I get these eggs back to you, what will you pay me?"

"But how can you recover them?"

"I don't know yet. But give me the right promises, and maybe I'll think of something."

Manmark was utterly confused. "What do you mean? If there are six of them, and if they defeated my security man . . . what hope do you have . . . ?"

"I fought in the war," Barrow replied.

"A lot of men fought."

"Not many did the kind of fighting that I did," the dragon hunter replied. "And few of them fought half as well either."

Manmark stared at the hard dark eyes. Then, because he had no choice, none whatsoever, he blurted, "Yes. Whatever it costs. Yes!"

⌐ *VI*

Here stood the best locomotive available on short notice—a soot-caked machine built of iron and fire, wet steam, and rhythmic noises not unlike the breathing of a great old beast. Since details mattered, Zephyr had hired workmen to paint dragon eyes on the front end and little red wings on its sides, and when the job wasn't done with the proper accuracy, he commissioned others to fix what was wrong. Two engineers stoked the fire, while a third sat on top of the tender, ready to spell whomever tired first. Behind the locomotive was the armored car hired to move spleens and scales—a wheeled fortress encased in steel and nearly empty, carrying nothing but seven white eggs and six mercenaries armed with enough munitions to hold off a regiment. And trailing behind was Zephyr's private car, luxurious and open in appearance, except for the small windowless room at the rear that served as a bath.

The original plan for the dragons' spleens was to travel east. But the eggs were too precious to risk losing among the barbarians. Which was why Zephyr ordered his little train to head for the mountains and the Westlands beyond. A telegraph message dressed in code had been sent ahead. By the time he arrived at the Great Bay, a steamer would be waiting, ready to carry him back to the land of fables and childhood memories.

"I haven't been home for years," he confessed to his companion.

The young woman smiled at him, and once again, she said, "Thank you for taking me."

"It was the very least I could do," Zephyr allowed. "You were wise to ask, in fact. If Manmark realized you were responsible—"

"And for this," she interrupted, letting her fat coin purse jingle in an agreeable fashion.

"You have earned every mark. For what you have done to help me, madam, I will always be in your gratitude . . ."

There was only one set of tracks, with the occasional sidings and rules of conduct between oncoming trains. But Zephyr had sprinkled the world before them with bribes, and for the time being, there might as well be no other train in the world. As they picked up speed—as the engine quickened its breathing and its pace—he looked through the thick window glass, watching a hand-painted sign pass on their right. "You are leaving Summer Gulch," he read. "The fastest growing city between here and there."

What an odd, interesting thing to write. Zephyr laughed for a moment, and again mentioned, "I haven't been home since I was a young man."

"I'd love to see the Great Continent," the aboriginal girl reported.

What would become of this creature? Zephyr was of several minds on the subject, but his happy mood steered him to the more benevolent courses.

She slipped her purse out of sight.

"Do you know why we call it the Dragon River?" he asked.

"I don't," she replied.

Somehow he doubted that. But a prostitute makes her living by listening as much as anything, and this old man could do little else but talk with her, at least for the moment. "Of course there are some substantial beds of fossils along the river's course, yes. Dragon bones and claws and the great scales are part of my people's history. And we are an ancient nation, you know. The oldest in the world, perhaps. From the beginning, our gods have been dragons and our emperors have been their earthly sons and daughters."

The woman had bright, jade-colored eyes and a pleasant, luring smile.

"My favorite story, true or not, is about a young emperor from the Fifth Dynasty." Zephyr allowed his eyes to gaze off to the north, looking at the broken, rain-ripped country. "He found a flying dragon, it is said. The bones and scales were intact, as was her heart and spleen. And behind her spleen were eggs. At least two eggs, it is said. Some accounts mention as many as six, but only two of her offspring were viable. After three weeks of sitting above the ground, in the warming sun—and I should add, because the emperor was a very good man—the eggs finally hatched. Two baby dragons slithered into the world. Brothers, they were, and they belonged to him.

"The emperor had always been cared for by others. But

he made a wise decision. He refused to let others care for his new friends, raising them himself, with his own hands. A mistake took one of those hands from him, but that was a minor loss. He refused to let his guards kill the offending dragon. And for his kindness, the dragon and its brother loved the emperor for all of his days."

Zephyr paused for a moment, considering his next words.

"It was a weak time for my great nation," he reported. "Barbarians were roaming the steppe and mountains, and peoples from the sea were raiding the coasts. But it is said— by many voices, not just those of my people—that a one-handed emperor appeared in the skies, riding the winged monsters. They were huge beasts, swift and strange. They breathed a strange fire, and they were powerful, and they had to eat a thousand enemy soldiers every day just to feed their endless hunger. An unlikely, mythic detail, I always believed. Except now, when I read scientific papers about the biology of dragons, I can see where they must have had prodigious appetites."

The woman nodded, listening to every word.

"As a skeptical boy, I doubted the story about the emperor's warrior dragons. Great men didn't need monsters to save their nation, I believed. But I was wrong. I realized my error some time ago. Two monsters could save my people then, and think what seven dragons could do today . . . particularly if several of them are female, and fertile, and agreeable to mating with their brothers . . ."

The young woman gave a little shrug, saying nothing for a long moment.

The train continued to churn toward the west, the locomotive sounding steady and unstoppable.

"We have a story," she muttered. "My people do, I mean."

"About the dragons? Yes, I suppose you do."

"Since I was old enough to listen, I heard how the world holds thousands of dragons in its chest, and from time to time, for reasons known only to the gods, one of them is released. Which makes sense, I suppose. If what everyone tells me is true, and their eggs can sleep for an eternity in the ground."

Even from a single fertile female, only one egg at a time would be exposed by erosion. Yes, it was a reasonable explanation.

"The freed dragons die of loneliness, always." She spoke those words with sadness, as if she knew something about that particular pain. "They kill and burn because of their longing for others like themselves, and then they fly too high in order to end their own miserable lives, and that is why the dragons cannot come back into this world."

"This is a very common story," Zephyr assured her. "Maybe every place in the world tells fables much like that."

"But there is more to my story," she said, her tone defensive.

"Is there?"

"Much more," she promised.

Neither of them spoke for a long moment. The young woman didn't want to say anything else, and Zephyr wasn't in the mood to let another people's legends distract him. He looked out another window, toward the empty south, and then from somewhere up ahead came a dull *whump* as a heavy block of dynamite detonated. Instantly, the brakes were applied, and the little train started to shake and shiver, fighting its momentum to remain on the suddenly unstable tracks.

The young woman was thrown from her seat, as was Zephyr.

He stood first and heard the early shots coming from inside the armored car. Again he looked to the south, seeing nothing, and then he hunkered down and looked in the other direction. A solitary figure was approaching on foot, armed with a rifle that he hadn't bothered to fire. He was marching steadily across the stunted grasses, allowing the mercenaries to fire at him. And while most of their bullets struck, each impact made only sparks and a high-pitched snap that seemed to accomplish nothing. Because the attacker was wearing a suit made from overlapping dragon scales, Zephyr realized. And with an impressive eye for detail, the man had gone to the trouble of stretching cloth between his arms and chest, as if he had wings, while on his masked face were painted the large, malevolent eyes of an exceptionally angry dragon.

⌒ VII

This was what Barrow did during the war. With a platoon of picked soldiers, he would squeeze into his costume and pick up a gun that was always too heavy to carry more than a few steps, and after swallowing his fears as well as his common sense, he and his brethren would walk straight at the enemy, letting them shoot at will, waiting to reach a point where he could murder every idiot who hadn't yet found reason enough to run away.

This was the war all over again, and he hated it.

His suit wasn't as good as the one he wore in the war. Manmark's students were experts at arranging the scales and fixing them to his clothes—a consequence of spending weeks and years assembling old bones—but there hadn't been enough time to do a proper, permanent job. The scales were tilted in order to guide the bullets to one side or the other, but they weren't always tilted enough. Every impact caused a bruise. One and then another blow to the chest seemed to break a rib or two, and Barrow found himself staggering now, the weight of his clothes and his own fatigue making him wish for an end to his suffering.

That old platoon had been a mostly invincible bunch, but by the war's end, those who hadn't died from lucky shots and cannon fire were pretty much crazy with fear. Barrow was one of the few exceptions—a consequence of getting hit less often and doing a better job of killing those who wanted him dead.

Through the narrow slits of his mask, he stared at the firing ports built into the armored car. Then he paused, knelt, and with a care enforced by hours of practice, he leveled his weapon and put a fat slug of lead into one man's face.

Two more rounds hit Barrow, square in the chest and on the scalp.

He staggered, breathed hard enough to make himself lightheaded, and then aimed and fired again, killing no one but leaving someone behind the steel screaming in misery.

The surviving men finally got smart. One would cry out, and all would fire together, in a single volley.

Barrow was shoved back off his feet.

Again, there was a shout followed by the blow of a great hammer.

They would break every bone inside his bruised body if this continued. Barrow saw his doom and still could not make his body rise off the dusty earth. How had he come to this awful place? He couldn't remember. He sat upright, waiting for the next misery to find him . . . but a new voice was shouting, followed by the odd, high-pitched report of a very different gun.

The dirt before him rose up in a fountain and drifted away, and left lying between his legs was a single purple Claw of God.

Damn, somebody had a dragon-buster gun.

If he remained here, he would die. Reflexes and simple panic pushed Barrow up onto his feet, and on exhausted legs he ran, trying to count the seconds while he imagined somebody working with the breech of that huge, awful gun, inserting another expensive charge before sealing it up and aiming at him again.

When Barrow thought it was time, he abruptly changed direction.

The next claw screamed through the air, peeling off to the right.

Three engineers were cowering on the dragon-eyed locomotive. Plainly, they hadn't come here expecting to fight. Barrow pointed his rifle at each of their faces, just for a moment, and then they leaped down together and started running back toward town.

The men inside the armored car fired again. But Barrow

kept close to the tender, giving them no easy shots. A few steps short of them, he reached behind his back, removing a satchel that he had carried from the beginning, out of sight, and he unwrapped the fuse and laid it on the ground, shooting it at pointblank range to set it on fire. Then he bent low and threw the satchel with his free arm, skipping it under the car before he stepped back a little ways, letting the guards see him standing in front of them with barely a care.

"There's enough dynamite under you now to throw that car up high and break it into twenty pieces," he promised. Then he added, "It's a long fuse. But I wouldn't spend too much time thinking before you decide to do what's smart."

An instant later, the main door was unlocked and unlatched. Five men came tumbling out into the open, one of them bleeding from the shoulder and none of them armed.

"Run," Barrow advised.

The mercenaries started chasing the train crew down the iron rails.

The fuse continued to burn, reaching the canvas satchel and sputtering for a few moments before it died away.

Barrow stared into the windowless car. The seven eggs were set inside seven oak crates, and he didn't look at any of them. He was staring at the man whom he had shot through the face, his mind thinking one way about it, then another.

A breech closed somewhere nearby, and a big hammer was cocked.

Barrow turned too late, eyes focusing first on the cavernous barrel of the gun and then on the old foreign man who was fighting to hold it up. At this range, with any kind of dragon-round, death was certain. But Barrow's sense of things told him that if he didn't lift his own weapon, the man would hesitate. And another moment or two of life seemed like reason enough to do nothing.

"I am a creature of foresight," Zephyr remarked.

"You're smarter than me," agreed Barrow.

"Details," the old man muttered, two fingers wrapped around the long brass trigger. "The world is built upon tiny but critical details."

Behind him stood one detail—a rather pretty detail, just as Barrow had recalled—and using a purse full of heavy gold, she struck Zephyr on the top of his skull, and the long barrel dropped as the gun discharged, and a Claw of God came spinning out, burying itself once again inside the ancient earth.

⸺ VIII

Manmark had the freight wagon brought out of the draw, and he used a whip on the surviving camels, forcing them into a quick trot toward the motionless train. But there was a generous distance to be covered; open country afforded few safe places to hide. There was time to watch Barrow and the aboriginal girl with his binoculars, a little dose of worry nipping at him, and then Zephyr was awake again, sitting up and speaking at some length to the dragon hunter. All the while, Manmark's students were happily discussing their golden futures and what each planned to do with his little share of the fame. They spoke about the dragons soon to be born, and they discussed what kinds of cages would be required to hold the great beasts, and what would be a fair price for the public to see them, and what kinds of science could be done with these travelers from another age.

What was Zephyr saying to the dragon hunter?

Of course, the crafty old trader was trying to top Manmark's offers of wealth. And if he was successful? If Barrow abruptly changed sides . . . ?

"Look at that cloud," one student mentioned.

Somewhere to the south, hooves were slapping at the ground, lifting the dust into a wind that was blowing north, obscuring what was most probably a small herd of hard-running hyraxes.

Manmark found the little pistol in his pocket, considering his options for a long moment.

If it came to it, would he have the courage?

Probably not, no. If these last days had taught Manmark anything, it was that he had no stomach for mayhem and murder.

He put the pistol back out of sight and again used the binoculars, the jumpy images showing that Zephyr had fallen silent for now and Barrow was gazing off to the south and all of the talking was being done by the prostitute who stood between the two men, arms swirling in the air as she spoke on and on.

The worry that he felt now was nebulous and terrible.

Again, Manmark struck the big camels with his whip, and he screamed at everyone, telling them, "We need to hurry. Hurry!"

But the wagon was massive and one camel short, and there was still a long, empty distance to cover. The curtain of dust was nearly upon the motionless train, and inside it were dozens, or perhaps hundreds of aboriginal men riding on the backs of the half-wild ponies that they preferred to ride—an entire tribe galloping toward the treasures that Manmark would never see again.

⌒ IX

She spoke quietly, with force.

"My favorite fable of all promises that the dragons will come again to this world. They will rise up out of the Earth to claim what has always been theirs, and only those men and women who help them will be spared. All the other people of the world will be fought and killed and eaten. Only the chosen few will be allowed to live as they wish, protected beneath the great wings of the reawakened gods."

Zephyr rubbed his sore head, trying to focus his mind. But really, no amount of cleverness or any promise of money would help now. Even with a splitting headache, he understood that inescapable lesson.

Speaking to the man wearing dragon scales, she said, "Your ugly people came into my country and stole everything of worth. You gave us disease and drink, and you are murdering our herds. But now I intend to destroy everything you have built here, and my children will take back all the lands between the seas."

She was a clever, brutal girl, Zephyr decided. And she had done a masterful job of fooling everyone, including him.

Barrow turned and stared at the oncoming riders. He had pulled off his armored mask, but he was still breathing hard, winded by his fight and terrified. He might defeat half a dozen mercenaries, if he was lucky. But not a nation of wild men and women armed with rifles and a communal rage.

"You need me," he muttered.

The young woman didn't respond. It was Zephyr who said, "What do you mean? Who needs you?"

"She does," Barrow announced. Then he pointed at the riders, adding, "If they want to help themselves, they should accept my help."

The woman laughed and asked, "Why?"

"When I was a boy," said Barrow, "I kept baby birds. And I learned that my little friends would take my food and my love best if I wore a sock on my hand, painting it to resemble their lost mothers and fathers."

The rumbling of hooves grew louder, nearer.

"I'm a big man in this big costume," he remarked. "This costume is bigger than anything any of your people can wear, I would think. And I'm brave enough to do stupid things. And you will have seven dragons to care for now . . . to feed and protect, and to train, if you can . . . and wouldn't you like to take along somebody who's willing to risk everything on a daily basis . . . ?"

Zephyr laughed quietly now.

Clearly, this Barrow fellow was at least as surprising as the young woman, and maybe twice as bold.

The woman stared at the man dressed as a dragon, a look of interest slowly breaking across her face.

Zephyr had to laugh louder now.

Dust drifted across the scene, thick and soft, muting the

sound of their voices. And then the woman turned to her people, shouting to be heard.

"I have dragons to give you!" she called out.

"Eight, as it happens! Eight dragons to build a new world . . . !"

Miss Emily Gray

Theodora Goss

Theodora Goss (people.bu.edu/tgoss) lives in Brighton, Massachusetts, with her husband Kendrick, a scientist and artist, and their daughter, Ophelia. She is a recovering graduate of Harvard Law School currently finishing her doctorate in English at Boston University. Her web site is quite elaborate and includes such things as an anthology, entitled Poems of the Fantastic and Macabre. She is co-editing an anthology for the Interstitial Arts project (interstitialarts.org) with Delia Sherman. Her stories and poems have appeared in magazines and anthologies such as Realms of Fantasy, Strange Horizons, Polyphony, Alchemy, Fantastic Metropolis, and Lady Churchill's Rosebud Wristlet, and have been collected in The Rose in Twelve Petals, a chapbook from Small Beer Press.

"Miss Emily Gray," published in the excellent and attractive small press magazine Alchemy, is a tale in the Gothic mode set in what might be the late nineteenth century. The setup is fairy tale familiar: A sulky teenage girl whose mother has died feels that life has gone to pot for the family and looks for a magical solution to her problems. Instead she receives a governess who is definitely not Mary Poppins; the governess marries her father. But Goss gives it a most unfamiliar (and amusingly feminist) twist. It is intriguing to compare it to the Mary Poppins bit in the Neil Gaiman story later in this book.

～ I. A Lane in Albion

It was April in Albion. To the south, in the civilized counties, farmers were already putting their lambs out to pasture, and lakeshores were covered with the daffodils beloved of the Poet. The daffodils were plucked by tourists, who photographed the lambs, or each other with bunches of daffodils, or the cottage of the Poet, who had not been particularly revered until after his death. But this was the north of Albion, where sea winds blew from one side of the island to the other, so that even in the pastures a farmer could smell salt, and in that place April was not the month of lambs or daffodils or tourists, but of rain.

In the north of Albion, it was raining. It was not raining steadily. The night before had wrung most of the water out of the sky, and morning was now scattering its last drops, like the final sobs after a fit of weeping. The wind blew the drops of water here and there, into a web that a spider had, earlier that morning, carefully arranged between two slats of a fence, and over the leaves, dried by the previous autumn, that still hung from the branches of an oak tree. The branches of the oak, which had stood on that spot since William the Conqueror had added words like mutton and testament to the language, stretched over the fence and the lane that ran beside it. The lane was still sodden from the night's rains, and covered by a low gray mist.

Along this lane came a sudden gust of wind, detaching an oak leaf from its branch, detaching the spiderweb from its fence, sweeping them along with puffs of mist so that they tumbled together, like something one might find under a bureau: a tattered collection of gray fluff, brown paper, and string. As this collection tumbled down the lane, it began to extend upward like a whirlwind, and then to solidify. Soon, where there had been a leaf and a spiderweb speckled with rain, there was now a plain but neat gray dress with white collar and cuffs, and brown hair pulled back in a neat but very plain bun, and a small white nose, and a pair of serious but very clear gray eyes. Beneath the dress, held up by small white hands so that its hem would not touch the sodden lane, were a pair of plain brown boots. And as they stepped carefully among the puddles, sending the mist swirling before them, they gathered not a single speck of mud.

⌐ II. *Genevieve in a Mood*

When Genevieve was in a "mood," she went to the nursery, to sulk among the rocking horses and decapitated dolls. That was where Nanny finally found her, sitting on a settee with broken springs, reading *Pilgrim's Progress*.

"There you are, Miss Genevieve," she said. She puffed and patted a hand against her ample bosom. She had been climbing up and down stairs for the last half hour, and she was a short, stout woman, with an untidy bun of hair held together by hairpins that dropped out at intervals, leaving a trail behind her.

"Evidently," said Genevieve. Nanny was the only person with authority who would not send her to her room for using "that" tone of voice. Therefore, she used it with Nanny as often as possible.

"Supper's almost over. Didn't you hear the bell? Sir Edward is having a fit. One of these days he'll fall down dead from apoplexy, and you'll be to blame."

Genevieve had no doubt he would. She could imagine her father's face growing red and redder, until it looked like a slice of rare roast beef. He would shout, "Where have you been, young lady?" followed by "Don't use that tone of voice with me!" followed by "Up to your room, Miss!" Then she would have brown bread and water for supper. Genevieve rather liked brown bread, and liked even better imagining herself as a prisoner, a modern Mary, Queen of Scots.

"And what will Miss Gray think?"

"I don't care," said Genevieve. "I didn't ask for a bloody governess."

"Genevieve!" said Nanny. She did not believe in girls cursing, riding bicycles, or—heaven forbid—smoking cigarettes.

"Do you know who's going away to school? Amelia Thwaite. You know, Farmer Thwaite's daughter. Who used to milk our cows. Whose grandfather was our butler. She's going to Paris, to study art!" Genevieve shut *Pilgrim's Progress* with a bang and tossed it on the settee, where it landed in a cloud of dust.

"I know, my dear," said Nanny, smoothing her skirt, which Genevieve and occasionally Roland had spotted with tears when their father had refused them something they particularly wanted: in Roland's case, a brown pony and riding crop that Farmer Thwaite was selling at what seemed a ridiculously low price. "Sir Edward doesn't believe in girls going away to school, and I quite agree with him. Now come down and make your apologies to Miss Gray. How do you think she feels, just arrived from—well, wherever she arrived from—without a pupil to greet her?"

Genevieve did not much care, but the habit of obedience was strong, particularly to Nanny's comfortable voice, so she rose from the settee, kicking aside *Pilgrim's Progress*. This, although unintentional, sufficiently expressed her attitude toward the book, which Old Thwaite had read to her and Roland every Sunday afternoon, after church, while her father slept on the sofa with a handkerchief over his face. When she read the book herself, which was not often, she imagined him snoring. More often, when she was in a "mood," she would simply hold it open on her lap at the picture of Christian in the Slough of Despont, imagining interesting ways to keep him from reaching the Celestial City, which she believed must be the most boring place in the universe.

As she clattered down the stairs after Nanny, speculating that her father would not shout or send her to her room in front of the new governess, she began to imagine a marsh with green weeds that looked like solid ground. From it would rise seven women, nude and strategically covered with mud, with names like Desire and Foolishness. They would twine their arms around Christian and drag him downward into the muddy depths, where they would subject him to unspeakable pleasures. She did not think he would escape their clutches.

∽ III. *The Book in the Chimney*

It was not what she was, exactly. She was not anything, exactly. Genevieve could see her now, through the library window, sitting in a garden chair, embroidering something. Once, Genevieve had crept up behind her and seen that she was embroidering on white linen with white thread so fine that the pattern was barely perceptible.

Her gray dress was always neat, her white face was always solemn. Her irregular verbs, as far as Genevieve could judge, were always correct. She knew the principle exports of Byzantium. When Genevieve did particularly well on her botany or geography, she smiled a placid smile.

It was not, then, anything in particular, except that her hands were so small, and moved so quickly over the piano keys, like jumping spiders. She preferred to play Chopin.

No, it was something more mysterious, something missing. Genevieve reached into the back of the fireplace and carefully pulled out a loose brick. Behind it was an opening just large enough for a cigar box filled with dead beetles, which was what Roland had kept there, or a book, which was what she had kept there since Roland had left for Harrow and then the university. No fire had been lit in the library since her mother's death, when Genevieve was still young enough to be carried around in Nanny's arms. Her mother, who had liked books, had left her *Pilgrim's Progress* and a copy of *Clarissa* in one volume, which Genevieve read every night until she fell asleep. She never remembered what she had read the night before, so she always started again at the beginning. She had never made it past the first letter.

Out of the opening behind the brick, she pulled a book with a red leather cover, faded and sooty from its hiding place. On the cover, in gold lettering, Genevieve could still read the words *Practical Divination*. On the first page was written,

Practical Divination for the Adept or Amateur
By the Right Reverend Alice Widdicomb
Endorsed by the Theosophical Society

She brought the book to the library table, where she had set the basin and a bottle of ink. She was out of black ink, so it would have to be purple. Her father would shout at her when he discovered that she was out of ink again, but this time she could blame it on Miss Gray and irregular verbs.

She poured purple ink into the basin, then blew on it and repeated the words the Right Reverend Alice Widdicomb recommended, which sounded so much like a nonsense rhyme that she always wondered if they were strictly necessary. But she repeated them anyway. Then she stared at the purple ink until her eyes crossed, and said to the basin, as solemnly as though she were purchasing a railway ticket, "Miss Gray, please."

First, the purple ink showed her Miss Gray sitting in the garden, looking faintly violet. Sir Edward came up from behind and leaned over her shoulder, admiring her violet embroidery. Then it showed a lane covered with purple mud, by a field whose fence needed considerable repair, over which grew a purple oak tree. Rain came down from the lavender sky. Genevieve waited, but the scene remained the same.

"Perfectly useless," she said with disgust. It was probably the purple ink. Magic was like Bach. If you didn't play the right notes in the right order, it never came out right. She turned to the back of the book, where she had tucked in a piece of paper covered with spidery handwriting. On one side it said "To Biddy, from Alice. A Sovereign Remedy for the Catarrh." On the other side was "A Spell to Make Come True Your Heart's Desire." That had not worked either, although Genevieve had gathered the ingredients carefully, even clipping the whiskers from the taxidermed fox in the front hall. She read it over again, wondering where she had made a mistake. Perhaps it needed to be a live fox?

In the basin, Miss Gray was once again working on her violet embroidery. Genevieve frowned, rubbing a streak of purple ink across her cheek. What was it, exactly? She would have to find out another way.

~ IV. A Wedding on the Lawn

How, and this was the important question, had she done it? The tulle, floating behind her over the clipped lawn like foam. The satin, like spilled milk. The orange flowers brought from London.

Roland was drunk, which was only to be expected. He was standing beside the tea table, itself set beside the yew hedge, looking glum. Genevieve found it in her heart to sympathize.

"Oh, what a day," said Nanny, who was serving tea. She was upholstered in brown. A lace shawl that looked as though it had been yellowing in the attic was pinned to her bodice by a brooch handpainted, entirely unnecessarily, thought Genevieve, with daffodils. Genevieve was "helping."

"The Romans," said Roland.

Genevieve waited for him to say something further, but he merely took another mouthful of punch.

"To think," said Nanny. "Like the woman who nursed a serpent, until it bit her bosom so that she died. My mother told me that story, and never did she say a truer word. And she so plain and respectable."

Miss Gray, the plain and respectable, was now walking around the garden in satin and tulle, on Sir Edward's arm, nodding placidly to the farmers and gentry. In spite of her finery, she looked as neat and ordinary as a pin.

"The Romans," said Roland, "had a special room where they could go to vomit. It was called the vomitorium." He lurched forward and almost fell on the tea table.

"Take him away, won't you, Nanny," said Genevieve. "Lie him down before he gives his best imitation of a Roman." That would get rid of them both, leaving her to ponder the mystery that was Miss Gray, holding orange blossoms.

When Nanny had taken Roland into the library—she could hear through the window that he had developed a case of hiccups—Genevieve circled behind the hedge, to an overgrown holly that she had once discovered in a game of hide and seek with Roland. From the outside, the tree looked like a mass of leaves edged with needles that would prick anyone who ventured too close. If you pushed your way carefully inside, however, you found that the inner branches were sparse and bare. It was the perfect place to hide. And if you pushed a branch aside just slightly, you could see through the outer leaves without being seen. Roland had never found her, and in a fit of anger had decapitated her dolls. But she had never liked dolls anyway.

Miss Gray was listening to Farmer Thwaite, who was addressing her as Lady Trefusis. She was nodding and giving him one of her placid smiles. Sir Edward was looking particularly satisfied, which turned his face particularly red.

The old fool, thought Genevieve. She wondered what Miss Gray had up those capacious sleeves, which were in the latest fashion. Was it money she wanted?

That did not, to Genevieve's disappointment, seem to fit the Miss Gray who knew the parts of the flower and the principal rivers of Cathay.

Security? thought Genevieve. People often married for security. Nanny had said so, and in this at least she was willing to concede that Nanny might be right. The security of never again having to teach irregular verbs.

Genevieve pushed the holly leaves farther to one side. Miss Gray turned her head, with yards of tulle floating behind it. She looked directly at Genevieve, as though she could see through the holly leaves, and—she winked.

I must have imagined it, thought Genevieve a moment later. Miss Gray was smiling placidly at Amelia Thwaite, who looked like she had stepped out of a French fashion magazine.

She couldn't have seen me, thought Genevieve. And then, I wonder if she will expect me to call her mother?

⌒ V. A Meeting by Moonlight

Genevieve was on page four of *Clarissa* when she heard the voices.

First voice: "Angel, darling, you can't mean it."

Second voice: Inaudible murmur.

First voice, which obviously and unfortunately belonged to Roland: "If you only knew how I felt. Put your hand on my heart. Can you feel it? Beating and burning for you."

How embarrassing, having one's brother under one's bedroom window, mouthing banalities to a kitchenmaid.

Second voice, presumably the maid: Inaudible murmur.

Roland: "But you can't, you just can't. I would die without you. Don't you see what you've done to me? Emily, my own. Let me kiss this white neck, these little hands. Tell me you don't love him, tell me you'll run away with me. Tell me anything, but don't tell me to leave you. I can't do it any more than a moth can leave a flame." A convincing sob.

How was she supposed to read *Clarissa*? At this rate, she would never finish the first letter. Of course, she had never finished it on any other night, but it was the principle that mattered.

Genevieve put *Clarissa* down on the coverlet, open in a way that would eventually crack the spine, and picked up the pitcher, still full of tepid water, from her nightstand. She walked to the window. It was lucky that Nanny insisted on fresh air. She leaned out over the sill. Below, she could see the top of Roland's head. Beside him, her neck and shoulders white in the moonlight, stood Emily the kitchenmaid.

Except, thought Genevieve suddenly, that none of the maids was named Emily. The woman with the white shoulders looked up.

This time it was unmistakable. Miss Gray had winked at her. Genevieve lay on her bed for a long time, with *Clarissa* at an uncomfortable angle beneath her, staring at the ceiling.

∽ VI. The Burial of the Dead

"I am the resurrection and the life, saith the Lord."

"He was so handsome," whispered Amelia Thwaite to the farmer's daughter standing beside her, whose attention was absorbed in studying the pattern of the clocks on Amelia's stockings. "I let him kiss me once, before he went to Oxford. He asked me not to fall in love with anyone else while he was away, and I wouldn't promise, and he must have been so angry because when I saw him again this summer, he would barely speak to me. And I'm just sick with guilt. Because I really did think, in my heart, that I could love only him, and now I will never, ever have the chance to tell him so."

"Blessed are the dead who die in the Lord; even so saith the Spirit, for they rest from their labors."

"There's something behind it," whispered Farmer Thwaite to the farmer standing beside him, who had been up the night before with a sick ewe and was trying, with some success, not to fall asleep. "You mark my words." His neighbor marked them with a stifled yawn. "A gun doesn't go off, not just like that, not by itself. They say he was drunk, but he must of been pointing it at the old man for a reason. A strict enough landlord he was, and I'm not sorry to be rid of him, I tell you. The question is, whether our Ladyship will hold the reins as tightly. She's a pretty little thing in black satin, like a cat that's got into the pantry and is sitting looking at you, all innocent with the cream on its chin. But there's something behind it, you mark my words." His neighbor dutifully marked them.

"Why art thou so full of heaviness, O my soul? and why art thou so disquiet within me?"

It was inexplicable. Genevieve could hear the rustle of dresses, the shuffle of boots, the drone of the minister filling the chapel. Each window with its stained-glass saint was dedicated to a Trefusis. A Trefusis lay under each stone knight in his stone armor, each stone lady folding her hands over stone drapery. A plaque beside the altar commemorated Sir Roland Trefusis, who had come across the channel with William the Conqueror—some ungenerously whispered, as his cook.

"We must believe it was an accident," Mr. Herbert had said. "In that moment of confusion, he must have turned the pistol toward himself, examining it, unable to imagine how it could have gone off in his hands. And we have evidence, gentlemen," this to the constable and the magistrate of the county, "that the young man was intoxicated. What is the use, I put it to you, of calling it suicide under these circumstances? You have a son yourself," to the magistrate. "Would you want any earthly power denying him the right to rest in sacred ground?"

Nanny sniffed loudly into her handkerchief, which had a broad black border. "If it wasn't for that woman, that wicked, wicked woman, your dear father and that dear, dear boy would still be alive. I don't know how she done it, but she done it somehow, and if the good Lord don't smite her like he smote the witch of Endor, I'll become a Mahometan."

"By his last will and testament, signed and witnessed two weeks before the unfortunate—accident," Mr. Herbert had said, "your father left you to the guardianship of your stepmother, Lady Emily Trefusis. You will, of course, come into your own money when you reach the age of majority—or marry, with your guardian's permission. I don't suppose, Genevieve, that you've discussed any of this with your stepmother?"

Miss Gray turned, as though she had heard Nanny's angry whisper. For a moment she looked at Genevieve and then, inexplicably, she smiled, as though the two of them shared an amusing secret.

"There is a river, the streams whereof make glad the city of God, the holy place of the tabernacle of the Most High."

"I am quite certain it was an accident," the minister had said, patting Genevieve's hand. His palm was damp. "I knew young Roland when he was a boy. Oh, he would steal eggs from under a chicken for mischief, but there was no malice in his heart. Be comforted, my dear. They are in the Celestial City, singing hymns with the angels of the Lord."

Genevieve wondered. She was inclined, herself, to believe that Roland at least was most likely in Hell. It seemed, remembering Old Thwaite's Sunday lessons, an appropriate penalty for patricide.

She sniffed. She could not help it, fiercely as she was trying to hold whatever it was inside her so that it would not come out, like a wail. Because, as often as she thought of Mary, Queen of Scots, who had gone to her execution without hesitation or tears, she had to admit that she was very much afraid.

"For so thou didst ordain when thou createdst me, saying, dust thou art, and unto dust shalt thou return. All we go down to the dust; yet even at the grave we make our song: Alleluia."

It must, of course, be explicable. But she had hidden and watched and followed, and she was no closer to an explanation than that day on which, in a bowl of purple ink, she had watched violet clouds floating against a lavender sky.

For a moment she leaned her head against Nanny's arm, but found no comfort there. She would have, she realized, to confront the spider in its web. She would have to talk with Miss Gray.

~ VII. A Conversation with Miss Gray

"... and this prayer I make,
Knowing that Nature never did betray
The heart that loved her, 'tis her privilege,
Through all the years of this our life, to lead
From joy to joy: for she can so inform
The mind that is within us, so impress
With quietness and beauty, and so feed
With lofty thoughts, that neither evil tongues,

Rash judgements, nor the sneers of selfish men,
Nor greetings where no kindness is, nor all
The dreary intercourse of daily life,
Shall e'er prevail against us, or disturb
Our cheerful faith, that all which we behold
Is full of blessings."

Miss Gray shut her book. "Hello, Genevieve. Can you tell me what I have been reading?"

"Wordsworth," said Genevieve. Miss Gray always read Wordsworth.

She was sitting on a stone bench beside the yew hedge, dressed in black with a white collar and cuffs, looking plain but very neat. The holly was now covered with red berries.

"In these lines, the Poet is telling us that if we pray to Nature, our great mother, she will answer us, not by transporting us to a literal heaven, but by making a heaven for us here upon earth, in our minds and hearts. I'm afraid, my dear, that you don't read enough poetry."

Genevieve stood, not knowing what to say. It had rained the night before, and she could feel a dampness around her ankles, where her stockings had brushed against wet grass.

"Have you been studying your irregular verbs?"

Genevieve said, in a voice that to her dismay sounded hoarse and uncertain, "This won't do, you know. Talking about irregular verbs. We must have it out sometime." How, if Miss Gray said whatever do you mean Genevieve, would she respond? Her hands trembled, and she clasped them in front of her.

But Miss Gray said only, "I do apologize. I assumed it was perfectly clear."

Genevieve spread her hands in a silent question.

"I was sent to make come true your heart's desire."

"That's impossible," said Genevieve, and "I don't understand."

Miss Gray smiled placidly, mysteriously, like a respectable Mona Lisa. "You wanted to go to school, like Amelia Thwaite, and wear fine clothes, and be rid of your father."

"You're lying," said Genevieve. "It's not true," and "I

didn't mean it." Then she fell on her knees, in the wet grass. Her head fell forward, until it almost, but not quite, touched Miss Gray's unwrinkled lap.

"Hush, my dear," said Miss Gray, stroking Genevieve's hair and brushing away the tears that were beginning to fall on her dress. "You will go to school in Paris, and we will go together to Worth's, to find you an appropriate wardrobe. And we will go to the galleries and the Academy of Art . . ."

There was sobbing now, and tears soaking through to her knees, but she continued to stroke Genevieve's hair and said, in the soothing voice of a hospital nurse, "And my dear, although you have suffered a great loss, I hope you will someday come to think of me as your mother."

In the north of Albion, rain once again began to fall, which was no surprise, since it was autumn.

The Baum Plan for Financial Independence

~~~~~~~~

John Kessel

John Kessel (www4.ncsu.edu/~tenshi/index2.html) lives in Raleigh, North Carolina, where he has taught American literature, creative writing, science fiction, and fantasy at North Carolina State University since 1982. He published his first novel, Freedom Beach, *in 1985, co-authored with James Patrick Kelly. His novel* Good News From Outer Space *(1989) was a finalist for the Nebula Award. His most recent novel is* Corrupting Dr. Nice *(1997). His stories are collected in* Meeting in Infinity *(1992), named a notable book by the* New York Times Book Review, *and* The Pure Product *(1997). He is also the editor of an anthology of stories from the famous Sycamore Hill Writers' Conference (which he helps to run),* Intersections *(1996), co-edited with Mark L. Van Name and Richard Butner. His insightful and often witty criticism has appeared in* Science Fiction Eye, The Los Angeles Times Book Review, The New York Review of Science Fiction, *and elsewhere.*

"The Baum Plan for Financial Independence" is another story published by SciFiction, the leading electronic publisher of short SF and fantasy, so this is its first time in print. The story is what the Fantasy Encyclopedia *calls a portal fantasy, in which a gateway to another place is central to creating the fantasy. It is also clever and sometimes funny. A couple of crooks discover what might be described as the gravy train. This story contains several nice surprises.*

—for Wilton Barnhardt

When I picked her up at the Stop 'n' Shop on Route 28, Dot was wearing a short black skirt and red sneakers just like the ones she had taken from the bargain rack the night we broke into the Sears in Hendersonville five years earlier. I couldn't help but notice the curve of her hip as she slid into the front seat of my old T-Bird. She leaned over and gave me a kiss, bright red lipstick and breath smelling of cigarettes. "Just like old times," she said.

The Sears had been my idea, but after we got into the store that night all the other ideas had been Dot's, including the game on the bed in the furniture department, and me clocking the night watchman with the anodized aluminum flashlight I took from Hardware, sending him to the hospital with a concussion and me to three years in Central. When the cops showed up and hauled me off, Dot was nowhere to be found. That was all right. A man has to take responsibility for his own actions; at least that's what they told me in the group therapy sessions that the prison shrink ran on Thursday nights. But I never knew a woman who could make me do the things that Dot could make me do.

One of the guys at those sessions was Radioactive Roy Destry, who had a theory about how we were all living in a computer and none of this was real. Well if this isn't real, I told him, I don't know what real is. The softness of Dot's breast or the shit smell of the crapper in the Highway 28 Texaco, how can there be anything more real than that? Radioactive Roy and the people like him are just looking for an exit door. I can understand that. Everybody dreams of an exit door sometimes.

I slipped the car into gear and pulled out of the station

onto the highway. The sky ahead was red above the Blue Ridge, but the air blowing in the windows was dry and smoky with the ash of the forest fires burning a hundred miles to the northwest.

"Cat got your tongue, darlin'?" Dot said. I pushed the cassette into the deck and Willie Nelson was singing "Hello Walls."

"Where are we going, Dot?"

"Just point this thing west for twenty or so. When you come to a sign that says Potter's Glen, make a right on the next dirt road."

Dot pulled a pack of Kools out of her purse, stuck one in her mouth, and punched the car's cigarette lighter.

"Doesn't work," I said.

She pawed through her purse for thirty seconds, then clipped it shut. "Shit," she said. "You got a match, Sid?" Out of the corner of my eye I watched the cigarette bobble up and down as she spoke.

"Sorry, sweetheart, no."

She took the cigarette from her mouth, stared at it for a moment, and flipped it out her opened window.

Hello window. I actually had a box of Ohio Blue Tips in the glove compartment, but I didn't want Dot to smoke because it was going to kill her someday. My mother smoked, and I remember her wet cough and the skin stretched tight over her cheekbones as she lay in the upstairs bedroom of the big house in Lynchburg, puffing on a Winston between hacking up pieces of her lung. Whenever my old man came in to clear her untouched lunch he asked her if he could have one, and mother would smile at him, eyes big, and pull two more coffin nails out of the red-and-white pack with her nicotine-stained fingers.

One time after I saw this happen, I followed my father down to the kitchen. As he bent over to put the tray on the counter, I snatched the cigarettes from his breast pocket and crushed them into bits over the plate of pears and cottage cheese. I glared at him, daring him to get mad. After a few seconds he just pushed past me to the living room and turned on the TV.

That's the story of my life: me trying to save the rest of you—and the rest of you ignoring me.

On the other side of Almond it was all mountains. The road twisted and turned, the headlights flashing against the tops of trees on the downhill side and the cut earth on the uphill. I kept shifting and drifting over the double yellow line as we came in and out of turns, but the road was deserted. Occasionally we'd pass some broken-down house with a battered pickup in the dirt driveway and a rust-spotted propane tank outside in the yard.

The sign for Potter's Glen surged out of the darkness, and we turned off onto a rutted gravel track that was even more twisted than the paved road. The track rose steeply; the T-Bird's suspension was shot, and my rotten muffler scraped more than once when we bottomed out. If Dot's plan required us sneaking up on anybody, it was not going to work. But she had assured me that the house on the ridge was empty and she knew where the money was hidden.

Occasionally the branch of a tree would scrape across the windshield or side mirror. The forest here was dry as tinder after the summer's drought, the worst on record, and in my rearview mirror I could see the dust we were raising vanish in the taillights. We had been fifteen minutes on this road when Dot said, "Okay, stop now."

The cloud of dust that had been following us caught up and billowed, settling slowly in the headlight beams. "Kill the lights," Dot said.

In the silence and darkness that came, the whine of cicadas moved closer. Dot fumbled with her purse, and when she opened the car door to get out, in the domelight I saw she had a map written on a piece of notebook paper. I opened the trunk and got out a pry bar and pair of bolt cutters. When I came around to her side of the car, she was shining a flashlight on the map.

"It shouldn't be more than a quarter of a mile farther up this road," she said.

"Why can't we just drive right up there?"

"Someone might hear."

"But you said the place was deserted."

"It is. But there's no sense taking chances."

I laughed. Dot not taking chances? That was funny. She didn't think so, and punched me in the arm. "Stop it," she said, but then she giggled. I swept the arm holding the tools around her waist and kissed her. She pushed me away, but not roughly. "Let's go," she said.

We walked up the dirt road. When Dot shut off the flashlight, the only light was the faint moon coming through the trees, but after our eyes adjusted it was enough. The dark forest loomed over us. Walking through the woods at night always made me feel like I was in some teen horror movie. I expected a guy in a hockey mask to come shrieking from between the trees and cut us to ribbons with fingernails like straight razors.

Dot had heard about this summer cabin that was owned by the rich people she had worked for in Charlotte. They were Broyhills or related to the Broyhills, old money from the furniture business. Or maybe it was Dukes and tobacco. Anyway, they didn't use this house but a month or so out of the year. Some caretaker came by every so often, but he didn't live on the premises. Dot heard the daughter telling her friend that the family kept ten thousand dollars in cash up there in case another draft riot made it necessary for them to skip town for a while.

So we would just break in and find the money. That was the plan. It seemed a little dicey to me; I had grown up with money—my old man owned a car dealership, before he went bust. Leaving piles of cash lying around their vacation home did not seem like regular rich people behavior to me. But Dot could be very convincing even when she wasn't convincing, and my father claimed I never had a lick of sense anyway. It took us twenty minutes to come up on the clearing, and there was the house. It was bigger than I imagined it. Rustic, flagstone chimney and entranceway, timbered walls and slake shingles. Moonlight glinted off the windows in the three dormers that faced front, but all the downstairs windows were shuttered.

I took the pry bar to the hinges on one of the shuttered windows, and after some struggle they gave. The window was dead-bolted from the inside, but we knocked out one of the panes and unlatched it. I boosted Dot through the window and followed her in.

Dot used the flashlight to find the light switch. The furniture was large and heavy; there was a big oak coffee table that must have weighed two hundred pounds that we had to move in order to take up the rug and check to see whether there was a safe underneath. We pulled down all the pictures from the walls. One of them was a woodcut print of a Madonna and child, but instead of a child the woman was holding a fish; in the background of the picture, outside a window, a funnel cloud tore up a dirt road. The picture gave me the creeps. Behind it was nothing but plaster wall.

I heard the clink of glass behind me. Dot had opened the liquor cabinet and was pulling out bottles to see if there was a compartment hidden behind them. I went over, took down a glass, and poured myself a couple of fingers of Glenfiddich. I sat in a leather armchair and drank it, watching Dot search. She was getting frantic. When she came by the chair I grabbed her around the hips and pulled her into my lap.

"Hey! Lay off!" she squawked.

"Let's try the bedroom," I said.

She bounced off my lap. "Good idea." She left the room.

This was turning into a typical Dot odyssey, all tease and no tickle. I put down my glass and followed her.

I found her in the bedroom rifling through a chest of drawers, throwing clothes on the bed. I opened the closet. Inside hung a bunch of jackets and flannel shirts and blue jeans, with a pair of riding boots and some sandals lined up neatly on the floor. I pushed the hanging clothes apart, and there, set into the back wall, was a door. "Dot, bring that flashlight over here."

She came over and shined the flashlight into the closet. I ran my hand over the seam of the door. It was flush with the wall, the same off-white color, but was cool to the touch, made of metal. No visible hinges and no lock, just a flip up handle like on a tackle box.

"That's not a safe," Dot said.

"No shit, Sherlock."

She shouldered past me, crouched down, and flipped up the handle. The door pushed open onto darkness. She shined the flashlight ahead of her; I could not see past her. "Jesus Christ," she said.

"What?"

"Stairs." Dot moved forward, then stepped down. I pushed the clothes aside and followed her.

The carpet on the floor stopped at the doorjamb; inside was a concrete floor and then a narrow flight of stairs leading down. A black metal handrail ran down the right side. The walls and ceiling were of roughed concrete, unpainted. Dot moved ahead of me down to the bottom, where she stopped.

When I got there I saw why. The stairs let out into a large, dark room. The floor ended halfway across it, and beyond that, at either side, to the left and right, under the arching roof, were open tunnels. From one tunnel opening to the other ran a pair of gleaming rails. We were standing on a subway platform.

Dot walked to the end of the platform and shined the flashlight up the tunnel. The rails gleamed away into the distance.

"This doesn't look like the safe," I said.

"Maybe it's a bomb shelter," Dot said.

Before I could figure out a polite way to laugh at her, I noticed a light growing from the tunnel to the right. A slight breeze kicked up. The light grew like an approaching headlight, and with it a hum in the air. I backed toward the stairs, but Dot just peered down the tunnel. "Dot!" I called. She waved a hand at me, and though she dropped back a step she kept watching. Out of the tunnel glided a car that slid to a stop in front of us. It was no bigger than a pickup. Teardrop shaped, made of gleaming silver metal, its bright single light glared down the track. The car had no windows, but as we stood gaping at it a door slid open in its side. The inside was dimly lit, with plush red seats.

Dot stepped forward and stuck her head inside.

"What are you doing?" I asked.

"It's empty," Dot said. "No driver. Come on."

"Get serious."

Dot crouched and got inside. She turned and ducked her head to look at me out of the low doorway. "Don't be a pussy, Sid."

"Don't be crazy, Dot. We don't even know what this thing is."

"Ain't you ever been out of Mayberry? It's a subway."

"But who built it? Where does it go? And what the hell is it doing in Jackson County?"

"How should I know? Maybe we can find out."

The car just sat there, silent. The air was still. The ruby light from behind her cast Dot's face in shadow. I followed her into the car. "I don't know about this."

"Relax."

There were two bench seats, each wide enough to hold two people, and just enough space on the door side to move from one to the other. Dot sat on one of the seats with her big purse in her lap, calm as a Christian holding four aces. I sat down next to her. As soon as I did the door slid shut and the car began to move, picking up speed smoothly, pushing us back into the firm upholstery. The only sound was a gradually increasing hum that reached a middle pitch and stayed there. I tried to breathe. There was no clack from the rails, no vibration. In front of us the car narrowed to a bullet-nosed front, and in the heart of that nose was a circular window. Through the window I saw only blackness. After a while I wondered if we were still moving, until a light appeared ahead, first a small speck, then grew brighter and larger until it slipped off past us to the side at a speed that said the little car was moving faster than I cared to figure.

"These people who own the house," I asked Dot, "where on Mars did you say they came from?"

Dot reached in her purse and took out a pistol, set it down on her lap, and fumbled around in the bag until she pulled out a pack of Juicy Fruit. She pulled out a stick, then held the pack out to me. "Gum?"

"No thanks."

She put the pack back in the purse, and the pistol too. She slipped the yellow paper sleeve off her gum, unwrapped the foil, and stuck the gum into her mouth. After folding the foil neatly, she slid it back into the gum sleeve and set the now empty stick on the back of the seat in front of us.

I was about to scream. "Where the fuck are we going, Dot? What's going on here?"

"I don't have any idea where we're going, Sid. If I knew you were going to be such a wuss, I would never of called you."

"Did you know about any of this?"

"Of course not. But we're going to be somewhere soon, I bet."

I got off the seat and sat down on the bench in front of her. That didn't set my nerves any easier. I could hear her chewing her gum, and felt her eyes on the back of my neck. The car sped into blackness, broken only by the occasional spear of light flashing past. As we did not seem to be getting anywhere real soon, I had some time to contemplate the ways in which I was a fool, number one being the way I let an ex lap-dancer from Mebane lead me around by my imagination for the last ten years.

Just when I thought I couldn't get any more pissed, Dot moved up from the back seat, sat down next to me, and took my hand. "I'm sorry, Sid. Someday I'll make it up to you."

"Yeah?" I said. "So give me some of that gum." She gave me a stick. Her tidy gum wrapper had fallen onto the seat between us; I crumpled the wrapper of my own next to hers.

I had not started in on chewing when the hum of the car lowered and I felt us slowing down. The front window got a little lighter, and the car came to a stop. The door slid open.

The platform it opened onto was better lit than the one under the house in the Blue Ridge. Standing on it waiting were three people, two men and a woman. The two men wore identical black suits of the kind bankers with too

much money wore in downtown Charlotte: the suits hung
the way no piece of clothing had ever hung on me—tailored
closer than a mother's kiss. The woman, slender, with
blond hair done up tight as a librarian's—yet there was no
touch of the librarian about her—wore a dark blue dress.
They stood there for a moment, then one of the men said,
"Excuse me? You're here. Are you getting out?"

Dot got up and nudged me, and I finally got my nerveless
legs to work. We stepped out onto the platform, and the
three well-dressed people got into the car, the door slid
shut, and it glided off into the darkness.

It was cold on the platform, and a light breeze came from
an archway across from us. Instead of rough stone like the
tunnel under the house, here the ceiling and walls were
smooth stucco. Carved above the arch was a crouching man
wearing some kind of Roman or Greek toga, cradling a
book under one arm and holding a torch in the other. He
had a wide brow and a long, straight nose and looked like a
guard in Central named Pisarkiewicz, only a lot smarter.
Golden light filtered down from fixtures like frogs' eggs in
the ceiling.

"What now?" I asked.

Dot headed for the archway. "What have we got to
lose?"

Through the arch was a ramp that ran upward, switch-
backing every forty feet or so. A couple of women, as well
dressed as the one we'd seen on the platform, passed us
going the other way. We tried to look like we belonged
there, though Dot's hair was a greasy rat's nest, I was
dressed in jeans and sneakers, I had not shaved since morning, and my breath smelled of scotch and Juicy Fruit.

At the top of the third switchback, the light brightened.
From ahead of us came the sound of voices, echoing as if
coming from a very large room. We reached the final archway, the floor leveled off, and we stepped into the hall.

I did not think there were so many shades of marble. The
place was as big as a train station, a great open room with
polished stone floors, a domed ceiling a hundred feet above
us, a dozen Greek half-columns set into the far wall. Bright

sun shining through tall windows between them fell on baskets of flowers and huge potted palms. Around the hall stood a number of booths like information kiosks, and grilled counters like an old-fashioned bank at which polite workers in pale green shirts dealt with the customers. But it was not all business. Mixed among people carrying briefcases stood others in groups of three or four holding pale drinks in tall glasses or leaning casually on some counter chatting one-on-one with those manning the booths. In one corner a man in a green suit played jazz on a grand piano.

It was a cross between Grand Central Station and the ballroom at the Biltmore House. Dot and I stood out like a pair of plow horses at a cotillion. The couple hundred people scattered through the great marble room were big-city well dressed. Even the people who dressed down wore hundred-dollar chinos with cashmere sweaters knotted casually around their necks. The place reeked of money.

Dot took my hand and pulled me into the room. She spotted a table with a fountain and a hundred wine glasses in rows on the starched white tablecloth. A pink marble cherub with pursed lips like a cupid's bow poured pale wine from a pitcher into the basin that surrounded his feet. Dot handed me one of the glasses and took one for herself, held it under the stream falling from the pitcher.

She took a sip. "Tastes good," she said. "Try it."

As we sipped wine and eyed the people, a man in a uniform shirt with a brass name pin that said, "Brad" came up to us. "Would you like to wash and brush up? Wash and Brush Up is over there," he said, pointing across the hall to another marble archway. He had a British accent.

"Thanks," said Dot. "We just wanted to wet our whistles first."

The man winked at her. "Now that your whistle is wet, don't be afraid to use it any time I can be of service." He smirked at me. "That goes for you too, sir."

"Fuck you," I said.

"It's been done already," the man said, and walked away.

I put down the wine glass. "Let's get out of here," I said.

"I want to go to see what's over there."

Wash and Brush Up turned out to be a suite of rooms where we were greeted by a young woman in green named Elizabeth and a young man named Martin. You need to clean up, they said, and separated us. I wasn't going to have any of it, but Dot seemed to have lost her mind—she went off with Martin. After grumbling for a while, I let Elizabeth take me to a small dressing room, where she made me strip and put on a robe. After that came the shower, the haircut, the steambath, the massage. Between the steambath and massage they brought me food, something like a cheese quesadilla only much better than anything like it I had ever tasted. While I ate, Elizabeth left me alone in a room with a curtained window. I pulled the curtain aside and looked out.

The window looked down from a great height on a city unlike any I had ever seen. It was like a picture out of a kid's book, something Persian about it, and something Japanese. Slender green towers, great domed buildings, long, low structures like warehouses made of jade. The sun beat down pitilessly on citizens who went from street to street between the fine buildings with bowed heads and plodding steps. I saw a team of four men in purple shirts pulling a cart; I saw other men with sticks herd children down to a park; I saw vehicles rumble past tired street workers, kicking up clouds of yellow dust so thick that I could taste it.

The door behind me opened, and Elizabeth stuck her head in. I dropped the curtain as if she had caught me whacking off. "Time for your massage," she said.

"Right," I said, and followed.

When I came out, there was Dot, tiny in her big plush robe, her hair clean and combed out and her finger and toenails painted shell pink. She looked about fourteen.

"Nice haircut," she said to me.

"Where are our clothes?" I demanded of Martin.

"We'll get them for you," he said. He gestured to one of the boys. "But for now, come with me."

Then they sat us down in front of a large computer screen and showed us a catalog of clothes you could not find outside of a Neiman Marcus. They had images of us, like paper dolls, that they called up on the screen and that they could dress any way they liked so you could see how you would look. Dot was in hog heaven. "What's this going to cost us?" I said.

Martin laughed as if I had made a good joke. "How about some silk shirts?" he asked me. "You have a good build. I know you're going to like them."

By the time we were dressed, the boy had come back with two big green shopping bags with handles. "What's this?" Dot asked, taking hers.

"Your old clothes," Martin said.

I took mine. I looked at myself in the mirror. I wore a blue shirt, a gray tie with a skinny knot and a long, flowing tail, ebony cuff links, a gunmetal gray silk jacket, and black slacks with a crease that would cut ice. The shoes were of leather as soft as a baby's skin and as comfortable as if I had broken them in for three months. I looked great.

Dot had settled on a champagne-colored dress with a scoop neckline, pale pumps, a simple gold necklace, and earrings that set off her dark hair. She smelled faintly of violets and looked better than lunch break at a chocolate factory.

"We've got to get out of here," I whispered to her.

"Thanks for stopping by!" Elizabeth and Martin said in unison. They escorted us to the door. "Come again soon!"

The hall was only slightly less busy than it had been. "All right, Dot. We head right for the subway. This place gives me the creeps."

"No," said Dot. She grabbed me by the arm that wasn't carrying my old clothes and dragged me across the floor toward one of the grilled windows. No one gave us a second glance. We were dressed the same as everyone else there, now, and fit right in.

At the window another young woman in green greeted us. "I am Miss Goode. How may I help you?"

"We came to get our money," said Dot.

"How much?" Miss Goode asked.

Dot turned to me. "What do you say, Sid? Would twenty million be enough?"

"We can do that," said Miss Goode. "Just come around behind the counter to my desk."

Dot started after her. I grabbed Dot's shoulder. "What the fuck are you talking about?" I whispered.

"Just go along and keep quiet."

Miss Goode led us to a large glass-topped desk. "We'll need a photograph, of course. And a number." She spoke into a phone: "Daniel, bring out two cases . . . That's right." She called up a page on her computer and examined it. "Your bank," she said to me, "is Banque Thaler, Geneva. Your number is PN68578443. You'll have to memorize it eventually. Here, write it on your palm for now." She handed me a very nice ball point pen. Then she gave another number to Dot.

While she was doing this, a man came out of a door in the marble wall behind her. He carried two silver metal briefcases and set them on the edge of Miss Goode's desk in front of Dot and me.

"Thank you, Daniel," she said. She turned to us. "Go ahead. Open them!"

I pulled the briefcase toward me and snapped it open. It was filled with tight bundles of crisp new one hundred dollar bills. Thirty of them.

"This is wonderful," Dot said. "Thank you so much!"

I closed my case and stood up. "Time to go, Dot."

"Just a minute," said Miss Goode. "I'll need your full name."

"Full name? What for?"

"For the Swiss accounts. All you've got there is three hundred thousand. The rest will be in your bank account. We'll need your photograph too."

Dot tugged my elegant sleeve. "Sid forgot about that," she explained to Miss Goode. "Always in such a hurry. His name is Sidney Xavier Dubose. D-U-B-O-S-E. I'm Dorothy Gale."

I had reached my breaking point. "Shut up, Dot."

"Now for the photographs . . ." Miss Goode began.

"You can't have my photograph." I pulled away from Dot. I had the briefcase in my right hand and shoved my bag of clothes under my left.

"That's all right," said Miss Goode. "We'll use your photographs from the tailor program. Just run along. But come again!"

I was already stalking across the floor, my new shoes clipping along like metronomes. People parted to let me by. I went right for the ramp that led to the subway. A thin man smoking a long cigarette watched me curiously as I passed one of the tables; I put my hand against his chest and knocked him down. He sprawled there in astonishment, but did nothing; nor did anyone else.

By the time I hit the ramp I was jogging. At the bottom the platform was deserted; the bubble lights still shone gold, and you could not tell whether it was night or day. Dot came up breathlessly behind me.

"What is wrong with you!" she shouted.

I felt exhausted. I could not tell how long it had been since we broke into the mountain house. "What's wrong with me? What's wrong with this whole setup? This is not sane. What are they going to do to us? This can't be real; it has to be some kind of scam."

"If you think it's a scam, just give me that briefcase. I'll take care of it for you, you stupid redneck bastard."

I stood there sullenly. I didn't know what to say. She turned from me and went to the other end of the platform, as far away as she could get.

After a few minutes the light grew in the tunnel, and the car, or one just like it, slid to a stop before us. The door opened. I got in immediately, and Dot followed. We sat next to each other in silence. The door shut, and the vehicle picked up speed until it was racing along as insanely as it had so many hours ago.

Dot tried to talk to me, but I just looked at the floor. Under the seat I saw the two gum wrappers, one of them crumpled into a knot, the other neatly folded as if it were still full.

That was the last time I ever saw Dot. I live in France now, but I have a house in Mexico and one in Toronto. In Canada I can still go to stock car races. Somehow that doesn't grab me the way it used to.

Instead I drink wine that comes in bottles that have corks. I read books. I listen to music that has no words. All because, as it turned out, I did have a ten-million-dollar Swiss bank account. The money changed everything, more than I ever could have reckoned. It was like a sword hanging over my head, like a wall between me and who I used to be. Within a month I left North Carolina: It made me nervous to stay in the state knowing that the house in the Blue Ridge was still there.

Sometimes I'm tempted to go back and see whether there really is a door in the back of that closet.

When Dot and I climbed the concrete stairs and emerged into the house, it was still night. It might have been only a minute after we went down. I went out to the living room, sat in the rustic leather chair, picked up the glass I had left next to it, and filled it to the brim with scotch. My briefcase full of three hundred thousand dollars stood on the hardwood floor beside the chair. I was dressed in a couple of thousand dollars' worth of casual clothes; my shoes alone probably cost more than a month's rent on any place that I had ever lived.

Dot sat on the sofa and poured herself a drink too. After a while she said, "I told you I'd make it up to you someday."

"How did you know about this?" I asked. "What is it?"

"It's a dream come true," Dot said. "You don't look a dream come true in the mouth."

"One person's dream come true is somebody else's nightmare," I said. "Somebody always has to pay." I had never thought that before, but as I spoke it I realized it was true.

Dot finished her scotch, picked up her briefcase and the green bag with her old skirt, sweater, and shoes, and headed for the door. She paused there and turned to me. She looked like twenty million bucks. "Are you coming?"

I followed her out. There was enough light from the moon that we were able to make our way down the dirt road to my car. The crickets chirped in the darkness. Dot opened the passenger door and got in.

"Wait a minute," I said. "Give me your bag."

Dot handed me her green bag. I dumped it out on the

ground next to the car, then dumped my own out on top of it. I crumpled the bags and shoved them under the clothes for kindling. On top lay the denim jacket I had been wearing the night I got arrested in the Sears, that the state had kept for me while I served my time, and that I had put back on the day I left stir.

"What are you doing?" Dot asked.

"Bonfire," I said. "Goodbye to the old Dot and Sid."

"But you don't have any matches."

"Reach in the glove compartment. There's a box of Blue Tips."

Lizzy Lou

Barbara Robson

Barbara Robson (www.clw.csiro.au/staff/RobsonB/) lives in Canberra, Australia. After completing a Ph.D. focusing on interactions between hydrodynamics and cyanobacterial blooms in a shallow, microtidal estuary, through the University of New South Wales in 2000, she spent three years as a postdoctoral research associate at the Centre for Water Research, University of Western Australia. Her work there included three-dimensional modeling of Western Australian wetlands. She works at the Black Mountain Laboratory of CSIRO Land and Water as a member of the Aquatic Ecosystem Modelling research team. Her fiction has appeared in the online magazines Antipodean SF, Andromeda Spaceways, *and* The Phone Book.*

"Lizzy Lou" was published in Borderlands, *an ambitious small press magazine publishing Australian science fiction, fantasy, and horror. This brief and lovely story of a little sister who gets littler has a literal fantasy level and yet reads like magic realism. It also reminds us of Lucy Clifford's classic children's story, "Wooden Tony."*

My sister was very small. In her second year of school, she was smaller even than me, sixteen months her junior and myself by far the smallest in my class. My sister said she overheard a doctor tell my mother that had our family been poorer and less well-spoken, it would have been labeled a case of "failure to thrive." I looked that up much later—it implied an unprovable suspicion of unspecified neglect. My sister might have been taken away, though she was well fed and well loved; healthy apart from a slight anemia. Another doctor said my sister's size was nothing to worry about: he had seen it before and she would grow up to be six feet tall.

My parents did worry, of course. Our family argued over the dinner table. My sister and I would sit, unhungry and unwilling in front of large plates piled with meat, spinach and vegetables. My parents would make us sit there for hours, rather than give in and allow us to leave our meals unfinished. We'd shake our heads and fold our arms and grumpily watch the food in front of us grow cold and congealed. But in the end, we'd have to eat it.

As kids do, I kept growing. I didn't catch up with my classmates, but I got closer. Lizzy, on the other hand, just got further and further behind.

It wasn't until after her seventh birthday that she actually started to shrink. I was the first to notice. Lizzy used to come up to my eyebrows, but by the end of the week, her head came no higher than my nose. We told Mum, but she laughed. "People don't shrink," she said. "It must have been you who has grown, Kate." I knew that I hadn't, though. Not by much. I still couldn't reach the second branch of the melaleuca in the back yard.

I was getting stronger and faster every week. Lizzy and I

would play with the other kids on our block: jump rope and hopscotch, Red Rover and Mother, May I? Before long, we won the piggy-back races every time. I was still kind of little, but Lizzy Lou was so small it was a cinch to carry her. She was quiet and shy, and getting quieter every day. The teachers liked her, but the kids at school started to pick on her. She was a soft target: she didn't fight back, and in those days, grown-ups wouldn't intervene in the playground. Maybe for fist-fights, but not for anything less.

The grown-ups in our lives had other things on their minds anyway. Mum was expecting a new baby and Dad was working late every day to pay the bills. Lizzy was a head and a half smaller than me when she started wagging school. I thought she'd get into big trouble, but she was too smart for that. Dad had an old typewriter and Lizzy practiced Mum's signature until she could copy it perfectly. She wrote her own sick notes and her teacher never picked up on it. Lizzy had always been good at spelling.

I'd meet her in the park after school, and we would play for a while on the swings before we went home. I wasn't brave enough to skip school myself. Besides; I liked school. I asked Lizzy what she did all day, but she wouldn't tell me.

The baby was born in October, just as the last school term started. Lizzy was moved into my room so Sarah could have a room of her own. I thought it was unfair, but Lizzy never complained. Lizzy Lou got quieter every day.

Lizzy looked like an angel; that's what Dad always said. I looked like Mary Anne Bugg, the bushranger. In the school Christmas pageant, Lizzy got to be baby Jesus and I got to be a sheep. That was more fun anyway. My parents came to watch, but Sarah cried all through the show.

In the last week of January, Mum took us shopping to buy new school books and new uniforms. I'd outgrown my old one. Lizzy had to have one specially hemmed up and taken in at the waist. Mum frowned at that, but there wasn't anything she could do about it. Mum frowned a lot lately where Lizzy was concerned, but she didn't take her to the doctor anymore. Anyway, we had to hurry home before it was time for Sarah's lunch.

While Mum was busy with Sarah in the front room, I sat on the floor of the study and looked through my new books. I was eager to read them all straight away, but Lizzy didn't seem interested in hers. She stood on the chair in front of Dad's typewriter, tapping away. I asked her what she was writing. Lizzy moved aside so I could see, and helped me with the hard words. It was a letter to our school, saying that Lizzy was transferring to another school and wouldn't be coming back. Lizzy said it meant she would never have to go to school again.

I was really worried. Nobody could get away with that. I didn't understand why she didn't like school anyway. There was always the library if the kids got too rough. I wondered whether I should tell Mum. But Lizzy always knew what she wanted and somehow when it mattered, she always quietly got her own way.

She put the letter in an envelope and used her pocket money to buy a stamp. I had to put it in the post box, because Lizzy Lou was too small to reach.

The letter seemed to work. Every day, we'd get into our uniforms and leave for school and every day, I'd get to school alone. No-one ever asked where Lizzy was. I'd meet her in the park on the way home and we'd play on the swings or down by the creek until it got late enough that Mum might worry. Even if I offered her all my sweets, Lizzy would never tell me where she'd been all day.

We were down by the lake for the Easter egg hunt, Lizzy Lou now half my size. Mum and Dad were with the other grown-ups by the barbeque and we were watching the ducks and playing with pebbles by the shore. Lizzy looked up at me with her sweetest little-girl smile, so I knew she was up to something. I was a bit surprised when she suggested a race. I always won races. She pointed out a tree at the other end of the park. It was a long run, but I could handle it. I offered to give Lizzy a head start, but she shook her head and smiled. I put my head down and ran.

I was halfway to the tree when Lizzy raced past me, her feet scarcely seeming to touch the ground. I couldn't believe it: She had never run faster than me. I ran as fast as I could, but I couldn't keep up. I puffed and panted, running harder than I ever had before. Lizzy looked back from fifty yards ahead, her laughter tinkling like glass bells in the wind.

It was then that I saw them, like cellophane glinting in the sunlight. I stopped running, outraged. "You cheat!" I yelled. "You flew!"

Lizzy's smile broke like china and I was sorry at once. She folded her wings away and I never saw them again.

Lizzy Lou kept on getting smaller, until one day we lost her in a field of long grass among the butterflies. Mum was busy rubbing dirt from Sarah's face with a hanky. She didn't seem too concerned. "She'll come back," said Mum, "when she's ready."

The End of the World as We Know It

Dale Bailey

Dale Bailey (www.dalebailey.com) lives in Hickory, North Carolina, with his wife and daughter. He teaches English at Lenoir–Rhyne College. He says on his website, "Ten years after I collected my first personal rejection letter (from Stanley Schmidt, God bless him, at Analog), I attended the Clarion Writers Workshop at Michigan State University in 1992." *That's where he sold his first story. He has published two horror novels—*The Fallen *(2002) and* House of Bones *(2003)—and a third,* Sleeping Policemen, *is forthcoming in 2006. Most of his fiction has appeared in* F&SF, *but he has also been published in* Amazing Stories, Pulphouse, Alchemy, *and* SciFiction, *and some of his best are collected in* The Resurrection Man's Legacy and Other Stories *(2003). His story "The Resurrection Man's Legacy" was a Nebula nominee, and "Death and Suffrage" won a 2003 International Horror Guild Award.*

"The End of the World as We Know It" was published in F&SF, *which had a particularly strong year in fantasy fiction in 2004. This is an especially topical postmodern fantasy about the nature of disaster. It even talks about tsunamis. It is a sad story, as befits the topic, and also a full-scale attack on the conventions of genre end-of-the-world stories. It is in addition a fascinating comparison and contrast to Kit Reed's "Perpetua," later in this book.*

Between 1347 and 1450 A.D., bubonic plague overran Europe, killing some 75 million people. The plague, dubbed the Black Death because of the black pustules that erupted on the skin of the afflicted, was caused by a bacterium now known as *Yersinia pestis*. The Europeans of the day, lacking access to microscopes or knowledge of disease vectors, attributed their misfortune to an angry God. Flagellants roamed the land, hoping to appease His wrath. "They died by the hundreds, both day and night," Agnolo di Tura tells us. "I buried my five children with my own hands . . . so many died that all believed it was the end of the world."

Today, the population of Europe is about 729 million.

Evenings, Wyndham likes to sit on the porch, drinking. He likes gin, but he'll drink anything. He's not particular. Lately, he's been watching it get dark—really *watching* it, I mean, not just sitting there—and so far he's concluded that the cliché is wrong. Night doesn't fall. It's more complex than that.

Not that he's entirely confident in the accuracy of his observations.

It's high summer just now, and Wyndham often begins drinking at two or three, so by the time the Sun sets, around nine, he's usually pretty drunk. Still, it seems to him that, if anything, night *rises*, gathering first in inky pools under the trees, as if it has leached up from underground reservoirs, and then spreading, out toward the borders of the yard and up toward the yet-lighted sky. It's only toward the end that anything falls—the blackness of deep space, he supposes, unscrolling from high above the Earth. The two planes of darkness meet somewhere in the middle, and that's night for you.

That's his current theory, anyway.

It isn't his porch, incidentally, but then it isn't his gin

either—except in the sense that, in so far as Wyndham can tell anyway, *everything* now belongs to him.

End-of-the-world stories usually come in one of two varieties.

In the first, the world ends with a natural disaster, either unprecedented or on an unprecedented scale. Floods lead all other contenders—God himself, we're told, is fond of that one—though plagues have their advocates. A renewed ice age is also popular. Ditto drought.

In the second variety, irresponsible human beings bring it on themselves. Mad scientists and corrupt bureaucrats, usually. An exchange of ICBMs is the typical route, although the scenario has dated in the present geo-political environment.

Feel free to mix and match:

Genetically engineered flu virus, anyone? Melting polar ice caps?

On the day the world ended, Wyndham didn't even realize it *was* the end of the world—not right away, anyway. For him, at that point in his life, pretty much *every* day seemed like the end of the world. This was not a consequence of a chemical imbalance, either. It was a consequence of working for UPS, where, on the day the world ended, Wyndham had been employed for sixteen years, first as a loader, then in sorting, and finally in the coveted position of driver, the brown uniform and everything. By this time the company had gone public and he also owned some shares. The money was good—very good, in fact. Not only that, he liked his job.

Still, the beginning of every goddamn day started off feeling like a cataclysm. *You* try getting up at 4:00 A.M. every morning and see how you feel.

This was his routine:

At 4:00 A.M., the alarm went off—an old-fashioned alarm, he wound it up every night. (He couldn't tolerate the radio before he drank his coffee.) He always turned it off right away, not wanting to wake his wife. He showered in the spare bathroom (again, not wanting to wake his wife; her name was Ann), poured coffee into his thermos, and ate

something he probably shouldn't—a bagel, a Pop Tart—
while he stood over the sink. By then, it would be 4:20,
4:25 if he was running late.

Then he would do something paradoxical: He would go
back to his bedroom and wake up the wife he'd spent the
last twenty minutes trying not to disturb.

"Have a good day," Wyndham always said.

His wife always did the same thing, too. She would screw
her face into her pillow and smile. "Ummm," she would
say, and it was usually such a cozy, loving, early-morning
cuddling kind of "ummm" that it almost made getting up
at four in the goddamn morning worth it.

Wyndham heard about the World Trade Center—*not* the
end of the world, though to Wyndham it sure as hell felt
that way—from one of his customers.

The customer—her name was Monica—was one of Wyndham's regulars: a Home Shopping Network fiend, this
woman. She was big, too. The kind of woman of whom
people say "She has a nice personality" or "She has such a
pretty face." She did have a nice personality, too—at least
Wyndham thought she did. So he was concerned when she
opened the door in tears.

"What's wrong?" he said.

Monica shook her head, at a loss for words. She waved
him inside. Wyndham, in violation of about fifty UPS regulations, stepped in after her. The house smelled of sausage
and floral air freshener. There was Home Shopping Network shit everywhere. I mean, *everywhere.*

Wyndham hardly noticed.

His gaze was fixed on the television. It was showing an
airliner flying into the World Trade Center. He stood there
and watched it from three or four different angles before he
noticed the Home Shopping Network logo in the lower
right-hand corner of the screen.

That was when he concluded that it must be the end of
the world. He couldn't imagine the Home Shopping Network preempting regularly scheduled programming for
anything less.

The Muslim extremists who flew airplanes into the World

Trade Center, into the Pentagon, and into the unyielding earth of an otherwise unremarkable field in Pennsylvania, were secure, we are told, in the knowledge of their imminent translation into paradise.

There were nineteen of them.

Every one of them had a name.

Wyndham's wife was something of a reader. She liked to read in bed. Before she went to sleep she always marked her spot using a bookmark Wyndham had given her for her birthday one year: It was a cardboard bookmark with a yarn ribbon at the top, and a picture of a rainbow arching high over white-capped mountains. *Smile*, the bookmark said. *God loves you.*

Wyndham wasn't much of a reader, but if he'd picked up his wife's book the day the world ended he would have found the first few pages interesting. In the opening chapter, God raptures all true Christians to Heaven. This includes true Christians who are driving cars and trains and airplanes, resulting in uncounted lost lives as well as significant damages to personal property. If Wyndham *had* read the book, he'd have thought of a bumper sticker he sometimes saw from high in his UPS truck. *Warning*, the bumper sticker read, *In case of Rapture, this car will be unmanned.* Whenever he saw that bumper sticker, Wyndham imagined cars crashing, planes falling from the sky, patients abandoned on the operating table—pretty much the scenario of his wife's book, in fact.

Wyndham went to church every Sunday, but he couldn't help wondering what would happen to the untold millions of people who *weren't* true Christians—whether by choice or by the geographical fluke of having been born in some place like Indonesia. What if they were crossing the street in front of one of those cars, he wondered, or watering lawns those planes would soon plow into?

But I was saying:

On the day the world ended Wyndham didn't understand right away what had happened. His alarm clock went off the way it always did and he went through his normal routine. Shower in the spare bath, coffee in the thermos, breakfast over the sink (a chocolate donut, this time, and gone a little stale). Then he went back to the bedroom to say goodbye to his wife.

"Have a good day," he said, as he always said, and, leaning over, he shook her a little: not enough to really wake her, just enough to get her stirring. In sixteen years of performing this ritual, minus federal holidays and two weeks of paid vacation in the summer, Wyndham had pretty much mastered it. He could cause her to stir without quite waking her up just about every time.

So to say he was surprised when his wife didn't screw her face into her pillow and smile is something of an understatement. He was shocked, actually. And there was an additional consideration: She hadn't said, "Ummm," either. Not the usual luxurious, warm-morning-bed kind of "ummm," and not the infrequent but still familiar stuffy, I-have-a-cold-and-my-head-aches kind of "ummm," either.

No "ummm" at all.

The air-conditioning cycled off. For the first time Wyndham noticed a strange smell—a faint, organic funk, like spoiled milk, or unwashed feet.

Standing there in the dark, Wyndham began to have a very bad feeling. It was a different kind of bad feeling than the one he'd had in Monica's living room watching airliners plunge again and again into the World Trade Center. That had been a powerful but largely impersonal bad feeling—I say "largely impersonal" because Wyndham had a third cousin who worked at Cantor Fitzgerald. (The cousin's name was Chris; Wyndham had to look it up in his address book every year when he sent out cards celebrating the birth of his personal savior.) The bad feeling he began to have when his wife failed to say "ummm," on the other hand, was powerful and *personal*.

Concerned, Wyndham reached down and touched his wife's face. It was like touching a woman made of wax, lifeless and cool, and it was at that moment—that moment precisely—that Wyndham realized the world had come to an end.

Everything after that was just details.

Beyond the mad scientists and corrupt bureaucrats, characters in end-of-the-world stories typically come in one of three varieties.

The first is the rugged individualist. You know the type: self-reliant, iconoclastic loners who know how to use firearms and deliver babies. By story's end, they're well on their way to Reestablishing Western Civilization—though they're usually smart enough not to return to the Bad Old Ways.

The second variety is the post-apocalyptic bandit. These characters often come in gangs, and they face off against the rugged survivor types. If you happen to prefer cinematic incarnations of the end-of-the-world tale, you can usually recognize them by their penchant for bondage gear, punked-out haircuts, and customized vehicles. Unlike the rugged survivors, the post-apocalyptic bandits embrace the Bad Old Ways—though they're not displeased by the expanded opportunities to rape and pillage.

The third type of character—also pretty common, though a good deal less so than the other two—is the world-weary sophisticate. Like Wyndham, such characters drink too much; unlike Wyndham, they suffer badly from *ennui*. Wyndham suffers too, of course, but whatever he suffers from, you can bet it's not *ennui*.

We were discussing details, though:

Wyndham did the things people do when they discover a loved one dead. He picked up the phone and dialed 9-1-1. There seemed to be something wrong with the line, however; no one picked up on the other end. Wyndham took a deep breath, went into the kitchen, and tried the extension. Once again he had no success.

The reason, of course, was that, this being the end of the world, all the people who were supposed to answer the phones were dead. Imagine them being swept away by a tidal wave if that helps—which is exactly what happened to more than three thousand people during a storm in Pakistan in 1960. (Not that this is *literally* what happened to the operators who would have taken Wyndham's 9-1-1 call, you understand; but more about what *really* happened to them later—the important thing is that one moment they had been alive; the next they were dead. Like Wyndham's wife.)

Wyndham gave up on the phone.

He went back into the bedroom. He performed a fumbling version of mouth-to-mouth resuscitation on his wife for fifteen minutes or so, and then he gave that up, too. He walked into his daughter's bedroom (she was twelve and her name was Ellen). He found her lying on her back, her mouth slightly agape. He reached down to shake her—he was going to tell her that something terrible had happened; that her mother had died—but he found that something terrible had happened to her as well. The same terrible thing, in fact.

Wyndham panicked.

He raced outside, where the first hint of red had begun to bleed up over the horizon. His neighbor's automatic irrigation system was on, the heads whickering in the silence, and as he sprinted across the lawn, Wyndham felt the spray, like a cool hand against his face. Then, chilled, he was standing on his neighbor's stoop. Hammering the door with both fists. Screaming.

After a time—he didn't know how long—a dreadful calm settled over him. There was no sound but the sound of the sprinklers, throwing glittering arcs of spray into the halo of the street light on the corner.

He had a vision, then. It was as close as he had ever come to a moment of genuine prescience. In the vision, he saw the suburban houses stretching away in silence before him. He saw the silent bedrooms. In them, curled beneath the sheets, he saw a legion of sleepers, also silent, who would never again wake up.

Wyndham swallowed.

Then he did something he could not have imagined doing even twenty minutes ago. He bent over, fished the key from its hiding place between the bricks, and let himself inside his neighbor's house.

The neighbor's cat slipped past him, mewing querulously. Wyndham had already reached down to retrieve it when he noticed the smell—that unpleasant, faintly organic funk. Not spoiled milk, either. And not feet. Something worse: soiled diapers, or a clogged toilet.

Wyndham straightened, the cat forgotten.

"Herm?" he called. "Robin?"

No answer.

Inside, Wyndham picked up the phone, and dialed 9-1-1. He listened to it ring for a long time; then, without bothering to turn it off, Wyndham dropped the phone to the floor. He made his way through the silent house, snapping on lights. At the door to the master bedroom, he hesitated. The odor—it was unmistakable now, a mingled stench of urine and feces, of all the body's muscles relaxing at once—was stronger here. When he spoke again, whispering really—

"Herm? Robin?"

—he no longer expected an answer.

Wyndham turned on the light. Robin and Herm were shapes in the bed, unmoving. Stepping closer, Wyndham stared down at them. A fleeting series of images cascaded through his mind, images of Herm and Robin working the grill at the neighborhood block party or puttering in their vegetable garden. They'd had a knack for tomatoes, Robin and Herm. Wyndham's wife had always loved their tomatoes.

Something caught in Wyndham's throat.

He went away for a while then.

The world just grayed out on him.

When he came back, Wyndham found himself in the living room, standing in front of Robin and Herm's television. He turned it on and cycled through the channels, but there was nothing on. Literally nothing. Snow, that's all. Seventy-five channels of snow. The end of the world had always been televised in Wyndham's experience. The fact that it wasn't being televised now suggested that it really *was* the end of the world.

This is not to suggest that television validates human experience—of the end of the world or indeed of anything else, for that matter.

You could ask the people of Pompeii, if most of them hadn't died in a volcano eruption in 79 A.D., nearly two millennia before television. When Vesuvius erupted, sending lava thundering down the mountainside at four miles a minute, some sixteen thousand people perished. By some freakish geological quirk, some of them—their shells, anyway—were preserved, frozen inside casts of volcanic ash.

Their arms are outstretched in pleas for mercy, their faces frozen in horror.

For a fee, you can visit them today.

Here's one of my favorite end-of-the-world scenarios by the way:

Carnivorous plants.

Wyndham got in his car and went looking for assistance—a functioning telephone or television, a helpful passer-by. He found instead more non-functioning telephones and televisions. And, of course, more non-functioning people: lots of those, though he had to look harder for them than you might have expected. They weren't scattered in the streets, or dead at the wheels of their cars in a massive traffic jam—though Wyndham supposed that might have been the case somewhere in Europe, where the catastrophe—whatever it was—had fallen square in the middle of the morning rush.

Here, however, it seemed to have caught most folks at home in bed; as a result, the roads were more than usually passable.

At a loss—numb, really—Wyndham drove to work. He might have been in shock by then. He'd gotten accustomed to the smell, anyway, and the corpses of the night shift—men and women he'd known for sixteen years, in some cases—didn't shake him as much. What *did* shake him was the sight of all the packages in the sorting area: He was struck suddenly by the fact that none of them would ever be delivered. So Wyndham loaded his truck and went out on his route. He wasn't sure why he did it—maybe because he'd rented a movie once in which a post-apocalyptic drifter scavenges a U.S. Postal uniform and manages to Reestablish Western Civilization (but not the Bad Old Ways) by assuming the postman's appointed rounds. The futility of Wyndham's own efforts quickly became evident, however.

He gave it up when he found that even Monica—or, as he more often thought of her, the Home Shopping Network Lady—was no longer in the business of receiving packages. Wyndham found her face down on the kitchen floor, clutching a shattered coffee mug in one hand. In death she had neither a pretty face nor a nice personality. She did have that same ripe unpleasant odor, however. In spite of it, Wyndham stood looking down at her for the longest time. He couldn't seem to look away.

When he finally *did* look away, Wyndham went back to the living room where he had once watched nearly three thousand people die, and opened her package himself. When it came to UPS rules, the Home Shopping Network Lady's living room was turning out to be something of a post-apocalyptic zone in its own right.

Wyndham tore the mailing tape off and dropped it on the floor. He opened the box. Inside, wrapped safely in three layers of bubble wrap, he found a porcelain statue of Elvis Presley.

Elvis Presley, the King of Rock 'n' Roll, died August 16, 1977, while sitting on the toilet. An autopsy revealed that he had ingested an impressive cocktail of prescription drugs—including codeine, ethinimate, methaqualone, and various barbiturates. Doctors also found trace elements of Valium, Demerol, and other pharmaceuticals in his veins.

For a time, Wyndham comforted himself with the illusion that the end of the world had been a local phenomenon. He sat in his truck outside the Home Shopping Network Lady's house and awaited rescue—the sound of sirens or approaching choppers, whatever. He fell asleep cradling the porcelain statue of Elvis. He woke up at dawn, stiff from sleeping in the truck, to find a stray dog nosing around outside.

Clearly rescue would not be forthcoming.

Wyndham chased off the dog and placed Elvis gently on the sidewalk. Then he drove off, heading out of the city. Periodically, he stopped, each time confirming what he had already known the minute he touched his dead wife's face: The end of the world was upon him. He found nothing but non-functioning telephones, non-functioning televisions, and non-functioning people. Along the way he listened to a lot of non-functioning radio stations.

You, like Wyndham, may be curious about the catastrophe that has befallen everyone in the world around him. You may even be wondering why Wyndham has survived.

End-of-the-world tales typically make a big deal about such things, but Wyndham's curiosity will never be satisfied. Unfortunately, neither will yours.

Shit happens.

It's the end of the world after all.

The dinosaurs never discovered what caused *their* extinction, either.

At this writing, however, most scientists agree that the dinosaurs met their fate when an asteroid nine miles wide plowed into the Earth just south of the Yucatan Peninsula, triggering gigantic tsunamis, hurricane-force winds, worldwide forest fires, and a flurry of volcanic activity. The crater is still there—it's 120 miles wide and more than a mile deep—but the dinosaurs, along with seventy-five percent of the other species then alive, are gone. Many of them died in the impact, vaporized in an explosion equivalent to thousands of megatons. Those that survived the initial cataclysm would have perished soon after as acid rain poisoned the world's water, and dust obscured the Sun, plunging the planet into a years-long winter.

For what it's worth, this impact was merely the most dramatic in a long series of mass extinctions; they occur in the fossil record at roughly thirty million-year intervals. Some scientists have linked these intervals to the solar system's periodic journey through the galactic plane, which dislodges millions of comets from the Oort cloud beyond

Pluto, raining them down on Earth. This theory, still contested, is called the Shiva Hypothesis in honor of the Hindu god of destruction.

The inhabitants of Lisbon would have appreciated the allusion on November 1, 1755, when the city was struck by an earthquake measuring 8.5 on the Richter Scale. The tremor leveled more than twelve thousand homes and ignited a fire that burned for six days.

More than sixty thousand people perished.

This event inspired Voltaire to write *Candide*, in which Dr. Pangloss advises us that this is the best of all possible worlds.

Wyndham could have filled the gas tank in his truck. There were gas stations at just about every exit along the highway, and *they* seemed to be functioning well enough. He didn't bother, though.

When the truck ran out of gas, he just pulled to the side of the road, hopped down, and struck off across the fields. When it started getting dark—this was before he had launched himself on the study of just how it is night falls—he took shelter in the nearest house.

It was a nice place, a two-story brick set well back from the country road he was by then walking on. It had some big trees in the front yard. In the back, a shaded lawn sloped down to the kind of woods you see in movies, but not often in real life: enormous, old trees with generous, leaf-carpeted avenues. It was the kind of place his wife would have loved, and he regretted having to break a window to get inside. But there it was: It was the end of the world and he had to have a place to sleep. What else could he do?

Wyndham hadn't planned to stay there, but when he woke up the next morning he couldn't think of anywhere to go. He found two non-functional old people in one upstairs bedroom and he tried to do for them what he had not been able to do for his wife and daughter: Using a spade from the garage, he started digging a grave in the front yard. After an hour or so, his hands began to blister and crack. His muscles—soft from sitting behind the wheel of a UPS truck for all those years—rebelled.

He rested for a while, and then he loaded the old people

into the car he found parked in the garage—a slate-blue
Volvo station wagon with 37,312 miles on the odometer.
He drove them a mile or two down the road, pulled over,
and laid them out, side by side, in a grove of beech trees. He
tried to say some words over them before he left—his wife
would have wanted him to—but he couldn't think of anything appropriate so he finally gave it up and went back to
the house.

It wouldn't have made much difference: Though Wyndham didn't know it, the old people were lapsed Jews. According to the faith Wyndham shared with his wife, they
were doomed to burn in hell for all eternity anyway. Both
of them were first-generation immigrants; most of their
families had already been burned up in ovens at Dachau
and Buchenwald.

Burning wouldn't have been anything new for them.

Speaking of fires, the Triangle Shirt Waist Factory in
New York City burned on March 25, 1911. One hundred
and forty-six people died. Many of them might have survived, but the factory's owners had locked the exits to prevent theft.

Rome burned, too. It is said that Nero fiddled.

Back at the house, Wyndham washed up and made himself a drink from the liquor cabinet he found in the kitchen.
He'd never been much of a drinker before the world ended,
but he didn't see any reason not to give it a try now. His experiment proved such a success that he began sitting out on
the porch nights, drinking gin and watching the sky. One
night he thought he saw a plane, lights blinking as it arced
high overhead. Later, sober, he concluded that it must have
been a satellite, still whipping around the planet, beaming
down telemetry to empty listening stations and abandoned
command posts.

A day or two later the power went out. And a few days
after that, Wyndham ran out of liquor. Using the Volvo, he
set off in search of a town. Characters in end-of-the-world
stories commonly drive vehicles of two types: The jaded so-
phisticates tend to drive souped-up sports cars, often racing
them along the Australian coastline because what else do

they have to live for; everyone else drives rugged SUVs.
Since the 1991 Persian Gulf War—in which some twenty-
three thousand people died, most of them Iraqi conscripts
killed by American smart bombs—military-style Humvees
have been especially coveted. Wyndham, however, found
the Volvo entirely adequate to his needs.

No one shot at him.

He was not assaulted by a roving pack of feral dogs.

He found a town after only fifteen minutes on the road.
He didn't see any evidence of looting. Everybody was too
dead to loot; that's the way it is at the end of the world.

On the way, Wyndham passed a sporting goods store
where he did not stop to stock up on weapons or survival
equipment. He passed numerous abandoned vehicles, but
he did not stop to siphon off some gas. He *did* stop at the
liquor store, where he smashed a window with a rock and
helped himself to several cases of gin, whiskey, and vodka.
He also stopped at the grocery store, where he found the
reeking bodies of the night crew sprawled out beside carts
of supplies that would never make it onto the shelves. Holding a handkerchief over his nose, Wyndham loaded up on
tonic water and a variety of other mixers. He also got some
canned goods, though he didn't feel any imperative to stock
up beyond his immediate needs. He ignored the bottled
water.

In the book section, he *did* pick up a bartender's guide.

Some end-of-the-world stories present us with two post-
apocalypse survivors, one male and one female. These two
survivors take it upon themselves to Repopulate the Earth,
part of their larger effort to Reestablish Western Civilization without the Bad Old Ways. Their names are always
artfully withheld until the end of the story, at which point
they are invariably revealed to be Adam and Eve.

The truth is, almost all end-of-the-world stories are at
some level Adam-and-Eve stories. That may be why they
enjoy such popularity. In the interests of total disclosure, I
will admit that in fallow periods of my own sexual life—and,
alas, these periods have been more frequent than I'd care to
admit—I've often found Adam-and-Eve post-holocaust fan-

tasies strangely comforting. Being the only man alive significantly reduces the potential for rejection in my view. And it cuts performance anxiety practically to nothing.

There's a woman in this story, too.

Don't get your hopes up.

By this time, Wyndham has been living in the brick house for almost two weeks. He sleeps in the old couple's bedroom, and he sleeps pretty well, but maybe that's the gin. Some mornings he wakes up disoriented, wondering where his wife is and how he came to be in a strange place. Other mornings he wakes up feeling like he dreamed everything else and this has always been his bedroom.

One day, though, he wakes up early, to gray pre-dawn light. Someone is moving around downstairs. Wyndham's curious, but he's not afraid. He doesn't wish he'd stopped at the sporting goods store and gotten a gun. Wyndham has never shot a gun in his life. If he did shoot someone—even a post-apocalyptic punk with cannibalism on his mind—he'd probably have a breakdown.

Wyndham doesn't try to disguise his presence as he goes downstairs. There's a woman in the living room. She's not bad looking, this woman—blonde in a washed-out kind of way, trim, and young, twenty-five, thirty at the most. She doesn't look extremely clean, and she doesn't smell much better, but hygiene hasn't been uppermost on Wyndham's mind lately, either. Who is he to judge?

"I was looking for a place to sleep," the woman says.

"There's a spare bedroom upstairs," Wyndham tells her.

.

The next morning—it's really almost noon, but Wyndham has gotten into the habit of sleeping late—they eat breakfast together: a Pop Tart for the woman, a bowl of dry Cheerios for Wyndham.

They compare notes, but we don't need to get into that. It's the end of the world and the woman doesn't know how it happened anymore than Wyndham does or you do or anybody ever does. She does most of the talking, though.

Wyndham's never been much of a talker, even at the best of times.

He doesn't ask her to stay. He doesn't ask her to leave.

He doesn't ask her much of anything.

That's how it goes all day.

Sometimes the whole sex thing *causes* the end of the world.

In fact, if you'll permit me to reference Adam and Eve just one more time, sex and death have been connected to the end of the world ever since—well, the beginning of the world. Eve, despite warnings to the contrary, eats of the fruit of the Tree of Knowledge of Good and Evil and realizes she's naked—that is, a sexual being. Then she introduces Adam to the idea by giving him a bite of the fruit.

God punishes Adam and Eve for their transgression by kicking them out of Paradise and introducing death into the world. And there you have it: the first apocalypse, *eros* and *thanatos* all tied up in one neat little bundle, and it's all Eve's fault.

No wonder feminists don't like that story. It's a pretty corrosive view of female sexuality when you think about it.

Coincidentally, perhaps, one of my favorite end-of-the-world stories involves some astronauts who fall into a time warp; when they get out they learn that all the men are dead. The women have done pretty well for themselves in the meantime. They no longer need men to reproduce and they've set up a society that seems to work okay without men—better in fact than our messy two-sex societies ever have.

But do the men stay out of it?

They do not. They're men, after all, and they're driven by their need for sexual dominance. It's genetically encoded so to speak, and it's not long before they're trying to turn this Eden into another fallen world. It's sex that does it, violent male sex—rape, actually. In other words, sex that's more about the violence than the sex.

And certainly nothing to do with love.

Which, when you think about it, is a pretty corrosive view of male sexuality.

The more things change the more they stay the same, I guess.

Wyndham, though.

Wyndham heads out on the porch around three. He's got some tonic. He's got some gin. It's what he does now. He doesn't know where the woman is, doesn't have strong feelings on the issue either way.

He's been sitting there for hours when she joins him. Wyndham doesn't know what time it is, but the air has that hazy underwater quality that comes around twilight. Darkness is starting to pool under the trees, the crickets are tuning up, and it's so peaceful that for a moment Wyndham can almost forget that it's the end of the world.

Then the screen door claps shut behind the woman. Wyndham can tell right away that she's done something to herself, though he couldn't tell you for sure what it is: that magic women do, he guesses. His wife used to do it, too. She always looked good to him, but sometimes she looked just flat-out amazing. Some powder, a little blush. Lipstick. You know.

And he appreciates the effort. He does. He's flattered even. She's an attractive woman. Intelligent, too.

The truth is, though, he's just not interested.

She sits beside him, and all the time she's talking. And though she doesn't say it in so many words, what she's talking about is Repopulating the World and Reestablishing Western Civilization. She's talking about Duty. She's talking about it because that's what you're supposed to talk about at times like this. But underneath that is sex. And underneath that, way down, is loneliness—and he has some sympathy for that, Wyndham does. After a while, she touches Wyndham, but he's got nothing. He might as well be dead down there.

"What's wrong with you?" she says.

Wyndham doesn't know how to answer her. He doesn't know how to tell her that the end of the world isn't about any of that stuff. The end of the world is about something else, he doesn't have a word for it.

So, anyway, Wyndham's wife.

She has another book on her nightstand, too. She doesn't read it every night, only on Sundays. But the week before the end of the world the story she was reading was the story of Job.

You know the story, right?

It goes like this: God and Satan—the Adversary, anyway; that's probably the better translation—make a wager. They want to see just how much shit God's most faithful servant will eat before he renounces his faith. The servant's name is Job. So they make the wager, and God starts feeding Job shit. Takes his riches, takes his cattle, takes his health. Deprives him of his friends. On and on. Finally—and this is the part that always got to Wyndham—God takes Job's wife and his children.

Let me clarify: In this context "takes" should be read as "kills."

You with me on this? Like Krakatoa, a volcanic island that used to exist between Java and Sumatra. On August 27, 1883, Krakatoa exploded, spewing ash fifty miles into the sky and vomiting up five cubic miles of rock. The concussion was heard three thousand miles away. It created tsunamis towering one hundred twenty feet in the air. Imagine all that water crashing down on the flimsy villages that lined the shores of Java and Sumatra.

Thirty thousand people died.

Every single one of them had a name.

Job's wife and kids. Dead. Just like thirty thousand nameless Javanese.

As for Job? He keeps shoveling down the shit. He will not renounce God. He keeps the faith. And he's rewarded: God gives him back his riches, his cattle. God restores his health, and sends him friends. God replaces his wife and kids.

Pay attention: Word choice is important in an end-of-the-world story.

I said "replaces," not "restores."

Different wife. Different kids.

The other wife, the other kids? They stay dead, gone, non-functioning, erased forever from the Earth, just like the dinosaurs and the twelve million undesirables incinerated by the Nazis and the five hundred thousand slaughtered in Rwanda and the 1.7 million murdered in Cambodia and the sixty million immolated in the Middle Passage.

That merry prankster God.

That jokester.

That's what the end of the world is about, Wyndham wants to say. The rest is just details.

By this point the woman (You want her to have a name? She deserves one, don't you think?) has started to weep softly. Wyndham gets to his feet and goes into the dark kitchen for another glass. Then he comes back out to the porch and makes a gin and tonic. He sits beside her and presses the cool glass upon her. It's all he knows to do.

"Here," he says. "Drink this. It'll help."

Leaving His Cares Behind Him

〜〜〜

Kage Baker

*Kage Baker (www.kagebaker.com) lives in Pismo Beach,
California, which she describes as "the Clam Capital of the
World." She is best known for her series of SF stories about
The Company, time travelers from our future who delve
into various periods of our past to rescue lost art and other
treasures. Her novels include* In the Garden of Iden *(1997)*,
Sky Coyote *(1999)*, Mendoza in Hollywood *(2000)*, The
Graveyard Game *(2001)*, The Life of the World to Come
(2004) and Children of the Company *(2005), with more in
the works. There is also a collection of Company Stories,*
Black Projects, White Knight: The Company Dossiers
(2002). Her first fantasy novel, The Anvil of the World,
was published in 2003, and another collection, Mother Ae-
gypt and Other Stories *(2004), and several small press
books and chapbooks have appeared in the last three years.
She is an engaging storyteller.*

*"Leaving His Cares Behind Him," a fun, nasty little
story, appeared in* Asimov's. *According to Baker, "Leaving
His Cares Behind Him" and the wastrel rogue Lord
Ermenwyr—who was also prominent in* The Anvil of the
World—*were inspired by the song "Back to the Family"
from Jethro Tull's album* Stand Up, *as well as by other
early Tull songs and by Ian Anderson, the band's Puckish
lead singer and flutist. No self-indulgence is too base for
Ermenwyr, and so even though his father is a demon, some
parental discipline must be enforced.*

The young man opened his eyes. Bright day affronted them. He groaned and rolled over, pulling his pillow about his ears.

After thirty seconds of listening to his brain pound more loudly than his heart, he rolled over again and stared at his comfortless world.

It shouldn't have been comfortless. It had originally been a bijou furnished residence, suitable for a wealthy young person-about-town. That had been when one could see the floor, however. Or the sink. Or the tabletops. Or, indeed, anything but the chilly wasteland of scattered clothing, empty bottles and unwashed dishes.

He regarded all this squalor with mild outrage, as though it belonged to someone else, and crawled from the strangling funk of his sheets. Standing up was a mistake; the top of his head blew off and hit the ceiling. A suitable place to vomit was abruptly a primary concern.

The kitchen? No; no room in the sink. Bathroom? Too far away. He lurched to the balcony doors, flung them wide and leaned out. A delicate peach soufflé, a bowl of oyster broth, assorted brightly colored trifles that did not yield their identities to memory and two bottles of sparkling wine spattered into the garden below.

Limp as a rag he clung to the rail, retching and spitting, shivering in his nakedness. Amused comment from somewhere roused him; he lifted his eyes and saw that half of Deliantiba (or at least the early-morning tradesmen making their way along Silver Boulevard) had watched his performance. He glared at them. Spitting out the last of the night before, he stood straight, turned his affronted back and went inside, slamming the balcony doors behind him.

With some effort, he located his dressing gown (finest velvet brocade, embroidered with gold thread) and matching slippers. The runner answered his summoning bell sooner than he had expected and her thunder at his door brought on more throbbing in his temples. He opened to see the older one, not the young one who was so smitten with him, and cursed his luck.

"Kretia, isn't it?" he said, smiling nonetheless. "You look lovely this morning! Now, I'd like a carafe of mint tea, a plate of crisp wafers and one green apple, sliced thin. Off you go, and if you're back within ten minutes you'll have a gratuity of your very own!"

She just looked at him, hard-eyed. "Certainly, sir," she replied. "Will that be paid for in advance, sir?"

"There goes *your* treat," he muttered, but swept a handful of assorted small coins from the nearest flat surface and handed them through the doorway. "That should be enough. Kindly hurry; I'm not a well man."

He had no clean clothing, but while poking through the drifts of slightly less foul linen he found a pair of red silk underpants he was fairly certain did not belong to him, and pulling them on cheered him up a great deal. By the time he had breakfasted and strolled out to meet the new day, Lord Ermenwyr was nearly himself again, and certainly capable of grappling with the question of how he was going to pay his rent for another month.

And grappling was required.

The gentleman at Firebeater's Savings and Loan was courteous, but implacable: no further advances on my lord's quarterly allotment were to be paid, on direct order of my lord's father. Charm would not persuade him; neither would veiled threats. Finally the stop payment order itself was produced, with its impressive and somewhat frightening seal of black wax. Defeated, Lord Ermenwyr slunk out into the sunshine and stamped his foot at a pigeon that was unwise enough to cross his path. It just stared at him.

He strode away, hands clasped under his coattails, thinking very hard. By long-accustomed habit his legs bore him to a certain pleasant villa on Goldwire Avenue, and when he realized where he was, he smiled and rang at the gate. A laconic porter admitted him to Lady Seelice's garden. An anxious-looking maidservant admitted him to Lady Seel-ice's house. He found his own way to Lady Seelice's boudoir.

Lady Seelice was sitting up in bed, going over the books of her shipping company, and she had a grim set to her mouth. Vain for him to offer to distract her with light con-versation; vain for him to offer to massage her neck, or brush her hair. He perched on the foot of her bed, looking as winsome as he could, and made certain suggestions. She declined them in an absent-minded sort of way.

He helped himself to sugared comfits from the exquisite little porcelain jar on her bedside table, and ate them quite amusingly, but she did not laugh. He pretended to play her corset like an accordion, but she did not laugh at that ei-ther. He fastened her brassiere on his head and crawled around the room on his hands and knees meowing like a kitten, and when she took absolutely no notice of that, he stood up and asked her outright if she'd loan him a hundred crowns.

She told him to get out, so he did.

As he was stamping downstairs, fuming, the anxious maidservant drifted into his path.

"Oh, dear, was she cross with you?" she inquired.

"Your mistress is in a vile mood," said Lord Ermenwyr resentfully, and he pulled her close and kissed her very hard. She leaned into his embrace, making soft noises, stroking his hair. When they came up for air at last, she looked into his eyes.

"She's been in a vile mood these three days. Something's wrong with her stupid old investments."

"Well, if she's not nicer soon, she'll find that her nimble little goat has capered off to greener pastures," said Lord Ermenwyr, pressing his face into the maidservant's bosom. He began to untie the cord of her bodice with his teeth.

"I've been thinking, darling," said the maidservant slowly, "that perhaps it's time we told her the truth about . . . you know . . . *us*."

Unseen under her chin, the lordling grimaced in dismay. He spat out a knot and straightened up at once.

"Well! Yes. Perhaps." He coughed, and looked suddenly pale. "On the other hand, there is the danger—" He coughed again, groped hurriedly for a silk handkerchief and held it to his lips. "My condition is so, ah, *tentative*. If we were to tell of our forbidden love—and then I were to collapse unexpectedly and die, which I might at any moment, how could I rest in my grave knowing that your mistress had turned you out in the street?"

"I suppose you're right," sighed the maidservant, watching as he doubled over in a fit of coughing. "Do you want a glass of wine or anything?"

"No, my darling—" Wheezing, Lord Ermenwyr turned and made his unsteady way to the door. "I think—I think I'd best pay a call on my personal physician!"

Staggering, choking, he exited, and continued in that wise until he was well out of sight at the end of the avenue, at which time he stood straight and walked on. A few paces later the sugared comfits made a most unwelcome return, and though he was able to lean quickly over a low wall, he looked up directly into the eyes of someone's outraged gardener.

Running three more blocks did not improve matters much. He collapsed on a bench in a small public park and fumed, considering his situation.

"I'm fed up with this life," he told a statue of some Deliantiban civic leader. "Independence is all very well, but perhaps . . ."

He mulled over the squalor, the inadequacy, the creditors, the wretched *complications* with which he had hourly to deal. He compared it with his former accustomed comforts, in a warm and loving home where he was accorded all the consideration his birth and rank merited. Within five minutes, having given due thought to all arguments pro and con, he rose briskly to his feet and set off in the direction of Silver Boulevard.

Ready cash was obtained by pawning one of the presents Lady Seelice had given him (amethysts were not really his color, after all). He dined pleasantly at his favorite restaurant that evening. When three large gentlemen asked at the door whether or not Lord Ermenwyr had a moment to speak with them, however, he was obliged to exit through a side door and across a roof.

Arriving home shortly after midnight, he loaded all his unwashed finery into his trunks, lowered the trunks from his window with a knotted sheet, himself exited in like manner, and dragged the trunks a quarter-mile to the caravan depot. He spent the rest of the night there, dozing fitfully in a corner, and by dawn was convinced he'd caught his death of cold.

But when his trunks were loaded into the baggage cart, when he had taken his paid seat amongst the other passengers, when the caravan master had mounted into the lead cart and the runner signaled their departure with a blast on her brazen trumpet—then Lord Ermenwyr was comforted, and allowed himself to sneer at Deliantiba and all his difficulties there as it, and they, fell rapidly behind him.

The caravan master drew a deep breath, deciding to be patient.

"Young man, your friends must have been having a joke at your expense," he said. "There aren't any country estates around here. We're in the bloody *Greenlands*. Nobody's up here but bandits, and demons and wild beasts."

"No need to be alarmed on my behalf, good fellow," the young man assured him. "There'll be bearers along to meet me in half an hour. That's their cart-track right there, see?"

The caravan master peered at what might have been a rabbit's trail winding down to the honest paved road. He followed it up with his eyes until it became lost in the immensity of the forests. He looked higher still, at the black mountain towering beyond, and shuddered. He knew what lay up there. It wasn't something he told his paying passengers about, because if he were ever to do so, no amount of bargain fares could tempt them to take this particular shortcut through the wilderness.

"Look," he said, "I'll be honest with you. If I let you off here, the next thing anyone will hear of you is a note demanding your ransom. *If* the gods are inclined to be merciful! There's a Red House station three days on. Ride with us that far, at least. You can send a message to your friends from there."

"I tell you this is my stop, Caravan Master," said the young man, in such a snide tone the caravan master thought: *To hell with him.*

"Offload his trunks, then!" he ordered the keymen, and marched off to the lead cart and resumed his seat. As the caravan pulled away, the other passengers looked back, wondering at the young man who sat down on his luggage with an air of unconcern and pulled out a jade smoking-tube, packing it with fragrant weed.

"I hope his parents have other sons," murmured a traveling salesman. Something howled in the depths of the forest, and he looked fearfully over his shoulder. In doing so, he missed seeing the young man lighting up his smoke with a green fireball. When he looked back, a bend in the road had already hidden the incautious youth.

Lord Ermenwyr, in the meanwhile, sucked in a double lungful of medicinal smoke and sighed in contentment. He leaned back, and blew a smoke ring.

"That's my unpaid rent and cleaning fee," he said to himself, watching it dissipate and wobble away. He sucked smoke and blew another.

"That's my little misunderstanding with Brasshandle the moneylender," he said, as it too faded into the pure air. Giggling to himself, he drew in a deep, deep store of smoke and blew three rings in close formation.

"Your hearts, ladies! All of you. Bye-bye now! You'll find another toy to amuse yourselves, I don't doubt. All my troubles are magically wafting away—oh, wait, I should blow one for that stupid business with the public fountain—"

When he heard the twig snap, however, he sat up and gazed into the darkness of the forest.

They were coming for him through the trees, and they were very large. Some were furred and some were scaled, some had great fanged pitilessly grinning mouths, some had eyes red as a dying campfire just before the night closes in.

Some bore spiked weapons. Some bore treebough clubs. They shared no single characteristic of feature or flesh, save that they wore, all, livery black as ink.

"It's about time you got here," said Lord Ermenwyr. Rising to his feet, he let fall the glamor that disguised his true form.

"Master!" cried some of that dread host, and "Little Master!" cried others, and they abased themselves before him.

"Yes, yes, I'm glad to see you too," said Lord Ermenwyr. "Take special care with my trunks, now. I'll have no end of trouble getting them to close again, if they're dropped and burst open."

"My little lord, you look pale," said the foremost creature, doffing his spiked helmet respectfully. "Have you been ill again? Shall we carry you?"

"I haven't been well, no," the lordling admitted. "Perhaps you ought."

The leader knelt immediately, and Lord Ermenwyr hopped up on his shoulder and clung as he stood, looking about with satisfaction from the considerable height.

"Home!" he ordered, and that uncouth legion bore him, and his trunks, and his unwashed linen, swiftly and with chants of praise to the great black gate of his father's house.

The Lord Ermenwyr was awakened next morning by an apologetic murmur, as one of the maidservants slipped from his bed. He acknowledged her departure with a sleepy grunt and a wave of his hand, and rolled over to luxuriate in dreams once more. Nothing disturbed his repose further until the black and purple curtains of his bed were drawn open, reverently, and he heard a sweet chime that meant his breakfast had just arrived on a tray.

"Tea and toast, little Master," someone growled gently. "The toast crisp, just as you like it, and a pot of hyacinth jam, and Hrekseka the Appalling remembered you like that shrimp-egg relish, so here's a puff pastry filled with it for a savory. Have we forgotten anything? Would you like the juice of blood oranges, perhaps?"

The lordling opened his eyes and smiled wide, stretched lazily.

"Yes, thank you, Krasp," he said, and the steward—who resembled nothing so much as an elderly werewolf stuck in mid-transformation—bowed and looked sidelong at an attendant, who ran at once to fetch a pitcher of juice. He meanwhile set about arranging Lord Ermenwyr's tray on his lap, opening out the black linen napery and tucking it into the lace collar of the lordling's nightshirt, and pouring the tea.

"And may I say, Master, on behalf of the staff, how pleased we are to see you safely returned?" said Krasp, stepping back and turning his attention to laying out a suit of black velvet.

"You may," said Lord Ermenwyr. He spread jam on his toast, dipped it into his tea and sucked at it noisily. "Oh, bliss. It's good to be back, too. I trust the parents are both well?"

Krasp genuflected. "Your lord father and your lady mother thrive, I rejoice to say."

"Mm. Of course. Siblings all in reasonably good health, I suppose?"

"The precious offspring of the Master and his lady continue to grace this plane, my lord, for which we in the servants' hall give thanks hourly."

"How nice," said Lord Ermenwyr. He sipped his tea and inquired further: "I suppose nobody's run a spear through my brother Eyrdway yet?"

The steward turned with a reproachful look in his sunken yellow eye. "The Variable Magnificent continues alive and well, my lord," he said, and held up two pairs of boots of butter-soft leather. "The plain ones, my lord, or the ones with the spring-loaded daggers in the heels?"

"The plain ones," Lord Ermenwyr replied, yawning. "I'm in the bosom of my family, after all."

When he had dined, when he had been washed and lovingly groomed and dressed by a succession of faithful retainers, when he had admired his reflection in a long mirror and pomaded his beard and moustaches—then Lord Ermenwyr strolled forth into the corridors of the family manse, to see what amusement he might find.

He sought in vain.

All that presented itself to his quick eye was the endless maze of halls, hewn through living black basalt, lit at intervals by flickering witchlight or smoking flame, or here and there by a shaft of tinted sunbeam, from some deep-hewn arrowslit window sealed with panes of painted glass. At regular intervals armed men—well, armed *males*—stood guard, and each bowed respectfully as he passed, and bid him good-morning.

He looked idly into the great vaulted chamber of the baths, with its tiled pools and scented atmosphere from the orchids that twined, luxuriant, on trellises in the steamy air; but none of his sisters were in there.

He leaned on a balustrade and gazed down the stairwell, at the floors descending into the heart of the mountain. There, on level below level to the vanishing point of perspective, servants hurried with laundry, or dishes, or firewood. It was reassuring to see them, but he had learned long since that they would not stop to play.

He paused by a window and contemplated the terraced gardens beyond, secure and sunlit, paradise cleverly hidden from wayfarers on the dreadful slopes below the summit. Bees droned in white roses, or blundered sleepily in orchards, or hovered above reflecting pools. Though the bowers of his mother were beautiful beyond the praise of poets, they made Lord Ermenwyr want to scream with ennui.

He turned, hopeful, at the sound of approaching feet.

"My lord." A tall servant bowed low. "Your lord father requests your presence in his accounting chamber."

Lord Ermenwyr bared his teeth like a weasel at bay. All his protests, all his excuses, died unspoken at the look on the servant's face. He reflected that at least the next hour was unlikely to be boring.

"Very well, then," he said, and followed where the servant led him.

By the time he had crossed the threshold, he had adopted a suitably insouciant attitude and compiled a list of clever things to say. All his presence of mind was required to remember them, once he had stepped into the darkness beyond.

His father sat in a shaft of light at the end of the dark hall, behind his great black desk, in his great black chair. For all that was said of him in courts of law, for all that was screamed against him in temples, the Master of the Mountain was not in his person fearful to look upon. For all that his name was spoken in whispers by the caravan-masters, or used to frighten their children, he wore no crown of sins nor cloak of shades. He was big, black-bearded, handsome in a solemn kind of way. His black eyes were calm, patient as a stalking tiger's.

Lord Ermenwyr, meeting those eyes, felt like a very small rabbit indeed.

"Good morning, Daddy," he said, in the most nonchalant voice he could summon.

"Good afternoon, my son," said the Master of the Mountain.

He pointed to a chair, indicating that Lord Ermenwyr should come forward and sit. Lord Ermenwyr did so, though it was a long walk down that dark hall. When he had seated himself, a saturnine figure in nondescript clothing stepped out of the shadows before him.

"Your report, please," said the Master of the Mountain. The spy cleared his throat once, then read from a sheaf of notes concerning Lord Ermenwyr's private pastimes for the last eight months. His expenses were listed in detail, to the last copper piece; his associates were named, their addresses and personal histories summarized; his favorite haunts named too, and the amount of time he spent at each.

The Master of the Mountain listened in silence, staring at his son the whole time, and though he raised an eyebrow now and then he made no comment. Lord Ermenwyr, for his part, with elaborate unconcern, drew out his smoking-tube, packed it, lit it, and sat smoking, with a bored expression on his face.

Having finished at last, the spy coughed and bowed slightly. He stepped back into the darkness.

"Well," said Lord Ermenwyr, puffing smoke, "I don't know why you bothered giving me that household accounts book on my last birthday. He kept *much* better records than I did."

"Fifteen pairs of high-heeled boots?" said the Master of the Mountain, with a certain seismic quality in the bass reverberation of his voice.

"I can explain that! There's only one cobbler in Deliantiba who can make really comfortable boots that give me the, er, dramatic presence I need," said Lord Ermenwyr. "And he's poor. I felt it was my duty to support an authentic craftsman."

"I can't imagine why he's poor, at these prices," retorted his father.

"When I was your age, I'd never owned a pair of boots. Let alone boots 'of premium-grade elkhide, dyed purple in the new fashion, with five-inch heels incorporating the unique patented Comfort-Spring lift.' "

"You missed out on a lot, eh? If you wore my size, I'd give you a pair," said Lord Ermenwyr, cool as snowmelt, but he tensed to run all the same.

His father merely stared at him, and the lordling exhaled another plume of smoke and studied it intently. When he had begun to sweat in spite of himself, his father went on:

"Is your apothecary an authentic craftsman too?"

"You can't expect me to survive without my medication!" Lord Ermenwyr cried. "And it's damned expensive in a city, you know."

"For what you spent, you might have kept three of yourselves alive," said his father.

"Well—well, but I've been ill. More so than usually, I mean. I had fevers—and I've had this persistent racking cough—blinding headaches when I wake up every morning—and see how pale I am?" Lord Ermenwyr stammered. His father leaned forward and grinned, with his teeth very white in his black beard.

"There's nothing wrong with you, boy, that a good sweat won't cure. The exercise yard, quick march! Let's see if you've remembered your training."

* * *

"Just what I expected," said the Master of the Mountain, as his son was carried from the exercise yard on a stretcher. Lord Ermenwyr, too winded to respond, glared at his father.

"And get that look off your face, boy. This is what comes of all those bottles of violet liqueur and vanilla éclairs," continued his father, pulling off his great gauntlets. "And the late nights. And the later mornings." He rubbed his chin thoughtfully, where a bruise was swelling. "Your reflexes aren't bad, though. You haven't lost any of your speed, I'll say that much for you."

"Thank you," Lord Ermenwyr wheezed, with as much sarcasm as he could muster.

"I want to see you out there again tomorrow, one hour after sunrise. We'll start with saber drill, and then you'll run laps," said the Master of the Mountain.

"On my sprained ankle?" Lord Ermenwyr yelled in horror.

"I see you've got your breath back," replied his father. He turned to the foremost guard bearing the stretcher. "Take my son to his mother's infirmary. If there's anything really the matter with him, she'll mend it."

"But—!" Lord Ermenwyr cried, starting up. His father merely smiled at him, and strode off to the guardroom.

By the time they came to his mother's bower, Lord Ermenwyr had persuaded his bearers to let him limp along between them, rather than enter her presence prostrate and ignominious.

But as they drew near to that place of sweet airs, of drowsy light and soft perfumes, those bearers must blink and turn their faces away; and though they propped him faithfully, and were great and horrible in their black livery and mail, the two warriors shivered to approach the Saint of the World. Lord Ermenwyr, knowing well that none of his father's army could meet his mother's gaze, sighed and bid them leave him.

"But, little Master, we must obey your lord father," groaned one, indistinctly through his tusks.

"It's all right; most of the time I can't look her in the eye, myself," said Lord Ermenwyr. "Besides, you were only told to bring me to the *infirmary*, right? So there's a semantic loophole for you."

Precise wording is extremely important to demons. Their eyes (bulging green and smoldering red respectively) met, and after a moment's silent debate the two bowed deeply and withdrew, murmuring their thanks. Lord Ermenwyr sighed, and tottered on through the long grass alone.

He saw the white-robed disciples walking in the far groves, or bending between the beds of herbs, gathering, pruning, planting. Their plainchant hummed through the pleasant air like bee song, setting his teeth on edge somehow. He found his mother at last, silhouetted against a painfully sunlit bower of blossoming apple, where she bent over a sickbed.

". . . the ointment every day, do you understand? You must have patience," she was saying, in her gentle ruthless voice. She looked over her shoulder and saw her son. He felt her clear gaze go through him, and he stood still and fidgeted as she turned back to her patient. She laid her hand upon the sufferer's brow, murmured a blessing; only then did she turn her full attention to Lord Ermenwyr.

He knelt awkwardly. "Mother."

"My child." She came forward and raised him to his feet. Having embraced him, she said:

"You haven't sprained your ankle, you know."

"It hurts," he said, and his lower lip trembled. "You think I'm lying again, I suppose."

"No," she said, patiently. "You truly believe you're in pain. Come and sit down, child."

She led him into the deeper shade, and drew off his boot (looking without comment on its five-inch heel). One of her disciples brought him a stoneware cup of cold spring water, and watched with wide eyes as she examined Lord Ermenwyr's ankle. Where her fingers passed, the lordling felt warmth entering in. His pain melted away like frost under sunlight, but he braced himself for what else her healing hands would learn in their touch.

"I know what you'll tell me next," he said, testily. "You'll say I haven't been exercising enough. You'll tell me I've been eating and drinking too much. You'll tell me I shouldn't wear shoes with heels this high, because it doesn't matter how tall I am. You'll tell me I'm wasting myself on pointless self-indulgences that leave me sick and depressed and penniless."

"Why should I tell you what you already know?" his mother replied. He stared sullenly into his cup of water.

"And you'll *reproach* me about Lady Seelice and Lady Thyria. And the little runner, what's-her-name, you'll be especially sorrowful that I can't even remember the name of a girl I've seduced. Let alone chambermaids without number. And . . . and you'll tell me about all those poor tradesmen whose livelihoods depend on people like me paying bills on time, instead of skipping town irresponsibly."

"That's true," said his mother.

"And, of course, you'll tell me that I don't really need all those drugs!" Lord Ermenwyr announced. "You'll tell me that I imagine half of my fevers and coughs and wasting diseases, and that neither relief nor creative fulfillment will come from running around artists' salons with my pupils like pinpoints. And that it all comes from my being bored and frustrated. And that I'd feel better at once if I found some honest work putting my *tremendous* talents to good use."

"How perceptive, my darling," said his mother.

"Have I left anything out?"

"I don't think so."

"You see?" Lord Ermenwyr demanded tearfully, turning to the disciple. "She's just turned me inside out, like a sock. I can't keep one damned secret from her."

"All things are known to Her," said the disciple, profoundly shocked at the lordling's blasphemy. He hadn't worked there very long.

"And now, do you know what else she's going to do?" said Lord Ermenwyr, scowling at him. "She's going to nag at me to go to the nursery and visit my bastard children."

"Really?" said the disciple, even more shocked.

"Yes," said his mother, watching as he pulled his boot back on. He started to stamp off, muttering, but turned back hastily and knelt again. She blessed him in silence, and he rose and hurried away.

"My son is becoming wise," said the Saint of the World, smiling as she watched him go.

The way to the nursery was mazed and obscured, for the Master of the Mountain had many enemies, and hid well where his seed sheltered. Lord Ermenwyr threaded the labyrinth without effort, knowing it from within. As he vaulted the last pit, as he gave the last password, his heart grew more cheerful. He would shortly behold his dear old nurse again!

Twin demonesses guarded the portal, splendid in black livery and silver mail. The heels of their boots were even higher than his, and much sharper. They grinned to see him, baring gold-banded fangs in welcome.

"Ladies, you look stunning today," he told them, twirling his moustaches. "Is Balnshik on duty?"

"She is within, little lord," hissed the senior of the two, and lifted her blade to let him pass.

He entered quite an ordinary room, long and low, with a fire burning merrily in the hearth behind a secure screen. Halfway up the walls was a mural painted in tones of pink and pale blue, featuring baby rabbits involved in unlikely pastimes.

Lord Ermenwyr curled his lip. Three lace-gowned infants snuffled in cots here; four small children sat over a shared game there, in teeny-tiny chairs around a teeny-tiny table; another child rocked to and fro on a ponderous wooden beast bright-painted; three more sat before a comfortable-looking chair at the fireside, where a woman in a starched white uniform sat reading to them.

". . . but the people in *that* village were very naughty and tried to ambush his ambassadors, so he put them all to the sword," she said, and held up the picture so they could all see.

"Ooo," chorused the tots.

She, having meanwhile noticed Lord Ermenwyr, closed the book and rose to her feet with sinuous grace.

"Little Master," she said, looking him up and down. "You've put on weight."

He winced.

"Oh, Nursie, how unkind," he said.

"Nonsense," Balnshik replied. She was arrogantly beautiful. Her own body was perfect, ageless, statuesque and bosomy as any little boy's dream, or at least Lord Ermenwyr's little boy dreams, and there was a dangerous glint in her dark eye and a throaty quality to her voice that made him shiver even now.

"I've come about the, er, the . . . those children I—had," he said. "For a sort of visit."

"What a delightful surprise!" Balnshik said, in well-bred tones of irony. She turned and plucked from the rocking beast a wretched-looking little thing in a green velvet dress. "Look who's come to see us, dear! It's our daddy. We scarcely knew we had one, did we?"

Baby and parent stared at one another in mutual dismay. The little boy turned his face into Balnshik's breast and screamed dismally.

"Poor darling," she crooned, stroking his limp curls. "We've been teething again and we're getting over a cold, and that makes us fretful. We're just like our daddy, aren't we? Would he like to hold us?"

"Perhaps not," said Lord Ermenwyr, doing his best not to run from the room. "I might drop it. Him. What do you mean, he's just like me?"

"The very image of you at that age, Master," Balnshik assured him, serenely unbuttoning her blouse. "Same pasty little face, same nasty look in his dear little eyes, same tendency to shriek and drum his little heels on the floor when he's cross. And he gets that same rash you did, all around his little—"

"Wasn't there another one?" inquired Lord Ermenwyr desperately.

"You know perfectly well there is," said Balnshik, watching tenderly as the baby burrowed toward comfort. "Your lord father's still paying off the girl's family, and your lady sister will never be able to hold another slumber party for her sorority. Where is he?" She glanced over at the table. "There we are! The one in the white tunic. Come and meet your father, dear."

The child in question, one of those around the table, got up reluctantly. He came and clung to Balnshik's leg, peering up at his father.

"Well, you look like a fine manly little fellow, anyway," said Lord Ermenwyr.

"You look like a very bad man," stated the child.

"And he's clever!" said Lord Ermenwyr, preening a bit. "Yes, my boy, I am rather a bad man. In fact, I'm a famous villain. What else have you heard about your father?"

The boy thought.

"Grandpapa says when I'm a man, I can challenge you to a fight and beat you up," he said gravely. "But I don't think I want to."

"You don't, eh?" A spark of parental feeling warmed in Lord Ermenwyr's heart. "Why not, my boy?"

"Because then I will be bigger than you, and you will be old and weak and have no teeth," the child explained. "It wouldn't be fair."

Lord Ermenwyr eyed him sourly. "That hasn't happened to your Grandpapa, has it?"

"No," the child agreed, "But he's twice as big as you." He brightened, remembering the other thing he had heard about his father. "And Grandmama says you're so smart, it's such a shame you don't do something with your life!"

Lord Ermenwyr sighed, and pulled out his jade tube. "Do you mind if I smoke in here?" he asked Balnshik.

"I certainly do," she replied, mildly but with a hint of bared fangs.

"Pity. Well, here, son of mine; here's my favorite ring for your very own." He removed a great red cabochon set in silver, and presented it to the child. "The top is hinged like a tiny box, see the clever spring? You can hide sleeping powders in it to play tricks on other little boys. I emptied out the poison, for heaven's sake," he added indignantly, seeing that the hint of bared fangs was now an open suggestion.

"Thank you, Father," piped the child.

Disconsolate, Lord Ermenwyr wandered the black halls.

He paused at a window that looked westward, and regarded the splendid isolation of the Greenlands. Nothing to be seen for miles but wave upon wave of lesser mountains, forested green as the sea, descending to the plain. Far away, far down, the toy cities behind their walls were invisible for distance, and when night fell their sparkling lights would glimmer in vain, like lost constellations, shrouded from his hopeful eye.

Even now, he told himself, even now down there the taverns would be opening. The smoky dark places would be lighting their lanterns, and motherly barmaids would serve forth wine so raw it took the paint off tables. The elegant expensive places would be firing up the various patent devices that glared in artificial brilliance, and the barmaids there were all thin, and young, and interestingly depraved-looking. What *they* served forth could induce visions, or convulsions and death if carelessly indulged in.

How he longed, this minute, for a glass of dubious green liqueur from the Gilded Clock! Or to loll with his head in the lap of an anonymous beauty who couldn't care less whether he did something worthwhile with his life. What had he been thinking, to desert the cities of the plain? They had everything his heart could desire. Theaters. Clubs. Ballrooms. Possibilities. Danger. Fun. . . .

Having made his decision to depart before the first light of dawn, Lord Ermenwyr hurried off to see that his trunks were packed with new-laundered clothes. He whistled a cheery little tune as he went.

* * *

The Master and the Saint sat at their game.

They were not Good and Evil personified, nor Life and Death; certainly not Order and Chaos, nor even Yin and Yang. Yet most of the world's population believed that they were. Their marriage, therefore, had done rather more than raise eyebrows everywhere.

The Master of the Mountain scowled down at the game board. It bore the simplest of designs, concentric circles roughly graven in slate, and the playing pieces were mere pebbles of black marble or white quartz. The strategy was fantastically involved, however.

So subtle were the machinations necessary to win that this particular game had been going on for thirty years, and a decisive conquest might never materialize.

"What are we going to do about the boy?" he said.

The Saint of the World sighed in commiseration, but was undistracted. She slid a white stone to a certain position on the board.

High above them, three white egrets peered down from the ledge that ran below the great vaulted dome of the chamber. Noting the lady's move, they looked sidelong at the three ravens that perched opposite, and stalked purposefully along the ledge until the ravens were obliged to sidle back a pace or two.

"To which of your sons do you refer, my lord?" the Saint inquired.

"The one with the five-inch heels to his damned boots," said the Master of the Mountain, and set a black stone down, *click*, between a particular pair of circles. "Have you seen them?"

One of the ravens bobbed its head derisively, spread its coal-black wings and soared across the dome to the opposite ledge.

"Yes, I have," admitted the Saint.

"They cost me a fortune, and they're purple," said the Master of the Mountain, leaning back to study the board.

"And when you were his age, you'd never owned a pair of boots," said the Saint serenely, sliding two white stones adjacent to the black one.

Above, one egret turned, retraced its way along the ledge, and the one raven cocked an eye to watch it. Three white stars shone out with sudden and unearthly light, in the night heavens figured on the surface of the arching dome.

"When I was his age, I wore chains. I never had to worry about paying my tailor; only about living long enough to avenge myself," said the Master of the Mountain. "I wouldn't want a son of mine educated so. But we've spoiled the boy!"

He moved three black stones, lining them up on successive rings. The two ravens flew to join their brother. Black clouds swirled under the dome, advanced on the floating globe of the white moon.

"He needs direction," said the Saint.

"He needs a challenge," said the Master. "Pitch him out naked on the mountainside, and let him survive by his wits for a few years!"

"He would," pointed out the Saint. "Do we want to take responsibility for what would happen to the innocent world?"

"I suppose not," said the Master with a sigh, watching as his lady moved four white stones in a neat line. The white egrets advanced on the ravens again. The white moon outshone the clouds.

"But he does need a challenge," said the Saint. "He needs to put that mind of his to good use. He needs *work*."

"Damned right he does," said the Master of the Mountain. He considered the board again. "Rolling up his sleeves. Laboring with his hands. Building up a callus or two."

"Something that will make him employ his considerable talent," said the Saint.

There was a thoughtful silence. Their eyes met over the board. They smiled. Under the vaulted dome, all the birds took flight and circled in patterns, white wings and black.

"I'd better catch him early, or he'll be down the mountain again before cockcrow," said the Master of the Mountain. "To bed, madam?"

* * *

Lord Ermenwyr rose sprightly by candlelight, congratulating himself on the self-reliance learned in Deliantiba: for now he could dress himself without a valet. Having donned apparel suitable for travel, he went to his door to rouse the bearers, that they might shoulder his new-laden trunks down the gorge to the red road far below.

Upon opening the door, he said:

"Sergeant, kindly fetch—Ack!"

"Good morning, my son," said the Master of the Mountain. "So eager for saber drill? Commendable."

"Thank you," said Lord Ermenwyr. "Actually, I thought I'd just get in some practice lifting weights, first."

"Not this morning," said his father. "I have a job for you, boy. Walk with me."

Gritting his teeth, Lord Ermenwyr walked beside his father, obliged to take two steps for every one the Master of the Mountain took. He was panting by the time they emerged on a high rampart, under faint stars, where the wall's guard were putting out the watch-fires of the night.

"Look down there, son," said the Master of the Mountain, pointing to three acres' space of waste and shattered rock, hard against the house wall.

"Goodness, is that a bit of snow still lying in the crevices?" said Lord Ermenwyr, watching his breath settle in powdered frost. "So late in the year, too. What unseasonably chilly weather we've had, don't you think?"

"Do you recognize the windows?" asked his father, and Lord Ermenwyr squinted down at the arrowslits far below. "You ought to."

"Oh! Is that the nursery, behind that wall?" Lord Ermenwyr said. "Well, what do you know? I was there only yesterday. Visiting my bastards, as a matter of fact. My, my, doesn't it look small from up here?"

"Yes," said the Master of the Mountain. "It does. You must have noticed how crowded it is, these days. Balnshik is of the opinion, and your mother and I concur with her, that the children need more room. A place to play when the weather is fine, perhaps. This would prevent them from growing up into stunted, pasty-faced little creatures with no stamina."

"What a splendid idea," said Lord Ermenwyr, smiling with all his sharp teeth. "Go to it, old man! Knock out a few walls and expand the place. Perhaps Eyrdway would be willing to give up a few rooms of his suite, eh?"

"No," said the Master of the Mountain placidly. "Balnshik wants an *outdoor* play area. A garden, just there under the windows. With lawns and a water feature, perhaps."

He leaned on the battlement and watched emotions conflict in his son's face. Lord Ermenwyr's eyes protruded slightly as the point of the conversation became evident to him, and he tugged at his beard, stammering:

"No, no, she can't be serious! What about household security? What about your enemies? Can't put the little ones' lives in danger, after all. Mustn't have them out where they might be carried off by, er, eagles or efrits, can we? Nursie means well, of course, but—"

"It's an interesting problem," said the Master of the Mountain. "I'm sure you'll think of a solution. You're such a clever fellow, after all."

"But—!"

"Krasp has been instructed to let you have all the tools and materials you need," said the Master of the Mountain. "I do hope you'll have it finished before high summer. Little Druvendyl's rash might clear up if he were able to sunbathe."

"Who the hell is Druvendyl?" cried Lord Ermenwyr.

"Your infant son," the Master of the Mountain informed him. "I expect full-color renderings in my study within three days, boy. Don't dawdle."

Bright day without, but within Lord Ermenwyr's parlor it might have been midnight, so close had he drawn his drapes. He paced awhile in deep thought, glancing now and then at three flat stones he had set out on his hearth-rug. On one, a fistful of earth was mounded; on another, a small heap of coals glowed and faded. The third stone held a little water in a shallow depression.

To one side he had placed a table and chair.

Having worked up his nerve as far as was possible, he went at last to a chest at the foot of his bed and rummaged there. He drew out a long silver shape that winked in the light from the few coals. It was a flute. He seated himself in the chair and, raising the flute to his lips, began to play softly.

Summoning music floated forth, cajoling, enticing, music to catch the attention. The melody rose a little and was imperious, beckoned impatiently, wheedled and just hinted at threatening; then was coy, beseeched from a distance.

Lord Ermenwyr played with his eyes closed at first, putting his very soul into the music. When he heard a faint commotion from his hearth, though, he opened one eye and peered along the silver barrel as he played.

A flame had risen from the coals. Brightly it lit the other two stones, so he had a clear view of the water, which was bubbling upward as from a concealed fountain, and of the earth, which was mounding up too, for all the world like a molehill.

Lord Ermenwyr smiled in his heart and played on, and if the melody had promised before, it gave open-handed now; it was all delight, all ravishment. The water leaped higher, clouding, and the flame rose and spread out, dimming, and the earth bulged in its mound and began to lump into shape, as though under the hand of a sculptor.

A little more music, calling like birds in the forest, brightening like the sun rising over a plain, galloping like the herds there in the morning! And now the flame had assumed substance, and the water had firmed beside it. Now it appeared that three naked children sat on Lord Ermenwyr's hearth, their arms clasped about their drawn-up knees, their mouths slightly open as they watched him play. They were, all three, the phantom color of clouds, a shifting glassy hue suggesting rainbows. But about the shoulders of the little girl ran rills of bright flame, and one boy's hair swirled silver, and the other boy had perhaps less of the soap bubble about him, and more of wet clay.

Lord Ermenwyr raised his mouth from the pipe, grinned craftily at his guests, and set the pipe aside.

"No!" said the girl. "You must keep playing."

"Oh, but I'm tired, my dears," said Lord Ermenwyr. "I'm all out of breath."

"You have to play," the silvery boy insisted. "Play right now!"

But Lord Ermenwyr folded his arms. The children got to their feet, anger in their little faces, and they grew up before his eyes. The boys' chests deepened, their limbs lengthened, they overtopped the girl; but she became a woman shapely as any he'd ever beheld, with flames writhing from her brow.

"Play, or we'll kill you," said the three. "Burn you. Drown you. Bury you."

"Oh, no, that won't do," said Lord Ermenwyr. "Look here, shall we play a game? If I lose, I'll play for you again. If I win, you'll do as I bid you. What do you say to that?"

The three exchanged uncertain glances.

"We will play," they said. "But one at a time."

"Ah, now, is that fair?" cried Lord Ermenwyr. "When that gives you three chances to win against my one? I see you're too clever for me. So be it." He picked up the little table and set it before him. Opening a drawer, he brought out three cards.

"See here? Three portraits. Look closely: this handsome fellow is clearly me. This blackavised brigand is my father. And *this* lovely lady—" he held the card up before their eyes, "is my own saintly mother. Think you'd recognize her again? Of course you would. Now, we'll turn the cards face down. Can I find the lady? Of course I can; turn her up and here she is. That's no game at all! But if you find the lady, you'll win. So, who'll go first? Who'll find the lady?"

He took up the cards and looked at his guests expectantly. They nudged one another, and finally the earthborn said: "I will."

"Good for you!" Lord Ermenwyr said. "Watch, now, as I shuffle." He looked into the earthborn's face. "You're searching for the lady, understand?"

"Yes," said the earthborn, meeting his look of inquiry. "I understand."

"Good! So, here she is, and now here, and now here, and now—where?" Lord Ermenwyr fanned out his empty hands above the cards, in a gesture inviting choice.

Certain he knew where the lady was, the earthborn turned a card over.

"Whoops! Not the lady, is it? So sorry, friend. Who's for another try? Just three cards! It ought to be easy," sang Lord Ermenwyr, shuffling them again. The earthborn scowled in astonishment, as the others laughed gaily, and the waterborn stepped up to the table.

"Stop complaining," said Lord Ermenwyr, dipping his pen in ink. "You lost fairly, didn't you?"

"We never had a chance," said the earthborn bitterly. "That big man on the card, the one that's bigger than you. He's the Soul of the Black Rock, isn't he?"

"I believe he's known by that title in certain circles, yes," said Lord Ermenwyr, sketching in a pergola leading to a reflecting pool. "Mostly circles chalked on black marble floors."

"He's supposed to be a *good* master," said the waterborn. "How did he have a son like you?"

"You'll find me a good master, poppets," said Lord Ermenwyr. "I'll free you when you've done my will, and you've my word as my father's son on that. You're far too expensive to keep for long," he added, with a severe look at the fireborn, who was boredly nibbling on a footstool.

"I hunger," she complained.

"Not long to wait now," Lord Ermenwyr promised. "No more than an hour to go before the setting of the moon. And look at the pretty picture I've made!" He held up his drawing. The three regarded it, and their glum faces brightened.

When the moon was well down, he led them out, and they followed gladly when they saw that he carried his silver flute.

The guards challenged him on the high rampart, but once they recognized him they bent in low obeisance. "Little master," they growled, and he tapped each lightly on the helmet with his flute, and each grim giant nodded its head between its boots and slept.

"Down there," he said, pointing through the starlight, and the three that served him looked down on that stony desolation and wondered. All doubt fled, though, when he set the flute to his lips once more.

Now they knew what to do! And gleeful they sprang to their work, dancing under the wide starry heaven, and the cold void warmed and quickened under their feet, and the leaping silver music carried them along. Earth and Fire and Water played, and united in interesting ways.

Lord Ermenwyr was secure in bed, burrowed down under blankets and snoring, by the time bright morning lit the black mountain. But he did not need to see the first rays of the sun glitter on the great arched vault below the wall, where each glass pane was still hot from the fire that had passionately shaped it, and the iron frame too cooled slowly.

Nor did he need to see the warm sleepy earth under the vault, lying smooth in paths and emerald lawns, or the great trees that had rooted in it with magical speed. Neither did he need to hear the fountain bubbling languidly. He knew, already, what the children would find when they straggled from the dormitory, like a file of little ghosts in their white nightgowns.

He knew they would rub their eyes and run out through the new doorway, heedless of Balnshik's orders to remain, and knew they'd rush to pull down fruit from the pergola, and spit seeds at the red fish in the green lily-pool, or climb boldly to the backs of the stone wyverns, or run on the soft grass, or vie to see how hard they could bounce balls against the glass without breaking it. Had he not planned all this, to the last detail?

The Master of the Mountain and the Saint of the World came to see, when the uneasy servants roused them before breakfast.

"Too clever by half," said the Master of the Mountain, raising his eyes to the high vault, where the squares of bubbled and sea-clear glass let in an underwater sort of light. "Impenetrable. Designed to break up perception and confuse. And . . . what's he done to the time? Do you feel that?"

"It's slowed," said the Saint of the World. "Within this garden, it will always be a moment or so in the past. As inviolate as memory, my lord."

"Nice to know he paid attention to his lessons," said the Master of the Mountain, narrowing his eyes. Two little boys ran past him at knee level, screaming like whistles for no good reason, and one child tripped over a little girl who was sprawled on the grass pretending to be a mermaid.

"You see what he can do when he applies himself?" said the Saint, lifting the howling boy and soothing him.

"He still cheated," said the Master of the Mountain.

It was well after noon when Lord Ermenwyr consented to rise and grace the house with his conscious presence, and by then all the servants knew. He nodded to them as he strolled the black halls, happily aware that his personal legend had just enlarged. Now, when they gathered in the servants' halls around the balefires, and served out well-earned kraters of black wine at the end of a long day, *now* they would have something more edifying over which to exclaim than the number of childhood diseases he had narrowly survived or his current paternity suit.

"By the Blue Pit of Hasrahkhin, it was a miracle! A whole garden, trees and all, in the worst place imaginable to put one, and it had to be secret and secure—and the boy

did it in just one night!" That was what they'd say, surely.

So it was with a spring in his step that nearly overbalanced him on his five-inch heels that the lordling came to his father's accounting chamber, and rapped briskly for admission.

The doorman ushered him into his father's presence with deeper than usual obeisances, or so he fancied. The Master of the Mountain glanced up from the scroll he studied, and nodded at Lord Ermenwyr.

"Yes, my son?"

"I suppose you've visited the nursery this morning?" Lord Ermenwyr threw himself into a chair, excruciatingly casual in manner.

"I have, as a matter of fact," replied his lord father. "I'm impressed, boy. Your mother and I are proud of you."

"Thank you." Lord Ermenwyr drew out his long smoking-tube and lit it with a positive jet of flame. He inhaled deeply, exhaled a cloud that writhed about his head, and fixed bright eyes upon the Master of the Mountain. "Would this be an auspicious time to discuss increasing an allowance, O my most justly feared sire?"

"It would not," said the Master of the Mountain. "Bloody hell, boy! A genius like you ought to be able to come up with his own pocket money."

Lord Ermenwyr stalked the black halls, brooding on the unfairness of life in general and fathers in especial.

"Clever enough to come up with my own pocket money, am I?" he fumed. "I'll show *him*."

He paused on a terrace and looked out again in the direction of the cities on the plain, and sighed with longing.

The back of his neck prickled, just as he heard the soft footfall behind him.

He whirled around and kicked, hard, but his boot sank into something that squelched. Looking up into the yawning, dripping maw of a horror out of legend, he snarled and said:

"Stop it, you moron! Slug-Hoggoth hasn't scared me since I was six."

"It has too," said a voice, plaintive in its disappointment. "Remember when you were twelve, and I hid behind the door of your bedroom? You screamed and screamed."

"No, I didn't," said Lord Ermenwyr, extricating his boot.

"Yes, you did, you screamed just like a girl," gloated the creature. "Eeeek!"

"Shut up."

"Make me, midget." The creature's outline blurred and shimmered; dwindled and firmed, resolving into a young man.

He was head and shoulders taller than Lord Ermenwyr, slender and beautiful as a beardless god, and stark naked except for a great deal of gold and silver jewelry. That having been said, there was an undeniable resemblance between the two men.

"Idiot," muttered Lord Ermenwyr.

"But prettier than you," said the other, throwing out his arms. "Gorgeous, aren't I? What do you think of my new pectoral? Thirty black pearls! And the bracelets match, look!"

Lord Ermenwyr considered his brother's jewelry with a thoughtful expression.

"Superb," he admitted. "You robbed a caravan, I suppose. How are you, Eyrdway?"

"I'm always in splendid health," said Lord Eyrdway. "Not like you, eh?"

"No indeed," said Lord Ermenwyr with a sigh. "I'm a wreck. Too much fast life down there amongst the Children of the Sun. Wining, wenching, burning my candle at both ends! I'm certain I'll be dead before I'm twenty-two, but what memories I'll have."

"Wenching?" Lord Eyrdway's eyes widened.

"It's like looting and raping, but nobody rushes you," explained his brother. "And sometimes the ladies even make breakfast for you afterward."

"I know perfectly well what wenching is," said Lord Eyrdway indignantly. "What's *burning your candle at both ends*?"

"Ahhh." Lord Ermenwyr lit up his smoking tube. "Let's go order a couple of bottles of wine, and I'll explain."

Several bottles and several hours later, they sat in the little garden just outside Lord Ermenwyr's private chamber. Lord Ermenwyr was refilling his brother's glass.

". . . so then I said to her, 'Well, madam, if you insist, but I really ought to have another apple first,' and that was the exact moment they broke in the terrace doors!" he said.

"Bunch of nonsense. You can't do that with an apple," Lord Eyrdway slurred.

"Maybe it was an apricot," said Lord Ermenwyr. "Anyway, the best part of it was, I got out the window with both the bag *and* the jewel case. Wasn't that lucky?"

"It sounds like a lot of fun," said Lord Eyrdway wistfully, and drank deep.

"Oh, it was. So then I went round to the Black Veil Club—but of course you know what goes on in *those* places!" Lord Ermenwyr pretended to sip his wine.

"'Course I do," said his brother. "Only maybe I've forgot. You tell me again, all right?"

Lord Ermenwyr smiled. Leaning forward, lowering his voice, he explained about all the outré delights to be had at a Black Veil Club. Lord Eyrdway began to drool. Wiping it away absent-mindedly, he said at last:

"You see—you see—that's what's so awful unfair. Unfair. All this fun you get to have. 'Cause you're totally worthless and nobody cares if you go down the mountain. You aren't the damn Heir to the Black Halls. Like me. I'm so really important Daddy won't let me go."

"Poor old Way-Way, it isn't fair at all, is it?" said Lord Ermenwyr. "Have another glass of wine."

"I mean, I'd just love to go t'Deliatitatita, have some fun," said Lord Eyrdway, holding out his glass to be refilled, "but, you know, Daddy just puts his hand on my shoulder n' says, 'When you're older, son,' but I'm older'n you by four years, right? Though of course who cares if *you* go, right? No big loss to the Family if *you* get an arrow through your liver."

"No indeed," said Lord Ermenwyr, leaning back. "Tell me something, my brother. Would you say I could do great things with my life if I only applied myself?"

"What?" Lord Eyrdway tried to focus on him. "You? No! I can see three of you right now, an' not one of em's worth a damn." He began to snicker. "Good one, 'eh? Three of you, get it? Oh, I'm sleepy. Just going to put my head down for a minute, right?"

He laid his head down and was promptly unconscious. When Lord Ermenwyr saw his brother blur and soften at the edges, as though he were a waxwork figure that had been left too near the fire, he rose and began to divest him of his jewelry.

"Eyrdway, I truly love you," he said.

The express caravan came through next dawn, rattling along at its best speed in hopes of being well down off the mountain by evening. The caravan master spotted the slight figure by the side of the road well in advance, and gave the signal to stop. The lead keyman threw the brake; sparks flew as the wheels slowed, and stopped.

Lord Ermenwyr, bright-eyed, hopped down from his trunks and approached the caravan master.

"Hello! Will this buy me passage on your splendid conveyance?" He held forth his hand. The caravan master squinted at it suspiciously. Then his eyes widened.

"Keymen! Load his trunks!" he bawled. "Lord, sir, with a pearl like that you could ride the whole route three times around. Where shall we take you? Deliantiba?"

Lord Ermenwyr considered, putting his head on one side.

"No . . . not Deliantiba, I think. I want to go somewhere there's a lot of trouble, of the proper sort for a gentleman. If you understand me?"

The caravan master sized him up. "There's a lot for a gentleman to do in Karkateen, sir, if his tastes run a certain way. You've heard the old song, 'right, about what *their* streets are paved with?"

Lord Ermenwyr began to smile. "I have indeed. Karkateen it is, then."

"Right you are, sir! Please take a seat."

So with a high heart the lordling vaulted the side of the first free cart, and sprawled back at his ease. The long line of carts started forward, picked up speed, and clattered on down the ruts in the red road. The young sun rose and shone on the young man, and the young man sang as he sped through the glad morning of the world.

The Problem of Susan

Neil Gaiman

Neil Gaiman (www.neilgaiman.com) lives in Menominee, Wisconsin. He is famous in many fields, but the foundation of his reputation is comics. For over twenty years as a professional writer, Neil Gaiman has been one of the top writers in modern comics. He is now a best-selling novelist, whose most recent novel, American Gods, was awarded the Hugo, Nebula, Bram Stoker, SFX and Locus awards, while his children's novel Coraline, has been an international bestseller and an enormous critical success. Some of his short fiction is collected in Angels and Visitations (1993), Smoke and Mirrors: Short Fictions and Illusions (1997), and Adventures in the Dream Trade (2002).

"The Problem of Susan" appeared in Flights, edited by Al Sarrantonio, the best original fantasy anthology of the year. A young journalist interviews a distinguished retired scholar of children's books, whose successful life has been marred by an early tragedy. Both have read the Narnia books of C. S. Lewis, and discuss a particular point. The core of the story is framed by dreams, something fantastic happens, and the result of the whole is a literary critique of some power, with a couple of really nasty moments. It is also interesting to see how Joel Lane uses a similar structure in his story later in this book.

She has the dream again that night.

In the dream, she is standing, with her brothers and her sister, on the edge of the battlefield. It is summer, and the grass is a peculiarly vivid shade of green: a wholesome green, like a cricket pitch or the welcoming slope of the South Downs as you make your way north from the coast. There are bodies on the grass. None of the bodies are human; she can see a centaur, its throat slit, on the grass near her. The horse half of it is a vivid chestnut. Its human skin is nut-brown from the sun. She finds herself staring at the horse's penis, wondering about centaurs mating, imagines being kissed by that bearded face. Her eyes flick to the cut throat, and the sticky red-black pool that surrounds it, and she shivers.

Flies buzz about the corpses.

The wildflowers tangle in the grass. They bloomed yesterday for the first time in, how long? A hundred years? A thousand? A hundred thousand? She does not know.

All this was snow, she thinks, as she looks at the battlefield.

Yesterday, all this was snow. Always winter, and never Christmas.

Her sister tugs her hand and points. On the brow of the green hill they stand, deep in conversation. The lion is golden, his hands folded behind his back. The witch is dressed all in white. Right now she is shouting at the lion, who is simply listening. The children cannot make out any of their words, not her cold anger or the lion's thrum-deep replies. The witch's hair is black and shiny; her lips are red.

In her dream she notices these things.

They will finish their conversation soon, the lion and the witch. . . .

123

* * *

There are things about herself that the professor despises. Her smell, for example. She smells like her grandmother smelled, like old women smell, and for this she cannot forgive herself, so on waking, she bathes in scented water and, naked and towel-dried, dabs several drops of Chanel toilet water beneath her arms and on her neck. It is, she believes, her sole extravagance.

Today she dresses in her dark brown dress suit. She thinks of these as her interview clothes, as opposed to her lecture clothes or her knocking-about-the-house clothes. Now she is in retirement, she wears her knocking-about-the-house clothes more and more. She puts on lipstick.

After breakfast, she washes a milk bottle, places it at her back door. She discovers that next-door's cat has deposited a mouse head, and a paw, on the doormat. It looks as though the mouse is swimming through the coconut matting, as though most of it is submerged. She purses her lips, then she folds her copy of yesterday's *Daily Telegraph*, and she folds and flips the mouse head and the paw into the newspaper, never touching them with her hands.

Today's *Daily Telegraph* is waiting for her in the hall, along with several letters, which she inspects, without opening any of them, and then places on the desk in her tiny study. Since her retirement, she visits her study only to write. Now she walks into the kitchen and seats herself at the old oak table. Her reading glasses hang about her neck, on a silver chain, and she perches them on her nose, and begins with the obituaries.

She does not actually expect to encounter anyone she knows there, but the world is small, and she observes that, perhaps with cruel humor, the obituarists have run a photograph of Peter Burrell Gunn as he was in the early 1950s, and not at all as he was the last time the professor had seen him, at a *Literary Monthly* Christmas party several years before, all gouty and beaky and trembling, and reminding her of nothing so much as a caricature of an owl. In the photograph, he is very beautiful. He looks wild, and noble.

She had spent an evening once kissing him in a summer house: she remembers that very clearly, although she cannot remember for the life of her in which garden the summer house had belonged.

It was, she decides, Charles and Nadia Reid's house in the country. Which meant that it was before Nadia ran away with that Scottish artist, and Charles took the professor with him to Spain, although she was certainly not a professor then. This was many years before people commonly went to Spain for their holidays; it was exotic then. He asked her to marry him, too, and she is no longer certain why she said no, or even if she had entirely said no. He was a pleasant-enough young man, and he took what was left of her virginity on a blanket on a Spanish beach, on a warm spring night. She was twenty years old, and had thought herself so old. . . .

The doorbell chimes, and she puts down the paper, and makes her way to the front door, and opens it.

Her first thought is how young the girl looks.

Her first thought is how old the woman looks. "Professor Hastings?" she says. "I'm Greta Campion. I'm doing the profile on you. For the *Literary Chronicle*."

The older woman stares at her for a moment, vulnerable, and ancient; then she smiles. It's a friendly smile, and Greta warms to her. "Come in, dear," says the professor. "We'll be in the sitting room."

"I brought you this," says Greta. "I baked it myself." She takes the cake tin from her bag, hoping its contents haven't disintegrated en route. "It's a chocolate cake. I read online that you liked them."

The old woman nods, and blinks. "I do," she says. "How kind. This way."

Greta follows her into a comfortable room, is shown to her armchair, and told, firmly, not to move. The professor bustles off and returns with a tray, on which are teacups and saucers, a teapot, a plate of chocolate biscuits, and Greta's chocolate cake.

Tea is poured, and Greta exclaims over the professor's brooch, and then she pulls out her notebook and pen, and a copy of the professor's last book, *A Quest for Meanings in Children's Fiction*, bristling with Post-it notes and scraps of paper. They talk about the early chapters, in which the hypothesis is set forth that there was originally no distinct branch of fiction that was intended only for children, until the Victorian notions of the purity and sanctity of childhood demanded that fiction for children be made . . .

". . . well, pure," says the professor.

"And sanctified?" asks Greta, with a smile.

"And sanctimonious," corrects the old woman. "It is difficult to read *The Water Babies* without wincing."

And then she talks about ways that artists used to draw children—as adults, only smaller, without considering the child's proportions—and how Grimm's stories were collected for adults and, when the Grimms realized the books were being read in the nursery, were bowdlerized to make them more appropriate. She talks of Perrault's "Sleeping Beauty in the Wood," and of its original coda in which the prince's cannibal ogre mother attempts to frame the Sleeping Beauty for having eaten her own children, and all the while Greta nods and takes notes, and nervously tries to contribute enough to the conversation that the professor will feel that it is a conversation or at least an interview, not a lecture.

"Where," asks Greta, "do you feel your interest in children's fiction came from?"

The professor shakes her head. "Where do any of our interests come from? Where does *your* interest in children's books come from?"

Greta says, "They always seemed the books that were most important to me. The ones that mattered. When I was a kid, and when I grew. I was like Dahl's *Matilda*. . . . Were your family great readers?"

"Not really . . . I say that, it was a long time ago that they died. Were killed. I should say."

"All your family died at the same time? Was this in the war?"

"No, dear. We were evacuees, in the war. This was in a train crash, several years after. I was not there."

"Just like in Lewis's Narnia books," says Greta, and immediately feels like a fool, and an insensitive fool. "I'm sorry. That was a terrible thing to say, wasn't it?"

"Was it, dear?"

Greta can feel herself blushing, and she says, "It's just I remember that sequence so vividly. In *The Last Battle.* Where you learn there was a train crash on the way back to school, and everyone was killed. Except for Susan, of course."

The professor says, "More tea, dear?" and Greta knows that she should leave the subject, but she says, "You know, that used to make me so angry."

"What did, dear?"

"Susan. All the other kids go off to Paradise, and Susan can't go. She's no longer a friend of Narnia because she's too fond of lipsticks and nylons and invitations to parties. I even talked to my English teacher about it, about the problem of Susan, when I was twelve."

She'll leave the subject now, talk about the role of children's fiction in creating the belief systems we adopt as adults, but the professor says "And tell me, dear, what did your teacher say?"

"She said that even though Susan had refused Paradise then, she still had time while she lived to repent."

"Repent *what?*"

"Not believing, I suppose. And the sin of Eve."

The professor cuts herself a slice of chocolate cake. She seems to be remembering. And then she says, "I doubt there was much opportunity for nylons and lipsticks after her family was killed. There certainly wasn't for me. A little money—less than one might imagine—from her parents' estate, to lodge and feed her. No luxuries . . ."

"There must have been something else wrong with Susan," says the young journalist, "something they didn't tell us. Otherwise she wouldn't have been damned like that—denied the Heaven of further up and further in. I mean, all the people she had ever cared for had gone on to their reward, in a world of magic and waterfalls and joy. And she was left behind."

"I don't know about the girl in the books," says the professor, "but remaining behind would also have meant that she was available to identify her brothers' and her little sister's bodies. There were a lot of people dead in that crash. I was taken to a nearby school—it was the first day of term, and they had taken the bodies there. My older brother looked okay. Like he was asleep. The other two were a bit messier."

"I suppose Susan would have seen their bodies, and thought, they're on holidays now. The perfect school holidays. Romping in meadows with talking animals, world without end."

"She might have done. I remember thinking what a great deal of damage a train can do, when it hits another train, to the people who were travelling. I suppose you've never had to identify a body, dear?"

"No."

"That's a blessing. I remember looking at them and thinking, *What if I'm wrong, what if it's not him after all?* My younger brother was decapitated, you know. A god who would punish me for liking nylons and parties by making me walk through that school dining room, with the flies, to identify Ed, well . . . he's enjoying himself a bit too much, isn't he? Like a cat, getting the last ounce of enjoyment out of a mouse. Or a gram of enjoyment, I suppose it must be, these days. I don't know, really."

She trails off. And then, after some time, she says, "I'm sorry, dear. I don't think I can do anymore of this today. Perhaps if your editor gives me a ring, we can set a time to finish our conversation."

Greta nods and says of course, and knows in her heart, with a peculiar finality, that they will talk no more.

That night, the professor climbs the stairs of her house, slowly, painstakingly, floor by floor. She takes sheets and blankets from the airing cupboard and makes up a bed in the spare bedroom, in the back. It is empty but for a wartime austerity dressing table, with a mirror and drawers, an oak bed, and a dusty applewood wardrobe, which contains only coat hangers and a dusty cardboard box. She places a vase on the dressing table, containing purple rhododendron flowers, sticky and vulgar.

She takes from the box in the wardrobe a plastic bag containing four old photographic albums. Then she climbs into the bed that was hers as a child, and lies there between the sheets, looking at the black-and-white photographs, and the sepia photographs, and the handful of unconvincing color photographs. She looks at her brothers, and her sister, and her parents, and she wonders how they could have been that young, how anybody could have been that young.

After a while she notices that there are several children's books beside the bed, which puzzles her slightly, because she does not believe she keeps books on the bedside table in that room. Nor, she decides, does she have a bedside table. On the top of the pile is an old paperback book—it must be over forty years old: the price on the cover is in shillings. It shows a lion, and two girls twining a daisy chain into its mane.

The professor's lips prickle with shock. And only then does she understand that she is dreaming, for she does not keep those books in the house. Beneath the paperback is a hardback, in its jacket, of a book that, in her dream, she has always wanted to read: *Mary Poppins Brings in the Dawn*, which P. L. Travers had never written while alive.

She picks it up and opens it to the middle, and reads the story waiting for her. Jane and Michael go with Mary Poppins on her day off, to Heaven, and they meet the boy Jesus, who is still slightly scared of Mary Poppins because she was once his nanny, and the Holy Ghost, who complains that he has not been able to get his sheet properly white since Mary Poppins left, and God the Father, who says,

> "There's no making her do anything. Not her. *She's* Mary Poppins."

"But you're God," said Jane. "You created everybody and everything. They have to do what you say."

"Not her," said God the Father once again, and he scratched his golden beard flecked with white. "I didn't create *her*. She's Mary Poppins."

And the professor stirs in her sleep, and dreams that she is reading her own obituary. It has been a good life, she thinks, as she reads it, discovering her life laid out in black-and-white. Everyone is there. Even the people she had forgotten.

Greta sleeps beside her boyfriend in a small flat in Camden, and she, too, is dreaming.

In the dream, the lion and the witch come down the hill together.

She is standing on the battlefield, holding her sister's hand. She looks up at the golden lion, and the burning amber of his eyes. "He's not a tame lion, is he?" she whispers to her sister, and they shiver.

The witch looks at them all; then she turns to the lion and says, coldly, "I am satisfied with the terms of our agreement. You take the girls: for myself, I shall have the boys."

She understands what must have happened, and she runs, but the beast is upon her before she has covered a dozen paces. The lion eats all of her except her head, in her dream. He leaves the head, and one of her hands, just as a house cat leaves the parts of a mouse it has no desire for, for later, or as a gift.

She wishes that he had eaten her head, then she would not have had to look. Dead eyelids cannot be closed, and she stares, unflinching, at the twisted thing her brothers have become. The great beast ate her little sister more slowly, and it seemed to her, with more relish and pleasure, than it had eaten her; but then, her little sister had always been its favorite.

The witch removes her white robes, revealing a body no less white, with high, small breasts, and nipples so dark, they are almost black. The witch lies back upon the grass, spreads her legs. Beneath her body, the grass becomes rimed with frost.

"Now," she says.

The lion licks her white cleft with its pink tongue, until she can take no more of it, and she pulls its huge mouth to hers, and wraps her icy legs into its golden fur. . . .

Being dead, the eyes in the head on the grass cannot look away. Being dead, they miss nothing.

And when they are done, sweaty and sticky and sated, only then does the lion amble over to the head on the grass, and devour it in its huge mouth, crunching her skull in its powerful jaws, and it is then, only then, that she wakes.

Her heart is pounding. She tries to wake her boyfriend, but he snores and grunts, and will not rouse.

It's true, Greta thinks, irrationally, in the darkness. *She grew up. She carried on. She didn't die. . . .*

She imagines the professor, waking in the night, and listening to the noises coming from the old applewood wardrobe in the corner: to the rustlings of all these gliding ghosts, which might be mistaken for the scurries of mice or rats, and to the padding of enormous velvet paws, and the distant, dangerous music of a hunting horn.

She knows she is being ridiculous, although she will not be surprised when she reads of the professor's demise. *Death comes in the night*, she thinks, before she returns to sleep. *Like a lion*.

The white witch rides naked on the lion's golden back. Its muzzle is spotted with fresh, scarlet blood. Then the vast pinkness of its tongue wipes around its face, and once more it is perfectly clean.

Stella's Transformation

Kim Westwood

Kim Westwood lives in Canberra, Australia, and attended the 2004 Clarion South writing workshop, which inaugurated Clarions in Australia. In a recent convention bio, she writes, "Until quite recently, Kim Westwood had been published only once before: a totally true Girl's Own Motorcycle Story in Two Wheels *magazine. Parked as it was between Matho's informative article on speed triples and Smithy's hot revs exposé of fat-wheeled mega motor Dukes, it felt like a real coup.... Thinking that the term 'speculative' might apply to her, she sent a potentially true story off to a competition and won The Canberra Speculative Fiction Group's Gregor Samsa Prize for Short Speculative Fiction. 'Oracle' was then published in* Redsine 9 *and won the 2002 Aurealis Award for best horror short story. (www.conflux.org.au/2004con/2004panels/#kimwest)"*

"Stella's Transformation" was published in Australia, in the original anthology Encounters. *Like the Gaiman story, it is not quite category fantasy, but certainly a fantasy about the fantastic in real life. A woman who is read to sleep by the right person with the correct magical touch leads a much better life; we really like the concept of reading at bedtime becoming a therapy for adults. Office coworkers notice improvements and some surprising changes during her transformation.*

The whole of Sam's City Gym had stopped to watch Stella, who'd caught her t-shirt in the Universal Multi-station again. As a high tight ponytail sped her way, she didn't like to remember why she had agreed to a personal trainer. It had been an act of desperation, post-relationship, in the tunnel no light.

"Stella, don't you think it's time we lost the family tent?"

She bunched what wasn't caught in the Universal around her knees in case the ponytail tried to rip it off her.

"Not yet—I'm not ready yet."

Evie snorted. "Well get it out yourself this time." She checked herself from all sides simultaneously in the wall-to-wall mirrors and bobbed off to pick on someone braver.

Stella braced herself and tugged, leaving half her t-shirt in the low pulley of the high-low bar. The gym resumed its nightly rhythm; the Universal clanged with the exertions of people who had loved and lost.

Freshly purged of impurities, Stella stood outside Sam's gym under a dull pink neon, on steps littered with last-minute cigarette butts. Across the road a video shop illumed the dusk, rows of naked bulbs burning moths against the latest blockbuster titles.

The counter attendant, a gangly youth with a predatory smirk, knew her better than she wished he did.

"Hi-ya Stel, what's on tonight? Surprise me."

She handed over the video.

"Oh," he said, showing all four incisors, "a *chick flick*."

She smiled painfully, unsuccessfully avoiding contact with his hand as he gave her change.

When she got home, her neighbor was out topiarising his privet hedge. He came over to give her his daily reminder.

"Celeste wasn't the right girl for you," he said cheerfully, handing her fresh-cut flowers. "Blue Moon—hybrid tea rose."

They sat in the kitchen eating fish and chips straight from the wrappers.

"Remember what they say about these and the sea," Howard waved a piece of battered cod at her, "and those awful dreams will stop. Now, what video are we watching?"

That night she dreamt Celeste was working out in Sam's City Gym with Evie. They were doing coordinated abdominal crunches, smiling at each other through gritted teeth and clenched buttocks. Then Evie was pressing her tight ribby torso against Celeste's suddenly naked breasts while Stella, stuck in the spaghettied arms of the Universal, was forced to watch a dozen simultaneous versions. She woke up whimpering, the sheet twisted around her body. On her way to work, she dumped the video through the returns chute. Next time, she promised, it would be *Kill Bill*.

At Fletcher & League Investment Advisers, Andrew Fletcher Jr., part-owner and unrepentant office leech, liked to stand too close to Stella while she photocopied.

"Great how an arts degree can give a career a leg-up, isn't it," he said, idly fingering the photocopy paper. "Just remember it wasn't me who decided to hire you."

Andrew's older business partner, Max League, wore sensible shoes and striped ties and liked to stare for long periods at the Rothko print on his wall. He found it helped him decide between income and growth investment strategies.

"Two colors with a dividing line," he said as she handed him the daily haul of mail. "What do you see?"

Stella, who saw a city drowning in fog, didn't want to say. She liked Max—he reminded her of an oversized wombat.

"So how's it going? Everything okay?" He'd noticed that the rather interesting young woman who used to arrive at her desk at the end of each day hadn't appeared for several weeks, and that she was looking a little peaky. He pulled a packet labelled "Hester's Herbals" out of a filing cabinet.

"That's my wife," he said, pointing to the smiling picture of health. "Ever tried valerian tea? Tastes like hell, but it works wonders on the nerves."

He wanted to tell her that he knew she was being wasted at work, but that it would get better.

"Hang in there," he said. "Week's nearly over."

Stella snuck off to the workers' cafeteria and sat with a cappuccino tipped against her lips, newspaper spread out on the laminex in front of her. The advertisement wafted into focus through the coffee steam: *Having trouble sleeping? Bad dreams? Home visits—guaranteed satisfaction.*

On Saturday, washing and vacuuming, she thought about it. All Sunday, windexing and gumptioning, she tried not to think about it. On Monday she raced home, leapt into the shower and scrubbed wildly.

She was switching between the parrot lamp and ceiling lights when the doorbell sounded. Her nervous system SOSed a desperate, last-minute Morse code to her extremities, sending some of them numb just as she opened the door.

Standing on her welcome mat was a mid-thirties swot carrying a battered leather briefcase.

"I'm Vince," he said.

He turned off the parrot lamp. Settling her on the living room couch before seating himself beside her, he opened his briefcase and took out a small book.

Vince read to Stella in the darkness with a caver's torch on his forehead, turning the pages like an archaeologist separating papyrus, a voice like warm honey pouring her slowly into dream. By the time he had packed his briefcase and gone, she was sleeping, curled in the arms of the Universal in a blissfully empty Sam's Gym.

Things began to pick up. Evie quit the gym to be a cheerleader, and the Universal was replaced by something with pink vinyl bucket seats called a Femitron—slimline, center-stage and abandoned. Stella switched to the treadmills with snag-free moving parts from where she could watch reruns of *Xena* on large TV monitors.

Vince came to read every Monday evening, always leaving so gently and with such enviable ecology that he could have been an ad for Greenpeace.

One night after he'd gone, she was called out of sleep. A briny perfume wafted from the open window where a muscular woman in gold lamé rested, her fishtail propped against the frame.

"That Vince is awfully good, isn't he," she said. "How are you with heights?"

When Stella dived back into dream, she went headfirst down, spearing toward a distant stipple-pattern of white dots. They unfurled into long petals and fanned out, becoming bodies with legs scissoring around a shiny blue gap at the center. Stella hit the gap in a swoosh of effervescence then, turning back between the neat frill of pointed feet, she rose, the resplendent centerpiece of a big smiling daisy.

The next morning a spray of tiny gold sequins like fish scales were still clinging to her skin.

Stella started to look forward to sleep. Plummeting like a gull toward fish, she would aim at the bright kaleidoscope of swimmers and surface each time into a new tableau: a lakeful of fluffy-bottomed swans; abalone divers in diaphanous loincloths standing athwart boats rocking in a bathtub sea; painted supplicants to the gods leaping off polystyrene cliffs into a deep, lapis lazuli basin.

Once, looking below the cloudless surface of a coral-edged pool, she thought she saw the woman with the mermaid tail reclining in a pearly clam amongst some kelp, but lost her as a bombardment of women in flamingo costumes dropped off trapezes into the water around her.

The concise figure writing quietly at the edge of the scenery was always there, but when she tried to approach, Vince would shimmer and fade just as she reached him.

* * *

Stella liked to walk past the bright, stucco perimeter of the public baths, but she'd never been in her local pool due to a lifetime fear that she wasn't airtight enough. School swimming carnivals had left memories of dog-paddling desperately to nowhere, afraid that the water would gurgle in and leave her bloated and bobbing on the surface before she could reach land.

One afternoon she could no longer resist. Cerulean walls, swept into shark-fin peaks, pointed her through to where the wet quietly smacked against strings of tricolor floats, while lane lines beckoned crookedly from below.

She swam in a costume and goggles hauled out of the lost property box, slipstreaming along in a sluice of blue that left the fast-lane boys swallowing her wake. One, with metallic purple goggles and "Australia" across his buttocks, accused her of wearing flippers in a Feet Only lane, then checked below the water.

"What are they?" he spluttered, "turbocharged?" before launching into the middle of the lane, his legs chopping the water like a cook with onions.

Howard brought out one of his animal teapots into his little back garden and asked her if she'd changed her diet recently.

"You're looking rather unusual—rather scintillatingly unusual," he said, about to pour tea through the nostrils of a fat Friesian cow. "You haven't met a nice girl or anything, have you?"

Howard was always hoping that. When she was with Celeste he'd hoped that. She shook her head. The bees mumbled in the japonica, grass kissed her bare feet.

He sighed, tipping a bellyful of Friesian into white, udder-shaped cups sitting in their saucers on pudgy pink teats. "Then I hope you haven't resorted to anything anabolic in your search for better definition have you dear?"

She smiled and said nothing—she knew how he loved to be in on secrets.

"Russian Caravan, for mysterious you," said Howard.

People began to regard Stella with interest: submarine eyes cruised her at cafés and bus stops, and followed her down grocery aisles. Howard, noticing their interest and her lack of response, decided to take her to his favorite nightclub.

His Paddington Bear body packed into blue jeans and western shirt, he organized her a drink and a bar stool, reminded her of the glorious opportunities surrounding her and headed for the dance floor. Lights pulsed across shiny black surfaces as a synthetic mix of sweaty bodies danced around silver bat poles.

"Have you ever had an orgasm using a finger on the palm of your hand?" The woman was buckled into a sleeveless, studded leather flying suit, "Amelia" inside a purple heart tattooed on her left shoulder.

"No, never." Looking at kohled, opaline eyes, Stella remembered the mermaid beckoning from the mouth of a shell the night before.

The woman must have seen reflected the image of the mermaid's digit, rather than hers, circling Stella's palm. "Oh," she said disappointedly, and shifted her gaze to survey the crowd over Stella's shoulder before moving off in the direction of another aviatrix lounging against the jukebox, smoke drifting a slow halo around her flying cap.

The next day, in his buttercup-yellow kitchen, teapots arranged in size order along the mantelpiece, Howard looked at Stella's dazzlingly white rubber swim cap through the steam of poached eggs, eyeballs up, on their plates.

"Don't we think that we might be going a little too far? Think of the sun dear, I do hope that you'll be using 30-plus on that."

Stella laced the chinstrap securely through its metal buckle. She'd found it at the local opportunity shop and planned to wear it to bed from now on.

* * *

At work, strange things began to happen with machinery. The photocopy paper went in white and came out blue, computer screens sloshed their color when Stella walked past, the hot water jug in the work kitchenette kept boiling after it was turned off. Andrew Fletcher, Jr. brushed past her in his usual accidental-on-purpose way and recoiled, looking injured.

"You just gave me a nasty electric shock," he said accusingly.

She said terribly sorry as the ceiling lights dulled then brightened. His phone began to ring and kept ringing after he picked it up. He smashed it down and stared balefully at her across the way.

Word got around that one of the workers at Fletcher & League glowed a bit blue at the edges. Andrew, having recently been born again, decided that she was possessed and tried to convince Max, a lifetime atheist, to get rid of her.

"On what grounds Andrew?"

"You know on what grounds: she's *paranormal*. And she deliberately gives me electric shocks."

"Maybe it's your shoes. They got rubber soles? Show me."

Max looked at him blandly, waiting, and Andrew knew that it was pointless. He slouched off to his office.

The night air coming through the bedroom windows was humid and smelt of city. Stella, lying curled against her pillows, flapped out the sheet and let it parachute back down. Vince was sitting in the armchair beside her bed, short sleeves revealing a surprising half-moon at each bicep. She traced a ribbon vein all the way down to where it estuaried at his fingertips.

"Vince?" The head torch panned her way. "Why can't I ever remember what you read?"

He smiled, and she had a sudden image of words flaking like filagree off each page and falling coruscant to ground as he read each book until it was empty, then gently gathered the little piles of shiny sentences into his briefcase before leaving.

The cyclops of light on his forehead picked out the pinks of neatly manicured nails as one finger stretched out to capture the corner of a page and slid behind it. Already she was diving slow motion toward a disintegrating daisy, the white kicking legs disappearing into a hazy reflective sheet that buckled and warped as it swallowed her.

When she surfaced, breaking the meniscus with a soft slap, she was in the municipal pool. Above her, halogen bulbs glowed an early lusterware pink, lighting empty lanes with large onyx moons. She swam to where the water shallowed into a curve of steps.

At the other end, backdropped by a teal and purple dusk, Vince sat writing on a chaise longue. Above him the mermaid—now with legs—kicked off the high board into a graceful backward curve, before being sucked splashless through one of the moons.

She climbed out to where Stella was standing. "I'm Cairo," she said, dripping phosphorescence onto Stella's bare feet. "Nice cap."

Stella was confused. "Nobody else talks to me," she said.

"Well, they're obviously props."

"How can you tell the difference?"

"They never look lost."

Stella wanted to laugh but felt too embarrassed by the truth. The water was making disconcerting wave patterns on the other woman's skin.

"Does he read to you too?"

"Every Thursday."

"So will we both be here again?"

"That depends on Vince, and how long his Esther Williams phase lasts, but I'm sure he'll find other places to write for us."

Stella liked the "us" a lot.

Cairo was a deep, shimmering blue. Strips of silver appeared along the length of her. "Try the diving board," she said.

Stella stood with her toes curled over the edge of the board. The shirring on her swimsuit was shot with an opalescent thread, and gleamed under the halogen. As Vince sliced ink across paper, she followed his neat calligraphy into the water, splintering its thick pearly surface, then stroking smoothly back to the edge of the pool.

"You look fabulous in lamé," said Cairo, reaching out a hand.

Stella woke with shirring marks like ripples across her belly, and printed on her left forearm was a perfect iridescent-blue hand. She imagined bruising all over from Cairo's touch.

Howard, on a mission, summonsed her to one of his regular weekend matchmaking dinners, promising a selection of lovely girls and boys. "All proclivities, in case you've been holding out on me in that regard," he'd said, watching her for a blush response.

Looking down through the smoked-glass table, she could see a variety of legs arranging themselves beneath the dinnerware. Howard was nudging her and reluctantly she lifted her gaze.

"Young Benjamin over there was asking what your secret was." Young Benjamin was wearing a paisley body shirt and a big stretchy smile.

"Secret?"

"To that rather special shine you seem to have—he's an aspiring alchemist."

She firmly closed Vince's briefcase in her mind and attempted to wipe away the traces of blue from her forearm on one of Howard's snowy linen serviettes.

Benjamin, watching her through the glass, saw all the signs of a trade secret and conspiratorially tapped the side of his nose with his forefinger before turning away.

"He'll be wanting to souvenir that serviette now," Howard whispered.

* * *

It was another bad beginning to the week at Fletcher & League: for the second time that morning, the lights went out.

Max looked up at the flickering emergency exit sign and sighed. He knew the cause. The frosted glass around his office picked out the electric tinge of Stella's outline beautifully, and whenever she was near, his screensaver would feature tropical fish. He sighed again. Any moment now, Andrew would storm in demanding things: an on-site electrician, a brand new building, an exorcist.

Andrew flung open the door and Max, not for the first time, wondered what exactly it was about his newest employee that he liked so damn much.

Outside, Stella was having trouble with her concentration. Sequins were falling like molt—a pearly cascade sent fluttering to ground every time she moved, and the blue was beginning to fade. Early that morning she'd woken to find Cairo standing at the end of her bed, resting a burn-seared boot up on the doona. Ammunition rounds had laced one muscular shoulder and she'd smelt of sweat and gunpowder.

"Guess what?" she'd said. "Swimming carnival's over."

Stella walked home past the pool, but the blue had lost its allure. A distant frontier was reaching in from the edges of the city, sharpening her senses to other things: the glint of metal on passers-by, debris gathering shadows below walls speckled with sun. The spurs on her boots tsssked gently.

The words had stopped falling off the page. Vince sat giving them careful thought as Stella rested between wakefulness and dream.

"Dry heat must suit you both," he said finally, holding up the little book. *Stella's Transformation* blazed in brand new script across its front and limned the contours of his face a seraphic gold.

"—That's if you're ready to go."

"Will I ever get to come back?"

"If you find someone who needs a new story." He handed

her a notebook from his briefcase, the cover unmarked and soft as chamois, the pages empty.

Then he paused. "Unless you'd rather I stop?"

Stella thought of Cairo, the musky sniff of leather on her. "No, go right ahead," she said.

He began to read, and Stella felt herself tipped irrevocably into dive. As she fell, speeding toward a distance filled with midnight, she hoped that Howard would forgive her for never having let him in on the secret.

The plains rippled with heat, far hills smudging into a bleached sky. Cairo was kicking dirt over the campfire.

"I don't see Vince anywhere," Stella said as they loaded pearl-handled six-shooters and checked girth and stirrup straps on restless horses.

Cairo smiled broadly as she swung into the saddle. "Looks like this one is all ours."

Max leaned in the doorway of his office. Lately the Rothko had started to resemble a cityscape. He looked across at Stella's empty chair. The electrics in the building had been back to normal for several days and no one was complaining of king tides on their computer screens anymore. He had thought about filing a missing persons report but for the message that had appeared on his screensaver: the tropical fish had been replaced by a gunslinger in a white bathing cap, a speech balloon beside her.

"Adios Max," it said.

Charlie the Purple Giraffe
Was Acting Strangely

David D. Levine

David Levine (www.spiritone.com/~dlevine/) and his wife, Kate Yule, live in Portland, Oregon, are active in science fiction fandom, and publish the SF fanzine Bento. *A life-long science fiction reader and writer, he attended the Clarion West SF Writing Workshop in 2000 and has been publishing short stories since 2001. He's now a winner of the James White Award, the Writers of the Future Contest, and the Phobos Fiction Contest, and his stories regularly appear in the magazines and in small press and theme anthologies. His work is entertaining and shows a growing depth of thematic resonances.*

"Charlie the Purple Giraffe Was Acting Strangely" appeared in Realms of Fantasy, *which remained at the top of the fantasy fiction field alongside* F&SF *in 2004. It is an amusing tale of comic cartoon characters—one of whom begins to intuit an audience, and fall into existential anxiety. It is pleasant to read and has some real punch, in the way of some of those absurd early stories by Philip K. Dick, such as "Roog."*

Jerry the orange squirrel was walking down the sidewalk one day when he saw some word balloons floating above the hedge beside him. It was the voice of his friend Charlie the purple giraffe. "A man has to have a proper garden, doesn't he?" Charlie was saying. "And what makes a proper garden? Proper plants! And what do you need for proper plants?"

After each question, Charlie seemed to be waiting for an answer. But no response was visible.

"You need proper dirt!" Charlie continued. "And what do you have to have for proper dirt?"

Intrigued, Jerry scampered to the top of the hedge and stared down. What he saw made the little lines of surprise come out of his head.

"You have to have proper worms!" Bent double, Charlie was busily tying a Windsor knot around the neck of a common garden worm. Beside him, a large tin can—its ragged-edged lid tilted at a rakish angle—squirmed with hundreds of worms in tiny top hats, spats, and bustles.

It wasn't the worms that surprised Jerry, though—Charlie did that sort of thing all the time. It was the fact that Charlie was speaking into the thin air.

"Who ya talkin' to, Charlie?" said Jerry.

Charlie was so startled that his eyes momentarily jumped out of his head. But he quickly regained his composure. "The worms?"

"Worms don't have ears."

"Uh . . . I was talkin' to *you*, Jerry."

"You didn't even know I was here."

"Sure I did! I was just pretendin' I didn't."

"Uh huh." Jerry's words dripped frost. One linen-clad worm raised a parasol against the drips.

"As a matter of fact, I was just about to invite you in for tea. Care to join me?"

"Yeah. We can have a nice chat."

They walked from the yard into Charlie's cozy one-room bungalow. It was pink today, with cheerful curves to its walls and roof, and was surrounded by smiling purple flowers. The entire interior was wallpapered in blue and yellow stripes, which clashed with the green and black stripes of Charlie's suit.

Charlie poured tea for the two of them, holding the tiny teapot delicately between white-gloved finger and thumb. A musical note came from the pot as he set it down. He seated himself and lifted his cup, pinky raised—though he did not drink, for his arms were too short to reach his head. "What brings you out on this fine morning?" he asked. His words were sprinkled with rainbows and candy canes.

Jerry sipped his tea for a moment. "Charlie . . . you have to admit you've been acting a little strange lately."

"Strange?" Charlie's eyes darted to one side, then returned to Jerry.

Jerry set down his cup. "You've been talking to yourself."

"Me? Talk to myself?" He slapped his knee and laughed, not very convincingly. "Why should I talk to myself, when you're so much more interesting than I am?"

"I've seen you do it. Like just now."

"I told you, I was talking to you."

"What about last week, when you were working on your car? I saw you from three blocks away. Every once in a while you'd wave your wrench and pontificate. It was like you were trying to convince someone of something, but there was nobody there."

"I was . . . rehearsing. I'm giving a speech to the Rotary Club next week."

Jerry hopped up on the table. "Charlie, there is no Rotary Club in this town."

"It's in . . . another town."

"What other town?"

Charlie passed his cup from hand to hand. He stared fixedly at a point on the wall. It was as though he were staring out a window, but there wasn't even a painting there—just the wallpaper, which was now patterned in pink and white polka-dots. His expression was grim, almost angry. Finally he brought his head down to Jerry's level, cupped his glove to his mouth, and whispered, "I wasn't talking to myself."

"Oh?"

Charlie peered theatrically from side to side, then leaned in even closer. "I was talking to the readers."

Jerry crossed his arms on his chest. "There's nobody here by that name."

"It's not a name. It's . . . what they do. Readers. People who read."

"Who read what?"

A change came over Charlie then, like a cloud passing in front of the sun. He placed his hands flat in his lap, straightened his neck, and took a deep breath. "Us," he said at last. "They read us."

"I don't understand."

Charlie stood up and began to pace, his hands tightly clenched behind his back. His strides were long, and the house was tiny; he could only take two or three steps in each direction before having to turn around. "Jerry," he began, then paused. "Look . . . do you ever ask yourself, why am I here? What is the meaning of life?"

"Sure. Sometimes. Doesn't everyone?"

Charlie stopped pacing, turned suddenly, and leaned down to Jerry again. "We make them laugh." His tone was deadly serious.

"Them."

"The readers. We were created to entertain them."

Jerry waved his tiny paws in a broad gesture of negation. "Whoa there, big guy. Jerry the squirrel is nobody's creation and nobody's patsy. I'm here for *me*."

"Sorry, Jerry, but it's the honest truth. We're just characters in a comic book."

Jerry fixed Charlie with a hard, beady stare. "Prove it."

Charlie's eyes closed and his shoulders slumped. He turned away from Jerry. "I can't."

"Then how do you know it's true?"

"I've always known, I think, in the back of my head

somewhere. But then one day . . ." He turned back to Jerry, and his eyes were two black pits of fear and despair. "I had just said good-bye to Hermione the hedgehog, I turned back to go into my house, and then . . . suddenly everything was black. I couldn't move. I couldn't see. I was squashed flat. But somehow I knew that all around me, piled above and below me like a huge stack of pancakes, was everyone and everything I have ever cared about. They were all squashed flat too, but I was the only one who knew it. That went on for a moment that seemed like forever. And then I was right back in my house, as though nothing had happened."

A thought balloon appeared above Jerry's head: "He's bonkers!"

"I know it sounds crazy. But it was as real as anything. And ever since then . . . I know we're being read, and we're being laughed at."

"I get it," Jerry said with false cheer. "When you talk to yourself you are telling them jokes!"

"No!" Charlie's hands bunched into fists, and he pounded the air ineffectually. "I'm trying to *explain* myself!"

Jerry scratched his head, and a few question marks came out. "You certainly aren't doing a very good job of it now."

"Well, for instance . . . last week, when I was working on my car. I was just putting the engine back in for the third time, and I was explaining to the readers that this was a very delicate operation and had to be performed with the utmost care. Not funny at all."

"Charlie, you were pounding it in place with a sledge hammer. That's pretty funny. And calling it a delicate operation just makes it funnier."

Charlie stood stock-still for a moment, his lip quivering. Then he collapsed into his chair, his purple neck arching high as he dropped his head into his hands. "I know!" he sobbed, big blue teardrops running down between his fingers. "No matter what I do, no matter how hard I try to be serious, it comes out hilarious. And I'm tired of them laughing at me!"

Jerry offered his handkerchief, and Charlie blew his nose in it with an immense orange HONK.

"These 'readers' . . . can you hear them? Can you see them?"

"No." He didn't raise his head from his hands.

"Then how do you know they're laughing at you?"

"I just know. The same way I know they're there."

"Where are they, exactly?"

"Right now? Over there."

Jerry followed Charlie's pointing finger, but there was nothing there but the green and white flowered wallpaper. At least it was prettier than the pink and white polka-dots that had been there before. "I don't see anything."

"Neither do I. But they're there. They're always there."

"Always?"

"Well, most of the time." He lifted his head and tried to return the sodden handkerchief, but Jerry gestured for him to keep it. "I don't think they watch anyone else. I mean, they're watching you now, because you're with me. And they might watch you for a while after you leave here. But eventually they'll come back to me. I'm the main character in their little comic book."

Jerry's tail bristled. "Why you? Why not me?"

"I don't know. I wish I did. That's just the way it is, I guess."

Jerry paced back and forth on the table for a time, thinking. Finally he spoke. "I think you ought to talk with Dr. Nocerous about this."

Charlie shook his head, a slow rueful motion. "OK . . . but I don't think it will do any good."

Doctor Nocerous's office walls were completely covered in diplomas, from such institutions as THE SCHOOL OF AARD VARKS and WAZUPWIT U. The doctor himself was a stout gray rhino, nearly as wide as he was tall, whose wire-rimmed glasses perched incongruously at the top of his horn. He wore a white lab coat, and a small round mirror was strapped to his forehead. He never used the mirror in any way. "Hmm," he said as he held his stethoscope to the side of Charlie's neck, and "Hmm" again as he stood on a stepladder to peer down Charlie's throat, and "Hmm" one more time as he held Charlie's lapel between two fingers and looked at his watch.

"Well, Doctor," said Jerry when the exam was finished, "what's wrong with him?"

"My examination has discovered no physical infirmities whatsoever. Superficially, he is salubrious as an equine."

"What?" said Charlie.

"Healthy as a horse," explained the doctor.

"I told you."

"But he's *seeing* things!" said Jerry.

"Indeed. These phantasmagorical manifestations are most worrisome," the doctor muttered, puffing on his pipe. A few small pink bubbles emerged as he pondered. "I recommend that we keep your friend under observation."

"How ironic," Charlie said to the wall, then returned his gaze to the doctor. "I am not seeing things, or hearing things! I just *know* things. Is that so bad?"

Jerry jumped up on the doctor's desk. "Charlie, listen to me. I'm your friend, right? I've never steered you wrong?"

"Of course not."

"Then get this through your thick purple skull: *There are no 'readers.'* You are not the 'main character' in anyone's 'comical book.' You're just a person like anyone else, and you're here to muddle through your life the same as the rest of us. Nothing more."

"The veracity of your diminutive companion's statement is incontrovertible," said the doctor, waving his pipe. "These megalomaniacal misapprehensions must be immediately terminated. They jeopardize your physical integrity and the overall stability of the community."

"What?"

"You're a danger to yourself and others."

Charlie jumped out of his seat. "I'm no danger to anyone! So what if I talk to myself? That doesn't mean I'm going to pick up a big mallet and start flattening people!"

"Solipsistic delusions are frequently merely the initial manifestation of a general insensitivity to the legitimacy, even the existence, of external personalities. If allowed to go unchecked, these tendencies could escalate into antisocial or even injurious behavior!"

"What?"

"He thinks you might pick up a big mallet and start flattening people," said Jerry.

Charlie stood with his feet planted wide and his fists clenched. The white fabric of his gloves was bunched and strained. He stared at the wall. "You think this is funny, don't you?"

"Nobody's making any jokes here, Charlie," said Jerry. "We're serious."

"I wasn't talking to you." He turned around, pointed at a different spot on the wall. "This has all been arranged for *your* amusement! Are you happy?"

Jerry and Dr. Nocerous looked at each other.

Charlie pulled a big mallet from his pocket and began pounding on the wall. "Are you laughing now? Huh? Are you?" The WHAM of the mallet on the wall was huge and black. "Just let me get out there and I'll show you what comedy is all about!"

"This situation necessitates immediate incarceration!" said the doctor as he ran behind his desk.

"Ditto!" said Jerry as he dived under a chair.

The doctor pressed a button under the desk; no sound came out, but a few small lightning bolts appeared. Moments later two enormous gorillas, their white coats stretched taut over bulging muscles, burst through the door. There was a swirl of motion, and when it cleared Charlie was on the floor, trussed in a strait jacket.

"Don't let them put me away!" Charlie cried.

"It's for your own good," said Jerry, and waved encouragingly as the gorillas hustled Charlie away. But as soon as they were gone, Jerry's shoulders slumped. "What are you going to do, Doctor?"

"His prognosis is not encouraging. However, he will be the recipient of the most advanced experimental treatments modern medical technology has to offer." From his pocket, the doctor drew one end of a set of heavy jumper cables. Sparks flew from the sharp copper teeth as he touched them together, and a small, strange grin appeared on his face.

Charlie's sad, desperate eyes peered through the slot in the metal door. "You've got to get me out of here, Jerry." His word balloons squeezed through the slot like bubbles from a sinking ship.

"Hang in there, buddy. Dr. Nocerous tells me you're coming along nicely."

"He's been saying that for weeks." Charlie shook his head, bringing his blackened horns briefly into view. "But I know the score. I'm not going to get out of here until I show some improvement, but since there's nothing wrong with me I'm never going to get any better than I am now."

"Charlie, you must accept that you have a problem. It's the first step on the road to recovery."

Charlie chuckled ruefully. "I have a problem, all right. I've learned that there are worse things than being laughed at."

"Nobody's laughing at you, Charlie. You need to understand that these 'readers' are nothing more than a projection of your own feelings of self-doubt and inconsequentiality."

"That's just what the rhino told you to say. But you're right—nobody's laughing at me. The *readers* aren't laughing at me. And that's the problem."

"I thought you didn't want them to laugh at you."

"I didn't. But since I've been here in this padded cell, tied up in this strait jacket all day long with nothing to do . . . they're *bored*."

"Well, that's an improvement, isn't it? Maybe now they'll watch someone else instead."

"They've tried. But—no insult intended—none of you guys are as funny as I am." Jerry's tail bristled. "So they're leaving. They're going away completely. And that scares me."

"You should be glad to be rid of them!" Jerry fumed.

Charlie's eyes closed for a moment. When they opened

again, Jerry saw a bit of the old manic fervor. "Listen . . . do you ever think about the nature of time?"

"What?"

"Time. How it passes, from moment to moment. Haven't you ever noticed how some things change when you aren't looking at them?"

"Like the wallpaper?"

"Exactly. I believe that time is . . . divided. Into moments, or segments. Within each segment we are alive and awake, but in between . . . there are gaps. That's when things change."

"What does this have to do with anything?"

"I think the readers live their lives in the gaps between our time segments. They live in our time too, somehow—I know because they can see us. But in the gaps . . . they have the universe to themselves."

"Charlie, you're not making any sense."

"I know it sounds crazy. But I'm dead serious. And here's the important part: When the readers aren't watching us . . . *we don't exist!*"

Jerry shook his head and turned away, but after a moment's thought he turned back. "OK. Suppose I accept this theory of yours. Suppose there *are* gaps between moments. But time still *feels* continuous to us. See?" He waved a paw rapidly back and forth. "So it doesn't really matter!"

"It doesn't matter as long as they keep coming back. But if too many of them get bored . . . if they all go away and don't come back . . . then the gap will just go on and on, and we'll never exist again. It'll be the end of the world, Jerry. Squashed flat in the dark, forever." Charlie's eyes were desperate, sincere, pleading. "You've got to get me out of here. I'll joke, I'll pratfall, I'll do anything to keep the readers coming back. To keep us all alive. Please."

Jerry closed his eyes, unable to bear his friend's gaze. "There are no readers, Charlie."

In the end, he was right.

Pat Moore

~~~~~~

Tim Powers

Tim Powers (www.theworksoftimpowers.com—tribute site) lives with his wife, Serena, in San Bernadino, California. He first became known as one of a circle of three SF writers (Powers, James P. Blaylock, K. W. Jeter) in Southern California in the early 1970s, who were the Philip K. Dick circle, and later, in the early 1980s, became the core of the SF described as "Steampunk." His tenth and most recent novel, Declare *(2000), was a winner of both the World Fantasy Award and the International Horror Guild Award. His previous novels* Last Call *(1992),* Expiration Date *(1995), and* Earthquake Weather *(1997) are a trilogy about gambling in Las Vegas, and the center of his work for that decade. Though he has published one collection of his short fiction,* Night Moves and Other Stories, *he is primarily a novelist and rarely writes short fiction. This is his first appearance in* The Year's Best Fantasy.*

"Pat Moore," which was published in Flights, *is set in the same noir fantasy milieu as his three novels of gambling. Pat Moore is a poker player in the San Francisco Bay Area. When he gets a chain letter using a Pat Moore as a warning example, his life is immediately in danger, from the living and the dead. The pace is fast and Powers' sure hand with detail and the nuances of character make this one a winner.*

"Is it okay if you're one of the ten people I send the letter to," said the voice on the telephone, "or is that redundant? I don't want to screw this up. 'Ear repair' sounds horrible."

Moore exhaled smoke and put out his Marlboro in the half-inch of cold coffee in his cup. "No, Rick, don't send it to me. In fact, you're screwed—it says you have to have ten friends."

He picked up the copy he had got in the mail yesterday, spread the single sheet out flat on the kitchen table and weighted two corners with the dusty salt and pepper shakers. It had clearly been photocopied from a photocopy, and originally composed on a typewriter.

> This has been sent to you for good luck. The original is in San Fransisco. You must send it on to ten friend's, who, you think need good luck, within 24 hrs of receiving it.

"I could use some luck," Rick went on. "Can you loan me a couple of thousand? My wife's in the hospital, and we've got no insurance."

Moore paused for a moment before going on with the old joke; then, "Sure," he said, "so we won't see you at the lowball game tomorrow?"

"Oh, I've got money for *that*." Rick might have caught Moore's hesitation, for he went on quickly, without waiting for a dutiful laugh, "Mark 'n' Howard mentioned the chain letter this morning on the radio. You're famous."

> The luck is now sent to you—you will receive Good Luck within three days of receiving this, provided you send it on. Do not send money, since luck has no price.

155

On a Wednesday dawn five months ago now, Moore had poured a tumbler of Popov Vodka at this table, after sitting most of the night in the emergency room at—what had been the name of the hospital in San Mateo, not Saint Lazarus, for sure—and then he had carefully lit a Virginia Slims from the orphaned pack on the counter and laid the smoldering cigarette in an ashtray beside the glass. When the untouched cigarette had burned down to the filter and gone out, he had carried the full glass and the ashtray to the back door and set them in the trash can, and then washed his hands in the kitchen sink, wondering if the little ritual had been a sufficient good-bye. Later he had thrown out the bottle of vodka and the pack of Virginia Slims too.

A young man in Florida got the letter, it was very faded, and he resolved to type it again, but he forgot. He had many troubles, including expensive ear repair. But then he typed ten copy's and mailed them, and he got a better job.

"Where you playing today?" Rick asked.

"The Garden City in San Jose, probably," Moore said, "the six- and twelve-dollar Hold 'Em. I was just about to leave when you called."

"For sure? I could meet you there. I was going to play at the Bay on Bering, but if we were going to meet there, you'd have to shave—"

"And find a clean shirt, I know. But I'll see you at Larry's game tomorrow, and we shouldn't play at the same table anyway. Go to the Bay."

"Naw, I wanted to ask you about something. So you'll be at the Garden City. You take the 280, right?"

Pat Moore put off mailing the letter and died, but later found it again and passed it on, and received threescore and ten.

"Right."

"If that crapped-out Dodge of yours can get up to freeway speed."

"It'll still be cranking along when your Saturn is a planter somewhere."

"Great, so I'll see you there," Rick said. "Hey," he added with forced joviality, "you're famous!"

Do not ignore this letter
ST LAZARUS

"Type up ten copies with your name in it, you can be famous too," Moore said, standing up and crumpling the letter. "Send one to Mark 'n' Howard. See you."

He hung up the phone and fetched his car keys from the cluttered table by the front door. The chilly sea breeze outside was a reproach after the musty staleness of the apartment, and he was glad he'd brought his denim jacket.

He combed his hair in the rearview mirror while the old slant-six engine of the Dodge idled in the carport, and he wondered if he would see the day when his brown hair might turn gray. He was still thirty years short of threescore and ten, and he wasn't envying the Pat Moore in the chain letter.

The first half hour of the drive down the 280 was quiet, with a Gershwin CD playing the *Concerto in F* and the pines and green meadows of the Fish and Game Refuge wheeling past on his left under the gray sky, while the pastel houses of Hillsborough and Redwood City marched across the eastern hills. The car smelled familiarly of Marlboros and Doublemint gum and engine exhaust.

Just over those hills, on the 101 overlooking the Bay, Trish had driven her Ford Grenada over an unrailed embankment at midnight, after a Saint Patrick's Day party at the Bayshore Meadows. Moore was objectively sure he would drive on the 101 some day, but not yet.

Traffic was light on the 280 this morning, and in his rearview mirror he saw the little white car surging from side to side in the lanes as it passed other vehicles. Like most modern cars, it looked to Moore like a computer mouse. He clicked up his turn signal lever and drifted over the lane-divider bumps and into the right lane.

The white car—he could see the blue Chevy cross on its hood now—swooped up in the lane Moore had just left, but instead of rocketing on past him, it slowed, pacing Moore's old Dodge at sixty miles an hour.

Moore glanced to his left, wondering if he knew the driver of the Chevy—but it was a lean-faced stranger in sunglasses, looking straight at him. In the moment before Moore recognized the thing as a shotgun viewed muzzle-on, he thought the man was holding up a microphone; but instantly another person in the white car had blocked the driver—Moore glimpsed only a purple shirt and long dark hair—and then with squealing tires the white Chevy veered sharply away to the left.

Moore gripped the hard green plastic of his steering wheel and looked straight ahead; he was braced for the sound of the Chevy hitting the center-divider fence, and so he didn't jump when he heard the crash—even though the seat rocked under him and someone was now sitting in the car with him, on the passenger side against the door. For one unthinking moment he thought someone had been thrown from the Chevrolet and had landed in his car.

He focused on the lane ahead and on holding the Dodge Dart steady between the white lines. Nobody could have come through the roof, or the windows or the doors. Must have been hiding in the backseat all this time, he thought, and only now jumped over into the front. What timing. He was panting shallowly, and his ribs tingled, and he made himself take a deep breath and let it out.

He looked to his right. A dark-haired woman in a purple dress was grinning at him. Her hair hung in a neat pageboy cut, and she wasn't panting.

"I'm your guardian angel," she said. "And guess what my name is."

Moore carefully lifted his foot from the accelerator—he didn't trust himself with the brake yet—and steered the Dodge onto the dirt shoulder. When it had slowed to the point where he could hear gravel popping under the tires, he pressed the brake; the abrupt stop rocked him forward, though the woman beside him didn't shift on the old green upholstery.

"And guess what my name is," she said again.

The sweat rolling down his chest under his shirt was a sharp tang in his nostrils. "Hmm," he said, to test his voice; then he said, "You can get out of the car now."

In the front pocket of his jeans was a roll of hundred-dollar bills, but his left hand was only inches away from the .38 revolver tucked into the open seam at the side of the seat. But both the woman's hands were visible on her lap, and empty. She didn't move.

The engine was still running, shaking the car, and he could smell the hot exhaust fumes seeping up through the floor. He sighed, then reluctantly reached forward and switched off the ignition.

"I shouldn't be talking to you," the woman said in the sudden silence. "*She* told me not to. But I just now saved your life. So don't tell me to get out of the car."

It had been a purple shirt or something, and dark hair. But this was obviously not the person he'd glimpsed in the Chevy. A team, twins?

"What's your name?" he asked absently. A van whipped past on the left, and the car rocked on its shock absorbers.

"Pat Moore, same as yours," she said with evident satisfaction. He noticed that every time he glanced at her, she looked away from something else to meet his eyes; as if whenever he wasn't watching her, she was studying the interior of the car, or his shirt, or the freeway lanes.

"Did you—get threescore and ten?" he asked. Something more like a nervous tic than a smile was twitching his lips. "When you sent out the letter?"

"That wasn't me, that was *her*. And she hasn't got it yet. And she won't, either, if her students kill all the available Pat Moores. You're in trouble every which way, but I like you."

"Listen, when did you get into my car?"

"About ten seconds ago. What if he had backup, another car following him? You should get moving again."

Moore called up the instant's glimpse he had got of the thing in front of the driver's hand—the ring had definitely been the muzzle of a shotgun, twelve-gauge, probably a pistol grip. And he seized on her remark about a backup car because the thought was manageable and complete. He clanked the gearshift into Park, and the Dodge started at the first twist of the key, and he levered it into Drive and gunned along the shoulder in a cloud of dust until he had got up enough speed to swing into the right lane between two yellow Stater Bros. trucks.

He concentrated on working his way over to the fast lane, and then when he had got there, his engine roaring, he just watched the rearview mirror and the oncoming exit signs until he found a chance to make a sharp right turn across all the lanes and straight into the exit lane that swept toward the southbound 85. A couple of cars behind him honked.

He was going too fast for the curving interchange lane, his tires chirruping on the pavement, and he wrestled with the wheel and stroked the brake.

"Who's getting off behind us?" he asked sharply.

"I can't see," she said.

He darted a glance at the rearview mirror and was pleased to see only a slow-moving old station wagon, far back.

"A station wagon," she said, though she still hadn't looked around. Maybe she had looked in the passenger-side door mirror.

He had got the car back under control by the time he merged with the southbound lanes, and then he braked, for the 85 was ending ahead, at a traffic signal by the grounds of some college.

"Is your neck hurt?" he asked. "Can't twist your head around?"

"It's not that. I can't see anything you don't see."

He tried to frame an answer to that, or a question about it, and finally just said, "I bet we could find a bar fairly readily. Around here."

"I can't drink. I don't have any ID."

"You can have a Virgin Mary," he said absently, catching

a green light and turning right just short of the college. "Celery stick to stir it with." Raindrops began spotting the dust on the windshield.

"I'm not so good at touching things," she said. "I'm not actually a living person."

"Okay, see, that means what? You're a *dead* person, a ghost?"

"Yes."

Already disoriented, Moore flexed his mind to see if anything in his experience or philosophies might let him believe this; and there was nothing that did. This woman, probably a neighbor, simply knew who he was, and she had hidden in the back of his car back at the apartment parking lot. She was probably insane. It would be a mistake to get further involved with her.

"Here's a place," he said, swinging the car into a strip-mall parking lot to the right. "Pirate's Cove. We can see how well you handle peanuts or something before you try a drink."

He parked around behind the row of stores, and the back door of the Pirate's Cove led them down a hallway stacked with boxes before they stepped through an arch into the dim bar. There were no other customers in the place at this early hour, and the long room smelled more like bleach than like beer; the teenaged-looking bartender barely gave them a glance and a nod as Moore led the woman across the worn carpet and the parquet square to a table under a football poster. There were four low stools instead of chairs.

The woman couldn't remember any movies she'd ever seen, and claimed not to have heard about the war in Iraq, so when Moore walked to the bar and came back with a glass of Budweiser and a bowl of popcorn, he sat down and just stared at her. She was easier to see in the dim light from the jukebox and the neon bar signs than she had been out in the gray daylight. He would guess that she was about thirty—though her face had no wrinkles at all, as if she had never laughed or frowned.

"You want to try the popcorn?" he asked as he un-snapped the front of his denim jacket.

"Look at it so I know where it is."

He glanced down at the bowl, and then back at her. As always, her eyes fixed on his as soon as he was looking at her. Either her pupils were fully dilated, or else her irises were black.

But he glanced down again when something thumped the table and a puff of hot salty air flicked his hair, and some popcorn kernels spun away through the air.

The popcorn still in the bowl had been flattened into little white jigsaw-puzzle pieces. The orange plastic bowl was cracked.

Her hands were still in her lap, and she was still looking at him. "I guess not, thanks."

Slowly he lifted his glass of beer and took a sip. That was a powerful raise, he thought, forcing himself not to show any astonishment—though you should have suspected a strong hand. Play carefully here.

He glanced toward the bar; but the bartender, if he had looked toward their table at all, had returned his attention to his newspaper.

"Tom Cruise," the woman said.

Moore looked back at her and after a moment raised his eyebrows.

She said, "That was a movie, wasn't it?"

"In a way." *Play carefully here.* "What did you—? Is something wrong with your vision?"

"I don't have any vision. No retinas. I have to use yours. I'm a ghost."

"Ah. I've never met a ghost before." He remembered a line from a Robert Frost poem: *The dead are holding something back.*

"Well, not that you could see. You can see me only because . . . I'm like the stamp you get on the back of your hand at Disneyland; you can't see me unless there's a black light shining on me. *She's* the black light."

"You're in her field of influence, like."

"Sure. There's probably dozens of Pat Moore ghosts in the outfield, and *she's* the whole infield. I'm the shortstop."

"Why doesn't . . . *she* want you to talk to me?" He never drank on days he intended to play, but he lifted his glass again.

"She doesn't want me to tell you what's going to happen." She smiled, and the smile stayed on her smooth face like the expression on a porcelain doll. "If it was up to me, I'd tell you."

He swallowed a mouthful of beer. "But."

She nodded, and at last let her smile relax. "It's not up to me. She'd kill me if I told you."

He opened his mouth to point out a logic problem with that, then sighed and said instead, "Would she know?" She just blinked at him, so he went on, "Would she know it, if you told me?"

"*Oh* yeah."

"How would she know?"

"You'd be doing things. You wouldn't be sitting here drinking a beer, for sure."

"What would I be doing?"

"I think you'd be driving to San Francisco. If I told you— if you asked—" For an instant she was gone, and then he could see her again; but she seemed two-dimensional now, like a projection on a screen—he had the feeling that if he moved to the side, he would just see this image of her get narrower, not see the other side of her.

"What's in San Francisco?" he asked quickly.

"Well if you asked me about Maxwell's Demon-n-n-n—"

She was perfectly motionless, and the drone of the last consonant slowly deepened in pitch to silence. Then the popcorn in the cracked bowl rattled in the same instant that she silently disappeared like the picture on a switched-off television set, leaving Moore alone at the table, his face suddenly chilly in the bar's air-conditioning. For a moment *air-conditioning* seemed to remind him of something, but he forgot it when he looked down at the popcorn—the bowl was full of brown BBs, unpopped dried corn. As he watched, each kernel slowly opened in white curls and blobs until all the popcorn was as fresh-looking and un-crushed as it had been when he had carried it to the table. There hadn't been a sound, though he caught a strong whiff of gasoline. The bowl wasn't cracked anymore.

He stood up and kicked his stool aside as he backed away from the table. She was definitely gone.

The bartender was looking at him now, but Moore hurried past him and back through the hallway to the stormy gray daylight.

What if she had backup? he thought as he fumbled the keys out of his pocket; and, *She doesn't want me to tell you what's going to happen.*

He realized that he'd been sprinting only when he scuffed to a halt on the wet asphalt beside the old white Dodge, and he was panting as he unlocked the door and yanked it open. Rain on the pavement was a steady tex-tured hiss. He climbed in and pulled the door closed, and had rammed the key into the ignition—

—when the drumming of rain on the car roof abruptly went silent, and a voice spoke in his head: *Relax. I'm you. You're me.*

And then his mouth had opened and the words were coming out of his mouth: "We're Pat Moore, there's noth-ing to be afraid of." His voice belonged to someone else in this muffled silence.

His eyes were watering with the useless effort to breathe more quickly.

He knew this wasn't the Pat Moore he had been in the bar with. This was the *her* she had spoken of. A moment later the thoughts had been wiped away, leaving nothing but an insistent pressure of *all-is-well.*

Though nothing grabbed him, he found that his head was turning to the right, and with dimming vision he saw that his right hand was moving toward his face.

But *all-is-well* had for some time been a feeling that was alien to him, and he managed to resist it long enough to make his infiltrated mind form a thought—*it's crowding me out.*

And he managed to think too: *Alive or dead, stay whole.*
He reached down to the open seam in the seat before he
could lose his left arm too, and he snatched up the revolver
and stabbed the barrel into his open mouth. A moment later
he felt the click through the steel against his teeth when he
cocked the hammer back. His belly coiled icily, as if he
were standing on the coping of a very high wall and looking up.

The intrusion in his mind paused, and he sensed confusion, and so he threw at it the thought, *One more step, and
I blow my head off.* He added, *Go ahead and call this bet,
please. I've been meaning to drive the 101 for a while now.*

His throat was working to form words that he could only
guess at, and then he was in control of his own breathing
again, panting and huffing spit into the gun barrel. Beyond
the hammer of the gun, he could see the rapid distortions of
rain hitting the windshield, but he still couldn't hear anything from outside the car.

The voice in his head was muted now: *I mean to help you.*

He let himself pull the gun away from his mouth, though he
kept it pointed at his face, and he spoke into the wet barrel
as if it were a microphone. "I don't want help," he said hoarsely.

I'm Pat Moore, and I want help.

"You want to . . . take over, possess me."

I want to protect you. A man tried to kill you.

"That's your pals," he said, remembering what the ghost
woman had told him in the car. "Your students, trying to
kill all the Pat Moores—to keep you from taking one over, I
bet. Don't joggle me now." Staring down the rifled barrel,
he cautiously hooked his thumb over the hammer and then
pulled the trigger and eased the hammer down. "I can still
do it with one pull of the trigger," he told her as he lifted his
thumb away. "So you—what, you put off mailing the letter,
and died?"

*The letter is just my chain mail. The only important thing
about it is my name, and the likelihood that people will reproduce it and pass it on. Bombers evade radar by throwing clouds of tinfoil. The chain mail is my name, scattered
everywhere so that any blow directed at me is dissipated.*

"So you're a ghost too."

A prepared ghost. I know how to get outside of time.

"Fine, get outside of time. What do you need me for?"

You're alive, and your name is mine, which is to say your identity is mine. I've used too much of my energy saving you, holding you. And you're the most compatible of them all—you're a Pat Moore identity squared, by marriage.

"Squared by—" He closed his eyes and nearly lowered the gun. "Everybody called her Trish," he whispered. "Only her mother called her Pat." He couldn't feel the seat under him, and he was afraid that if he let go of the gun, it would fall to the car's roof.

Her mother called her Pat.

"You can't have me." He was holding his voice steady with an effort. "I'm driving away now."

You're Pat Moore's only hope.

"You need an exorcist, not a poker player." He could move his right arm again, and he started the engine and then switched on the windshield wipers.

Abruptly the drumming of the rain came back on, sounding loud after the long silence. She was gone.

His hands were shaking as he tucked the gun back into its pocket, but he was confident that he could get back onto the 280, even with his wornout windshield wipers blurring everything, and he had no intention of getting on the 101 any time soon; he had been almost entirely bluffing when he told her, *I've been meaning to drive the 101 for a while now.* But like an alcoholic who tries one drink after long abstinence, he was remembering the taste of the gun barrel in his mouth: *That was easier than I thought it would be,* he thought.

He fumbled a pack of Marlboros out of his jacket pocket and shook one out.

As soon as he had got onto the northbound 85, he became aware that the purple dress and the dark hair were blocking the passenger-side window again, and he didn't jump at all. He had wondered which way to turn on the 280, and now he steered the car into the lane that would take him back north, toward San Francisco. The grooved interchange lane gleamed with fresh rain, and he kept his speed down to forty.

"One big U-turn," he said finally, speaking around his lit cigarette. He glanced at her; she looked three-dimensional again, and she was smiling at him as cheerfully as ever.

"I'm your guardian angel," she said.

"Right, I remember. And your name's Pat Moore, same as mine. Same as everybody's, lately." He realized that he was optimistic, which surprised him; it was something like the happy confidence he had felt in dreams in which he had discovered that he could fly and leave behind all earthbound reproaches. "I met *her,* you know. She's dead too, and she needs a living body, and so she tried to possess me."

"Yes," said Pat Moore. "That's what's going to happen. I couldn't tell you before."

He frowned. "I scared her off, by threatening to shoot myself." Reluctantly he asked, "Will she try again, do you think?"

"Sure. When you're asleep, probably, since this didn't work. She can wait a few hours—a few days, even, in a pinch. It was just because I talked to you that she switched me off and tried to do it right away, while you were still awake. *Jumped the gun,*" she added, with the first laugh he had heard from her. It sounded as if she were trying to chant in a language she didn't understand.

"Ah," he said softly. "That raises the ante." He took a deep breath and let it out. "When did you . . . die?"

"I don't know. Some time besides now. Could you put out the cigarette? The smoke messes up my reception; I'm still partly seeing that bar, and partly a hilltop in a park somewhere."

He rolled the window down an inch and flicked the cigarette out. "Is this how you looked, when you were alive?"

She touched her hair as he glanced at her. "I don't know."

"When you were alive—did you know about movies, and current news? I mean, you don't seem to know about them now."

"I suppose I did. Don't most people?"

He was gripping the wheel hard now. "Did your mother call you Pat?"

"I suppose she did. It's my name."

"Did your . . . friends, call you Trish?"

"I suppose they did."

I suppose, I suppose! He forced himself not to shout at her. She's dead, he reminded himself, she's probably doing the best she can.

But again he thought of the Frost line: *The dead are holding something back.*

They had passed under two gray concrete bridges, and now he switched on his left turn signal to merge with the northbound 280. The pavement ahead of him glittered with reflected red brake lights.

"See, my wife's name was Patricia Moore," he said, trying to sound reasonable. "She died in a car crash five months ago. Well, a single-car accident. Drove off a freeway embankment. She was drunk." He remembered that the popcorn in the Pirate's Cove had momentarily smelled like spilled gasoline.

"I've been drunk."

"So has everybody. But—you might be her."

"Who?"

"My wife. Trish."

"I might be your wife."

"Tell me about Maxwell's Demon."

"I would have been married to you, you mean. We'd *really* have been Pat Moore then. Like mirrors reflecting each other."

"That's why *she* wants me, right. So what's Maxwell's Demon?"

"It's . . . she's dead, so she's like a smoke ring somebody puffed out in the air, if they were smoking. Maxwell's Demon keeps her from disappearing like a smoke ring would, it keeps her . . ."

"Distinct," Moore said when she didn't go on. "Even though she's got no right to be distinct anymore."

"And me. Through her."

"Can I kill him? Or make him stop sustaining her?" And you, he thought; it would stop him sustaining you. Did I stop sustaining you before? Well, obviously.

Earthbound reproaches.

"It's not a *him*, really. It looks like a sprinkler you'd screw onto a hose, to water your yard, if it would spin. It's in her house, hooked up to the air-conditioning."

"A sprinkler." He was nodding repeatedly, and he made himself stop. "Okay. Can you show me where her house is? I'm going to have to sleep sometime."

"She'd kill me."

"Pat—Trish—" Instantly he despised himself for calling her by that name. "—you're already dead."

"She can get outside of time. Ghosts aren't really in time anyway. I'm wrecking the popcorn in that bar in the future as much as in the past, it's all just cards in a circle on a table, none in front. None of it's really now or not-now. She could make me not ever—she could take my thread out of the carpet—you'd never have met me, even like this."

"Make you never have existed."

"Right. Never was any me at all."

"She wouldn't dare—Pat." Just from self-respect, he couldn't bring himself to call her Trish again. "Think about it. If you never existed, then I wouldn't have married you, and so I wouldn't be the Pat Moore squared that she needs."

"If you *did* marry me. *Me*, I mean. I can't remember. Do you think you did?"

She'll take me there, if I say yes, he thought. She'll believe me if I say it. And what's to become of me, if she doesn't? That woman very nearly crowded me right out of the world five minutes ago, and I was wide awake.

The memory nauseated him.

What becomes of a soul that's pushed out of its body, he thought, as *she* means to do to me? Would there be *anything* left of *me*, even a half-wit ghost like poor Pat here?

Against his will came the thought, You always did lie to her.

"I don't know," he said finally. "The odds are against it."

There's always the 101, he told himself, and somehow the thought wasn't entirely bleak. Six chambers of it, hollow-point .38s. Fly away.

"It's possible, though, isn't it?"

He exhaled, and nodded. "It's possible, yes."

"I think I owe it to you. Some Pat Moore does. We left you alone."

"It was my fault." In a rush he added, "I was even glad you didn't leave a note." It's true, he thought. I was grateful.

"I'm glad she didn't leave a note," this Pat Moore said.

He needed to change the subject. "*You're* a ghost," he said. "Can't you make *her* never have existed?"

"No. I can't get far from real places or I'd blur away, out of focus, but she can go way up high, where you can look down on the whole carpet, and—twist out strands of it; bend somebody at right angles to *everything,* which means you're gone without a trace. And anyway, she and her students are all blocked against that kind of attack, they've got ConfigSafe."

He laughed at the analogy. "You know about computers?"

"No," she said emptily. "Did I?"

He sighed. "No, not a lot." He thought of the revolver in the seat, and then thought of something better. "You mentioned a park. You used to like Buena Vista Park. Let's stop there on the way."

Moore drove clockwise around the tall, darkly-wooded hill that was the park, while the peaked roofs and cylindrical towers of the old Victorian houses were teeth on a saw passing across the gray sky on his left. He found a parking space on the eastern curve of Buena Vista Avenue, and he got out of the car quickly to keep the Pat Moore ghost from having to open the door on her side; he remembered what she had done to the bowl of popcorn.

But she was already standing on the splashing pavement in the rain, without having opened the door. In the ashy daylight, her purple dress seemed to have lost all its color, and her face was indistinct and pale; he peered at her, and he was sure the heavy raindrops were falling right through her.

He could imagine her simply dissolving on the hike up to the meadow. "Would you rather wait in the car?" he said. "I won't be long."

"Do you have a pair of binoculars?" she asked. Her voice too was frail out here in the cold.

"Yes, in the glove compartment." Cold rain was soaking his hair and leaking down inside his jacket collar, and he wanted to get moving. "Can you . . . *hold* them?"

"I can't hold anything. But if you take out the lens in the middle you can catch me in it, and carry me."

He stepped past her to open the passenger-side door and bent over to pop open the glove compartment, and then he knelt on the seat and dragged out his old leather-sleeved binoculars and turned them this way and that in the wobbly gray light that filtered through the windshield.

"How do I get the lens out?" he called over his shoulder.

"A screwdriver, I guess," came her voice, barely audible above the thrashing of the rain. "See the tiny screw by the eyepiece?"

"Oh. Right." He used the small blade from his pocketknife on the screw in the back of the left barrel, and then had to do the same with a similar screw on the forward side of it. The eyepiece stayed where it was, but the big forward lens fell out, exposing a metal cross on the inside; it was held down with a screw that he managed to rotate with the knife tip—and then a triangular block of polished glass fell out into his palm.

"That's it—that's the lens," she called from outside the car.

Moore's cell phone buzzed as he was stepping backward to the pavement, and he fumbled it out of his jacket pocket and flipped it open. "Moore here," he said. He pushed the car door closed and leaned over the phone to keep the rain off it.

"Hey Pat," came Rick's voice, "I'm sitting here in your Garden City Club in San Jose, and I could be at the Bay. Where are you, man?"

The Pat Moore ghost was moving her head, and Moore looked up at her. With evident effort, she was making her head swivel back and forth in a clear *no* gesture.

The warning chilled Moore. Into the phone he said, "I'm—not far, I'm at a bar off the 85. Place called the Pirate's Cove."

"Well, don't chug your beer on my account. But come over here when you can."

"You bet. I'll be out of here in five minutes." He closed the phone and dropped it back into his pocket.

"They made him call again," said the ghost. "They lost track of your car after I killed the guy with the shotgun." She smiled, and her teeth seemed to be gone. "That was good, saying you were at that bar. They can tell truth from lies, and that's only twenty minutes from being true."

Guardian angel, he thought. "You killed him?"

"I think so." Her image faded, then solidified again. "Yes."

"Ah. Well—good." With his free hand he pushed the wet hair back from his forehead. "So what do I do with this?" he asked, holding up the lens.

"Hold it by the frosted sides, with the long edge of the triangle pointed at me; then look at me through the two other edges."

The glass thing was a blocky right-triangle, frosted on the sides but polished smooth and clear on the thick edges; obediently he held it up to his eye and peered through the two slanted faces of clear glass.

He could see her clearly through the lens—possibly more clearly than when he looked at her directly—but this was a mirror image: the dark slope of the park appeared to be to the left of her.

"Now roll it over a quarter turn, like from noon to three," she said.

He rotated the lens ninety degrees—but her image in it rotated a full 180 degrees, so that instead of seeing her horizontal, he saw her upside down.

He jumped then, for her voice was right in his ear. "Close your eyes, and put the lens in your pocket."

He did as she said, and when he opened his eyes again, she was gone—the wet pavement stretched empty to the curbstones and green lawns of the old houses.

"You've got me in your pocket," her voice said in his ear. "When you want me, look through the lens again and turn it back the other way."

It occurred to him that he believed her. "Okay," he said, and sprinted across the street to the narrow stone stairs that led up into the park.

His leather shoes tapped the ascending steps and they splashed in the mud as he took the uphill path to the left. The city was gone now, hidden behind the dense overhanging boughs of pine and eucalyptus, and the rain echoed under the canopy of green leaves. The cold air was musky with the smells of mulch and pine and wet loam.

Up at the level playground lawn, the swing sets were of course empty, and in fact he seemed to be the only living soul in the park today. Through gaps between the trees, he could see San Francisco spread out below him on all sides, as still as a photograph under the heavy clouds.

He splashed through the gutters that were made of fragments of old marble headstones—keeping his head down, he glimpsed an incised cross filled with mud in the face of one stone, and the lone phrase IN LOVING MEMORY on another—and then he had come to the meadow with the big old oak trees he remembered.

He looked around, but there was still nobody to be seen in the cathedral space, and he hurried to the side and crouched to step in under the shaggy foliage and catch his breath.

"It's beautiful," said the voice in his ear.

"Yes," he said, and he took the lens out of his pocket. He held it up and squinted through the right-angle panels, and there was the image of her, upside down. He rotated it counterclockwise ninety degrees, and the image was upright, and when he moved the lens away from his eye, she was standing out in the clearing.

"Look at the city some more," she said, and her voice now seemed to come from several yards away. "So I can see it again."

One last time, he thought. Maybe for both of us; it's nice that we can do it together.

"Sure." He stepped out from under the oak tree and walked back out into the rain to the middle of the clearing and looked around.

A line of trees to the north was the panhandle of Golden Gate Park, and past that he could see the stepped levels of Alta Vista Park; more distantly to the left he could just make out the green band that was the hills of the Presidio, though the two big piers of the Golden Gate Bridge were lost behind miles of rain; he turned to look southwest, where the Twin Peaks and the TV tower on Mount Sutro were vivid above the misty streets; and then far away to the east the white spike of the Transamerica Pyramid stood up from the skyline at the very edge of visibility.

"It's beautiful," she said again. "Did you come here to look at it?"

"No," he said, and he lowered his gaze to the dark mulch under the trees. Cypress, eucalyptus, pine, oak—even from out here he could see that mushrooms were clustered in patches and rings on the carpet of wet black leaves, and he walked back to the trees and then shuffled in a crouch into the aromatic dimness under the boughs.

After a couple of minutes, "Here's one," he said, stooping to pick a mushroom. Its tan cap was about two inches across, covered with a patch of white veil. He unsnapped his denim jacket and tucked the mushroom carefully into his shirt pocket.

"What is it?" asked Pat Moore.

"I don't know," he said. "My wife was never able to tell, so she never picked it. It's either *Amanita lanei,* which is edible, or it's *Amanita phalloides,* which is fatally poisonous. You'd need a real expert to know which this is."

"What are you going to do with it?"

"I think I'm going to sandbag *her.* You want to hop back into the lens for the hike down the hill?"

* * *

He had parked the old Dodge at an alarming slant on Jones Street on the south slope of Russian Hill, and then the two of them had walked steeply uphill past close-set gates and balconies under tall sidewalk trees that grew straight up from the slanted pavements. Headlights of cars descending Jones Street reflected in white glitter on the wet trunks and curbstones, and in the wakes of the cars the tire tracks blurred away slowly in the continuing rain.

"How are we going to get into her house?" he asked quietly.

"It'll be unlocked," said the ghost. "She's expecting you now."

He shivered. "Is she. Well, I hope I'm playing a better hand than she guesses."

"Down here," said Pat, pointing at a brick-paved alley that led away to the right between the Victorian-gingerbread porches of two narrow houses.

They were in a little alley now, overhung with rosebushes and rosemary, with white-painted fences on either side. Columns of fog billowed in the breeze, and then he noticed that they were human forms—female torsos twisting transparently in the air, blank-faced children running in slow motion, hunched figures swaying heads that changed shape like water balloons.

"The outfielders," said the Pat Moore ghost.

Now Moore could hear their voices: *Goddam car—I got yer unconditional right here—Excuse me, you got a problem?—He was never there for me—So I told him, you want it, you come over here and take it—Bless me, Father, I have died—*

The acid smell of wet stone was lost in the scents of tobacco and jasmine perfume and liquor and old, old sweat.

Moore bit his lip and tried to focus on the solid pavement and the fences. "Where the hell's her place?" he asked tightly.

"This gate," she said. "Maybe you'd better—"

He nodded and stepped past her; the gate latch had no padlock, and he flipped up the catch. The hinges squeaked as he swung the gate inward over flagstones and low-cut grass.

He looked up at the house the path led to. It was a one-story 1920s bungalow, painted white or gray, with green wicker chairs on the narrow porch. Lights were on behind stained glass panels in the two windows and the porch door.

"It's unlocked," said the ghost.

He turned back toward her. "Stand over by the roses there," he told her, "away from the . . . the outfielders. I want to take you in in my pocket, okay?"

"Okay."

She drifted to the roses, and he fished the lens out of his pocket and found her image in the right-angle faces, then twisted the lens and put it back into his pocket.

He walked slowly up the path, stepping on the grass rather than on the flagstones, and stepped up to the porch.

"It's not locked, Patrick," came a woman's loud voice from inside.

He turned the purple-glass knob and walked several paces into a high-ceilinged kitchen with a black-and-white tiled floor; a blond woman in jeans and a sweatshirt sat at a Formica table by the big old refrigerator. From the next room, beyond an arch in the white-painted plaster, a steady whistling hiss provided an irritating background noise, as if a tea kettle were boiling.

The woman at the table was much more clearly visible than his guardian angel had been, almost aggressively three-dimensional—her breasts under the sweatshirt were prominent and pointed, and her nose and chin stood out perceptibly too far from her high cheekbones, and her lips were so full that they looked distinctly swollen.

A bottle of Wild Turkey bourbon stood beside three *Flintstones* glasses on the table, and she took it in one hand and twisted out the cork with the other. "Have a drink," she said, speaking loudly, perhaps in order to be heard over the hiss in the next room.

"I don't think I will, thanks," he said. "You're good with your hands." His jacket was dripping on the tiles, but he didn't take it off.

"I'm the solidest ghost you'll ever see."

Abruptly she stood up, knocking her chair against the refrigerator, and then she rushed past him, her Reeboks beating on the floor—and her body seemed to rotate as she went by him, as if she were swerving away from him, though her course to the door was straight. She reached out one lumpy hand and slammed the door.

She faced him again and held out her right hand. "I'm Pat Moore," she said, "and I want help."

He flexed his fingers, then cautiously held out his own hand. "I'm Pat Moore too," he said.

Her palm touched his, and though it was moving very slowly, his own hand was slapped away when they touched.

"I want us to become partners," she said. Her thick lips moved in ostentatious synchronization with her words.

"Okay," he said.

Her outlines blurred for just an instant; then she said, in the same booming tone, "I want us to become one person. You'll be immortal, and—"

"Let's do it," he said.

She blinked her black eyes. "You're—agreeing to it," she said. "You're accepting it, now?"

"Yes." He cleared his throat. "That's correct."

He looked away from her and noticed a figure sitting at the table—a transparent old man in an overcoat, hardly more visible than a puff of smoke.

"Is he Maxwell's Demon?" Moore asked.

The woman smiled, baring huge teeth. "No, that's . . . a soliton. A poor little soliton who's lost its way. I'll show you Maxwell's Demon."

She lunged and clattered into the next room, and Moore followed her, trying simultaneously not to slip on the floor and to keep an eye on her and on the misty old man.

He stepped into a parlor, and the hissing noise was louder in here. Carved dark wood tables and chairs and a modern exercise bicycle had been pushed against a curtained bay window in the far wall, and a vast carpet had been rolled back from the dusty hardwood floor and humped against the chair legs. In the high corners of the room and along the fluted top of the window frame, things like translucent cheerleaders' pom-poms grimaced and waved tentacles or locks of hair in the agitated air. Moore warily took a step away from them.

"Look over here," said the alarming woman.

In the near wall, an air-conditioning panel had been taken apart, and a red rubber hose hung from its machinery and was connected into the side of a length of steel pipe that lay on a TV table. Nozzles on either end of the pipe were making the loud whistling sound.

Moore looked more closely at it. It was apparently two sections of pipe, one about eight inches long and the other about four, connected together by a blocky fitting where the hose was attached, and a stove stopcock stood half-open near the end of the longer pipe.

"Feel the air," the woman said.

Moore cupped a hand near the end of the longer pipe and then yanked it back—the air blasting out of it felt hot enough to light a cigar. More cautiously he waved his fingers over the nozzle at the end of the short pipe; and then he rolled his hand in the air jet, for it was icy cold.

"*It's* not supernatural," she boomed, "even though the air conditioner's pumping room temperature air. A spiral washer in the connector housing sends air spinning up the long pipe; the hot molecules spin out to the sides of the little whirlwind in there, and it's them that the stopcock lets out. The cold molecules fall into a smaller whirlwind inside the big one, and they move the opposite way and come out at the end of the short pipe. Room-temperature air is a mix of hot and cold molecules, and this device separates them out."

"Okay," said Moore. He spoke levelly, but he was wishing he had brought his gun along from the car. It occurred to him that it was a rifled pipe that things usually come spinning out of, but which he had been ready to dive into. He wondered if the gills under the cap of the mushroom in his pocket were curved in a spiral.

"But this is counterentropy," she said, smiling again. "A Scottish physicist named Maxwell p-postulay-postul—guessed that a Demon would be needed to sort the hot molecules from the cold ones. If the Demon is present, the effect occurs, and vice versa—if you can make the effect occur, you've summoned the Demon. Get the effect, and the cause has no choice but to be present." She thumped her chest, though her peculiar breasts didn't move at all. "And once the Demon is present, he—he—"

She paused, so Moore said, "Maintains distinctions that wouldn't ordinarily stay distinct." His heart was pounding, but he was pleased with how steady his voice was.

Something like an invisible hand struck him solidly in the chest, and he stepped back.

"You don't touch it," she said. Again there was an invisible thump against his chest. "Back to the kitchen."

The soliton old man, hardly visible in the bright overhead light, was still nodding in one of the chairs at the table.

The blond woman was slapping the wall, and then a white-painted cabinet, but when Moore looked toward her, she grabbed the knob on one of the cabinet drawers and yanked it open.

"You need to come over here," she said, "and look in the drawer."

After the things he'd seen in the high corners of the parlor, Moore was cautious; he leaned over and peered into the drawer—but it contained only a stack of typing paper, a felt-tip laundry-marking pen, and half a dozen yo-yos.

As he watched, she reached past him and snatched out a sheet of paper and the laundry marker; and it occurred to him that she hadn't been able to see the contents of the drawer until he was looking at them.

I don't have any vision, his guardian angel had said. *No retinas. I have to use yours.*

The woman had stepped away from the cabinet now. "I was prepared, see," she said loudly enough to be heard out on Jones Street, "for my stupid students killing me. I knew they might. We were all working to learn how to transcend time, but I got there first, and they were afraid of what I would do. So *boom-boom-boom* for Mistress Moore. But I had already set up the Demon, and I had Xeroxed my chain mail and put it in addressed envelopes. Bales of them, the stamps cost me a fortune. I came back strong. And I'm going to merge with you now and get a real body again. You accepted the proposal—you said 'Yes, that's correct'—you didn't put out another bet this time to chase me away."

The cap flew off the laundry marker, and then she had slapped the paper down on the table next to the Wild Turkey bottle. "Watch me!" she said, and when he looked at the piece of paper, she began vigorously writing on it. Soon she had written *Pat* in big sprawling letters and was embarked on *Moore*.

She straightened up when it was finished. "Now," she said, her black eyes glittering with hunger, "you cut your hand and write with your blood, tracing over the letters. Our name is us, and we'll merge. Smooth as silk through a goose."

Moore slowly dug the pocketknife out of his pants pocket. "This is new," he said. "You didn't do this name-in-blood business when you tried to take me in the car."

She waved one big hand dismissively. "I thought I could sneak up on you. You resisted me, though—you'd probably have tried to resist me even in your sleep. But since you're accepting the inevitable now, we can do a proper contract, in ink and blood. Cut, cut!"

"Okay," he said, and unfolded the short blade and cut a nick in his right forefinger. "*You've* made a new bet now, though, and it's to me." Blood was dripping from the cut, and he dragged his finger over the *P* in her crude signature.

He had to pause halfway through and probe again with the blade tip to get more freely flowing blood; and as he was painfully tracing the *R* in *Moore,* he began to feel another will helping his hand to push his finger along, and he heard a faint drone like a radio carrier wave starting up in his head. Somewhere he was crouched on his toes on a narrow, outward-tilting ledge with no handholds anywhere, with vast volumes of emptiness below him—and his toes were sliding—

So he added quickly, "And I raise back at you."

By touch alone, looking up at the high ceiling, he pulled

the mushroom out of his shirt pocket and popped it into his mouth and bit down on it. Check and raise, he thought. Sandbagged. Then he lowered his eyes, and in an instant her gaze was locked on to his.

"What happened?" she demanded, and Moore could hear the three syllables of it chug in his own throat. "What did you do?"

"*Amanita,*" said the smoky old man at the table. His voice sounded like nothing organic—more like sandpaper on metal. "It was time to eat the mushroom."

Moore had resolutely chewed the thing up, his teeth grating on bits of dirt. It had the cold-water taste of ordinary mushrooms, and as he forced himself to swallow it, he forlornly hoped, in spite of all his bravura thoughts about the 101 freeway, that it might be the *lanei* rather than the deadly *phalloides.*

"He ate a mushroom?" the woman demanded of the old man. "You never told me about any mushroom! Is it a poisonous mushroom?"

"I don't know," came the rasping voice again. "It's either poisonous or not, though, I remember that much."

Moore was dizzy with the first twinges of comprehension of what he had done. "Fifty-fifty chance," he said tightly. "The death-cap *Amanita* looks just like another one that's harmless, both grown locally. I picked this one today, and I don't know which it was. If it's the poison one, we won't know for about twenty-four hours, maybe longer."

The drone in Moore's head grew suddenly louder, then faded until it was imperceptible. "You're telling the truth," she said. She flung out an arm toward the back porch, and for a moment her bony forefinger was a foot long. "Go vomit it up, now!"

He twitched, like someone mistaking the green left-turn arrow for the green light. No, he told himself, clenching his fists to conceal any trembling. Fifty-fifty is better than zero. You've clocked the odds and placed your bet. Trust yourself.

"No good," he said. "The smallest particle will do the job, if it's the poisonous one. Enough's probably been absorbed already. That's why I chose it." This was a bluff, or a guess, anyway, but this time she didn't scan his mind.

He was tense, but a grin was twitching at his lips. He nodded toward the old man and asked her, "Who *is* the lost sultan, anyway?"

"Soliton," she snapped. "He's you, you—dumb-brain." She stamped one foot, shaking the house. "How can I take you now? And I can't wait twenty-four hours just to see if I *can* take you!"

"Me? How is he me?"

"My name's Pat Moore," said the gray silhouette at the table.

"Ghosts are solitons," she said impatiently, "waves that keep moving all-in-a-piece after the living push has stopped. Forward or backward doesn't matter to them."

"I'm from the *future*," said the soliton, perhaps grinning.

Moore stared at the indistinct thing, and he had to repress an urge to run over there and tear it apart, try to set fire to it, stuff it in a drawer. And he realized that the sudden chill on his forehead wasn't from fright, as he had at first assumed, but from profound embarrassment at the thing's presence here.

"I've blown it all on you," the blond woman said, perhaps to herself even though her voice boomed in the tall kitchen. "I don't have the . . . sounds like *courses* . . . I don't have the energy reserves to go after another living Pat Moore *now*. You were perfect, Pat Moore squared—why did you have to be a die-hard suicide fan?"

Moore actually laughed at that—and she glared at him in the same instant that he was punched backward off his feet by the hardest invisible blow yet.

He sat down hard and slid, and his back collided with the stove; and then, though he could still see the walls and the old man's smoky legs under the table across the room and the glittering rippled glass of the windows, he was somewhere else. He could feel the square tiles under his palms, but in this other place he had no body.

In the now-remote kitchen, the blond woman said, "Drape him," and the soliton got up and drifted across the floor toward Moore, shrinking as it came so that its face was on a level with Moore's.

Its face was indistinct—pouches under the empty eyes, drink-wrinkles spilling diagonally across the cheekbones, petulant lines around the mouth—and Moore did not try to recognize himself in it.

The force that had knocked Moore down was holding him pressed against the floor and the stove, unable to crawl away, and all he could do was hold his breath as the soliton ghost swept over him like a spiderweb.

You've got a girl in your pocket, came the thing's raspy old voice in his ear.

Get away from me, Moore thought, nearly gagging.

Who get away from who?

"I can get another living Pat Moore," the blond woman was saying, "if I never wasted any effort on you in the first place, if there was never a *you* for me to notice." He heard her take a deep breath. "I can do this."

Her knee touched his cheek, slamming his head against the oven door. She was leaning over the top of the stove, banging blindly at the burners and the knobs, and then Moore heard the triple click of one of the knobs turning, and the faint thump of the flame coming on. He peered up and saw that she was holding the sheet of paper with the ink and blood on it, and then he could smell the paper burning.

Moore became aware that there was still the faintest drone in his head only a moment before it ceased.

"Up," she said, and the ghost was a net surrounding Moore, lifting him up off the floor and through the intangible roof and far away from the rainy shadowed hills of San Francisco.

He was aware that his body was still in the house, still slumped against the stove in the kitchen, but his soul, indistinguishable now from his ghost, was in some vast region where *in front* and *behind* had no meaning, where the once-apparent dichotomy between *here* and *there* was a discarded optical illusion, where comprehension was total but didn't depend on light or sight or perspective, and where even *ago* and *to come* were just compass points; everything was in stasis, for motion had been left far behind with sequential time.

He knew that the long braids or vapor trails that he encompassed and that surrounded him were lifelines, stretching from births in that direction to deaths in the other—some linked to others for varying intervals, some curving alone through the non-sky—but they were more like long electrical arcs than anything substantial even by analogy; they were stretched across time and space, but at the same time, they were coils too infinitesimally small to be perceived, if his perception had been by means of sight; and they were electrons in standing waves surrounding an unimaginable nucleus, which also surrounded them—the universe, apprehended here in its full volume of past and future, was one enormous and eternal atom.

But he could feel the tiles of the kitchen floor beneath his fingertips. He dragged one hand up his hip to the side pocket of his jacket, and his fingers slipped inside and touched the triangular lens.

No, said the soliton ghost, a separate thing again.

Moore was still huddled on the floor, still touching the lens—but he and his ghost were sitting on the other side of the room at the kitchen table too, and the ghost was holding a deck of cards in one hand and spinning cards out with the other. It stopped when two cards lay in front of each of them. The Wild Turkey bottle was gone, and the glow from the ceiling lamp was a dimmer yellow than it had been.

"Hold 'Em," the ghost rasped. "Your whole lifeline is the buy-in, and I'm going to take it away from you. You've got a tall stack there, birth to now, but I won't go all-in on you right away. I bet our first seven years—Fudgsicles, our dad flying kites in the spring sunsets, the star decals in constellations on our bedroom ceiling, our mom reading the Narnia books out loud to us. Push 'em out." The air in the kitchen was summery with the pink candy smell of Bazooka gum.

Hold 'Em, thought Moore. *I'll raise.*

Trish killed herself, he projected at his ghost, *rather than*

live with us anymore. Drove her Granada over the embank-
ment off the 101. The police said she was doing ninety, with
no touch of the brake. Again he smelled spilled gasoline—

—and so, apparently, did his opponent; the pouchy-faced
old ghost flickered but came back into focus. "I make it
more," said the ghost. "The next seven. Bicycles, the Albert
Payson Terhune books, hiking with Joe and Ken in the oil
fields, the Valentine from Theresa Thompson. Push 'em out,
or forfeit."

Neither of them had looked at their cards, and Moore
hoped the game wouldn't proceed to the eventual arbitrary
showdown—he hoped that the frail ghost wouldn't be able
to keep sustaining raises.

I can't hold anything, his guardian angel had said.

It hurt Moore, but he projected another raise at the
ghost: *When we admitted we had deleted her poetry files*
deliberately, she said "You're not a nice man." She was
drunk, and we laughed at that when she said it, but one day
after she was gone, we remembered it, and then we had to
pull over to the side of the road because we couldn't see
through the tears to drive.

The ghost was just a smoky sketch of a midget or a mon-
key now, and Moore doubted it had enough substance even
to deal the next three cards. In a faint birdlike voice it said,
"The next seven. College, and our old motorcycle, and—"

And Trish at twenty, Moore finished, grinding his teeth
and thinking about the mushroom dissolving in his stomach. *We talked her into taking her first drink. Pink gin,*
Tanqueray with Angostura bitters. And we were pleased
when she said, "Where has this been all my life?"

"All my life," whispered the ghost, and then it flicked
away like a reflection in a dropped mirror.

The blond woman was sitting there instead. "What did
you have?" she boomed, nodding toward his cards.

"The winning hand," said Moore. He touched his two
facedown cards. "The pot's mine—the raises got too high
for him." The cards blurred away like fragments left over
from a dream.

Then he hunched forward and gripped the edge of the table, for the timeless vertiginous gulf, the infinite atom of the lifelines, was a sudden pressure from outside the world, and this artificial scene had momentarily lost its depth of field.

"I can twist your thread out, even without his help," she told him. She frowned, and a vein stood out on her curved forehead, and the kitchen table resumed its cubic dimensions and the light brightened. "Even dead, I'm more potent than you are."

She whirled her massive right arm up from below the table and clanked down her elbow, with her forearm upright; her hand was open.

Put me behind her, Pat, said the Pat Moore ghost's remembered voice in his ear.

He made himself feel the floor tiles under his hand and the stove at his back, and then he pulled the triangular lens out of his pocket; and when he held it up to his eye, he was able to see himself and the blond woman at the table across the room, and the Pat Moore ghost was visible upside down behind the woman. He rotated the glass a quarter turn, and she was now upright.

He moved the lens away and blinked, and then he was gripping the edge of the table and looking across it at the blond woman, and at her hand only a foot away from his face. The fingerprints were like comb-tracks in clay. Peripherally he could see the slim Pat Moore ghost, still in the purple dress, standing behind her.

"Arm wrestling?" he said, raising his eyebrows. He didn't want to let go of the table, or even move—this localized perspective seemed very frail.

The woman only glared at him out of her irisless eyes. At last he leaned back in the chair and unclamped the fingers of his right hand from the table edge; and then he shrugged and raised his right arm and set his elbow beside hers. With her free hand she picked up his pocketknife and hefted it. "When this thing hits the floor, we start." She clasped his hand, and his fingers were numbed as if with a hard impact.

Her free hand jerked, and the knife was glittering in a

fantastic noneuclidean parabola through the air, and though he was braced all the way through his torso from his firmly planted feet, when the knife clanged against the tiles, the massive power of her arm hit his palm like a falling tree.

Sweat sprang out on his forehead, and his arm was steadily bending backward and the whole world was rotating too, narrowing, tilting away from him to spill him, all the bets he and his ghost had made, into zero.

In the car, the Pat Moore ghost had told him, *She can bend somebody at right angles to* everything, *which means you're gone without a trace.*

We're not sitting at the kitchen table, he told himself; we're still dispersed in that vaster comprehension of the universe.

And if she rotates me ninety degrees, he was suddenly certain, I'm gone.

And then the frail Pat Moore ghost leaned in from behind the woman and clasped her diaphanous hand around Moore's; and together they were Pat Moore squared, their lifelines linked still by their marriage, and he could feel her strong pulse in supporting counterpoint to his own.

His forearm moved like a counterclockwise second hand in front of his squinting eyes as the opposing pressure steadily weakened. The woman's face seemed in his straining sight to be a rubber mask with a frantic animal trapped inside it, and when only inches separated the back of her hand from the Formica tabletop, the resistance faded to nothing, and his hand was left poised empty in the air.

The world rocked back to solidity with such abruptness that he would have fallen down if he hadn't been sitting on the floor against the stove.

Over the sudden pressure-release ringing in his ears, he heard a scurrying across the tiles on the other side of the room, and a thumping on the hardwood planks in the parlor.

The Pat Moore ghost still stood across the room, beside the table; and the Wild Turkey bottle was on the table, and he was sure it had been there all along.

He reached out slowly and picked up his pocketknife. It was so cold that it stung his hand.

"Cut it," said the ghost of his wife.

"I can't cut it," he said. Barring hallucinations, his body had hardly moved for the past five or ten minutes, but he was panting. "You'll die."

"I'm dead already, Pat. This"—she waved a hand from her shoulder to her knee—"isn't any good. I should be gone." She smiled. "I think that was the *lanei* mushroom."

He knew she was guessing. "I'll know tomorrow."

He got to his feet, still holding the knife. The blade, he saw, was still folded out.

"Forgive me," he said awkwardly. "For everything."

She smiled, and it was almost a familiar smile. "I forgave you in midair. And you forgive me too."

"If you ever did anything wrong, yes."

"Oh, I did. I don't think you noticed. Cut it."

He walked back across the room to the arch that led into the parlor, and he paused when he was beside her.

"I won't come in with you," she said, "if you don't mind."

"No," he said. "I love you, Pat."

"Loved. I loved you too. That counts. Go."

He nodded and turned away from her.

Maxwell's Demon was still hissing on the TV table by the disassembled air conditioner, and he walked to it one step at a time, not looking at the forms that twisted and whispered urgently in the high corners. One seemed to be perceptibly more solid than the rest, but all of them flinched away from him.

He had to blink tears out of his eyes to see the air hose clearly, and when he did, he noticed a plain ON-OFF toggle switch hanging from wires that were still connected to the air-conditioning unit. He cut the hose and switched off the air conditioner, and the silence that fell then seemed to spill out of the house and across San Francisco and into the sky.

He was alone in the house.

He tried to remember the expanded, timeless perspective he had participated in, but his memory had already simplified it to a three-dimensional picture, with himself floating like a bubble in one particular place.

Which of the . . . jet trails or arcs or coils was mine? He wondered now. How long is it?

I'll be better able to guess tomorrow, he thought. At least I know it's there, forever—and even though I didn't see which one it was, I know it's linked to another.

Perpetua

Kit Reed

Kit Reed [www.kitreed.net] lives in Middletown, Connecticut. Since the late 1950s, she has published short fiction of striking high quality and originality in the SF and fantasy magazines, as well as a number of novels both in and out of genre. Her recent SF novels are Little Sisters of the Apocalypse *(1994), and* @Expectations *(2000). Story collections include* Mister Da V. and Other Stories *(1967),* The Killer Mice *(1976),* Other Stories and . . . The Attack of the Giant Baby *(1981),* The Revenge of the Senior Citizens *(1986),* Thief of Lives *(1992),* Weird Women, Wired Women *(1997), and* Seven for the Apocalypse *(1999). Her near-future satirical SF novel,* Thinner Than Thou, *was published in 2004.*

"Perpetua" was published in Flights. *It is a wildly fantastic story set just after the apocalypse begins (perhaps the one from Biblical prophecy, perhaps not). A father has gathered his four daughters together and shrunk the family so they will fit inside an alligator named Perpetua so that they can survive. And survive in style, with gourmet meals consumed wearing Prada. It is a feminist story, told from the point of view of the rebellious daughter, filled with striking images, and is a marvelous contrast to Dale Bailey's end-of-the-world story earlier in this book.*

We are happy to be traveling together in the alligator. To survive the crisis in the city outside, we have had ourselves made *very small*.

To make our trip more pleasant, the alligator herself has been equipped with many windows, cleverly fitted between the armor plates so we can look out at the disaster as we ride along. The lounge where we are riding is paneled in mahogany and fitted with soft leather sofas and beautifully sculpted leather chairs where we recline until seven, when the chef Father engaged calls us to a sit-down dinner in the galley lodged at the base of our alligator's skull. Our vehicle is such a technical masterpiece that our saurian hostess zooms along unhampered, apparently at home in the increasingly treacherous terrain. If she knows we're in here, and if she guesses that tonight we will be dining on Boeuf Wellington and asparagus terrine with Scotch salmon and capers while she has to forage, she rushes along as though she doesn't care. We hear occasional growls and sounds of rending and gnashing over the Vivaldi track Father has chosen as background for this first phase of our journey; she seems to be finding plenty to eat outside.

Inside, everything is arranged for our comfort and happiness, perhaps because Father knows we have reservations about being here. My sisters and I can count on individualized snack trays, drugs of choice and our favorite drinks, which vary from day to day. Over our uniform jumpsuits, we wear monogrammed warm-up jackets in our favorite colors—a genteel lavender for Lily, which Ella apes because she's too young to have her own ideas; jade for Stephanie and, it figures, my aggressively girlish sister Anna is in Passive Pink; Father doesn't like it, but I have chosen black.

"Molly, that color doesn't become you."

"Nobody's going to see me, what difference does it make?"

"I like my girls to look nice."

I resent this because we all struggled to escape the family and made it, too. We'd still be out there if it wasn't for this. "Your girls, your girls—we haven't been your girls in years."

Father: "You will always be my girls." That smile.

OK, I am the family gadfly. "This crisis. Is there something funny going on that we don't know about?"

"Molly," he thunders. "Look out the windows. Then tell me if you think there's anything funny about this."

"I mean, is this a trick to get us back?"

"If you think I made this up, send a goddamn e-mail. Search the Web or turn on the goddamn TV!"

The chairs are fitted with wireless connections so we can download music and e-mail our loved ones, although we never hear back, and at our fingertips are multimedia remotes. We want for nothing here in the alligator. Nothing material, that is. I check my sources, and Father is right. It is a charnel house out there while in here with Father, we are pampered and well fed and snug.

It is a velvet prison, but look at the alternative! Exposure to thunderstorms and fires in collision, vulnerability to mudslides and flooding of undetermined origin; our alligator slithers through rivers of bloody swash, and our vision is obscured by the occasional collision with a severed limb. We can't comprehend the nature or the scope of the catastrophe, only that it's all around us, while here inside the alligator, we are safe.

Her name is Perpetua. Weird, right? Me knowing? But I do.

So we are safe inside Perpetua, and I guess we have Father to thank. Where others ignored the cosmic warnings, he took them to heart. Got ready. Spared no expense. I suppose we should be glad.

If it weren't for the absence of certain key loved ones from our table and from our sumptuous beds in the staterooms aft of the spiny ridge, we probably would.

It's Father's fault. Like a king summoning his subjects, he brought us back from the corners of the earth, where we strayed after we grew up and escaped the house. He brought us in from West Hollywood (Stephanie) and Machu Picchu (Lily) and (fluffy Anna) Biarritz and Farmington, for our baby sister Ella attends the exclusive Miss Porter's School. And Father reached me . . . where? When Father wants you, it doesn't matter how far you run, you will come back.

Emergency, the message said, *Don't ask. Just come*, and being loyal daughters, we did. With enormous gravity, he sat us down in the penthouse.

"My wandering daughters." He beamed. Then he explained. He even had charts. The catastrophe would start here, he said, pointing to the heart of the city. Then it would blossom, expanding until it blanketed the nation and finally, the world. Faced with destruction, would you dare take your chances outside? Would we?

He was not asking. "You will come."

"Of course, Father," we said, although even then I was not sure.

Anna the brownnose gilded the lily with that bright giggle. "Anything you say, Father. Anything to survive."

Mother frowned. "What makes you think you'll survive?"

"Erna!"

"What if this is the Last Judgment?" she had Father's Gutenberg Bible in her lap.

He shouted: "Put that thing down!"

She looked down at the book and then up at him. "What makes you think anybody will survive?"

"That's enough!"

"More than enough, Richard." She raked him with a smile. "I think I'll take my chances here."

He and Mother have never been close. He shrugged. "As you wish. But, you girls . . ."

Anna said, "Daddy, can we bring our jewelry?"

Stephanie laid her fingertip in the hollow of Father's throat. "I'm fresh out of outfits—can I go to Prada and pick up a few things?"

I said, "It's not like we'll be going out to clubs."

"Daddy?"

"Molly, watch your tone." Stephanie is Father's favorite.

He told her, "Anything you want, sweet, but be back by four."

Little Ella asked if she could bring all her pets—a litter of kittens and a basset hound. The cat is the natural enemy of the alligator, Father explained; even in miniature—and we were about to be miniaturized—the cats would be an incipient danger, but the dog's all right. Ella burst into tears.

"Can I bring my boyfriend?" Lily said.

Our baby sister punched her in the breast so hard, she yelled. "Not if I can't take Mittens."

"Boyfriends?" We girls chorused, "Of course."

Father shook his head.

You see, because we are traveling in elegant but close quarters, there's no room for anybody else. This meant no boyfriends, which strikes me as thoughtless if not a little small. When we protested, Father reminded us of our choices: death in the disaster or life in luxury with concomitant reknotting of family ties. He slammed his fist on the hunt table his decorator brought from Colonial Williamsburg at great expense. "Cheap at the price."

I was thinking of my boyfriend, whom I had left sleeping in Rangoon. Never guessing I was leaving forever, I stroked his cheek and slipped out. "But Derek!"

"Don't give it another thought."

"Daddy, what's going to happen to Derek?"

"He'll keep."

Stephanie, Anna and Lily said, "What's going to happen to Jimmy/David/Phil!"

"Oh, they'll keep," he said. Perceiving that he had given the wrong answer, he added, "Trust me. It's being taken care of."

"But, Daddy!"

Perceiving that he still hadn't said enough, he explained that although we were being miniaturized, his technicians would see to it that all our parts would match when we and our boyfriends were reunited, although he did not make clear whether we would be restored to normal size or the men we loved would be made extremely small. He said whatever it took to make us do what he wanted, patting us each with that fond, abstracted smile.

"I've got my best people on it. Don't worry. They'll be fine."

Anna did her loving princess act. "Promise?"

Now Father became impatient. "Girls, I am sparing no expense on this. Don't you think I have covered every little thing?"

None of us dares ask him what this all cost. Unlike most people in the city outside, we are, after all, still alive, but the money! How much will be left for us when Father dies?

Of course in normal times, the brass fixtures, the ceiling treatment and luxurious carpeting that line our temporary home would be expensive, but the cost of miniaturizing all these priceless objects and embedding them in our alligator? Who can guess!

One of us began to cry.

"Stop that," Father roared. "Enough is enough."

It probably is enough for him, riding along in luxury with his five daughters, but what about Stephanie and Anna and Lily and Ella and me?

The first few days, I will admit, passed pleasantly as we settled into our quarters and slipped into our routines. Sleep as late as we like and if we miss breakfast Chef leaves it outside our doors in special trays that keep the croissants moist, the juice cold and the coffee hot. There's even a flower on the tray. Late mornings in the dayroom, working puzzles or reading or doing needlework, a skill Father insisted we learn when we were small. Looking at what he's made of us, I have to wonder: five daughters at his beck and call, making a fuss over him and doing calligraphy that would have pleased blind old Milton; we all nap after lunch. We spend our afternoons in the music room followed by cocktails in the lounge and in the evening we say grace over a delicious meal at the long table, with Father like the Almighty at the head. Is this what he had in mind for us from the first?

I have never seen him happier.

This poses a terrible problem. Is the catastrophe outside a real unknitting of society and the city as we know it and, perhaps, the universe, or is it something Father manufactured to keep us in his thrall?

My sisters may be happy, but I am uncertain. I'm bored and dubious. I'm bored and suspicious and lonely as hell.

The others are in the music room with Father at the piano, preparing a Donizetti quartet. I looked in and saw them together in the warm light; with his white hair sparkling in the halogen glow of the piano lamp, he looked exalted. As if there were a halo around his head. Now, I love Father, but I was never his favorite. There's no part in the Donizetti piece for me. Why should I go in there and play along? Instead I have retreated to the lounge, where I strain at the window in hope. For hours I look out, staring in a passion of concentration because Derek is out there somewhere, whereas I . . . If I keep at this, I think, if I press my face to the glass and stare intently, if I can *just keep my mind on what I want*, then maybe I can become part of the glass or pass through it and find Derek.

With my head pressed against the fabric of our rushing host, I whisper:

"Oh, please."

Outside it is quite simply desolate. Mud and worse things splash on my window as the giant beast that hosts us lunges over something huge, snaps at some adversary in her path, worries the corpse and takes a few bites before she rushes on. God, I wish she'd slow down. I wish she would stop! I want her to lurch onto a peak and let me out!

Can't. On autopilot.

Odd. The glass is buzzing. Vibration or what? I brush my face, checking for bees. If I knew how, I'd run to the galley at the base of her skull and thump on the brushed steel walls until she got my message. Crucial question: Do alligators know Morse code?

No need.

"What?"

My God. She and I are in communication.

"Lady!"

The windowpane grows warm, as though I have made her blush. *It's Perpetua.*

"I know!"

I thought you did.

"Oh, lady, can you tell me what's going on?"

Either more or less than you think.

In a flash I understand the following: We are not, as I suspected—hoped!—being duped. Father has his girls back, all right—he has us at his fingertips in a tight space where he has complete control—but this is his response to the warnings, not something he made up. Although my best-case scenario would confirm my suspicions and make it easy to escape, we are not captive inside a submarine in perfectly normal New York City, witlessly doing his bidding while our vehicle sloshes around in a total immersion tank.

There really is a real disaster out there.

Soon enough, tidal waves will come crashing in our direction, to be followed by meteorite showers, with volcanic eruptions pending and worse to come. As for Father's contrivances, I am correct about one thing: the cablevision we watch and the Web we surf aren't coming in from the world outside; they are the product of the database deep in the server located behind our alligator's left eye.

"But what about Derek?"

I don't know.

"Can you find out?"

You have to promise to do what I want.

I whisper into the window set into her flank: "What do you want?"

Promise?

"Of course I promise!"

Then all that matters is your promise. It doesn't matter what I want.

"I need to know what's happening! Maybe Mother is right—maybe it really is the hand of God. Wouldn't you get sick of people like us and want to clean house?"

Not clear.

"Whether God is sick of us?"

Any of it. The only clear thing is what we have to do.

"What? What!"

She lets me know that although I left him in Rangoon, Derek is adrift somewhere in New York. Don't ask me whether he flew or came by boat or what I'm going to do. Just ask me what I think, and then ask me how I know.

You have to help me.

"You have to stop and let me out!"

I know what's out there because, my God, Perpetua is showing me. Images spill into my head and cloud my eyes: explosions mushrooming, tornadoes, volcanic geysers, what? In seconds I understand how bad it is, although Perpetua can't tell me whether we are in the grip of terrorists or space aliens or a concatenation of natural disasters or what; she shows me Derek standing in the ruins of our old building with his hand raised as if to knock on the skeletal door, I see looters and carnivores and all the predictable detritus of a disaster right down to the truck with the CNN remote, and I see that they won't be standing there much longer because the roiling clouds are opening for a fresh hailstorm unless it's a firestorm or a tremendous belching of volcanic ash.

You won't last a minute out there, not the way you are.

She's right. To survive the crisis in the city outside, we have had ourselves made very small.

You got it. You don't stand a chance.

"Oh God," I cry.

Not God, not by a long shot.

"Oh, lady!" I hear Father and the others chattering as they come in from the music room. I whisper into the glass. My mouth leaves a wet lip print frosted by my own breath. "What am I going to do?"

Our saurian hostess exits my consciousness so quickly that I have to wonder whether she was ever there. My only proof? I have her last words imprinted; *Find out how.*

Chef brings our afternoon snack trays, and my sisters and I graze, browsing contentedly, like farm animals. Father nods, and he and Chef exchange looks before Chef bows and backs out of the room.

It comes to me like a gift.

Passionately, I press my lips to the glass. "It's in the food."

Find the antidote. Take it when you get out.

"Are you? Are you, Perpetua?" I am wild with it. "Are you really going to stop and let me out?"

She doesn't answer. The whole vehicle that encloses our family begins to thrash. I hear magnified snarling and terrible rending noises as she snaps some enemy's spine and over Vivaldi I hear her giant teeth clash as she worries it to death.

We bide our time then, Perpetua and I, at least I do. What choice do I have?

But while I am waiting, her history is delivered to me whole. It is not so much discovered as remembered, as though it happened to me. Sleeping or waking, I can't say when or how she reaches me; her story seeps into my mind, and as it unfolds I understand why she and I are bonded. Rather, why she chose me. Rushing along through the night while Father plots and my sisters sleep, our alligator somehow drops me into the tremendous ferny landscape of some remote, prehistoric dawn, where I watch, astonished, as her early life unfolds under a virgin sun that turns the morning sky pink. Although I am not clear whether it is her past or a universal past that Perpetua is drawing, at some level I understand. She shows me the serpentine tangle of clashing reptiles and the emergence of a king, and she takes me beyond that to deliver me at the inevitable: that all fathers of daughters are kings. I see Perpetua's gigantic, armored father with his flaming jaws and his great teeth, and I join his delicate, scaly daughters as they slither here and there in the universe, apparently free but always under his power.

So you see.

I have the context, if not the necessity.

Then over the next few days while we float along in our comfortable dream world, she encourages me to explore.

While the others nap, I feel my way along the flexible vinyl corridors that snake through Perpetua's sinuous body, connecting the chambers where we sleep and the rooms where we eat and the ones where we entertain ourselves.

The tubing is transparent, and I see Perpetua's vitals pulsing wherever I flash my light. Finally I make my way to the galley—quietly, because Chef sleeps nearby. It's a hop, skip and a jump to the medicine chest, where I find unmarked glass capsules sealed in a case. I slip one into my pocket, in case. From the galley, I discover, there are fixed passageways leading up and a flexible one leading down. I open the hatch and descend.

Yes, Perpetua says inside my head and as I get closer to her destination, repeating like an orgasmic lover, *Yes, yes, yes!*

I have found the Destruct button.

It is located at the bottom of the long stairway that circumvents her epiglottis; opening the last hatch I find my way into the control center, which is lodged in her craw. And here it is. Underneath there is a neatly printed plate put there by Father's engineers: IN CASE OF EMERGENCY, BREAK GLASS.

Perpetua's great body convulses. *Yes.*

Trembling, I press my mouth to the wall: "Is this what you want?" I can't afford to wait for an answer. "It would be suicide!"

We have a deal.

"But what about me?"

When it's time, you'll see.

The next few days are extremely hard. Perpetua rushes on without regard for me while Chef bombards us with new delicacies and Father and my sisters rehearse Gilbert and Sullivan in the music room. I can't help but think of Mother, alone in the ruins of our penthouse. Is she all right, is she maybe in some safe place with my lover Derek, or did she die holding the Gutenberg Bible in an eternal *I told you so?* Mother! Is that the Last Judgment shaping up out there, or is it simply the end of the world? Whatever it is, I think, she and Derek are better off than I am, trapped in here.

Father asks, "What's the matter with you?"

"Nothing. I'm fine."

My sisters say, "Is it Derek? Are you worried about Derek? This is only the beginning, so get over it."

"I'm fine."

"Of course you are—we're terribly lucky," they say. Father has given them jewels to match their eyes. "We're lucky as hell, and everything's going to be fine."

I can hardly bear to be with them. "Whatever you want," I whisper to Perpetua, "let's do it."

When it's time.

Relief comes when you least expect it, probably because you aren't expecting it. Perpetua and I are of the Zen Archer school of life. She summons me out of a stone sleep.

It's time.

The alligator and I aren't one now, but we are thinking as one. Bending to her will, I pad along the corridors to the galley and descend to the control room. She doesn't have to explain. Predictably, the Destruct button is red. At the moment, it is glowing. I use the hammer to break the glass.

Now.

I push the button that sets the timer. The bottom falls out of the control room, spilling me into her throat, and she vomits me out. I crunch down on the breakable capsule that will bring me back to normal size.

My God, I'm back in the world! I'm back in the world, and it is terrible.

As I land in the muck, Perpetua rushes on like an express train roaring over me while I huddle on the tracks or the Concorde thundering close above as I lie on my back on the runway, counting the plates in its giant belly as it takes off. I have pushed the Destruct button. Is the timer working? Did it abort? Our alligator hostess is traveling at tremendous speeds, and as she slithers on, she whips her tail and opens her throat in a tremendous cry of grief that comes out of her in a huge, reptilian groan: *Nooooooo.*

Rolling out of her wake, I see the stars spiraling into the Hudson; in that second I think I see the proliferation and complexity of all creation dividing into gold and dross, unless it is light and dark, but which is which I cannot tell. A black shape on the horizon advances at tremendous speeds; it resolves into a monstrous reptile crushing everything in its path. The great mouth cracks wide as the huge beast approaches, blazing with red light that pours out from deep inside, and all at once I understand. This vast, dark shape is the one being Perpetua hates most, but she is helpless and rushing toward it all the same, and the terror is that she has no choice.

This is by no means God jerking her along; it is a stupendous alligator with its greedy jaws rimmed with blood, summoning Perpetua and its thousand other daughters into its path, preparing to devour them.

The thought trails after her like a pennant of fire. *The father is gathering us in.*

So I understand why the alligator helped me.

And I understand as well the scope of her gift to me: in another minute, I will become an orphan, as the monster alligator lunges for Perpetua and she stops it in its tracks, destructing in an explosion that lights up the apocalyptic skies. And because I am about to be free, and free of Father forever. . . .

I understand why I had to help her die.

Scared now.

It's OK.

I'll be fine.

Quarry

Peter S. Beagle

Peter S. Beagle (www.peterbeagle.com) lives in Oakland,
California. Everything you might want to know about his
work and upcoming publications (including "Two Hearts,"
the long-awaited follow-up to The Last Unicorn) can be
found at his website. He was born in 1939 and raised in the
Bronx, just a few blocks from Woodlawn Cemetery, the in-
spiration for his first novel, A Fine And Private Place.
Today, thanks to classic works such as The Last Unicorn
(and the fine animated movie based on it), he is acknowledged as one of America's greatest living fantasy authors—
a distinguished company that includes Lloyd Alexander,
Ray Bradbury, Ursula K. Le Guin, and Gene Wolfe—and
his dazzling abilities with language, characters, and magical
storytelling have earned him millions of readers.

"Quarry" was published in F&SF. It is part of the un-
named fantasy world that provided the setting for Beagle's
Giant Bones collection and his novel The Innkeeper's Song.
In the latter book we meet the eternally-pursued Soukyan
and his trickster mentor-companion after they have been
traveling together for a number of years. In the story presented here, Peter tells the tale of how the lives of these two
unlikely confederates first became entangled.

I never went back to my room that night. I knew I had an hour at most before they would have guards on the door. What was on my back, at my belt, and in my pockets was all I took—that, and all the *tilgit* the cook could scrape together and cram into my pouch. We had been friends since the day I arrived at *that place*, a scrawny, stubborn child, ready to die rather than ever admit my terror and my pain. "So," she said, as I burst into her kitchen, "running you came to me, twenty years gone, blood all over you, and running you leave. Tell me nothing, just drink this." I have no idea what was in that bottle she fetched from under her skirts and made me empty on the spot, but it kept me warm on my way all that night, and the *tilgit*—disgusting dried marshweed as it is—lasted me three days.

Looking back, I shiver to think how little I understood, not only the peril I was in, but the true extent of the power I fled. I did know better than to make for Sumildene, where a stranger stands out like a sailor in a convent; but if I had had the brains of a bedbug, I'd never have tried to cut through the marshes toward the Queen's Road. In the first place, that grand highway is laced with tollbridges, manned by toll-collectors, every four or five miles; in the second, the Queen's Road is so well-banked and pruned and well-maintained that should you be caught out there by daylight, there's no cover, nowhere to run—no rutted smuggler's alley to duck into, not so much as a proper tree to climb. But I didn't know that then, among other things.

What I did understand, beyond doubt, was that they could not afford to let me leave. I do not say *escape*, because they would never have thought of it in such a way. To their minds, they had offered me their greatest honor, never before granted one so young, and I had not only rejected it, but lied in their clever, clever faces, accepting so humbly, falteringly telling them again and again of my bewildered gratitude, unworthy peasant that I was. And even then I did know that they were not deceived for a single moment, and they knew I knew, and blessed me, one after the other, to let me know. I dream that twilight chamber still—the tall chairs, the cold stone table, the tiny green *tintan* birds murmuring themselves to sleep in the vines outside the window, those smiling, wise, gentle eyes on me—and each time I wake between sweated sheets, my mouth wrenched with pleas for my life. Old as I am, and still.

If I were to leave, and it became known that I had done so, and without any retribution, others would go too, in time. Not very many—there were as yet only a few who shared my disquiet and my growing suspicions—but even one unpunished deserter was more than they could afford to tolerate.

I had no doubt at all that they would grieve my death. They were not unkind people, for monsters.

The cook hid me in the scullery, covering me with aprons and dishrags. It was not yet full dark when I left, but she felt it risky for me to wait longer. When we said farewell, she shoved one of her paring knives into my belt, gave me a swift, light buffet on the ear, said, "So. On your way then," pushed me out of a hidden half-door into the dusk, and slapped it shut behind me. I felt lonelier in that moment, blinking around me with the crickets chirping and the breeze turning chill, and that great house filling half the evening sky, than I ever have again.

As I say, I made straight for the marshes, not only meaning to strike the Queen's Road, but confident that the boggy ground would hide my footprints. It might indeed have concealed them from the eyes of ordinary trackers, but not from those who were after me within another hour. I knew little of them, the Hunters, though over twenty years I had occasionally heard this whisper or that behind this or that slightly trembling hand. Just once, not long after I came to *that place*, I was sent to the woods to gather kindling, and there I did glimpse two small brown-clad persons in a tree. They must have seen me, but they moved neither foot or finger, nor turned their heads, but kept sitting there like a pair of dull brown birds, half-curled, half-crouched, gazing back toward the great house, waiting for something, waiting for someone. I never saw them again, nor any like them; not until they came for me.

Not those two, of course—or maybe they were the same ones; it is hard to be sure of any Hunter's age or face or identity. For all I know, they do not truly exist most of the time, but bide in their nowhere until *that place* summons them into being to pursue some runaway like me. What I do know, better than most, is that they never give up. You have to kill them.

I had killed once before—in my ignorance, I supposed the cook was the only one who knew—but I had no skill in it, and no weapon with me but the cook's little knife: nothing to daunt those who now followed. I knew the small start I had was meaningless, and I went plunging through the marshes, increasingly indifferent to how much noise I made, or to the animals and undergrowth I disturbed. Strong I was, yes, and swift enough, but also brainless with panic and hamstrung by inexperience. A child could have tracked me, let alone a Hunter.

That I was not taken that first night had nothing to do with any craft or wiliness of mine. What happened was that I slipped on a straggling *tilgit* frond (wild, the stuff is as slimy-slick as any snail-road), took a shattering tumble down a slope I never saw, and finished by cracking my head open against a mossy, jagged rock. Amazingly, I did not lose consciousness then, but managed to crawl off into a sort of shallow half-burrow at the base of the hill. There I scraped every bit of rotting vegetation within reach over myself, having a dazed notion of smothering my scent. I vaguely recall packing handfuls of leaves and spiderwebs against my bleeding wound, and making some sort of effort to cover the betraying stains, before I fainted away.

I woke in the late afternoon of the next day, frantically hungry, but so weak and sick that I could not manage so much as a mouthful of the *tilgit*. The bleeding had stopped—though I dared not remove my ragged, mushy poultice for another full day—and after a time I was able to stand up and stay on my feet, just barely. I lurched from my earthen shroud and stood for some while, lightheaded yet, but steadily more lucid, sniffing and staring for any sign of my shadows. Not that I was in the best shape to spy them out—giddy as I was, they could likely have walked straight up to me and disemboweled me with their empty hands, as they can do. But they were nowhere to be seen or sensed.

I drank from a mucky trickle I found slipping by under the leaves, then grubbed my way back into my poor nest again and slept until nightfall. For all my panicky blundering, I knew by the stars that I was headed in the general direction of the Queen's Road, which I continued to believe meant sanctuary and the start of my new and blessedly ordinary life among ordinary folk.

I covered more distance than I expected that night, for all my lingering faintness and my new prudence, trying now to make as little noise as possible, and leave as little trace of my passage. I met no one, and when I went to ground at dawn in a riverbank cave—some *sheknath*'s winter lair, by the smell of it—there was still no more indication of anyone trailing me than there had been since I began my flight. But I was not fool enough to suppose myself clear of pursuit, not quite. I merely hoped, which was just as bad.

The Queen's Road was farther away than I had supposed: for all the terrible and tempting knowledge that I and others like me acquired in *that place*, practical geography was unheard of. I kept moving, trailing after the hard stars through the marshes as intently as the Hunters were surely trailing me. More than once, the bog sucked both shoes off my feet, taking them down so deeply that I would waste a good half-hour fishing for them; again and again, a sudden screen of burly *jukli* vines or some sticky nameless creepers barred my passage, so I must either lower my head and bull on through, or else blunder somehow around the obstacle and pray not to lose the way, which I most often did.

Nearing dawn of the fourth day, I heard the rumble of cartwheels, like a faraway storm, and the piercing squawk, unmistakable, of their *pashidi* drivers' clan-whistles along with them, and realized that I was nearing the Queen's Road.

If the Hunters were following as closely as I feared, was this to be the end of the game—were they poised to cut me down as I raced wildly, recklessly, toward imaginary safety? Did they expect me to abandon all caution and charge forward into daylight and the open, whooping with joy and triumph? They had excellent reason to do so, as idiotic a target as I must have made for them a dozen times over. But even idiots—even terrified young idiots—may learn one or two things in four days of being pursued through a quagmire by silent, invisible hounds. I waited that day out under a leech-bush: few trackers will ever investigate one of those closely; and if you lie very still, there is a fairish chance that the serrated, brittle-seeming leaves will not come seeking your blood. At moonset I started on.

Just as the ground began to feel somewhat more solid, just as the first lights of the Queen's Road began to glimmer through the thinning vegetation . . . there they were, there they were, both of them, each standing away at an angle, making me the third point of a murderous triangle. They simply *appeared*—can you understand?—assembling themselves out of the marsh dawn: weaponless both, their arms hanging at their sides, loose and unthreatening. One was smiling; one was not—there was no other way to tell them apart. In the dimness, I saw laughter in their eyes, and a weariness such as even I have never imagined, and death.

They let me by. They turned their backs to me and let me pass, fading so completely into the gray sunrise that I was almost willing to believe them visions, savage mirages born of my own fear and exhaustion. But with that combination came a weary understanding of my own. They were playing with me, taking pleasure in allowing me to run loose for a bit, but letting me know that whenever they tired of the game I was theirs, in the dark marshes or on the wide white highway, and not a thing I could do about it. At my age, I am entitled to forget what I forget—terror and triumph alike, grief and the wildest joy alike—and so I have, and well rid of every one of them I am. But that instant, that particular recognition, remains indelible. Some memories do come to live with you for good and all, like wives or husbands.

I went forward. There was nothing else to do. The marshes fell away around me, rapidly giving place to nondescript country, half-ragged, halfway domesticated to give a sort of shoulder to the road. Farmers were already opening their fruit and vegetable stands along that border; merchants' boys from towns farther along were bawling their employers' wares to the carters and wagoners; and as I stumbled up, a *shukri*-trainer passed in front of me, holding his arms out, like a scarecrow, for folk to see his sharp-toothed pets scurrying up and down his body, and more of them pouring from each pocket as he strode along. Ragged, scabbed and filthy as I was, not one traveler turned his head as I slipped onto the Queen's Road.

On the one hand, I blessed their unconcern; on the other, that same indifference told me clearly that none of them would raise a finger if they saw me taken, snatched back before their eyes to *that place* and whatever doom might await me there. Only the collectors at their tollgates might be at all likely to mourn the fate of a potential contributor—and I had nothing for them anyway, which was going to be another problem in a couple of miles. But right then was problem enough for me: friendless on a strange road, utterly vulnerable, utterly without resources, flying—well, trudging—from the only home I had known since the age of nine, and from the small, satisfied assassins it had sent after me. And out of *tilgit* as well.

The Queen's Road runs straight all the way from Bitava to Fors na' Shachim, but in those days there was a curious sort of elbow: unleveled, anciently furrowed, a last untamed remnant of the original wagon-road, beginning just before the first tollgate I was to reach. I could see it from a good distance, and made up my mind to dodge away onto it—without any notion of where the path might come out, but with some mad fancy of at once eluding both the killers and the collectors. Sometimes, in those nights when the dreams and memories I cannot always tell apart anymore keep me awake, I try to imagine what my life would have been if I had actually carried my plan through. Different, most likely. Shorter, surely.

Even this early, the road was steadily growing more crowded with traffic, wheeled and afoot, slowing my pace to that of my closest neighbor—which, in this case, happened to be a bullock-cart loaded higher than my head with *jejebhai* manure. Absolutely the only thing the creatures are good for; we had a pair on the farm where I was a boy—if I ever was, if any of that ever happened. Ignoring the smell, I kept as close to the cart as I could, hoping that it would hide me from the toll-collectors' sight when I struck off onto that odd little bend. My legs were tensing for the first swift, desperate stride, when I heard the voice at my ear, saying only one word, "*No.*"

A slightly muffled voice, but distinctive—there was a sharpness to it, and a hint of a strange cold amusement, all in a single word. I whirled, saw nothing but the manure cart, determined that I had misheard a driver's grunt, or even a wheel-squeak, and set myself a second time to make my move.

Once again the voice, more insistent now, almost a bark: "*No, fool!*"

It was not the driver; he never looked at me. I was being addressed—commanded—by the manure pile.

It shifted slightly as I gaped, and I saw the eyes then. They were gray and very bright, with a suggestion of pale yellow far under the grayness. All I could make out of the face in which they were set was a thick white mustache below and brows nearly as heavy above. The man—for it was a human face, I was practically sure—was burrowed as deeply into the *jejebhai* dung as though he were lolling under the most luxurious of quilts and bolsters on a winter's night. He beckoned me to join him.

I stopped where I was, letting the cart jolt past me. The sharp voice from the manure was clearer this time, and that much more annoyed with me. "Boy, if you have any visions of a life beyond the next five minutes, you will do as I tell you. *Now.*" The last word was no louder than the others, but it brought me scrambling into that cartload of muck faster than ever I have since lunged into a warm bed, with a woman waiting. The man made room for me with a low, harsh chuckle.

"Lie still, so," he told me. "Lie still, make no smallest row, and we will pass the gate like royalty. And those who follow will watch you pass, and never take your scent. Thank me later—" I had opened my mouth to speak, but he put a rough palm over it, shaking his white head. "Down, down," he whispered, and to my disgust he pushed himself even farther into the manure pile, all but vanishing into the darkness and the stench. And I did the same.

He saved my life, in every likelihood, for we left that gate and half a dozen like it behind as we continued our malodorous excursion, while the driver, all unwitting, paid our toll each time. Only with the last barrier safely past did we slide from the cart, tumble to the roadside and such cover as there was, and rise to face each other in daylight. We reeked beyond the telling of it—in honesty, almost beyond the smelling of it, so inured to the odor had our nostrils become. We stank beyond anything but laughter, and that was what we did then, grimacing and howling and falling down on the dry grass, pointing helplessly at each other and going off again into great, ridiculous whoops of mirth and relief, until we wore ourselves out and could barely breathe, let alone laugh. The old man's laughter was as shrill and cold as the mating cries of *shukris*, but it was laughter even so.

He was old indeed, now I saw him in daylight, even under a crust of filth and all that still stuck to the filth—straw, twigs, dead spiders, bullock-hair. His own hair and brows were as white as his mustache, and the gray eyes streaked with rheum; yet his cheeks were absurdly pink, like a young girl's cheeks, and he carried himself as straight as any young man. Young as I was myself, and unwise as I was, when I first looked into his eyes, I already knew far better than to trust him. And nonetheless, knowing, I wanted to. He can do that.

"I think we bathe," he said to me. "Before anything else, I do think we bathe."

"I think so too," I said. "Yes." He jerked his white head, and we walked away from the Queen's Road, off back into the wild woods.

"I am Soukyan," I offered, but to that he made no response. He clearly knew the country, for he led me directly to a fast-flowing stream, and then to a pool lower down, where the water gathered and swirled. We cleaned ourselves there, though it took us a long time, so mucky we were; and afterward, naked-new as raw carrots, we lay in the Sun and talked for a while. I told truth, for the most part, leaving out only some minor details of *that place*—things I had good reason not to think about just then—and he . . . ah, well, what he told me of his life, of how he came to hail me from that dungheap, was such a stew of lies and the odd honesty that I've never studied out the right of it yet, no more than I have ever learned his own name. The truth is not in him, and I would be dearly disappointed if it should show its poor face now. He was there—leave it at that. He was there at the particular moment when I needed a friend, however, fraudulent. It has happened so since.

"So," he said at last, stretching himself in the Sun. "And what's to be done with you now?"—for all the world as though he had all the disposing of me and my future. "If you fancy that your followers have forsaken you, merely because we once stank our way past them, I'd greatly enjoy to have the writing of your will. They will run behind you until you die—they will never return to their masters without you, or whatever's left of you. On that you have my word."

"I know that well enough," said I, trying my best to appear as knowledgeable as he. "But perhaps I am not to be taken so easily." The old man snorted with as much contempt as I have ever heard in a single exhalation of breath, and rolled to his feet, deceptively, alarmingly graceful. He crouched naked on his haunches, facing me, studying me, smiling with pointed teeth.

"Without me, you die," he said, quite quietly. "You know it and I know it. Say it back to me." I only stared, and he snapped, "*Say it back.* Without me?"

And I said it, because I knew it was true. "Without you, I would be dead." The old man nodded approvingly. The yellow glint was stronger in the gray eyes.

"Now," he said. "I have my own purposes, my own small annoyance to manage. I could deal with it myself, as I've done many a time—never think otherwise—but it suits me to share roads with you for a little. It suits me." He was studying me as closely as I have ever been considered, even by those at *that place,* and I could not guess what he saw. "It suits me," he said for a third time. "We may yet prove of some use to each other."

"We may, or we may not," I said, more than a bit sharply, for I was annoyed at the condescension in his glance. "I may seem a gormless boy to you, but I know this country, and I know how to handle myself." The first claim was a lie; of the second, all I can say is that I believed it then. I went on, probably more belligerent for my fear: "Indeed, I may well owe you my life, and I will repay you as I can, my word on it. But as to whether we should ally ourselves . . . sir, I hope only to put the width of the world between myself and those who seek me—I have no plans beyond that. Of what your own plans, your own desires may be, you will have to inform me, for I have no notion at all."

He seemed to approve my boldness; at any rate, he laughed that short, yapping laugh of his and said, "For the moment, my plans run with yours. We're dried enough—dress yourself, so, and we'll be off and gone while our little friends are still puzzling over how we could have slipped their grasp. They'll riddle it out quickly enough, but we'll have the heels of them a while yet." And I could not help finding comfort in noticing that "your followers" had now become "our little friends."

So we ourselves were allies of a sort, united by common interests, whatever they were. Having no goal, nor any vision of a life beyond flight, I had no real choice but to go where he led, since on my own the only question would have been whether I should be caught before I stumbled into a swamp and got eaten by a *lourijakh.* For all his age, he marched along with an air of absolute serenity, no matter if we were beating our way through some near-impenetrable thornwood or crossing high barrens in the deepest night. Wherever he was bound—which was only one of the things he did not share with me—we encountered few other travelers on our way to it. An old lone wizard making his *lamisetha*; a couple of deserters from someone's army, who wanted to sell us their uniforms; a little band of prospectors, too busy quarreling over the exact location of a legendary hidden *drast* mine to pay overmuch attention to us. I think there was a water witch as well, but at this reach it is hard to be entirely sure.

By now I would not have trusted my woodcraft for half a minute, but it was obvious from our first day together that my new friend had enough of that for the pair of us. Every night, before we slept—turn and turn about, always one on watch—and every morning, before anything at all, he prowled the area in a wide, constantly shifting radius, clearly going by his nose as much as his sight and hearing. Most of the time he was out of my view, but on occasion I would hear a kind of whuffling snort, usually followed by a low, disdainful grunt. In his own time he'd come trotting jauntily up from the brushy hollow or the dry ravine, shaking his dusty white hair in the moonlight, to say, "Two weeks, near enough, and not up with us yet? Not taking advantage of my years and your inexperience to pounce on us in the dark hours and pull us apart like a couple of boiled chickens? Indeed, I begin to lose respect for our legendary entourage—as stupid as the rest, they are, after all." And what he meant by *the rest*, I could not imagine then.

Respect the Hunters or no, he never slackened our pace, nor ever grew careless in covering our tracks. We were angling eastward, into the first folds of the Skagats—the Burnt Hills, your people call them, I believe. At the time I had no name at all for them, nor for any other feature of this new landscape. For all the teachings I had absorbed at *that place*, for all the sly secret knowledge that was the true foundation of the great house, for all the wicked wisdom that I would shed even today, if I could, as a snake scours itself free of its skin against a stone...nevertheless, then I knew next to nothing of the actual world in which that knowledge moved. We were deliberately kept quite ignorant, you see, in certain ways.

He ridiculed me constantly about that. I see him still, cross-legged across the night's fire from me, jabbing out with a long-nailed forefinger, demanding, "And you mean to sit there and tell me that you've never heard of the Mildasi people, or the Achali? You know the lineage, the lovers and the true fate of every queen who ever ruled in Fors— you know the deep cause of the Fishermen's Rebellion, and what really came of it—you know the entire history of the Old Arrangement, which cannot be written—but you have absolutely no inkling where Byrnarik Bay's to be found, nor the Northern Barrens, nor can you so much as guess at the course of the Susathi. Well, you've had such an education as never was, that's all I can say. And it's worthless to us, all of it worthless, nothing but a waste of head-space, taking up room that could have been better occupied if you'd been taught to read track, steal a horse, or shoot a bow. *Worthless.*"

"I can shoot a bow," I told him once. "My father taught me."

"Oh, indeed? I must remember to stand behind you when you loose off." There was a deal more of that as we journeyed on. I found it tedious most often, and sometimes hurtful; but there was a benefit, too, because he began taking it on himself to instruct me in the nature and fabric of this new world—and this new life, as well—as though I were visiting from the most foreign of far-off lands. Which, in ways even he could not have known, I was.

One thing I did understand from the first day was that he was plainly a fugitive himself, no whit different from me, for all his conceit. Why else would he have been hiding in a dung-cart, eager to commandeer the company of such a bumpkin as I? Kindly concern for my survival in a dangerous world might be part of it, but he was hardly combing our backtrail every night on my behalf. I knew that much from the way he slept—when he slept—most often on his back, his arms and legs curled close and scrabbling in the air, running and running behind his closed eyes, just as a hound will do. I knew it from the way he would cry out, not in any tongue I knew, but in strange yelps and whimpers and near-growls that seemed sometimes to border on language, so close to real words that I was sure I almost caught them, and that if he only kept on a bit longer, or if I dared bend a bit closer, I'd understand who—or what—was pursuing him through his dreams. Once he woke, and saw me there, studying him; and though his entire body tensed like a crossbow, he never moved. The gray eyes had gone full yellow, the pupils slitted almost to invisibility. They held me until he closed them again, and I crept away to my blanket. In the morning, he made no mention of my spying on his sleep, but I never imagined that he had forgotten.

So young I was then, all that way back, and so much I knew, and he was quite right—none of it was to prove the smallest use in the world I entered on our journey. That nameless, tireless, endlessly scornful old man showed me the way to prepare and cook *aidallah,* which looks like a dungball itself, which is more nourishing than *tilgit,* and tastes far better, and which is poisonous if you don't strip every last bit of the inner rind. He taught me to carry my silly little knife out of sight in a secret place; he taught me how to sense a *sheknath*'s presence a good mile before winding it, and—when we were sneaking through green, steamy Taritaja country—how to avoid the mantraps those cannibal folk set for travelers. (I was on my way over the lip of two of them before he snatched me back, dancing with scorn, laughing his yap-laugh and informing me that no one would ever eat *my* brain to gain wisdom.) And, in spite of all my efforts, I cannot imagine forgetting my first introduction to the sandslugs of the Oriskany plains. There isn't a wound they can't clean out, nor an infection they can't digest; but it is not a comfortable process, and I prefer not to speak of it any further. Nevertheless, more than once I have come a very long way to find them again.

But cunning and knowing as that old man was, even he could detect no sign of the Hunters from the moment when we joined fortunes on the Queen's Road. Today I'd have the wit to be frightened more every day by their absence; but then I was for once too interested in puzzling out the cause of my companion's night terrors, and the identity of his pursuers, to be much concerned with my own. And on the twentieth twilight that we shared, dropping down from the Skagats into high desert country, I finally caught sight of it for a single instant: the cause.

It stalked out of a light evening haze on long bird legs— three of them. The third appeared to be more tail than leg—the creature leaned back on it briefly, regarding us— but it definitely had long toes or claws of its own. As for the head and upper body; I had only a dazed impression of something approaching the human, and more fearsome for that. In another moment, it was gone, soundless for all its size; and the old man was up out of a doze, teeth bared, crouching to launch himself in any direction. When he turned to me, I'd no idea whether I should have seen what I had, or whether it would be wisest to feign distraction. But he never gave me the chance to choose.

I cannot say that I actually saw the change. I never do, not really. Never anymore than a sort of sway in the air— you could not even call it a ripple—and there he is: there, like that first time: red-brown mask, the body a deeper red, throat and chest and tail-tip white-gold, bright yellow eyes seeing me—*me,* lost young Soukyan, always the same— seeing me truly and terribly, all the way down. Always. The fox.

One wild glare before he sprang away into the mist, and I did not see him again for a day and another night. Nor the great bird-legged thing either, though I sat up both nights, expecting its return. It was plainly seeking him, not me— whatever it might be, it was no Hunter—but what if it saw me as his partner, his henchman, as liable as he for whatever wrong it might be avenging? And what if I *had* become a shapeshifter's partner, unaware? Not all alliances are writ-ten, or spoken, or signed. Oh, I had no trouble staying awake those two nights. I thought it quite likely that I might never sleep again.

Or eat again, either, come to that. As I have told you, I never went back to my room at *that place,* which meant leaving my bow there. I wished now that I had chanced fetching it: not only because I had killed a man with that bow when I was barely tall enough to aim and draw, but because without it, on my own, I was bound to go very hungry indeed. I stayed close to our camp—what point in wandering off into unknown country in search of a half-mad, half-sinister old man?—and merely waited, making do with such scraps and stores as we had, drinking from a nearby waterhole, little more than a muddy footprint. Once, in that second night, something large and silent crossed the Moon; but when I challenged it there was no response, and nothing to see. I sat down again and threw more wood on my fire.

He came back in human form, almost out of nowhere, but not quite—I never saw that change, either, but I did see, far behind him, coming around a thicket beyond the waterhole, the two sets of footprints, man and animal, and the exact place where one supplanted the other. Plainly, he did not care whether I saw it or not. He sat down across from me, as always, took a quick glance at our depleted larder, and said irritably, "You ate every last one of the *sushal* eggs. Greedy."

"Yes. I did." Formal, careful, both of us, just as though we had never shared a dung-cart. We stared at each other in silence for some while, and then I asked him, most politely, "What are you?"

"What I need to be," he answered. "Now this, now that, as necessary. As are we all."

I was surprised by my own sudden fury at his blandly philosophical air. "We do not *all* turn into foxes," I said. "We do not *all* abandon our friends—" I remember that I hesitated over the word, but then came out with it strongly—"leaving them to face monsters alone. Nor do we *all* lie to them from sunup to sundown, as you have done to me. I have no use for you, and we have no future together. Come tomorrow, I go alone."

"Well, now, that would be an extremely foolish mistake,

and most probably fatal as well." He was as calmly judicial as any human could have been, but he was *not* human, *not* human. He said, "Consider—did I not keep you from your enemies, when they were as close on your heels as your own dirty skin? Have I not counseled you well during this journey you and I have made together? That *monster,* as you call it, did you no harm—nor even properly frighted you, am I right? Say honestly." I had no fitting answer, though I opened my mouth half a dozen times, while he sat there and smiled at me. "So. Now. Sit still, and I will tell you everything you wish to know."

Which, of course, he did not.

This is what he did tell me:

"What you saw—that was no monster, but something far worse. That was a Goro." He waited only a moment for me to show that I knew the name; quite rightly not expecting this, he went on. "The Goro are the bravest, fiercest folk who walk the Earth. To be killed by a Goro is considered a great honor, for they deign to slay only the bravest and fiercest of their enemies—merely to make an enemy of a Goro is an honor as well. However short-lived."

"Which is what you have done," I said, when he paused. He looked not at all guilty or ashamed, but distinctly embarrassed.

"You could say that, I suppose," he replied. "In a way. It was a mistake—I made a serious mistake, and I'm not too proud to admit it, even to you." I had never heard him sound as he did then: half-defiant, yet very nearly mumbling, like a child caught out in a lie. He said, "I stole a Goro's dream."

I looked at him. I did not laugh—I don't recall that I said anything—but he sneered at me anyway. His eyes were entirely gray now, narrow with disdain, and somewhat more angled than I had noticed before. "Mock me, then—why should you not? Your notion of dreams will have them all gossamer, all insubstantial film and gauze and wispy vapors. I tell you now that the dream of a Goro is as real and solid as your imbecile self, and each one takes solid form in our world, no matter if we recognize it or not for what it is.

Understand me, fool!" He had grown notably heated, and there was a long silence between us before he spoke again.

"Understand me. Your life may well depend on it." For just that moment, the eyes were almost pleading. "It happened that I was among the Goro some time ago, traveling in . . . that *shape* you have seen." In all the time that we have known each other, he has never spoken the word *fox*, not to me. He said, "A Goro's dream, once dreamed, will manifest itself to us as it chooses—a grassblade or a jewel, a weed or a log of wood, who knows why? In my case . . . in my case—pure chance, mind you—it turned out to be a shiny stone. The *shape* likes shiny things." His voice trailed away, again a guilty child's voice.

"So you took it," I said. "Blame the shape, if you like— no matter to me—but it was you did the stealing. I may be only a fool, but I can follow you that far."

"It is not so simple!" he began angrily, but he caught himself then, and went on more calmly. "Well, well, your morality's no matter to me either. What should matter to you is that a stolen dream cries out to its begetter. No Goro will ever rest until his dream is safe home again, and the thief gathered to his ancestors in very small pieces. Most often, some of the pieces are lacking." He smiled at me.

"A grassblade?" I demanded. "A stone—a stick of wood? To pursue and kill for a discarded stick, no use to anyone? You neglected to mention that your brave, fierce Goro are also quite mad."

The old man sighed, a long and elaborately despairing sigh. "They are no more mad than yourself—a good deal less so, more than likely. And a Goro's dream is of considerable use—to a Goro, no one else. They keep them all, can you follow *that*? A Goro will hoard every physical manifestation of every dream he dreams in his life, even if at the end it seems only to amount to a heap of dead twigs and dried flower petals. Because he is bound to present the whole unsightly clutter to his gods, when he goes to them. And if even one is missing—one single feather, candle-end, teacup, seashell fragment—then the Goro will suffer bitterly after death. So they believe, and they take poorly to having it named nonsense. Which I am very nearly sure it is."

When he was not railing directly at me, his arrogance trickled away swiftly, leaving him plainly uneasy, shapeshifter or no. I found this rather shamefully enjoyable. I said, "So. This one wants his shiny stone back, and it has called him all this way on your trail. It does seem to me—"

"That I might simply return it to him? Apologies—some small token gift, perhaps—and no harm done?" This time his short laugh sounded like a branch snapping in a storm. "Indeed, nothing would suit me better. It is only a useless pebble, as you say—the *shape* lost all interest in it long ago. Unfortunately, for such an offense against a Goro—such a sin, if you like—vengeance is required." Speaking those words silenced him again for a long moment: his eyes flicked constantly past and beyond me, and his whole body had grown so taut that I half-expected him to turn back into a fox as we sat together. For the first time in our acquaintance, I pitied him.

"Vengeance is required," he repeated presently. "It is a true sacrament among the Goro, much more than a matter of settling tribal scores. Something to do with evening all things out, restoring the proper balance of the world. Smoothing the rumples, you might say. Very philosophical, the Goro, when they have a moment." He was doing his best to appear composed, you see, though he must have known I knew better. He does that.

"All as may be," I said. "What's clear to me is that we now have two different sets of assassins to deal with, each lot unstoppable—"

"The Goro are *not* assassins," he interrupted me. "They are a civilized and honorable people, according to their lights." He was genuinely indignant.

"Splendid," I said. "Then by all means, you must stay where you are and allow yourself to be honorably slaughtered, so as to right the balance of things. For myself, I'll give them a run, in any case," and I was on my feet and groping for my belongings. Wonderful, what weeks of flight can do for a naturally mild temper.

He rose with me, nodding warningly, if such a thing can be. "Aye, we'd best be moving. I can't speak for your lot, but the day's coming on hot, and our Goro will sleep out the worst of it, if I know them at all. Pack and follow."

That brusquely—*pack and follow*. And so I did, for there was no more choice in the matter than there ever had been. The old man set a fierce pace that day, not only demanding greater speed from me than ever, but also doubling back, zigzagging like a hare with a *shukri* one jump behind; then inexplicably going to ground for half an hour at a time, absolutely motionless and silent until we abruptly started on again, with no more explanation than before. During those stretches he often slipped out of sight, each time hissing me to stillness, and I knew that he would take the fox-shape (or would it take him? which was real?) to scout back along the way we had come. But whether we were a trifle safer, or whether death was a little closer on our heels, I could never be sure. He never once said.

The country continued high desert, simmering with mirages, but there were moments in the ever-colder nights when I could smell fresh water; or perhaps I felt its presence in the water composing my own body. The old man did finally reveal that in less than a week, at our current rate, we should strike the Nai, the greatest river in this part of the country, which actually begins in the Skagats. There are always boats, he assured me—scows and barges and little schooners, going up and down with dried fish for this settlement, nails and harness for that one, a full load of lumber for the new town building back of the old port. Paying passengers were quite common on the Nai, as well as the non-paying sort—and here he winked elaborately at me, looking enough like the grandfather I still think I almost remember that I had to look away for a moment. Increasingly, as the years pass, I prefer the fox-shape.

"Not that this will lose our Goro friend," he said, "not for a moment. They're seagoing people—a river is a city street to the Goro. But they dislike rivers, exactly as a countryman dislikes the city, and the farther they are from the sea, the more tense and uneasy they become. Now the Nai will take us all the way to Druchank, which is a hellpit, unless it has changed greatly since I was last there. But from Druchank it's a long, long journey to the smell of salt, yet no more than two days to . . ."

And here he stopped. It was not a pause for breath or memory, not an instant's halt to find words—no interruption, but an end, as though he had never intended to say more. He only looked at me, not with his usual mockery, nor with any expression that I could read. But he clearly would not speak again until I did, and I had a strong sense that I did not want to ask what I had to ask, and get an answer. I said, at last, "Two days to where?"

"To the place of our stand." The voice had no laughter in it, but no fear either. "To the place where we turn and meet them all. Yours and mine."

It was long ago, that moment. I am reasonably certain that I did not say anything bold or heroic in answer, as I can be fairly sure that I did not shame myself. Beyond that . . . beyond that, I can only recall a sense that all the skin of my face had suddenly grown too tight for my head. The rest is stories. *He* might remember exactly how it was, but he lies.

I do recollect his response to whatever I finally said. "Yes, it *will* come to that, and we will not be able to avoid facing them. I thought we might, but I always look circumstance in the eye." (And would try to steal both eyes, and then charge poor blind circumstance for his time, but never mind.) He said, "Your Hunters and my Goro"—no more sharing of shadows, apparently—"there's no shaking them, none of them. I would know if there were a way." I didn't doubt that. "The best we can do is to choose the ground on which we make our stand, and I have long since chosen the Mihanachakali." I blinked at him. That I remember, blinking so stupidly, nothing to say.

The Mihanachakali was deep delta once—rich, bountiful farmland, until the Nai changed course, over a century ago. The word means *black river valley*—I suppose because the Nai used to carry so much sweet silt to the region when it flooded every year or two. You wouldn't know that now, nor could I believe it at the time, trudging away from

Druchank (which was just as foul a hole as he remembered, and remains so), into country grown so parched, so entirely dried out, that the soil had forgotten how to hold even the little mist that the river provided now and again. We met no one, but every turn in the road brought us past one more abandoned house, one more ruin of a shed or a byre; eventually the road became one more desiccated furrow crumbling away to the flat, pale horizon. The desert had never been anything but what it was; this waste was far wilder, far lonelier, because of the ghosts. Because of the ghosts that I could feel, even if I couldn't see them—the people who had lived here, tried to live here, who had dug in and hung on as long as they could while the Earth itself turned ghost under their feet, under their splintery wooden plows and spades. I hated it as instinctively and deeply and sadly as I have ever hated a place on Earth, but the old man tramped on without ever looking back for me. And as I stumbled after him over the cold, wrinkled land, he talked constantly to himself, so that I could not help but overhear.

"Near, near—they never move, once they . . . twice before, twice, and then that other time . . . listen for it, smell it out, find it, find it, so close . . . no mistake, it cannot have moved, I *will* not be mistaken, listen for it, reach for it, find it, find it, *find it!*" He crouched lower and lower as we plodded on, until he might as well have taken the fox-form, so increasingly taut, elongated and pointed had his shadow become. To me during those two days crossing the Mihanachakali, he spoke not at all.

Then, nearing sundown on the second day, he abruptly broke off the long mumbled conversation with himself. Between one stride and the next, he froze in place, one foot poised off the ground, exactly as I have seen a stalking fox do when the chosen kill suddenly raises its head and sniffs the air. "Here," he said quietly, and it seemed not so much a word but a single breath that had chosen shape on its own, like a Goro's dream. "Here," he said again. "Here it was. I remembered. I *knew*."

We had halted in what appeared to me to be the exact middle of anywhere. River off *that* way, give or take; a few

shriveled hills lumping up *that* way; no-color evening sky
baking above . . . I could never have imagined surroundings
less suitable for a gallant last stand. It wouldn't have taken
a Goro and two Hunters to pick us off as we stood there
with the sunset at our backs: two small, weary figures,
weaponless, exposed to attack on all sides, our only possible shelter a burned-out farmhouse, nothing but four walls,
a caved-in roof, a crumbling chimney, and what looked to
be a root cellar. A shepherd with a sling could have potted
us like sparrows.

"I knew," he repeated, looking much more like his former superior self. "Not whether it would *be* here, but that
it would be *here*." It made no sense, and I told him so, and
the yap-laugh sounded more elated than I had yet heard it.
"Think for once, idiot! No, no—*don't* think, forget about
thinking! Try remembering, try to remember something,
anything you didn't learn at that bloody asylum of yours.
Something your mother told you about such places—
something the old people used to say, something children
would whisper in their beds to frighten each other. Something even a fool just might already know—remember!
Remember?"

And I did. I remembered half-finished stories of houses
that were not quite . . . that were not there all the time . . .
rumors, quickly hushed by parents, of house-things blooming now and then from haunted soil, springing up like mushrooms in moonlight . . . I remembered an uncle's absently
mumbled account of a friend, journeying, who took advantage of what appeared to be a shepherd's mountain hut and
was not seen again—no more than the hut itself—and someone else's tale of bachelor cousins who settled into an empty
cottage no one seemed to want, lived there comfortably
enough for some years, and then . . . I did remember.

"Those are fables," I said. "Legends, nothing more. If
you mean *that* over there, I see nothing but a gutted hovel
that was most likely greatly improved by a proper fire. Let
it appear, let it vanish—either way, we are both going to
die. Of course, I may once again have missed something."

He could not have been more delighted. "Excellent. I

must tell you, I might have felt a trifle anxious if you had actually grasped my plan." The pale yellow glow was rising in his eyes. "The true nature of that house is not important, and in any case would take too long to explain to an oaf. What matters is that if once our pursuers pass its door, they will not ever emerge again—therefore, we two must become bait and deadfall together, luring them on to disaster." Everything obviously depended on our pursuers running us to this Earth at the same time; if they fell upon each other in their lust to slaughter us, so much the better, but he was plainly not counting on this. "Once we've cozened them into that corner," and he gestured toward the thing that looked so like a ruinous farmhouse, "why, then, our troubles are over, and no burying to plague us, either." He kicked disdainfully at the stone-hard soil, and the laugh was far more fox than human.

I said, as calmly and carefully as I could, "This is not going to work. There are too many unknowns, too many possibilities. What if they do *not* arrive together? What if, instead of clashing, they cooperate to hunt us down? Much too likely that we will be the ones trapped in your—your *corner*—with no way out, helpless and doomed. This is absurd."

Oh, but he was furious then! Totally enraged, how he stamped back and forth, glaring at me, even his mustache crouched to spring, every white hair abristle. If he had been in the fox-shape—well, who knows?—perhaps he might indeed have leaped at my throat. "Ignorant, ignorant! *Unknowns, possibilities*—you know nothing, you are *fit* for nothing but my bidding." He stamped a few more times, and then turned to stalk away toward the farmhouse . . . toward the thing that looked like a farmhouse. When I made to follow, he waved me back without turning his head. "Stay!" he ordered, as you command a dog. "Keep watch, call when they come in sight. You can do that much."

"And what then?" I shouted after him, as angry as he by now. "Have you any further instructions for the help? When I call to you, what then?"

Still walking, still not looking back, he answered, "Then you run, imbecile! Toward the house—*toward*, but not *into!* Do try to remember that." On the last words, he vanished into the shadow of the farmhouse. And I . . . why, I took up my ridiculous guard, stolidly patrolling the dead fields in the twilight, just as though I understood what I was to expect, and exactly what I would do when it turned up. The wind was turning steadily colder, and I kept tripping on the ruts and tussocks I paced, even falling on my face once. I am almost certain that he could not have seen me.

In an hour, or two hours, the half-Moon rose: the shape of a broken button, the color of a knife. I am grateful for it still; without it, I would surely never have seen the pair of them flitting across the dark toward me from different directions, dodging my glance, constantly dropping flat themselves, taking advantage of every dimness, every little swell of ground. The sight of them froze me, froze the tongue in my mouth. I could no more have cried out warning than I could have flown up to that Moon by flapping my arms. They knew it, too. I could see their smiles slicing through the moonlight.

I was not altogether without defenses. They had taught us somewhat of *kuj'mai*—the north-coast style—in *that place*, and I was confident that I could take passable care of myself in most situations. But not here, not in this situation, not for a minute, not against those two. My mind wanted to run away, and my body wanted to wet and befoul itself. Somehow I did neither, no more than I made a sound.

The worst moment—my stomach remembers it exactly, if my mind blurs details—was when I suddenly realized that I had lost sight of them, Moon or no. Then panic took me entirely, and I turned and fled toward the farmhouse-thing, as instructed, my eyes clenched almost shut, fully expecting to be effortlessly overtaken at any moment, as a *sheknath* drags down its victim from behind. They would be laughing—were laughing already, I knew it, even if I couldn't hear them. I could feel their laughter pulling me down.

When the first hand clutched at my neck, I did turn to fight them. I like to remember that. I did shriek in terror—

yes, I admit that without shame—but only once; then I whirled in that grasp, as I had been taught, and struck out with right hand and left foot, in proper *kuj'mai* style, aiming at once to shatter a kidney and paralyze a breathing center. I connected with neither, but found myself dangling in the air, screaming defiance into a face like no face I knew. It had a lizard's scales, almost purple in color, the round black eyes of some predatory bird—but glaring with a savage philosophy that never burdened the brain of any bird—a nose somewhere between a snout and a beak, and a long narrow muzzle fringed with a great many small, shy fangs. The Goro.

"Where is he?" it demanded in the Common Tongue. Its voice was higher than I had imagined, sounding as though it had scales on it as well, and it spoke with a peculiar near-lisp which would likely have been funny if I had not been hearing it with a set of three-inch talons very nearly meeting in my throat. The Goro said again, almost whispering, "Where is he? You have exactly three *daks* to tell me."

What measure of time a *dak* might be, I cannot tell you to this day, but it still sounds short. What I can say is that all that kept me from betraying the old man on the instant was the fact that I could barely make a sound, once I had heard that voice and the hissing, murderous wisdom in that voice. I managed to croak out, "Sir, I do not know, honestly"—I did say *sir*, I am sure of that anyway—but the Goro only gripped me the tighter, until I felt my tongue and eyes and even my teeth about to explode from my head. It wanted the shapeshifter's life, not mine; but to the wrath in that clench, what difference. In another moment I would be just as dead as if it had been I who stole a dream. The pure injustice of it would have made me weep, if I could have.

Then the Hunters hit him (or her, I never knew), one from either side. The Goro was so intent on strangling information out of me that it never sensed or saw them until they were upon it. It uttered a kind of soft, wheezing roar, hurled me away into a dry ditch, and turned on them, slashing out with claws at one, striking at the other's throat, all fangs bared to the yellow gums. But they were quicker: they spun away like dancers, lashing back with their weaponless hands—and, amazingly, hurting the creature. Its own attacks drew blood from exposed flesh, but theirs brought grunts of surprised pain from deep in the Goro's belly; and after that first skirmish it halted abruptly, standing quite still to take their measure properly. Still struggling for each breath, I found myself absurdly sympathetic. It knew nothing of Hunters, after all, while I knew a little.

But then again, they had plainly never encountered such an opponent. They seemed no more eager to charge a second time than it was to come at them. One took a few cautious steps forward, pausing immediately when the Goro growled. The Hunter's tone was blithe and merry, as I had always been told their voices were. "We have no dispute with you, friend," and he pointed one deadly forefinger at me as I cowered behind the creature who had so nearly killed me a moment before. The Hunter said, "We seek *him*."

"Do you so?" Those three slow words, in the Goro's voice, would have made me reconsider the path to paradise. The reply was implicit before the Goro spoke again. "He is mine. I need what he knows."

"Ah, but so do we, you see." The Hunter might have been lightly debating some dainty point of poetry or religion with a fine lady, such as drifted smokily now and then through the chill halls of *that place*. He continued, "What *we* need will come back to where it belongs. He will . . . stay here."

"Ah," said the Goro in turn, and the little sigh, coming from such a great creature, seemed oddly gentle, even wistful. The Goro said, "I also have no wish to kill you. You should go away now."

"We cannot." The other Hunter spoke for the first time, sounding almost apologetic. "There it is, unfortunately."

I had at that point climbed halfway out of the ditch, moving as cautiously and—I hoped—as inconspicuously as I possibly could, when the Goro turned and saw me. It uttered that same chilling wheeze, feinted a charge, which sent me diving back down to bang my head on stony mud, and then wheeled faster than anything that big should have been able to move, swinging its clawed tail to knock the nearer Hunter a good twenty feet away. He regained his feet swiftly enough, but he was obviously stunned, and only stood shaking his head as the Goro came at him again. The second Hunter leaped on its back, chopping and jabbing at it with those hands that could break bones and lay open flesh, but the Goro paid no more heed than if the Hunter had been pelting it with flowers. It simply shook him off and struck his dazed partner so hard—this time with a paw—that I heard his neck snap from where I stood. It does not, by the way, sound like a dry twig, as some say. Not at all.

I scrambled all the way out of the ditch on my second try, and poised low on the edge, ready to bolt this way or that, according to what the Goro did next. Vaguely I recalled that the old man had ordered me to run for the house once I had gained the attention of all parties; but, what with the situation having altered, I thought that perhaps I might not move much for some while—possibly a year, or even two. The surviving Hunter, mortally bound to avenge his comrade, let out a howl of purest grief and fury and sprang wildly at the Goro—who, amazingly, backed away so fast that the Hunter literally fell short, and very nearly sprawled at the Goro's feet, still crying vengeance. The Goro could have killed him simply by stepping on him, or with a quick slash of its tail, but it did no such thing. Rather, it backed farther, allowing him to rise without any hindrance, and the two of them faced each other under the half-Moon, the Hunter crouched and panting, the Goro studying him thoughtfully out of lidless black eyes.

The Hunter said, his voice still lightly amused, "I am not afraid of you. We have killed—" he caught himself then, and for a single moment, a splinter of a moment, I saw real, rending pain in his own pitiless eyes—"*I* have killed a score greater than you, and each time walked away unscathed. You will not live to say the same."

"Perhaps not," said the Goro, and nothing more than that. It continued to stand where it was, motionless as a long-legged *gantiya* waiting in the marshes for a minnow, while the Hunter, just as immobile, seemed to vibrate with bursting, famished energy. I began to ease away from the ditch, one slow-sliding foot at a time, freezing for what seemed hours between steps and wishing desperately now for the Moon to sink or cloud over. There came no sound or signal from the farmhouse-thing; for all I knew, the old man had taken full advantage of the Goro's distraction to abandon me to its mercy, and that of my own pursuer. Neither of them had yet paid any further heed to me, but each waited with a terrible patience for the other's eyes to make the first move. At the last, the eyes are all you have.

Gradually gaining an idiotic confidence in my chances of slipping off unnoticed, I forgot completely how I had earlier tripped in a rut and sprawled on my face, until I did it again. I made no sound, for all my certainty that I had broken my nose, but they heard me. The Hunter gave a sudden short laugh, far more terrifying than the Goro's strange, strangled roar, and came bounding at me, flying over those same furrows like a dolphin taking the sunset waves. I was paralyzed—I have no memory of reacting, until I found myself on my back, curled into a half-ball, as a *shukri* brought to bay will do, biting and clawing madly at an assailant too vast for the malodorous little beast even to conceive of. The Hunter was over me like nightfall: still perfectly efficient, for all his fury, contemptuously ignoring my flailing attempts at both attack and defense, while seeking the one place for the one blow he would ever need to strike. He found it.

He found it perhaps half a second after I found the cook's paring knife in the place where the old man had scornfully insisted that I carry it. Thought was not involved—the frantic, scrabbling thing at the end of my arm clutched the worn wooden handle and lunged blindly upward, slanting the blade along the Hunter's rib cage, which turned it like a melting candle. I felt the warm, slow trickle—*ah, they could bleed, then!*—but the Hunter's face never changed; if anything, he smiled with a kind of taunting triumph. *Yes, I can bleed, but that will not help you. Nothing will help you.* Nevertheless, he missed his strike, and I somehow rolled away, momentarily out of range and still, still alive.

The Hunter's hands were open, empty, hanging at his sides. The brown tunic was dark under his left arm, but he never stopped smiling. He said clearly, "There is no hope. No hope for you, no escape. You must know that."

"Yes," I said. "Yes, I know." And I did know, utterly, beyond any delusion. I said, "Come ahead, then."

To do myself some justice, he moved in rather more deliberately this time, as though I might have given him something to consider. I caught a moment's glimpse of the Goro standing off a little way, apparently waiting for us to destroy each other, as the old man had hoped it and the Hunters would do. The Hunter eased toward me, sideways-on, giving my paring knife the smallest target possible, which was certainly a compliment of a sort. I feinted a couple of times, left and right, as I had seen it done. He laughed, saying, "Good—very good. Really." A curious way to hear one's death sentence spoken.

Suddenly I had had enough of being quarry: the one pursued, the one hunted down, dragged down, the one helplessly watching his derisive executioner approach, himself unable to stir hand or foot. Without anything resembling a strategy, let alone a hope, I flung myself at the Hunter like a stone tumbling downhill. He stepped nimbly aside, but surprise slowed him just a trifle, and I hurtled into him, bringing us down together for a second time, and jarring the wind out of his laughter.

For a moment I was actually on top, clutching at the Hunter's throat with one hand, brandishing my little knife over him with the other. Then he smiled teasingly at me, like a father pretending to let a child pin him at wrestling, and he took the knife away from me and snapped it between his fingers. His face and clothes were splotched with blood now, but he seemed no whit weaker as he shrugged me aside and kneeled on my arms. He said kindly, "You gave us a better run than we expected. I will be quick."

Then he made a mistake.

Under the chuckling benignity, contempt, always, for

every living soul but Hunters. Under the gracious amusement, contempt, utter sneering contempt. They cannot help it, it is what they are, and it is their only weakness. He tossed the broken handle of the paring knife—with its one remaining jag of blade—lightly into my face, and raised a hand for the killing blow. When he did that, his body weight shifted—only the least bit, but his right knee shifted with it, and slipped in a smear of blood. My half-numb left arm pulled free.

There was no stabbing possible with that fraction of a knife—literally no point to it, as you might say. I thought only to *mark* him, to make him know that he had *not* killed a pitiful child, but a man grown. One last time I slashed feebly at his smiling face, but he turned his head slightly, and I missed my target completely, raking the side of his neck. I remember my disappointment—*well, failed at that, too, my last act in this world*. I remember.

It was no dribble this time, no ooze, but a fierce leap like a living animal over my hand—even Hunters have an artery there—followed immediately by a lover's triumphant blurt of breath into my face. The Hunter's eyes widened, and he started to say something, and he died in my arms.

I might have lain there for a little while—I don't know. It cannot have been long, because the body was abruptly snatched off mine and flung back and away, like a snug blanket on a winter's morning, when your mother wants you out feeding the *jejebhais*. The Goro hauled me to my feet.

"*Him,*" it said, and nothing more. It made no menacing gesture, uttered no horrifying threat; none of that was necessary. Now here is where the foolishness comes in. I had every hysterical intention of crying, "Lord, lord, please, do not slay me, and I will lead you straight to where he hides, only spare my wretched life." I meant to, I find no disgrace in telling you this, especially since what I actually heard myself say—quite politely, as I recall—was, "You will have to kill me, sir." For that miserable, lying, insulting, shapeshifting old man, I did that, and he jeered at me for it, later on. Ah, well, we begin as we are meant to continue, I suppose.

regarded me out of those eyes that could nei-
hough I saw a sort of pinkish membrane flick
across   from time to time) nor reveal the slightest feeling. It said, "That would serve no useful purpose. You will
take me to him."

As I have said, it raised no deadly paw, showed no more
teeth than the long muzzle normally showed. But I *felt* the
command, and the implacable will behind the command—I
felt the Goro in my mind and my belly, and to disobey was
not possible. Not possible . . . I can tell you nothing more.
Except, perhaps, that I was young. Today, withered relic
that I am become, I might yet perhaps hold that will at bay.
It was not possible then.

"Yes," I said. "Yes." The Goro came up to me, moving
with a curious shuffling grace, if one can say that, wrapping
that tail around its haunches as daintily as a lace shawl. It
gripped me between neck and shoulder and turned me. I
said nothing further, but started slowly toward the farmhouse that was not a farmhouse—or perhaps it was? what
did I know of anything's reality anymore? My ribs were so
badly bruised that I could not draw a full breath, and there
was something wrong with the arm that had killed the
Hunter. The half-Moon was setting now, silvering the shadows and filling the hard ruts with shivering, deceiving light,
and it was cold, and I was a child in a man's body, wishing
I were safe back in *that place*.

Nearing the farmhouse, the Goro halted, tightening its
clutch on my shoulder. Weary and bewildered as I was—no,
more than bewildered, half-mad, surely—I studied the
house, *looked* at it for the first time, and could not imagine
anyone ever having taken it for anybody's home. The dark
waiting beyond the sagging door sprang out to greet us
with a stench far beyond stench: not the smell that anciently
abandoned places have, of wood rotted into black slush,
blankets moldering on the skeleton of a bed, but of an un-
human awareness having nothing to do with our notions of
life or shelter, or even ordinary fear. The thing's
camouflage—how long in evolving? how can it have begun
to pass itself off as something belonging to this world?—

might serve well enough from a distance, on a dark night, but surely close to . . . ? Then I glanced back at the Goro.

The Goro had forgotten me completely, though its paw remembered. Its eyes continued to tell me nothing, but it was staring at the farmhouse-thing with an intensity that would have been rapture in a human expression. It lisped, much more to itself than to me, "He is in there. I have run him to earth at last."

"No," I said, once more to my own astonishment. "No. It is a trap. Believe me."

"I honor your loyalty," the Goro said. It bent its awful head and made a curious gesture with its free paw which I have never seen again, and which may have meant blessing, or merely a compliment. I try not to think about it. It said, "But you cannot know him as I do. He is here because what he stole from me is here. Because his honor demands that he face me to keep it, as mine demands that he pay the price of a stolen dream. We understand each other, we two."

"Nonsense," I said. I felt oddly lightheaded, and even bold, in the midst of my leg-caving, bladder-squeezing terror. "He has no honor, and he cares nothing for your dream, or for anything but his continual falsehearted existence. And that is no house, but a horror from somewhere more alien to you than you are to me. Please—I am trying to save *you*, not him. Believe me, please."

The Goro looked at me. I have no more idea now than I did then of what it could have been thinking, nor of what it made of my warning. Did it take me seriously and begin silently altering its plans? Had it assumed from the first that, as some sort of partner of its old enemy, nothing I said must ever be trusted for a moment? All I know is what happened—which is that out of the side of my eye I saw the fox burst from the shadows that the farmhouse was real enough to cast in this world, under this Moon, and come racing straight toward the Goro and me. In the moonlight, he shone red as the Hunter's blood.

He halted halfway, cocking his head to one side and grinning to show the small stone held in his jaws. I did not notice it immediately: it was barely more than a pebble, less bright than the sharp teeth that gripped it, or the mocking yellow eyes above it. The Goro's crystallized dream, the cause of the unending flight and pursuit that had called to me from a wagonload of manure. The fox tilted his head back, tossed the stone up at the sinking Moon, and caught it again.

And the Goro went mad. Nothing I had seen of its raging power, even when it was battling the two Hunters, could possibly have prepared me for what I saw in the next moment. The eyes, the lidless eyes that I had thought could never express any emotion . . . I was in a midnight fire at sea once, off Cape Dylee, when the waves themselves seemed alight to the horizon, all leaping and dancing with an air of blazing delight at our doom. The Goro's eyes were like that as it lunged forward, not shambling at all now, but charging like a rock-*targ*, full-speed with the second stride. It was making a sound that it had not made before: if an avalanche had breath, if an entire forest were to fall at once, you might hear something—*something*—like what I heard then. Not a roar, not a bellow, not a howl—no word in any language I know will suit that sound. Flesh never made that sound; it came through the Goro out of the tortured Earth, and that is all there is to that. That is what I believe.

The fox wheeled and raced away, his red brush joyously, insultingly high, and the Goro went after him. I stumbled forward, shouting, *"No!"* but I might as well have been crying out to a forest or an avalanche. Distraught, battered, uncertain of anything at all, it may be that I was deceived, but it seemed to me that the shadow of the farmhouse-thing reared up as they neared it, spreading out to shapelessness and *reaching* . . . I knew the fox well enough to anticipate his swerving away at the last possible minute, but I miscalculated, and so did he. The shadow's long, long arms cut off his escape on three sides, taking him in mid-leap, as a frog laps a fly out of the air. I thought I heard him utter a single small puppyish yelp, not like a fox at all.

The Goro went straight in after him, never trying to elude the shadow's grasp—I doubt it saw anything but the little dull pebble in the fox's jaws. It vanished as instantly and completely as he had, without a sound.

Telling you this tale, I notice that I am constantly pausing to marvel at my own stupidity. Each time I offer the same defense: I was young, I was inexperienced, I had been reared in a stranger place than any scoffer can possibly have known . . . all of it true, and none of it resembling an explanation for what I did next. Which was to plunge my naked hands into the devouring shadow, fumbling to rescue *anything* from its grip—the fox, the Goro, some poor creature consumed before we three ever came within its notice, within range of its desire. Today, I can only say that I pitied the Goro, and that the old man—the fox, as you will—was my guide, occasionally my mentor, and somehow nearly my friend, may the gods pity *me*. Have to do, won't it?

Where was I? Yes, I remember—groping blindly in the shadow on the chance of dragging one or the other of them back into the moonlight of this world. My arms vanished to the wrists, the forearms, past the elbows, into . . . into the flame of the stars? Into the eternal, unimaginable cold of the gulfs between them? I do not know to this day; for that, you must study my scarred old flesh and form your own opinion. What I know is that my hands closed on something they could not feel, and in turn I hauled them back, though I could not connect them, even in my mind, with a human body, mine or anyone else's. I screamed all the time, of course, but the pain had nothing to do with me—it was far too terrible, too *grand*, to belong to one person alone. I felt almost guilty keeping it for myself.

The shadow fought me. Whatever I had seized between my burning, frozen hands—and I could not tell whether it was as small a thing as the fox or as great as the Goro—the shadow wanted it back, and very nearly took it from me. And why I did not, *would* not, allow that to happen, I cannot put into words for you. I think it was the hands' decision, surely not my own. They were the ones who suffered, they were the ones entitled to choose—*yes, no, hang on, let go* . . . I was standing far—oh, very far indeed—to one side, looking on.

Did I pull what I held free by means of my pure heart and failing strength, or did the shadow finally give in, for its own reasons? I know what I believe, but none of that matters. What does matter is that when my hands came back to me, they held the fox between them. A seemingly lifeless fox, certainly; a fox without a breath or a heartbeat that I could detect; a fox beyond bedraggled, looking half his normal size, with most of his fur gone, the rest lying limply, and his proud brush as naked as a rat's tail. Indeed, the only indication that he still lived was the fact that he was unconsciously trying to shape-shift in my hands. The shiver of the air around him, the sudden slight smudging of his outline . . . I jumped back, as I had not recoiled from the house-thing's shadow, letting him fall to the ground.

He landed without the least thump, so insubstantial he was. The transformation simply faded and failed; though whether that means that the fox-shape was his natural form and the other nothing but a garment he was too weak to assume, I have never known. The Moon was down, and with the approach of false dawn, the shadow was retreating, the house-thing itself withering absurdly, like an overripe vegetable, its sides slumping inward while its insides—or whatever they might have been—seemed to ooze palely into the rising day, out to where the shadow had lain in wait for prey. Only for a moment . . . then the whole creature collapsed and vanished before my eyes, and the one trace of its passage was a dusty hole in the ground. A small hole, the sort of hole that remains when you have pulled a plant up by its roots. Or think you have.

There was no sign of the Goro. When I looked back at the fox, he was actually shaking himself and trying to get to his feet. It took him some while, for his legs kept splaying out from under him, and even when he managed to balance more or less firmly on all four of them, his yellow eyes were obviously not seeing me, nor much else. Once the fox-shape was finally under control, he promptly abandoned it for that of the old man, who looked just as much of a disaster, if not even more so. The white mustache appeared to have been chewed nearly away; one burly white eyebrow was altogether gone, as were patches of the white mane, and the skin of his face and neck might have been through fire or frostbite. But he turned to stare toward the place where the house that was not a house had stood, and he grinned like a skull.

"Exactly as I planned it," he pronounced. "Rid of the lot of them, we are, for good and all, thanks to my foresight. I *knew* it was surely time for the beast to return to that spot, and I *knew* the Goro would care for nothing else, once it caught sight of me and that stone." Amazingly, he patted my shoulder with a still-shaky hand. "And you dealt with your little friends remarkably well—far better than I expected, truth be told. I may have misjudged you somewhat."

"As you misjudged the thing's reach," I said, and he had the grace to look discomfited. I said, "Before you thank me—" which he had shown no sign of doing "—you should know that I was simply trying to save whomever I could catch hold of. I would have been just as relieved to see the Goro standing where you are."

"Not for long," he replied with that supremely superior air that I have never seen matched in all these years. "The Goro consider needing any sort of assistance—let alone having to be *rescued*—to be dishonorable in its very nature. He'd have quickly removed a witness to his sin, likely enough." I suspected that to be a lie—which it is, for the most part—but said nothing, only watching as he gradually recovered his swagger, if not his mustache. It was fascinating to observe, rather like seeing a newborn butterfly's wings slowly plumping in the Sun. He said then—oddly quietly, I remember—"You are much better off with me. Whatever you think of me."

When he said that, just for that moment, he looked like no crafty shapeshifter but such a senile clown as one sees in the wayside puppet plays where the young wife always runs off with a soldier. He studied my hands and arms, which by now were hurting so much that in a way they did not hurt at all, if you can understand that. "I know something that will help those," he said. "It will not help enough, but you will be glad of it."

Not yet true dawn, and I could feel how hot the day would be in that barren, utterly used-up land that is called the Mihanachakali. There was dust on my lips already, and sweat beginning to rise on my scalp. A few scrawny *rukshi* birds were beginning to circle high over the Hunters' bodies. I turned away and began to walk—inevitably back the way we had come, there being no other real road in any direction. The old man kept pace with me, pattering brightly at my side, cheerfully informing me, "The coast's what we want—salt water always straightens the mind and clears the spirit. We'll have to go back to Druchank—no help for that, alas—but three days farther down the Nai—"

I halted then and stood facing him. "Listen to me," I said. "Listen closely. I am bound as far from Goros and Hunters, from foxes that are not foxes and houses that are not houses as a young fool can get. I want nothing to do with the lot of you, or with anything that is like you. There must be a human life I am fit to lead, and I will find it out, wherever it hides from me. I will find my life."

"Rather like our recent companions seeking after us," he murmured, and now he sounded like his old taunting self, but somehow subdued also. "Well, so. I will bid you good luck and good-bye in advance, then, for all that we do appear to be traveling the same road—"

"We are *not*," I said, loud enough to make my poor head ache, and my battered ribs cringe. I began walking again, and he followed. I said, "Whichever road you take, land or water, I will go some other way. If I have to climb back into a manure wagon a second time, I will be shut of you."

"I have indeed misjudged you," he continued, as though I had never spoken. "There is promising stuff to you, and with time and tutelage you may blossom into adequacy yet. It will be interesting to observe."

"I will write you a letter," I said through my teeth. There would plainly be no ridding myself of him until Druchank, but I was determined not to speak further word with him again. And I did not, not until the second night, when we had made early camp close enough to Druchank to smell its foulness on a dank little breeze. Hungry and weary, I weakened enough to ask him abruptly, "That house—whatever it was—you called it *the beast*. It was alive, then? Some sort of animal?"

"Say *vegetable*, and you may hit nearer the mark," he answered me. "They come and go, those things—never many, but always where they grew before, and always in the exact guise they wore the last time. I have seen one that you would take for a grand, shady *keema* tree without any question, and another that looks like a sweet little dance pavilion in the woods that no one seems to remember building. I cannot say where they are from, nor what exactly becomes of their victims—only that it is a short blooming season, and if they take no prey they rot and die back before your eyes. As that one did." He yawned as the fox yawned, showing all his teeth, and added, "A pity, really. I have . . . made use of that one before."

"And you led me there," I said. "You told me nothing, and you led me there."

He shrugged cheerfully. "I tried to tell you—a little, anyway—but you did not care to hear. My fault?" I did not answer him. A breeze had come up, carrying with it the smell of the Nai—somewhat fresher than that of the town—and the bray of a boat horn.

"It had already taken the Goro," I said finally, "and still it died."

"Ah, well, a Goro's not to everybody's taste." He yawned again, and suddenly barked with laughter. "Probably gave the poor old thing a bellyache—no wonder!" He literally fell over on his back at the thought, laughing, waving his arms and legs in the air, purely delighted at the image, and more so with himself for creating it. I watched him from where I lay, feeling a curious mixture of ironic admiration, genuine revulsion, and something uncomfortably like affection, which shocked me when I made myself name it to myself. As it occasionally does even now.

"I tried to stop the Goro," I said. "I told him that it was a trick, that you were deceiving him. I begged him not to fall into your trap."

The old man did not seem even slightly perturbed. "Didn't listen, did he? They never do. That's the nature of a Goro. Just as not wanting to know things is the nature of humans."

"And your nature?" I challenged him. "What is the nature of whatever you are?"

He considered this for some time, still lying on his back with his arms folded on his chest in the formal manner of a corpse. But his eyes were wide open, and in the twilight they were more gray than fox-yellow just then.

"Deceptive," he offered at last. "That's fair enough— deceptive. Misleading, too, and altogether unreliable." But he seemed not quite satisfied with any of the words, and thought about it for a while longer. At last he said, "Illusory. Good as any, *illusory*. That will do."

I lay long awake that night, reflecting on all that I had passed through—and all that had passed through and over me—since I fled across another night from *that place*, with the Hunters behind me. Deceptive, misleading, illusory, even so he had done me no real ill, when you thought about it. Led me into peril, true, but preserved me from it more than once. And he had certainly taught me much that I needed to know, if I were to make my way forward to wherever I was making my way to in this world. I could have had worse counselors, and doubtless would yet, on my journey.

My hands and arms pained me still, but far less than they had, as I leaned to nudge him out of his usual twitchy fox-sleep. He had searched out a couple of fat-leaved weeds that morning, pounded them for a good hour, mixed the resulting mash with what I tried not to suspect was his own urine, and spread it from my palms to my shoulders, where it crusted cool and stiff. I had barely touched his own shoulder before his eyes opened, yellow as they always are when he first wakes. I wonder what his dreams would look like, if they were to take daylight substance, as a Goro's do.

"Three more days on the Nai brings us where?" I asked him.

Diva's Bones

~~~~~~

John Meaney

John Meaney (www.johnmeaney.tripod.com) lives in Kent, England. He holds a degree in physics and computer science—("I've still got a day-job in IT consultancy—teaching stuff, Java programming and the like—but it's part-time now,") and a black belt in Shotokan Karate. His novels include To Hold Infinity (1998), Paradox (1999), and Context (2001), the latter two titles being the first two books in the Nulapeiron Sequence. His fourth novel, Resolution, is out in 2005. His short fiction has appeared in Interzone. His novelette Sharp Tang was shortlisted for the British Science Fiction Association Award in 1995, and To Hold Infinity and Paradox were on the BSFA shortlists for Best Novel in 1999 and 2001, respectively. The Times called John Meaney "The first important new sf writer of the 21st century."

"Diva's Bones" appeared in Interzone, which has usually had a few first rate fantasy stories in any given year. But this year Interzone gave up the ghost, ceased publication, was sold, and resumed publication late in the year with a new look and under new editorship. So the field lost two of it's top magazine editors, Asimovs' Gardner R. Dozois and Interzone's David Pringle. Meaney's tale is a weird fantasy detective dream drug story, cleverly plotted, filled with atmospheric detail and surprises.

Reactors, formed of polished obsidian, moaned in the cavernous vaults. Supporting pillars of fluted bone stood in the shadows; around them, black flames licked upward, reaching toward the city above.

Necroflux hummed everywhere. Gelid air slid across my skin like a dead man's touch. (Do they think of this, up above? Not while they have lighting and warmth.) Down here, you can't ignore the facts.

I closed my mind to the whispers. They were strongest in the long aisles between the fusion piles, teasing the awareness. When I reached the wrought-iron stairs I climbed quickly, then caught my breath before entering the antechamber.

A uniformed flunky buzzed the director's office, and beckoned me toward a seat.

"Can I take your overcoat, Lieutenant?"

"I'm fine."

I don't like it here.

I forced the feeling aside. Pushing my hands in my suit pockets, I stared up at the black iron dragon on the wall: the glowering seal of the Energy Authority.

The heavy door clicked open, swung inward. I was halfway into the brightly lit office (checking out the deep-red carpet, the polished carvings from far Zuram) by the time he rose: lean, with a gray goatee, wearing a suit of heavy tweed. A silver watch-chain winking across his vest.

"Lieutenant O'Connor, is it?"

I nodded. "And you're Malfax Cortindo."

"Good evening." He shook my hand—I caught a whiff of bottled lavender, but his grip was stronger than I expected—and motioned me to an elegant chair. "Your commissioner was a trifle vague about how I might help."

"He said I could ask for technical advice." I hesitated.

"Perhaps I should tell you about my case, and you can tell me what occurs to you. In confidence, of course."

"Of course."

There had been four killings this year, in three different countries, involving famous stage performers. In each instance, the authorities spun a story of natural death on stage, which worked because none of the deaths was bloody: micro-caliber bullets in the first two cases, a neurotoxic dart in the more recent.

But journalists were not stupid, and their reports hinted at the truth without ever quite stating it in plain declarative sentences: a kind of muttering between the lines.

"You're investigating a homicide, I presume, lieutenant. Perhaps . . . a body being stolen?"

I looked at him for a long moment, not trusting him. But if I provided no information, what use was his advice?

In those four cases, two of the bodies disappeared immediately—one in the confusion as fire swept through the theater, the other because an ambulance crew of impostors calmly bore the deceased away—and someone stole the third body from the family mausoleum. (Masked men without ID tried to remove the fourth body from its vault, but that time there were armed guards who fired first and no one asked questions.)

"Let's say, a *potential* homicide." My job was to make sure it didn't happen.

"A conspiracy, then. Perhaps a death threat?"

"I—Sort of." I cleared my throat. "No one's threatened anything overtly. But we've a likely target making an appearance in the near future, based on previous patterns. I'm trying to understand the killers' motives."

Director Cortindo fingered his goatee, frowning. Then his face cleared.

"The Diva!" He beamed a delighted smile, startling in these necro-industrial surroundings. "Of course . . . Maria daLivnova is performing on stage, at the . . . Brazhinski Theatre, is it? It's the *Mort d'Arcturi*, and the Diva sings the part of Lady Elena."

Unsettled, I stared at him.

"You've heard the stories, then. About the murders of famous performing artists."

But how did you guess?

I didn't like the way his intuition leaped so far ahead of my explanation.

"It is my business, in a way," said Cortindo. And, sober now: "You'd better come with me, Lieutenant. You need to see something."

In the vault, he removed a polished walnut case. Then he flipped up the brass catches, pulled the lid back, and turned the case toward me.

Gray-white bones, dry-looking on a red silk lining.

"Go ahead," he said. "Pick one up."

I bit my lip.

"I'm not sure I—"

Cortindo's mouth twisted in an almost-smile.

"You'll never understand what you're facing, until you do this."

Peaceful paradise enveloped me.

I was warm and happy in my abstract dreams: emerald swirling light; golden shapes which drifted and called to me; divine human figures who laughed and played, and sang on a silver shore by waves of liquid cobalt. Music, sublime, brought tears to my . . .

Something was wrong.

A plot in Paradise?

No.

Something, someone, wanted to tear me away from all that was peaceful, all that was forgiveness, all that was simply love.

"NO!"

Images rippled and tore.

No . . .

And I hurled myself at the director with hands outstretched, going for the throat—

Die now!

—but he was too quick for me, snatching back the bones in his gauntlet-covered hands, backstepping and spinning away—*so fast*—then I came to my senses and stood there, chest heaving and panting, drenched with sweat.

Paradise. Fading now.

What the hell—?

"Well done, Lieutenant. Most people take longer to come to their senses."

I looked down at my empty hands.

At my palms, which had held those gray-white bones.

"I've trained since childhood in *pa-kua*," Director Cortindo added. "It's a soft martial art, heavy on circular avoidance techniques."

Squinting at him, I swallowed, and said: "I don't understand."

"Otherwise"—with a gentle smile—"I'd have had security guards in here with me. It's a wrench, when you leave the dream."

My eyes were watering, my head splitting with a stone-hard migraine.

A dream?

The bones induced a dream. A powerful alternative to reality.

"A wrench, you call it. That's a mild way of putting it."

If I wasn't here at the commissioner's suggestion—read: on his order—I'd be considering other words. Assault on a law officer. Obstruction while in the pursuit of official duties.

"The time"—Cortindo took out his antique silver pocket watch—"is half past three."

"I don't—"

But then I realized what he was saying.

I arrived at noon.

The bones' dreams had held me in their clutch for over three hours.

And I felt like weeping, that Cortindo tore me away so soon.

* * *

"He was an artist. Pedro d'Alquazar by name." Director Cortindo stared down at the bones. "Died in poverty before collectors discovered his talent, his true worth. Now his best pieces are priceless treasures, displayed in several national galleries."

He closed the walnut case, snapped the catches shut.

"Because he died penniless, d'Alquazar's body came in with a normal shipment. But one of our thanatocogs sensed his difference, and alerted a team to rescue his corpse."

I watched him replace the case on a shelf inside the vault—*please don't*—then step back out and swing the heavy door shut. It shifted the air pressure and my ears felt as if they might pop. I swallowed.

Then we left the vault's anteroom, climbed the steps into the cavernous main installation, while guards sealed up the iron door behind us.

"I'm still not sure I understand," I said.

Cortindo waved at the necrofusion piles that reared on all sides, nearly to the groined ceilings a hundred feet overhead.

"What a waste of artistic bones"—with a tiny shrug—"to be merely fuel for this."

We visited one of the two control rooms, situated half-way up one wall of the cathedral-like space. Technicians in black coats nodded at Cortindo, paid no attention to me as Cortindo gave brief explanations of the various instruments.

"These dials here," he said, "record the flux. You'll see they're calibrated in meganecrons per square yard, for convenience."

"Naturally."

He gave me a look. "Over here, we monitor for resonance overload. In life, shadow-particles act as standing waves, changing the microstructure of the bones. We want clean waves averaged out to useful harmonics. Deviations can be dangerous."

I thought of the flux sweeping through the bones, the

moaning, fragmented thoughts as necrofusion piles replayed shards of forgotten lives.

Cortindo's voice droned on but I, hands in pockets, wandered over to the window and stared down at the long rows of reactors. My skin prickled, but not from stray radiation.

So many dead.

Ten thousand or more incarcerated in each pile.

"If you could build a fusion reactor from a single person's bones," said Cortindo, coming to stand beside me, "you might obtain clarity. But in these jumbled piles stacked to critical mass, what you get is demonic chaos. The vector sum of a mob's primeval fears."

"And if you poked your head inside a reactor's cladding?"

"Oh, Lieutenant." Cortindo gave a tiny shudder. "You wouldn't want to do that."

Ordinary people—people like you and me—end up as part of the fusion piles, keeping those who live after us warm and happy. If any of our memories survive, replayed, they form nightmarish fragments of a vast demonic power harnessed for the common good. Nothing more than that.

But for the few, the gifted artistic few, the dreams laid down in their bones are beyond price.

And if you were a certain sort of collector, wouldn't you want to capture those sublime thoughts right now, when you yourself were alive to enjoy them, to be enwrapped in priceless visions?

Cortindo was right.

I needed to see that. Experience the dream.

Before, the motive was a vague, shadowy, theoretical thing: insufficient for the vast expense and risk involved. But now . . .

Hell, I understand it now.

But when it came to the modus operandi and the perpetrators' identity—must there be more than one?—I left the En-

ergy Authority feeling more ignorant than when I arrived.
Vision-remnants whirled in my mind, and that was bad.

Get control.

I stepped out onto a dank courtyard upon the surface,
where a department car was waiting for me.

"The airport, sir, is that right?"

"Quick as you can."

I slid into the back of the big old cruiser and slammed the
door shut. The uniformed officers in front took the hint: the
driver gunned the engine, screeched out of the courtyard,
and hacked his way through fog-bound streets, running
three stop lights in succession.

Someone's horn blared. Cheeky bastard.

Lucky we're in a hurry.

We got to the airport on time.

"Good job."

"Sir."

Someone opened the car door.

"There's coffee upstairs waiting for you, Lieutenant. I'm
afraid the flight's delayed. Another 20 minutes."

"Thank you, Sergeant."

A chilly breeze was pushing back the fog. I nodded to the
men on duty, and went inside.

From the control tower, I watched as paparazzi set up position on the cold tarmac, then stood around with hands in
overcoat pockets, breath steaming from beneath their hats,
waiting for the photo opportunity.

Finally, it landed, and uniformed groundstaff—already
vetted by the officers in place—wheeled the stairs to the forward hatch.

They won't try here. I was almost certain of it.

She was first off the flight: descending the steps to a chorus of flashbulbs popping white, while the plane's pro-
pellers still revolved.

Officers ringed her, and pushed through to the VIP lounge.
I nodded my thanks to the control room staff who had put
up with me, and headed off to meet Maria daLivnova, diva

extraordinaire, high-profile target and a perfect trophy for certain persons unknown.

Couldn't you have visited some other city?

She would be awkward, I was sure, with an artistic temperament having little to do with practical considerations. And when I met her, that turned out to be true, more or less.

But I couldn't have known . . .

I had no idea how stunningly beautiful she would be.

Officers surrounded her, but I did not see them. All that I could focus on was a pair of glistening dark enchanting eyes in an elegant ivory-skinned face. And that gaze, when turned on me, seemed to vibrate like a pure and wonderful perfect note.

But she was not beguiled by me.

"You'll allow me privacy, Lieutenant." With ice in her voice: "I require that. Meditation before the performance."

So beautiful.

This was a professional interview, and it would make life much easier if she agreed to the arrangements I described.

"I'll do my best, ma'am."

Dismissively: "Very well."

She scarcely registered my existence. No more than the furniture in the lounge, or the vehicle that was waiting for her outside. The Diva was wrapped up, I can only assume, in the coming performance and her part in it.

So very . . .

Yet I might be the one to step between her and a killer's bullet.

. . . beautiful.

There was an escort of half a dozen cars, with armed officers in uniform, to take the Diva to the Hotel Pacifica which we had already secured. Plainclothes detectives were in residence in the rooms above, below and to either side of her suite.

If she truly was in danger, and the pattern followed that

established in other countries, then the risk lay in the theater itself, during the performance.

So beautiful.

And in the middle of the night, that was where I went: the Brazhinski Theatre.

I prowled the galleries. I scoured private boxes and public balconies: tracking vectors, evaluating hiding-places, listing places of concealment and angles of attack, while the night-watchman and two patrolmen tracked my progress.

Too many places to hide.

There would be uniformed officers at the exits during the performance, and that helped. If the killer—if there was a killer—was willing to commit suicide, then the situation was fraught. But if he wanted to make an escape, all right: I could ensure that his egress was blocked, publicly and visibly. He could take the Diva's life only by giving up his own.

I still don't like it.

Because if someone was insane enough to want her dead in the first place—

They would sing beautifully . . .

I shook away the thought.

. . . so beautifully, her bones.

What I had to do boiled down to three things. First, put prominent, visible security in place: better to discourage the perpetrators from trying than to be a hero and aim for an arrest. Second, keep watch during the performance itself. Track the audience members constantly; watch for anything suspicious. Be prepared to use deadly force among an audience composed of the city's most wealthy and influential citizens, where any action at all could cost me my career, and a mistake—like a bullet which missed the killer and struck an innocent person—might be rewarded with the hangman's rope.

I don't want to become a fusion pile component.

Oh, yes. The third thing.

I should not get hung up on the performance itself. If someone wanted to stage—ha!—a very public killing, that would be an ideal place. But I'd better not take it for granted. They could go for her anywhere: in the dressing-room, in the car journey to or from the theater. In her hotel suite. Anywhere at all.

My headache was coming back.

In my dingy apartment, I hauled myself through chin-ups from the exposed ceiling pipes, press-ups on the worn gray floorboards, and sit-ups with my feet hooked under the iron-framed bed. Deep knee bends, trying to avoid splinters in my bare feet.

Then I showered in the tiny tin stall, under a miserable trickle which gave out before I'd finished rinsing off. Feeling scratchy, I sat down at the small kitchen table with half a pint of bourbon, twisted off the cap, and proceeded to drink.

That night I dreamed.

Of the Diva.

Day-shift started at eight. So it was at five o'clock—a.m.— that I ran through near-deserted streets in my threadbare tracksuit beneath pre-dawn skies, along slick wet sidewalks where cracked lamps flickered. Steam rose from manhole covers. Occasionally, a low moan sounded from a wall-mounted pipe.

At the orphanage school, old Sister Mary Thanatos taught us that the sounds are caused by the passage of steam, the expansion and contraction of metal piping, and bear no relation to the dark source of that power. "Thermodynamics," she used to say, "and the properties of metals." Nothing to do with necroflux or the reactors beneath our streets.

But I could not help comparing those eerie tones to the groans of the dying, the sobs of the bereaved.

I ran faster.

* * *

And finally, performance night. The cars drawing up: stretch limousines, with their glittering bodywork. The uniformed chauffeurs who stood respectfully out of the limelight as their clients walked in finery along the wide red carpet leading into the theater.

The crowds: watching and milling.

No sign of weapons, of scowling faces, of a professionally blank expression which might hide a calculating killer's mind.

If I were an assassin, where would I be?

I prowled, learning nothing.

But I was outside her door when the stage assistant, flushed and breathless with anxiety, tapped on her door and said:

"Miss daLivnova? Five minutes."

I checked my shoulder holster, drew my gun. Slid out the magazine, checked its shining load of copper-colored death-bringers, snapped it shut once more.

Reholstered.

"Why, the glamorous detective! It's . . ."

The dressing-room door was swinging open, and her flawless features glimmered with a magic I cannot describe. And then she smiled.

My breathing stopped.

". . . show time."

Nothing happened. Nothing untoward.

It was a miraculous performance, and the rousing finale paralyzed my heart. I was entranced, despite myself, by the spotlit apparition of the Diva on stage. For that moment she was unguarded—captivating the souls of the people who were supposed to be guarding her: the other officers were awestruck too—but no shot rang out from the crowd, from the shadows beyond the bright-lit stage.

And then the swirling party afterward, the headache of observing glittering guests—diamond tiaras, massive gold rings, bright smiles which widened with unaccustomed sincerity—followed by relief, watching the kaleidoscope wind down in the early hours of morning.

Dangerous relief: I kept prodding myself into alertness, in case the killer struck now, in the emotional aftermath as everyone lowered their exhausted guard.

Finally, Commissioner Treevor—rotund, dressed in his finest tuxedo with a crimson cummerbund: he had enjoyed the performance from his private box—came up and delivered congratulations on a job well done.

"Go home, rest." He waved a fat, unlit cigar. "You'll be busy again tomorrow."

"Yes, sir." Another night of being a glamorous detective.

But I waited one more hour, until all the guests were gone, then I followed the Diva and her twelve-strong uniformed escort to the hotel. She arrived safely.

Afterward, I stuffed my hands in my raincoat pockets, and shambled through the streets back to my tiny apartment where shadows waited for my return.

Some kind of glamour.

In this city, daytime never amounts to more than glimmering gray sky, forever weak. Dawn is a pimp's contract with the world.

What I hate about switching to night-shift is that it's hard to find a quiet place to run. Even when the city's office blocks are crammed with employees at their wooden desks fitted with pneumatic message-tubes, their important Bakelite phones, still the sidewalks are busy. I hate waiting at intersections for battered gray cars and purple taxis to pass, before running onward through the smog.

That's why I run the catacombs.

Only the rich can afford to bury their dead away from the fusion piles—the burial fee is 100,000 florins, which would pay my rent for decades—and that's one reason why the casings are of heavy polished brass, securely locked. They gleam as you run past, down ancient stone tunnels where few people tread.

Of course there are whispers.

One comes . . .

Usually, I can ignore them as I run. Today my skin crawled.

Danger.

Upping the pace.

Danger and . . .

I poured on the speed.

. . . the beauty of the drawing dark.

Foot splashing in a dank puddle.

Do you feel it, calling?

Sprinting now.

Do you feel the song?

And then I was into the larger caverns, away from the tunnels—relief!—as the strange whispers slid away. I slowed to a walk, sweat-soaked, heart pounding with more than exertion.

It's never been this bad.

And I wondered, as I dragged myself up the worn stone stairs, whether these rich folks' bones held knowledge as well as memory, echoed with more than fragments of a forgotten and extinct past.

Do you feel the song?

I reached the top, and banged on the door until the custodians let me out.

Second performance.

Lights, swirls: the songs, the magic. The spellbound audience. The darkness beyond, where the killer might wait.

The congratulations afterward.

Journalists. The fans.

And the wandering home alone when the glittering spell is done.

Next day, I ran along the sidewalks.

Neither pedestrians nor the traffic bothered me. Obstacles and smog, and waiting to cross the streets . . . they slowed my run, but they did not whisper, and that was good enough.

Afterward, the water in my shower remained hot, coming out of the nozzle in a strong jet, for as long as I wanted. Later, my freshly laundered shirt and suit felt good against my skin.

Perhaps it's going be OK.

But the third night was when it happened.

The final aria was sublime.

For all the magic of the previous performances, they might have been warm-ups, preliminary stages to a blinding spell which was surely the apex of the Diva's career: a conjuration of sound and emotion beyond anything else the world could offer.

Killers be damned . . . I stood frozen in the wings, paralyzed, unable to take my eyes off center-stage, and the glorious figure who drew magic with her voice. Pure, silver voice, delineating the Lady Elena's grief over the body of her dead king. Rose to dizzy heights, a lowering, then the true finale. Sweetness. And the drawing off, a post-coital lover's embrace. The honeyed, drawn-out ending of the song to end all songs.

Afterward, nothing.

Stunned silence. Not even breathing.

My God . . .

And then, a woman's sob.

Like one being, the audience rose to their feet, and began to clap.

And then the cheers and applause rose to thunderous crescendo, echoed back from the great theater's cathedral-like space, the opulent boxes and gold-leaf painted galleries, filled with consensual joy.

From the wings, blinking tears from my eyes, I watched her bow.

The applause faded, petered out. There was a final clap, embarrassed.

Then a gasp from the balcony.

* * *

This was no standing ovation.

The entire half-dozen rows at the front, some 300 people in gowns and tuxedos, were on their feet. In silence. They filed out from their seats, stood before the front row, and stopped.

Then, one slow pace at a time, they advanced in unspeaking unison upon the stage, a bright and fearful hunger glowing in their eyes.

No. It was never a killer.

Black glimmering in the air above them: a communal magic, strong enough to draw illusions to rewrite witnesses' memories. To make some into active servants, and to etch the minds of everyone here. Afterward, to alter their perceptions of what occurred.

Had the others died in this fashion?

Not a single killer.

That shining blackness held me frozen, like everybody else . . . then something snapped inside me—it felt like that, an audible crack in my brain as the trance-shift training finally kicked in: a professional reflex—and I was free to move.

Yes, move.

She was paralyzed too, the Diva.

Held in place not by the black spell, but by terror.

Move now!

I sprinted onto the stage.

My arm caught her by the waist, sheer momentum carrying us onward, and then she was keeping pace with me.

"Wait—"

A pause in the wings, while a threatening moan rose up from the audience—from the 300-strong ensorcelled segment at the front—but the Diva clung to me as she kicked off her shoes.

"All right. Which—?"

I tugged her toward the fire exit.

Run.
Sounds of pursuit, and a cold viscous shivering in the air.
Run hard.

Furious questions boiled in my brain as we tore along the dank alleyway, ducked among shadowed crates—*no, don't stop*—then left the hiding-place to run onward, into a darkened street where the lamps were cracked and rats scurried out of sight as we hurtled past.

Questions. Could the audience be responsible for the killings: all members of the same conspiracy? Unlikely. More probably, they were held in thrall by some dark power. But either way, could they follow us?

And were there others, partners or servants, who might hunt us down?

"I can't—" The Diva was gasping.

Can't stop.

I hauled her onward, along another deserted alley and then the narrow street, noting that her dress was ripped, catching a glimpse of ivory breast but discarding the vision, no time for messing around. Looking for the nondescript stone bunker I knew must stand nearby.

"Not much farther." I squeezed her upper arm tight enough to hurt. "Quickly, and we might survive this."

It crouched like a dark stone igloo, wrapped in shadows on the street corner.

Adrenaline must have powered her body because the Diva ran as fast as me, nearing the shelter. My police badge, shoved into the scanner slot, passed muster. The massive stone door swung open: silently, on well-oiled heavy-duty hinges.

Inside, I pressed the square red metal plate which caused the door to close behind us.

Safe? Perhaps.

It was quiet in here.

"Which way, Lieutenant?"

I pointed at the spiral stairs.

"Down."

* * *

She was drenched with sweat, leaning against me as we walked the catacombs, heading for the only safe place I could think of.

"Save me," she said, and the emotion in her miraculous eyes was genuine, even if it wasn't love.

"I will."

But even as we hurried on, whispers slid across my skin.

So beautiful, her songs.

I pushed her roughly, increased the pace.

So beautiful, her bones.

"Faster now."

Do you feel the song?

Moving through stone tunnels, past brass-doored tombs. Whispers of the dead tugging at my mind. Not enough to hide the clatter which sounded behind us.

"They're following!"

I drew my gun part-way out of the shoulder holster, replaced it. "I know."

There was blood on her feet, crimson and strangely beautiful against her elegant skin, but the Diva made no complaint. We hurried until the great black iron doors came into sight, and I knew we had a chance of getting out of this alive.

Dragon, iron, looking down on us.

"I don't like this place," the Diva whispered. "There's something here."

Drawing out my pistol, reversing it, I hammered the butt against the door.

"I know. But this is where we have to go."

Slowly—too slowly—the big doors swung inward, and a lean face peered out.

I flashed my badge as we half-fell inside.

"Close the doors and bar them. Don't let anyone else in."

"Yes, sir."

God help me, I froze *solid*.

A dozen fingers squeezed simultaneously, a dozen triggers travelled short arcs. A composite bang hammered the air. Bullets tore into her elegant torso, ripped her organs apart in a spattering gout of thick crimson blood.

That was the moment.

I'm sorry . . .

The moment I allowed to happen.

. . . my love.

And then the rage.

Do you feel the song?

It was too late for the director. I stabbed fingertips into his eyes, clawed with murderous rage, then grabbed his jaw and hair and twisted, hard, as I bent him across my knee. A loud crack as vertebrae snapped.

I dropped his corpse to the floor.

Do you feel . . . ?

Around me, parazombies toppled, comatose. In need of thaumatomedical care.

Dying, the Diva shivered once on a widening, glistening pool of wine-dark blood, and her mouth formed an accusation her shredded lungs could no longer voice.

You promised . . .

And then she died.

I don't know.

I will *never* know . . . whether I hesitated from fear, or held back for that split second because of sneaking whispers from the spirits who wanted her dead.

Because I wanted her to die?

She didn't love me, the bitch.

Such a hard thought isn't mine. Can't be mine.

I risked everything for her.

I'm a professional. I was doing my job.

Only my job.

But she was more than just another assignment.

If only she'd loved me.

Hot tears track down my cheeks as I pick up her fine, blood-soaked body. I step over the fallen men, carry her away from this place of the dead.

So beautiful . . .

Their whispers cling, try to draw me back, but I ignore them.

Do you feel the song?

On the surface now, I stand with my bloody burden in a small courtyard, beneath a blank night sky touched with emerald. The place is silent and deserted: whoever manned it, they're down below, among the fallen.

Three cars are parked here, and I choose one: big and black, with hard fins and a wide, malevolent grille across the front. The trunk opens at my touch. I roll the Diva's beautiful corpse inside, and slam the lid down.

Inside a booth, on hooks, I find the keys to all three cars. The unwanted ones go down a drain.

Do you feel the song?

The engine growls into life. I leave it running as I step over to the outer gates—heavy black iron, but finely balanced—and swing them open.

Then I get back inside the car, and drive out onto the dark, cobbled street beyond.

Driving.

Into the mist.

Where am I going?

I have a vacation home, beside a silent black lake where no fish survive. Inherited from my parents, single-story and built from slate, with a deep cold cellar. None of my colleagues—I think—are aware of its existence.

Do you . . .

There, I will clean my treasures, scrape them into a pristine state, and store them on cushions covered with the finest silk. To hold that skull against my temple. To pick up those elegant metacarpals and kiss them, while in my spirit the song to end all songs rises to sweet and glorious crescendo, forever mine.

. . . feel the song?

At least, until they track me down—my colleagues, or the dead director's secret allies—and we fight for the most miraculous prize.

Diva's bones.

The Seventh Daughter

Bruce McAllister

Bruce McAllister (www.geocities.com/bhmcallister/) lives in Redlands, California. His website describes him as "a California-based writer, interdisciplinary writing coach, book and screenplay consultant, workshop leader and 'agent finder' for both new and established writers of non-fiction, fiction and screenplays," and says, "At the University of Redlands in southern California, where he taught writing for over twenty years, he helped establish and direct the Creative Writing Program, was responsible for both the Professional Writing track of that program and its Communications Internship program, received various teaching and service awards, and was Edith R. White Distinguished Professor of Literature and Writing from 1990 to 1995." His first SF novel was Humanity Prime *(1971), in the famous Ace Special line, and his last was* Dream Baby *(1989). He has published stories since 1963, though infrequently in the last decade.*

"The Seventh Daughter" was published in F&SF. It is a beautifully compressed fantasy descended from fairy tale material, and from historical fact, from nostalgia, and a careful consideration of what it all might mean. It is also a love story.

The American boy lived with his parents in a small villa high on a hillside above a cove where young people danced at night, laughing and shouting, their voices rising through the olive trees to him as he fell asleep. Sometimes he did not know which was the real story. The Ligurian Sea below him in the night, where a poet had drowned long ago. The laughter and shouting below him that drowned out the whispers of that sea and the mutterings of that poet. The boyish face he saw in the mirror when he dared to look. The things he made of paint and clay and words that only he knew about. It didn't matter, he told himself—it was all real and yet it was not—but the question was always there as he fell asleep and woke.

In the top drawers of his bedroom dresser, with every color of modeling clay, he had made a world and knew its story perfectly. "The Seven Daughters of Satan," he called it. He'd built very carefully the valley, the forest, and the seven villages where the daughters of Satan, who had abandoned them, had grown up. The men of the villages were scared of the daughters, beautiful as they were, because they knew who they were. The daughters showed no dark gifts, no witch's skills or demonic tendencies, but the men of the villages felt it: *The waiting*. The waiting for *him*. The entire valley and the mountains that surrounded it were waiting. If you held your breath and stayed entirely still, you could even hear it: The ticking of God's great clock. The hour didn't matter. What mattered was that the ticking never stopped. The men heard it as they stared, hearts breaking, at the faces of the seven daughters, and did not take a step toward them. The daughters did not understand. They could not hear the ticking. They did not know how much the men wanted them.

The daughters kept more and more to themselves and the

men said less and less. A child might run up to one of the girls and say something, hand something to her, take something away, even play with her. But the adults never took such a chance. The daughters grew more sullen, their white faces and their red lips once like seven Sleeping Beauties, but now like fading ghosts. *He will return*, the villagers whispered to themselves. Inside their thatched house, in which the daughters had grown up and in which they slept side to side on mats on a clay floor, they had a deaf nanny to watch over them. The nanny could not hear the ticking either, and was growing blinder each year as well.

Each daughter had a dresser built years ago when the daughters were little by men from the villages. In each daughter's dresser there were seven drawers, and in the top drawer, made of clay and fashioned by the nanny's son (who lived with them but slept in a separate room) was a replica of the village in which the daughter had been conceived and born. The villagers knew that late at night little people of clay, homunculi, were brought to life by supernatural power and moved through the clay village in each drawer to entertain the lonely daughter it belonged to.

One day the boy, who was not from this valley but knew its story, found the smallest and prettiest of the daughters and stood before her, big and gangly in his dark suit, his skin on fire from self-consciousness. She was, he saw, as scared as he was.

"Are you my father?" she asked.

"No," he answered. "I am a boy."

She nodded, smiled a little, and let him take her in his arms, dancing her across the cobbles of the village square to music that came not from guitars or other instruments, but from the throats of the villagers as they stood and watched and began to hum, the sound soon filling the valley like the voice of God.

Before long every daughter was dancing and the clock stopped its ticking.

When strains of 1950s songs like "Diana" and "Heavenly Shades of Night" and "Candy Man" and all the others reached the boy from the *lido*, that outdoor dance floor in the cove far below his bedroom window, he would lie in bed thinking of the boys and girls—a few years older than he and flirting in another language—dancing. He would not get up. He would not turn on a light. He would listen to the songs until he fell asleep. As he slept he dreamed long, adventurous dreams of strange places, heroes and creatures worthy of legends, but also shorter dreams about hills covered with vipers and funerals of his relatives and a little boat in a storm, sinking, and it was these shorter dreams that came true. Why they did, he didn't know. It made no sense, but what did in life anyway? The longer dreams became stories which he wrote in longhand and kept secret from his parents in the drawer right below the seven daughters, which he also kept secret.

The ones that came true he never wrote down. It frightened him to do so. When he woke from his dreams, he would go to school with his friends from the village, or go down to the wharf by himself to find seashells among the colorful fish in the nets, or walk along the dirt road that led from his house past the walls with their brave green lizards to the Hotel Byron. One day his parents said it: "That hotel is too new. It *couldn't* be where they lived." "Who?" the boy asked. "Mary Shelley and her husband Percy," they answered. "The woman who wrote that book. The one about the monster. *Frankenstein.*" Not long after he would learn from someone that Percy, her husband, the poet, had drowned one stormy night in his little boat as he made his way from Viareggio up the coast back to this very village.

When the boy was back in his own country and the dreams—the ones that came true—had stopped, and he no longer wrote stories or made things of clay to put in drawers, he learned that that woman, Mary, had dreamed her dream—the one that had become her sad and terrible book—in that little fishing village, too.

Often, years later, when he was a man and had a wife and children, he would try to remember what had happened to the drawer and its mountains, valley, villages and people of clay. "The Seven Daughters of Satan," he had called it. This he could remember, but he could not remember what had happened to that clay. Did it matter? Weren't people—your wife, your children—what mattered? Then one night, as he lay beside his wife, she put her arm over him and whispered in the dark, *"Thank you for setting us free,"* and he knew which story it was and how there would never be anything as real (because love is what makes things real) as this.

Life in Stone

~~~~~

Tim Pratt

Tim Pratt (www.sff.net/people/timpratt/) lives in Oakland, California. He is an associate editor and book reviewer at Locus *magazine. He also creates chapbooks with fiancee Heather Shaw (see www.tropismpress.com), and co-edits a'zine with Heather,* Flytrap, *which he says fulfills his occasional urge to read slush and his more frequent desire to do layout. He has only been publishing for a few years, starting in 1999 in the small press and online, but is building an impressive body of short fantasy fiction. He published eleven stories in 2002, and fifteen in 2003. His fiction and poetry have appeared in* The Year's Best Fantasy and Horror, Strange Horizons, Realms of Fantasy, Asimov's, Lady Churchill's Rosebud Wristlet, *and* Year's Best Fantasy. *His first novel,* The Strange Adventures of Rangergirl, *is publishing in 2005. Some of his short fiction is collected in* Little Gods (2003).*

"Life in Stone" appeared in the online magazine Lenox Avenge *(www.lenoxavemag.com/lenoxavemag/issue3stone. htm). It is a fantasy adventure about immortality, filled with color and action, and even Lovecraftian echoes, guardians with tentacles. Mr. Zealand is an assassin hired to kill the immortal Archibald Grace. It's just a job—but like no other. Pratt's story is a deconstruction of this kind of fantasy as well as an example of it.*

After ascending seventy-two flights of iron stairs, creeping past tentacled sentinels lurking in pools filled with black water, and silently dispatching wizened old warriors armed with glaives and morningstars that proved a close match for his pistols and poisoned glass knives, Mr. Zealand at last stumbled into the uppermost room of Archibald Grace's invisible tower. All Zealand's earlier murders were mere journeyman work compared to this final assassination, the murder of a man who'd lived for untold centuries, who'd come to America and enslaved Buffalo spirits, who'd built this tower of ice and iron on the far side of the Rockies as a sanctuary and stronghold for his own precious life.

Zealand rested for a moment, catching his breath. He got winded so much more easily now than he had as a young man, and he didn't sleep well anymore, which made him jangly all day, most days. He leaned against a filigreed pillar of white ivory, a tusk or bone cut from some prehistoric—possibly even ahistorical—leviathan. Archibald Grace had doubtless slain whatever monster this ivory came from. He was a killer of such stature that even Zealand found himself humbled. Grace had murdered monsters, while Zealand had seldom killed anything but men. He ran his hand along the spiraled carving on the pillar, one of a dozen in the round tower room, and then he walked to the arched, open window. He looked down from the tower's lunatic height onto the small town of Cincaguas, just another little place in the valley, whose inhabitants were unaware of the magical edifice rising on the outskirts of town, an invisible spire so high that Zealand could look down on a slowly gliding California condor.

Having regained his breath, Zealand turned to face the center of the room. He unzipped his black canvas shoulder pack and reached inside to touch the haft of a stone-headed axe, an ancient implement fitted onto an unbreakable carbon-steel handle. Zealand approached the center of the room, passing the pillars, and saw what he'd been led to expect—a square box, two feet to a side, resting on an ivory pedestal. The box was a simple thing, made of aged wood worn so smooth that the grain was nearly invisible. Zealand drew one of his remaining knives, this one made of ceramic, and used the blade to pry open and lift the lid.

The box was empty. Zealand stared at the space inside for a long time, going so far as to probe the inner edges with his knife, looking for a false bottom, but there was no such concealment. The stone simply wasn't there. Despite all the effort he'd spent making his way to the top of this edifice, there would be no reward. He'd learned long ago that mere effort didn't guarantee success, but this was an especially bitter reminder of that fact.

Zealand sank to the floor, sitting cross-legged, resting his head in his hands. He was too old for this by at least a dozen years. In his younger, hungrier days, such a setback would only have infuriated and energized him, given him an adrenal surge and a slow-burning determination to soldier on, but he'd long since grown out of such dedication to his work for its own sake. For many years he'd crafted an image of himself as an implacable nightstalker, relentless avatar of death, and he'd seen his work as a sort of nightmarish inversion of a holy mission.

But he'd just turned forty-five, he suffered chronic lower back pain, he found it increasingly embarrassing to sleep with prostitutes less than half his age, and he'd spent the past dozen birthdays and New Year's Eves alone in his home amid the redwoods above Santa Cruz, California. He'd lost all illusions about his career. He was neither avenging angel nor cinematic assassin; he was simply a man who'd spent a lot of years killing people for money. This job was more of the same, despite certain baroque complications and supernatural curlicues.

Though there was the promise of something more than money as payment if he succeeded in taking Archibald Grace's life.

Zealand got to his feet. No use mourning the moment of failure. Better to push himself, weary or not, onward to the possibility of success. He reloaded his pistols and redistributed his knives. Now he had to make his way back down to the foot of the tower. Maybe the guards wouldn't harry him so, if he was only trying to leave. He could hope for that much.

The next day Zealand met his client, the thus-far-immortal Archibald Grace himself. They shared their usual booth at their usual Italian restaurant, Grace drinking cheap house wine, Zealand sticking to water.

"Damn," Grace said. "I thought for sure I'd left it there." Grace looked like a young man, with a neat black beard and eyes the clear blue of synthetic sapphires.

"You were sure you'd left it in Mammoth Caves, too," Zealand said with practiced patience. "Sure you'd left it in the Great Sequoia Forest, certain it was in your old summer palace at the bottom of Lake Champlain, and positive it was hidden behind Niagara Falls. I am beginning to suspect you need a tutorial in the proper meaning of the words 'sure,' 'certain,' and 'positive.'"

"I am sorry," Grace said, looking into his wine. "You can have ownership of the tower, of course, as usual."

"Oh, good," Zealand said. "It will go nicely with the mud-slimed cave full of ghosts behind Niagara, and the sinkhole decorated with obscene pictographs in Mammoth Caves. Though I admit the palace in Champlain is nice. If it weren't also the den of an aquatic monster, I might even go back there. I'd like the tower better if it weren't full of homicidal beasts and your wizened homunculi."

"There's a phrase, to stop them from attacking you," Grace said, making a familiar grasping motion with his left hand. "But I've forgotten it. I've forgotten so many things." He still stared into his wine, as if he might find his missing memories at the bottom of the glass.

Zealand, who was not a man given to casual gestures of

physical affection, reached across to touch Grace's hand. "Don't worry," he said. "I'll find your life, and I will crush it. You will die."

"I'm sure it's in North America," Grace said. "I moved everything with me when I came here. I came with the . . ." He made the grasping motion again.

"The Vikings," Zealand said, sitting back. "On the long-boats. You've told me."

"I brought my life, my soul, hidden in a stone. Or, perhaps, an egg." Grace cupped his hands around a half-remembered roundness. "All the wizards and witches and giants and monsters knew the trick, to put your life somewhere safe, so your body couldn't be killed. So long as your life is safe, you live. We used to hide our souls in tree trunks, until the witch hunters began putting whole forests to the torch. As the trees burned, the souls burned, and sorcerers screamed across the continent." He clucked his tongue. "Then, for a time, it was fashionable to hide your life in the head of a toad, but toads are stupid, and often get eaten, or die. I was always smart. I hid my life well."

"I know," Zealand said.

"But I've forgotten where I put it." Grace looked up from his wine, into Zealand's face, and for a moment it was clear he'd forgotten who Zealand was. "I've forgotten so many things. It's hard to know which things are worth remembering, when you don't have a soul."

"I know," Zealand said again.

"I used to be a giant." Grace looked wistful. "Before I was a man. I broke the spines of mammoths in my hands. But I've forgotten how to be a giant, and I don't want to be a man. I only want to die."

"I know," Zealand said, for the third time. Three times was usually enough to make Grace stop going over the usual elusive reminiscences again. "Where should I look next, do you think?"

"Look for what?" Grace said, blinking his beautiful eyes.

"Come, then," Zealand said. "I'll take you home."

* * *

Some weeks later, after another pair of fruitless searches for Grace's life, Zealand crunched through the snow-covered sand on the shore of Lake Tahoe. The water was still and blue, and though there was no wind, the cold was bitter and penetrating, making the inside of Zealand's nose burn with every breath. A woman stood on the edge of the water, a long black scarf hanging motionless down her back, her thick down coat the red of arterial spurt.

"Are you Hannah?" Zealand asked.

She turned, the lower half of her face covered by the scarf. "Mr. Zed?" she said, her accent British and precise. Her eyes were the color of the water, almost the color of Archibald Grace's own, which made sense, as Hannah claimed to be Grace's daughter. When she'd first contacted him, Zealand had been suspicious, partly because Grace's apparent sexual preference made the presence of offspring rather unlikely, but upon further consideration it was understandable that someone as old as Grace would have tried various partners and sexual permutations, probably many times over. Hannah had known things about Grace that Grace barely remembered about himself, and Zealand was reasonably certain her claim was true.

"You told me you know the whereabouts of your father's life," Zealand said. He was still fascinated by her eyes, so like Grace's.

"I do. I'll take you there, but you have to do something for me first."

"I'm not prepared to wait," Zealand said. His tone was polite, but the menace was implicit.

She laughed, harsh and hyena-like, quite unlike her urbane voice. "Father has lived for epochs. Another day or two won't matter."

"Nevertheless, I want you to tell me now."

She pulled the scarf down. Below the eyes, her face was inhuman, with two holes covered by membranous flaps where her nose should have been. Her mouth was lipless, filled by a score of two-inch-long interlocking incisors. She resembled nothing so much as a deep-sea fish, one of those horrors fishermen occasionally pulled up in their nets, and

Zealand recalled Grace's claim to have spent years living beneath the sea. When Hannah spoke again, her mouth did not open, and Zealand realized that her human voice was a magical contrivance, not something born of her own vocal cords at all. "My father is almost a god, and my mother was the mistress of black oceanic caves. I will decide where we go, and when."

Zealand drew a pistol and fired a shot, blowing off Hannah's right knee. She screamed, this time opening her mouth, and it was an inhuman, gurgling sound. She fell to the sand, throwing her head back into the snow, her monstrous teeth spreading apart, her long tongue lolling out as she shrieked. She had a bioluminescent bulb on the end of her tongue, glowing a sick yellow.

Zealand put his gun away, wondering if he'd made his point sufficiently. Hannah had stopped screaming, so perhaps not. Feeling himself cloaked in a kind of prevailing numbness, what he had long thought of as his "working state," Zealand put one heavy boot down on Hannah's right thigh, just above her destroyed knee, then bent over to grasp her ankle in both hands. He wrenched her leg upward, grunting and twisting, pulling on her ankle while pressing down on the thigh with his foot, until her lower leg came free with a sickening pop. Hannah lashed and flailed at him, but the pain made her imprecise. Zealand noted with interest that she didn't bleed, though the wound seeped clear water. He hurled her lower leg into the lake, then stepped away from her thrashing limbs. "I hope you're part starfish, or that leg might be gone forever. You'll tell me where to find your father's life now."

Tears ran from Hannah's eyes. Her screams had subsided to whimpers, and the whimpering didn't stop when she spoke in her magical human voice—both sounds emerged simultaneously. "I only wanted to see my father again. I wanted you to take me to him. I've hated him for too long, hated him for his essential nature, and I wanted him to know that I forgave him, if he would forgive me." Despite her obvious agony, her voice remained clear and barely modulated.

"Your father has something like Alzheimer's, but more profound. He doesn't even remember your existence." Zealand had asked Grace if he knew anyone named Hannah, and Grace had given him that blank, desperate look and grasped at the air, but that was all. He'd been quiet and morose for hours after Zealand asked him, though, and Zealand suspected that Hannah's name had set up unpleasant resonances deep inside Grace, below his conscious mind. "But since he doesn't remember you, it means he doesn't hold a grudge for whatever drove the two of you apart, if that's any comfort."

"His mind is gone?"

"Not entirely, but it is degrading more every day. I think it comes from having lived so long without his soul."

"You intend to restore his soul to him?"

Zealand shook his head.

Hannah stared up at him, her monstrous jaw clenched. "Then you will kill him, destroy his life?"

"It's what he wants. It's why he hired me." Zealand gestured with a gloved hand. "You've exhausted my patience once already. Are you trying to do so again? Direct me to your father's life."

"I have to show you."

Zealand sighed. He trudged up the shore to his car and returned with his tool bag. He withdrew a pair of bolt cutters and snapped off Hannah's teeth, one at a time.

Then he flipped her over onto her stomach and bound her hands behind her with thick plastic loops that tightened with a tug. He picked her up over his shoulder and carried her, his knees creaking under the combined weight of Hannah and his tool bag; at least she didn't thrash. He was breathing hard by the time they reached his car, an SUV rented under a false name. He put her in the passenger seat, and, after a moment's thought, pulled the scarf back up over the lower half of her face. Looking at her broken teeth and glowing tongue made him feel uncomfortable, and a little guilty, the latter an emotion that had plagued him more and more in recent years. His "working state" was already fading, and the emotions that replaced it were not welcome.

After he got into the driver's seat Zealand said, "Guide me."

Zealand crouched on the edge of a creek in a wilderness area in the mountains above the lake. Hannah lay on her side in the snow nearby. Zealand was exhausted. He'd carried her nearly two miles from the trailhead, most of that well off the path, falling twice when the treacherous snow and ice gave way beneath his footsteps. His knees ached, and his feet were numb inside his boots, but he'd made it. Hannah had led him to a pretty place of tall pines, cracked gray rock faces, and a rushing mountain stream.

"It's filled with rocks," Zealand said, staring down at the bottom of the wide, swiftly flowing stream.

"It's white, speckled with red, egg-shaped, almost as big as your fist," Hannah said.

Zealand saw the stone, half-buried among water-smoothed rocks. He pulled off his glove, pushed up his sleeve, and plunged his hand into the water. It was deeper than it seemed, and he had to submerge his arm past the elbow before he could reach the stone. He grasped it and pulled it out of the water. Zealand's whole arm was numbed by cold, and he thought briefly how nice it would be to feel that way all over, inside and out, just cold and aching nothingness, the way he felt on a job, but forever. He couldn't even feel the texture of the stone in his hand, just the weight, which was greater than he would have expected.

He held Archibald Grace's life in his hand.

Dropping the stone into his coat pocket, he walked to where Hannah lay in the snow. "Thank you," he said. "Would you like me to kill you now? I can be quick."

"No!" Hannah shouted, her eyes wide.

"Your wounds are grievous," Zealand said.

"I'll heal."

Zealand looked down at her for a moment, then nodded. He thought she probably would. She was Grace's daughter. He squatted on his heels in the snow. "Tell me, before I decide what to do with you, how did you find Grace's life?"

"It was in his tower, at Cincaguas. I used to play there, as a child—there's a room that opens onto the ocean, onto the caves where I was born, so I could travel freely between them. I went to the tower last year, and father hadn't changed the pass phrase, so the guards let me through."

Zealand interrupted her. "The pass phrase? What is it?"

Hannah hesitated, then said four syllables in a language Zealand did not recognize. He committed the sounds to memory. "Go on," he said. "Why did you take his soul?"

"I thought I could make my father talk to me if I had his life, that I could use the stone as leverage. But I couldn't even *find* him. Then I heard you were working for Father, that you'd been seen around his old haunts, searching for his life. I didn't know he'd hired you to kill him, so I contacted you."

"I suppose you regret that now."

"I only regret not being able to talk to my father. I'd gladly give up a leg for that chance."

"Life is disappointment," Zealand said, and he'd never meant any three words so completely. He pondered the possibility of mercy. "I can throw you into the stream," he said, "or I can leave you for the coyotes."

"Stream," she said, without hesitation.

"And if I let you live today, will you come for me later, and try to kill me?"

"Never."

"Liar," Zealand said, almost appreciatively. He picked her up by her one good leg and the straps that bound her wrists, swung her a few times, and tossed her into the stream. He stood in the snow long enough to watch her wriggle away, eel-like, and disappear over the falls, flowing back down toward the lake.

Zealand kissed Grace just behind his left ear, and Grace moaned and moved his body back against him.

"I found your life yesterday," Zealand said. "Not forty miles from here."

Grace went stiff in Zealand's arms. They lay together in a wide, soft bed, mountain morning light filling the window and the room. "And now you want to use it to control me," Grace said, his voice heavy with disappointment, but not surprise.

Zealand put his hand on Grace's slim, bare thigh. "No," he said. "I just wanted to spend one more night with you, before smashing your soul apart."

Grace relaxed. "Good. That's good. I've lived for eons. Another day doesn't matter much."

Zealand shifted uncomfortably at this echo of Hannah's words. He shouldn't have treated her with such brutality. He was tired of doing things he regretted, tired of feeling ashamed, tired of bad dreams. How nice it would be to become immortal, and let his regrets drain away, or freeze over.

Apropos of nothing obvious, Grace said, "It's easier to be a sorcerer when you don't have a soul. It's easier to do the awful things you have to do, when you know the true sensation and emotion will be forgotten in the aftermath."

Not for the first time, Zealand wondered if Grace could overhear his thoughts. "How does it feel?" he asked. "Putting your soul aside?" It was an important question, and one he hadn't asked before.

"It's been so long since I had my soul, I don't recall the difference." Grace rolled away and sat on the edge of the bed. Zealand looked at the muscles in his unblemished back. "Fear is the first to go, which is liberating. Then other feelings fade. Your memories go, but it's the bad memories first, so it seems a boon. Finally the conscious will to live erodes, and you become like a moss or a lichen, living for the sake of mere existence. But you retain your mind, and so there is some dissatisfaction, some sense of . . ." He grasped at the air. "Eventually, you long for death."

"Do you wish to die, even when you're with me?" Zealand said.

Grace shrugged. "Perhaps moss enjoys the sensation of falling rain, or the warmth of sunlight. But that's not meaning. It's just pleasure." Without turning around, he said,

"Do you still want your payment for killing me? Do you still want me to show you how to be immortal?"

Zealand didn't answer. It had seemed obvious, before. An immortal life, free from self-doubt, self-loathing, and fear—of course he wanted that. He touched Grace's back. Despite their time embracing, Grace's skin was cool, almost cold.

Zealand didn't answer Grace's question, and after a while, Grace forgot he'd asked, and went into the kitchen to get a piece of fruit.

After they made love a final time, after Grace taught Zealand the trick of putting his soul aside, they went out onto the deck that jutted over the cold blue vastness of Lake Tahoe. Here on the northern shore houses were fewer and farther apart than on the more tourist-friendly south shore, and they had a clear view of snowy mountains and evergreens. The brisk air made standing on the deck a bracing experience, and Zealand slit his eyes against the lake wind. He placed the spotted stone that held Grace's life on the redwood deck railing. Grace didn't seem interested in it; he just gazed, wide-eyed, at the mountains, as if seeing them for the first time. "Go ahead," he said. "I'm ready."

Zealand raised the old stone axe with its unbreakable handle. He thought about touching Grace, or kissing him, but the time for that had passed, and hesitation would only make this harder. He brought down the axe, and shattered Grace's life.

The spotted rock burst apart, and light the color of Grace's eyes shone forth, blazing so brightly that even when Zealand squeezed his eyes shut, he saw blue. After a moment the light faded, and Zealand opened his eyes.

Grace sagged against the railing, his whole body trembling, and when he spoke, his words were choked by sobs. "I have a daughter," he said, and then began pounding his head against the deck railing, slamming his forehead down so hard that the wood audibly cracked. Grace looked up at Zealand, his forehead gashed, blood running into his eyes, and screamed, "Finish it! Kill the body!"

Zealand lifted the axe again and brought it down between Grace's eyes. The man's forehead caved in, and the axe stuck there, embedded in Grace's skull, trapped fast in bone as old as the mountains. Grace fell back on the deck, dead.

Zealand went inside for the tarps and the chains he'd need to sink Grace to the lake bottom. His hands trembled as he wrapped Grace in the heavy plastic. The dead man had shaped nations, seduced monsters, and lived to the outer extremes of experience, but he'd died like anyone, like so many others at Zealand's hands—messily, and speaking only of regrets.

Zealand sat by Grace's corpse, holding the dead man's hand for a while, and contemplated the nature of immortality.

Zealand sat in the upper room of the tower at Cincaguas, holding an oblong piece of shaped marble in his hand. The stone was prepared according to Grace's instructions, as a receptacle for Zealand's life, and he could never make another—this was one-time magic, once and forever magic. Zealand heard the distant scrape and clang of weapons on the lower floors. He'd claimed possession of the tower with the pass phrase he'd learned from Hannah, and then he'd changed the phrase to one only he knew. But the guards were old, and Hannah knew her way around, so he was not surprised to see her limp in through the arched doorway. She apparently did have some starfish in her ancestry, because her leg had grown back, though it was knotty as coral, and a bit shorter than the other leg. She wore the slashed remains of a dark blue wetsuit, and she bled water from the wounds the guards had inflicted. Her teeth had grown back, too, though they curved off at strange angles, and some of them cut her face when she closed her mouth.

"You killed my father," she said, her voice emerging from the air before her, a calm statement of fact.

"He wanted me to," Zealand said. He didn't stand up.

"I don't care. Because of you, I never had a chance to talk to him, and make things right between us."

Zealand rolled the marble egg between his palms. "He mentioned you in his last words. He said he had a daughter, and I've never heard such anguish."

"He remembered me?"

"He remembered everything, and I think he wanted to die even more once he did."

"I came here to kill you," Hannah said, but she didn't come any closer.

"I thought you might." He held up the stone, so she could see it. "I've been up here for weeks, trying to decide if I should put my life in this rock. I've never been an indecisive person, but I've been balanced on the edge over this." He glanced up at her, then away, and said, "I'm sorry for the way I hurt you." He set the egg on the stone floor.

Hannah sat down beside him. She smelled strongly of salt water. "My father never told me he was sorry for anything."

"He wasn't capable of being sorry, not while his soul was put aside."

"I'm sure that made his life easier."

"Mmm," Zealand said. "Are you still going to kill me?"

"Perhaps. Did you love my father?"

"As well as I was able. But I may as well have loved a cloud, or the stars, for all the feeling was returned."

"I know how that feels." She picked up the marble egg. "I don't think I'll kill you. Not just now."

"I almost want you to. It would take the decision out of my hands. I wish I knew where to go from here."

She laughed, that harsh hyena sound, and Zealand realized that her laughter, unlike her voice, came from her own throat. "No one knows that." She put the marble egg back in Zealand's hand. "Not even my father knew where to go next. He just knew he was going to keep going on forever. Until you helped him find forever's end."

Zealand nodded. He stood and walked to the tower window, and looked down at the earth, far below. Hannah came and stood beside him.

"It's a long way down," Zealand said.

"Looked at another way," Hannah said, "we've come a long way *up*."

Zealand squeezed the stone in his hand. It was cold, and hard, and didn't yield at all under the pressure of his hand. He thought about irrevocable decisions.

Zealand dropped the marble egg out the window, and Hannah stood beside him as they watched it fall.

Many Voices

M. Rickert

*Mary Rickert lives in Saratoga Springs, New York. She
came to publish in the fantasy field by a circuitous route. In
an interview she says, "I was writing these weird little stories for years. The response I got for them was generally
something like, 'This is good but I don't know who would
publish such a thing.' My experience, from submitting to
small journals, was that no one did. . . . Eventually, I came
across the volumes of* The Year's Best Fantasy and Horror,
*edited by Ellen Datlow and Terri Windling. It was through
these volumes that I discovered there was a whole community of writers and readers interested in the kind of stories I
was interested in." Her short fiction has appeared often recently in* F&SF, *and last year in both our* Year's Best SF
and Year's Best Fantasy *volumes. We see her fantasy as
somewhere in the range of Kit Reed's and Shirley Jackson's
work. It could easily be mistaken for good literature.*

"Many Voices" appeared in F&SF. *It is a tale of fantasy
and escape which calls to mind C.S. Lewis's famous remark about the term escape being a pejorative only to jail-
ers. Rose sees auras revealing fates and also talks to angels.
Or perhaps she is crazy. She is on the night shift, left in
charge of thirty-eight mental patients. One dies. It seems to
us that this story ventures into Philip K. Dick territory.*

There are many kinds of prisons, and mine is not the worst one. I leave it in my sleep anyway, along with that body prison in repose, and travel the starry way to my garden, which even in closed blossom smells so sweet I cannot help but sigh. With ethereal fingers I commence weeding, hence my garden's reputation for being both beautiful and haunted. But I am not a ghost. I return to my body with clang of gate and prison noise, the shouts of women abandoned to this fate by a world of men, mostly men, who cannot accept our witchy ways, we who would direct our own fate, who have saved ourselves the best we can, only to be confined to the cuss and piss of this ugly place. I wake weary from my work. When I open my fist nothing is there. My palm reveals only the tremble of my faith.

"You are delusional," Laura said. "I want you to try to understand that."

"Your whole body is made of space," I said, "You are a solar system."

"Mental illness is nothing to be ashamed of. You, of all people, should know that."

"No."

"It's your best defense."

"Do what you want, it won't change anything."

Laura, with her red-gold hair that will not be tamed, though she tries valiantly, and so has a bubble of curls around her neatly made-up face. I stare at her until she looks away. She is twenty-six and I am her first big case. Huge. She will lose. It isn't really my neck she's worried about. Poor thing in her little blue suit, the beating of her heart in the pulse at her throat, like a sparrow.

"Hey Rose," Thalia whispers, "I got a friend. She got a problem."

"What sort of problem?"

"Like, is it true? What they say about you?"

"Some. Some not."

"She ass me to ass you if you could help."

"Not if she's afraid of me."

"Oh, it ain't against you personal, you know, it's just the way she is. She thinks you seem real nice though and not at all like the newspapers said you was."

"Thalia, I don't have much tolerance for bullshit."

"What?"

"Just say what you've got to say, all right?"

"It's her babies."

"Okay?"

"She killed them."

"What do you want?"

"She wants them back."

"Well, they already are back."

"What the fuck?"

"They're someone else's babies now."

"Bitch. Crazy white bitch."

" 'Course she's just a bitch," the new girl says and leans over to spit on me.

"Shut the fuck up," Marlo shouts, "I'm trying to watch this."

"Cunt," the new girl whispers.

A room full of women, a coven of sorts.

"Hey. I don't want you looking at me."

"Will you shut the fuck up?"

"She's throwing a hex."

"She ain't throwing a hex. It's just like they said. She's just crazy."

"Shut up! Shut up! Shut up!"

A storm of fists, and shouting. Guards come into the room and pull us apart. Thalia points at me. "It's all her fault. She put a hex on us."

"Shut the fuck up," says the guard. "Crazy witch."

I knew the jury would find me guilty even before they did. I could see it in the light around their bodies and what happened with it when they sat close together. I closed my eyes and the light around my body mingled with theirs.

Laura kept trying to get them to say I am crazy which tells you how well she understood what was going on. But they weren't buying it. They said I am a sane woman and knew exactly what I was doing, which is my personal victory.

"I refuse to take the blame for this," Laura said through clenched teeth and a sympathetic demeanor, her hand gently rubbing my back as she polled the jury. Each face, each parting mouth, each water soul dissolving said it, "Guilty. Guilty. Guilty."

I couldn't stop smiling.

"Rose, do you understand what is happening?"

The light around her body tells me she is tired and there is a black hole around the area of her throat. I have repeatedly warned her of this problem and she simply ignores me. There is nothing I can do in cases like these except love. I send love light to her through my forehead and heart and it makes a triangle, which closes the black hole but this is, of course, temporary, and she says, "Rose?"

"They say I'm sane."

"You're going to prison, Rose."

JOAN OF ARC KILLER FOUND GUILTY

"Her angels can go there with her," said Frank Wakind, husband of the victim.

Dear Rose,

Your father and me are sorry we could not be there for you at the trial. As you know we are having a hard enough time as it is so we couldn't just take off after you out there and leave everything to go to weed. We did talk to that man your lawyer sent down and told him all we could remember about your condition. He agreed with what your father been saying all along about the state of your mind and when he said that your father left the room and got back to plowing which as you know is his way of saying prayers and thanking Jesus for the truth about

you which you hated him for but now you see how
he was right all along and maybe you can begin for-
giving and I can finally have some peace because as
you know the truth shall set you free. Oh I almost
forgot to tell you I saw Catherine Shelby at the A and
P and she told me to tell you she prays for you but
now you gotta start praying to God and forget all
this other stuff and remember God loves you and I
do and so does your father and he loves you very
much dear.

When I think of you as a little girl I try to point to
when it happened and I remember that tragedy with
that boy and maybe I should of done something bet-
ter for you but your father says there is only one
place to fix the blame and mostly I think he is right
'cause you killed that lady. Oh, my little girl, you
need to stop this nonsense about angels because you
are not a saint my dear but a big sinner. I'm checking
bus schedules and will try to see you in October.

Love,
Your mother

The little girl in the apple orchard has red hair and that is
why her parents named her Rose and simply abandoned the
chosen name of Elinor when they adopted her already almost two years old and carrying a fancy store-bought baby
quilt that neither parent asked about or saved though Rose
has memorized each picture that contains it until she can
close her eyes and see the red-haired woman who bought it.
There are only six apple trees. Technically it is not an orchard but that is what everyone calls it. Rose calls it an orchard too but she also calls each tree by its name, which she
has learned through careful listening. It is in the spring of
her eighth year that the first angel appears to her, glorious
in her body of bright, beautiful in her wings. She appears to
Rose in her bedroom, murmuring things an eight-year-old
girl couldn't possibly understand. In later years angels will
appear to Rose anywhere, the kitchen, the bathroom,

school, the park, the grocery store, but in those first years they only appear in the bedroom and the apple orchard.

Sometimes her mother watches from the kitchen window or the distant field and the angels tell Rose to wave. Her father doesn't look at her most of the time. The angels try to shield her when he does, but when it comes right down to it there is little they can do with their amorphous wings against the awesome fact of his body. At the supper table he looks at his meatloaf and says, "How old're you now?"

The day she tells him she's ten, he says, "You'll come with us tomorrow and pick stones."

She knows better than to argue. She wakes in the dark. Goes to the orchard and tells the trees of her great love. A dozen angels circle her and take turns telling her her own life story, which makes her weep.

"But we'll always be with you," they say, their voices like bees.

That day Rose picks stones in the fields with her mother and a couple boys from the high school. The stones are rough and sharp. Some are heavy. Some are light. Her fingers hurt and the palm of her hand hurts and then her back hurts and her neck and the Sun is so hot, the straw hat little help, and besides, it itches. In the distance she can see the orchard, lonely without her.

She and her mother leave the men to make lunch. They make cheese sandwiches and ice tea.

"With the extra hands it's all getting done so quick," says her mother.

Rose looks at her hands. They don't belong to her anymore. They look like claws.

"Your father and the boys won't be in for another half hour."

Rose, who has already begun to see and understand things no one else does, will always be somewhat dense about understanding and seeing herself in the world.

"I wouldn't mind if you was to take a little break."

She loves her mother. She loves her so much she gives her a big hug that fills the room with pink until her mother says, sadly, "Oh Rose," and then she lets go and races out of the house. The screen door slams shut behind her and the chickens squawk and she runs to the orchard suddenly filled with light. She hugs all her friends. The angels stand at the edge of branches and pretend to fall off, only to swoop up at the last minute like owls diving for field mice, which is an old trick by now but still makes Rose gasp and then laugh which she does until she hears the clang of the bell, and sees the dark silhouettes of her father and the boys in the field coming home. It is then she sees the shadow on the right, the taller one who walks like he's pushing against a heavy wind, fall to the ground, his whole body torn apart as if clawed by a great beast. She covers her eyes. When she takes her hands away she sees him clearly, a freckled young man with close-set eyes.

"It's beginning," the angels say.

Rose walks slowly to the house. The boys are hungry and gobble the sandwiches without saying much. In the silence she tries to choose the best words.

"Frank?" she says.

The boy turns to her, an astonished look on his face, as if he's only just discovered her presence at the table, or already fears the truth of what she's going to say.

The other boy, Eddie she thinks his name is, laughs as if there is something funny in her voice but no one else seems to hear it, and he swallows the laugh with another bite of his sandwich. She looks at him, and sees how the light around his body is all mixed up, wild colors and a heavy dose of gray that spiral and jag into him. She has seen this before on other teenagers.

She turns back to Frank. He looks at her with those blue eyes, his pale face only slightly pinked by a scattering of freckles like brown sugar. She knows he is not considered a handsome boy but the light around his body is beautiful, like the angels, though not so bright of course, and even as she looks at it, she can see how it is becoming part of the air around him as if he is melting.

"You gotta be careful for the next couple a months," she says.

He raises his eyebrows.

She knows the way it sounded like a threat and not a warning. Her father glares at her across the table and Eddie starts laughing again but this time he muffles it behind his hand and his shoulders shake.

She thinks maybe she should explain but under the weight of the room she weakens. She looks down at her plate and picks up a small dot of cheese. She can feel her father looking at her and Eddie laughing and her mother taking a deep breath. Only Frank seems unconcerned.

At the end of the summer he falls into the threshing machine. She can hear his screams all the way in the apple orchard. She knows her father and Eddie are with him. Her mother is running to the house. She lies on the grass and looks through the leaves at the small bitter apples. He doesn't scream for long. In the silence she hears sirens.

"I should of listened to you better, I guess."

She's afraid to look at him. But he looks all right. Not bleeding at all. He squats down beside her. "You ain't like the rest, you know."

"Neither are you," she says.

He laughs and rubs the top of her head. She feels it faintly, as if a gentle breeze moved there. For a moment he looks the way boys do in movies before they kiss the girl, nothing like her dad, but then he stands up real fast. She has to shield her eyes because he stands in front of the Sun. He looks toward the field and sighs. "My mom is gonna throw a fit."

"I'm sorry," Rose says.

He shrugs. Puts his hands in his pockets. "I gotta go see if I can find her."

Just like that he is gone. Her mother finds her asleep in the orchard. "Come in now for supper," she says. Rose doesn't mention the specks of blood on her mother's wrist and throat and her mother doesn't mention Rose's warning. Rose thinks maybe it is forgotten until Eddie stops showing up for work and her father can't find anyone to help.

"I just don't understand these boys," she hears her mother say one morning as they walk past her bedroom.

"It's that Eddie Bikwell. If this thing had to happen why couldn't it happen to him?"

"George!"

"He's told everyone she's a witch."

"Well, no one believes in such things no more."

Their voices fade down the stairs. Rose watches the Sun rise. When it does, she dresses and goes downstairs to make breakfast. She makes scrambled eggs and bacon and toast. Then she goes to the yard and rings the bell that brings her parents to the house. They come in smelling like hay and manure. Between chores and school she doesn't have time for the orchard anymore. The angels visit her at home. They tell her to be careful but she doesn't really understand. When her father asks her who she's talking to she tells him.

"We got ourselves someone else's problem," she hears him tell her mother one night.

"She's ours, George, sent to us by God."

"Maybe we weren't meant for no children. Maybe this is a curse."

"She loves you like you was her born daddy."

"I just sayin' maybe they should of warned us if there was something like this in her family."

"We're her family."

"I'm just saying."

Could you just tell me a little about your professional background?

Well, I graduated from Victory High in 1988 and went to the University of Wisconsin, Milwaukee. I graduated there in 1991 with a degree in psychology.

How did you manage that in three years?

I took a full load. I went to summer school. It wasn't so hard. I just stay focused.

So, why the big hurry to graduate?

It was an economic consideration mostly. I just figured if I could do it in three instead of four, well, that's one less year of student loans.

Is that when you started working at St. Luke's?

I started working there my first year in college and I stayed there.

Doing what?

Oh, at first I was little more than a candy striper. You know, sort of an aid to the doctors and the play-group therapist. I helped get patients to their appointments. Passed out magazines. Changed the TV channel, stuff like that.

Let me back up here a little. What kind of a place is St. Luke's?

A facility for the mentally ill.

A hospital?

Not exactly. The people there are, it's been determined, not in need of hospital care but do need some kind of institutional care.

Sort of like a halfway house?

Well, sort of. Only in a halfway house the expectation is that the people will move on. Become self-sufficient. St. Luke's wasn't like that. Some of the people have been there twenty, thirty years.

By "some of the people" do you mean the patients?

Yes.

So you worked at St. Luke's all the time you were in college?

Yes.

And did your job description change over time?

Well, as I said, I started out doing sort of general stuff and then I got more and more responsibilities.

Such as?

Dispensing medicine. Watching—

Excuse me. You say you didn't even have a bachelor's degree yet, but you were given the task of dispensing medicine?

It's not really that complicated.

What else?

I started working night shift and more and more I became the person in charge.

You mean you were in charge of all the other workers at your level?

No. I was in charge of the patients.

Where was the administration, the doctors?

They went home.

How many patients were there?

Thirty-eight.

What was the night duty, when you were in charge, like?

Mostly quiet. I mean once in a while there'd be a wan-
derer. The people there are heavily drugged. They go to
sleep okay, mostly.

So what happened that changed your relationship with
the patients?

You mean Mrs. Tate?

Tell us about that.

Mrs. Tate started wandering. She just couldn't get to
sleep. She became quite agitated. She came up to me and
asked me to help her.

And what did you do?

I helped her.

How?

Well, I could see right away what a mess was around her,
in her aura there were these two lost souls. One was okay,
just a little baby, but the other was evil, an evil spirit, and it
was all attached to her like glue, like she'd walked through
it and was all sticky.

How did this happen? In your opinion?

Mrs. Tate's been in and out of institutions for years. I figured somewhere along the way someone died and he or she,
you can't tell the sex usually at this stage, attached itself to
the first vulnerable one to come along. Mrs. Tate was it.

So, what did you do for Mrs. Tate?

It wasn't really that complicated. The first one was easy. I
just reached in and grabbed it and gave it to one of my angels.

Your angel?

Yes.

Please, continue.

Well, as I was saying, that one went fine. She immediately
felt somewhat better. I told her about the other one though,
that it would take more time.

You told Mrs. Tate her aura was, what would you say,
being haunted by an evil spirit?

Well, I'd say invaded, but basically, yes.

What, well, how did Mrs. Tate react to this?

She wasn't surprised, if that's what you mean. She said

she'd known for years and had just given up on trying to tell anyone 'cause no one believed her when she did.

How did you proceed?

I told her to stop taking the night cocktail.

The night cocktail?

The drugs they, I dispensed at night. It wasn't anything she needed. Just sleeping medicine that wasn't working anymore and it was creating all these holes in her aura that this thing had attached itself to.

Well, but don't they usually make patients take their drugs right there, show the under tongue thing?

Yeah, but I was mostly the one doing the dispensing by then.

Right. So are you saying you took her off her medication entirely?

No. She needed some stuff. I'm not anti-medicine, if that's what you think.

So what happened? With Mrs. Tate?

She came every night. Every night I got a little more of the stickiness out.

And how did you do this?

Sort of like a massage. Only I didn't touch her.

Would you call it Reiki, or healing hands?

Well, I wouldn't. It's sort of like that, only messier.

What was the eventual outcome of this treatment of Mrs. Tate?

She got better. I mean she still has some problems but she got so improved that she lives on her own now. She got a job. She's working on getting her GED. She sort of feels bad though. She's the one who told Eva Wakind about me.

Mrs. Tate feels bad about what happened to Eva?

She feels bad about what's happening to me. If Eva hadn't written that note everything would have just kept going the way it was.

To Dr. Rain, Birth hurts like it does, and I remember mine and how I didn't want a go out there but I couldn't stop it no way, though I tried to hold back from that light which burned my skin and I would

*say that the first ever violent thing that happened to
me was my birth and it just all got worse from there.
Fuck you for trying to make me live because it makes
you feel better. I already told you about my daddy
and how my mama didn't believe me and then I got
pregnant but that baby died when I had the abortion
which I had to do by myself since what was I suppose to do borrow money from my mom? Fuck you
for saving my life last time I tried. I been seeing
someone else and she tells me I am not a victim and
she says if I need to die to get a decent start maybe
that's what I should do. She understands how it is
with me. Finally she says it is time. I have to be self
aware else I'll come back like in some fucking mess
again, like I'll pick you as a mother or some shit like
that. All you want me to do is cut pictures out of
magazines and glue them on paper and shit and talk
about my problems and she don't know it yet but I
pick her. After I die I'm coming back as her baby.*

Eva

I know right away he is the one. How can such a beautiful thing come from such a horrible act? My angels tell me
I can choose a different path. I see them before me, like rays
of Sun, the different courses of my life. But she is trying to
come to me. How can I refuse? In this cold place of gates
and chains, all these angry women, she comes and the first
thing I do for her in this incarnation is accept her. How else
could it happen here? With love? He leads me down the
hall. He thinks I suspect nothing. We all know. The angels.
Half the women here. He is the one who is ignorant. He un-
locks the door. We walk into the room. He locks it. I hear
the zip, the slap of leather. "Come here, cunt," he says.
"Don't try to fight." I don't. I lie down. When he touches
me I feel his sad and ugly life. My angels stay with me. He
feels them too. I know he does. But he does it anyway.
Don't get me wrong. I weep. I grit my teeth. I want it to be

over. When it is, I am pregnant. She is not my victim. She is me, reborn.

Rose, who did this to you?

I'm glad you've come. I have something important to say.

I'm listening.

I can't get out of here.

I'm working on the appeal but, Jesus Christ, Rose, who are you protecting?

You want a feel her kicking? She's kicking right now.

Rose, who?

Sometimes I go to my garden and pick flower petals but when I wake up my fist is empty. It's like I wasn't even there.

Those are dreams, Rose.

So, I'm running out of time. I mean if I can't travel with a rose petal I can't possibly hope to travel out of here with her. It's just taking longer than I thought.

Fucking justice.

So here's the thing. I've chosen you.

Well, good, Rose, that's good. But you have to help me, Rose, you have to help me help you.

You don't understand. You're the one.

Rose, what are you talking about?

After she's born she's coming to live with you.

Rose, my God, Rose, that's very kind, really, it's an honor. But I'm gone twelve hours a day. I didn't even think you liked me.

I'm stuck like glue.

Rose, you're not making sense.

Have you taken care of that throat problem?

JOAN OF ARC KILLER HAS BABY

In a shocking twist to the sensational trial of former health care worker Rose Miller, found guilty of murdering Eva Wakind, a patient at St. Luke's Home for the Mentally Ill, under what she said was the instruction of angels' voices, recently gave birth to a baby girl. Prison officials refuse to comment on the pregnancy and birth. Miss Wakind's former attorney, Laura Fagele, has begun the process of becoming the infant's legal guardian. Numerous phone calls to Ms. Fagele's residence were not returned.

Night after night I travel the starry way watching my baby sleep. The room is blue sky and painted clouds, a store-bought quilt of summer flowers. It smells of baby diapers and powder and sweet. She has my red hair, something in the shape of her face comes from the guard, something in the nose or the cheek reminds me of Eva, all these aspects innocent in her, present before ruin.

I am slowly disappearing. No one seems to notice. Laura comes to visit. The hole at her throat is black and huge. It is eating her face. She keeps repeating herself, "Fucking justice," she says. The words break apart in the air and fall to the ground like broken glass.

"The system," I say.

She leans forward, her eyes dark-circled and earnest. She coughs. The angels buzz around us, so loud I can hardly hear myself think. "What about the system?" she says.

"I can't figure how to break out of it."

"You can't break out, Rose." She coughs again. "Do you hear me, Rose? Do you understand anything I'm telling you?"

I learned young how to rise above my bed and escape the body's system of skin and bones, vulnerable and brittle, innocent. What I have not been so successful at is how to escape its sorrow.

I travel to my garden and breathe in the heavy scent of closed blossoms, rub my hands across the flowers, brushing the heavy scent upward, hyacinth, rose, dahlia, the heavy fragrance of dirt. In the distance I hear the voices; girls' voices whispering, shouting, weeping, pleading, accompanied by the angels murmuring like bees.

I wake up to the bright light noise of metal and chains, a

laugh, sharp and abrupt. I open my fist; a tiny red rose petal trembles there. I let it fall. It spirals slowly to the ground and lies against the hard gray floor. Later, Thalia finds it. She fingers it gently, then, with a furtive glance, stuffs it into her pocket. She sees me watching but I don't say anything about it and neither does she.

A Hint of Jasmine

Richard Parks

Richard Parks (www.dm.net/~richard-parks/) lives in Clinton, Mississippi, with his wife and their three cats. In his day job he's a computer network administrator. He says "I had one early sale to Amazing SF *in 1980, but I didn't start selling regularly until 1993. Since then I've had stories in* Realms of Fantasy, Asimov's SF, SF Age, Weird Tales, Black Gate, Fantastic Stories, Lady Churchill's Rosebud Wristlet, *and several anthologies." His stories are generally told in a comfortable adult tone, without much overt drama, but with clarity and intensity, a pleasure to read. His first collection,* The Ogre's Wife: Fairy Tales for Grownups, *was a World Fantasy Award nominee in 2003. He is currently assembling a second. His story "A Place to Begin" appeared in our* Year's Best Fantasy 2.*

"A Hint of Jasmine" appeared in Asimov's, *where it seemed a bit out of place, but stood out as a pure fantasy in a generally SF magazine. It is about a haunted house and old southern mansion, and a man who specializes in ghosts, in a kind of ordinary, rational way. But the ghosts are very real.*

Water Oaks Plantation was ten miles north of Canemill on Route 501. Eli kept the sensic in its case, even after he'd turned down the long tree-lined driveway leading to the house.

The ghosts at Water Oaks should be easy enough to find.

Eli had requested all the general data he could, on both the Stockard family and the plantation, but the plantation's history during the War of Secession was a little sketchy.

Especially around the time of the Water Oaks Massacre.

As for the Massacre itself, Eli knew only what everyone else who had grown up near Canemill knew: the few slaves remaining at Water Oaks near war's end staged a revolt. The master of the plantation, Captain John Stockard, was a prisoner of war after the siege of Vicksburg and absent. Stockard's wife Elizabeth, aided by a single loyal servant and a pair of her husband's pistols, reputedly ended the revolt by the simple expedient of killing every single one of the remaining slaves. Captain Stockard returned home to find only his wife, his infant son, and the one servant. There was one marked grave for his daughter Margaret, killed in the revolt. All the slaves were buried somewhere on the grounds in a single pit.

Details were also sketchy as to how many slaves were in that pit. Estimates ran from five to fifty, though no one seriously believed the latter. There had been talk of an exhumation, inquests, but in the confusion after the war and in light of Elizabeth Stockard's deteriorating mental state, it had never happened. Even the location of the grave was lost. After that, the legends grew: books, stories, songs. No one celebrated, but everyone remembered—in Canemill, almost as a personal memory, passed along like all others of those times by people who were not there, and could not know, but would forever believe in their hearts that they *did* know.

There was a gravel parking lot with a few other cars. Guests at the B&B that Water Oaks now was, Eli assumed. He parked his rental and got his first good look at Water Oaks in nearly thirty years.

The house wasn't a grand Greek Revival town home like Stanton Hall or Rosalie in Natchez; it was the center of a working plantation and was built in the French plantation style. Smaller, by comparison, and a little more practical, but still big enough. Eli crossed the lot to the front porch, carrying the sensic in its case hanging from a strap around his shoulder.

The stout oak boards barely creaked as he walked across the porch. The ceiling of the porch was painted blue in the old belief that the color discouraged wasps and spiders. Perhaps it worked, for Eli didn't notice either. In fact, the house was in much better shape in all details than Eli remembered: the white paint was clearly fresh, a rotting finial over the doorway had been replaced with an exact copy of the original. The grounds were immaculate.

Elizabeth's put some money into this.

Eli frowned. The Bed-and-Breakfast market around Canemill might be steady, but it wasn't such to support this kind of investment. Eli wondered what that meant, if anything, other than his old classmate Elizabeth was clearly doing well for herself. She must have been, to be able to repurchase the ancestral home in the first place. The Stockards, like so many planter families, had been completely ruined in the war and had lost Water Oaks for land taxes soon after war's end. When Eli knew them, those remnants of the old aristocracy were living in a modest old Victorian home not too far from Eli's own house.

The entranceway was grand; one thing this plantation home had in common with the Greek Revival-style houses was the central hallway, running from one end of the house to the other, connecting the front door and the rear door. The staircase leading to the second floor was off to the side so as not to block the flow of air through the house; there was no air conditioning in those days, and the homes were built to maximize what air flow there was.

Eli stepped just inside the doorway, hesitated.

"One," he said softly.

"One what?"

A young woman sat at a massive desk just beside the stairway. Eli recognized her, though he'd never seen her before. Elizabeth's daughter, Mary. The resemblance was uncanny.

Eli hesitated. "Just counting chandeliers. How many are there?"

The woman smiled. "Seven. And no you weren't. You just walked through the little girl, didn't you?"

Eli just stared at the woman for a moment or two, but there was really no doubt in his mind. She knew. "I'm Eli Mothersbaugh from the bureau of bio-Remnant Reconciliation," he said finally. "I believe you're expecting me."

The young woman was, as Eli had surmised, Elizabeth's daughter. The resemblance was indeed striking—the same jet black hair, brown eyes. The same tall, graceful elegance. Eli suddenly felt very, very old.

He asked the logical question as she showed him to his room upstairs. "How long have you known about the ghosts?"

She smiled. Eli remembered that smile. "Since the day Mother and I moved into Water Oaks. The little girl was just the first."

Eli considered this. "Do you see her?"

Mary shook her head. "No . . . it's a feeling, really. I've heard it described as a 'cold spot,' but it's not really cold. It's tingly like cold, and a bit hazy when you're standing there as if you're looking at everything through a mist."

Eli knew the feeling. In fact, he was feeling it at that exact moment. "Two," he said.

"That would be Ruth Benning," Mary said.

"The original Elizabeth Stockard's servant," Eli said. "Who was with her at the time of the Massacre by all accounts."

Mary stopped at the upstairs landing, and turned to look at him. "You've done your homework."

"Of course. Not that I really had to, except for the finer details. When I was growing up, people talked about the Stockards of Water Oaks like it all happened yesterday."

"They still do," Mary said.

"Now let me ask you a question: if you can't see them, how do you know who they are?"

Mary sighed. "I don't know for certain. It's what I feel . . . rather like being in the same room with someone you know. I can't explain any better than that. Oh, I know it's all very unscientific compared to what you're used to."

Eli shook his head. "The remnant signatures are very individual, and someone who can sense them at all can usually tell at least a little about them. Would you like to see if you're right?"

Mary's eyes widened slightly. "Yes, I would. How?"

Eli unzipped the sensic case. "It may not work if the remnant is too mobile. Still, I gather she tends to hang about the stairway?"

"She's not *always* here," Mary confirmed. "But most of the time."

The sensic's display came up. Eli pointed the sensor and changed the display from charting to mapping. The lines of numbers reformed themselves into an image. It was a little faint, blurred like an old-fashioned photographic negative slightly out of focus, but clear enough. A small black woman stood about mid-way up the staircase, looking straight down the stairwell to the floor below. She wore a plain gingham dress, and her head was covered in a white *tignon*, the cloth wrapped and secured just so. Her age was hard to tell, but she was clearly ancient. Eli turned the display so that Mary could see.

"That's Ruth Benning, no doubt," she said. "I've seen the pictures. Wait . . . if this is just some sort of energy field, why are there clothes?"

"Good question. No one's really answered it yet, though there are theories." Eli started to expound on a couple of them, but a glance at Mary told him that her mind was elsewhere.

"Can . . . can you show me the others?" she asked.

Eli didn't ask what Mary meant about the others. He assumed there were more than two, and, in any case, preferred to do his own count. "Probably."

Mary looked pensive. "Does Ruth know we're here?"

Eli switched the display back to charting, looked closely at the numbers. "Hard to say . . ." He looked up, saw Mary watching him intently. *She wants the truth,* he thought. He had no way of knowing this for sure, unlike his first impression of a remnant, which was almost always verifiable with the sensic. The living were always harder to read.

"No, I don't think so," he said finally. "Here, look. . . ." He switched the display back. "See these numbers? She's just repeating a particular series of actions: the hesitation . . . the look down the stairwell. Then it starts again. She's what we call a repeater."

"Repeater?"

"A remnant caught in some sort of traumatic or deeply significant sequence of events. Now she's not much more than a recording, like a tape loop that just runs."

"Until when?"

"Indefinitely. Or until whatever's holding her here goes away."

Mary nodded. "I think that's where you come in."

"Is she why you called the bureau? It *was* you, wasn't it?"

Mary nodded again. "I discussed it with Mother first, of course. She wasn't too happy about it, but finally gave in."

"Have the guests been complaining?"

Mary laughed. "Most don't even notice, and the ones that do rather enjoy it, I think. Adds atmosphere to the place . . . not that it really needs any."

"Then what's the problem?"

"Three days ago *something* tried to push my mother down the stairs."

Eli frowned. "Who saw this?"

"I did. I was standing beside Mother when it happened. I heard something hit her, like a slap, and she almost went down head-first. If I hadn't been there to catch her . . . well, I'm afraid of what might have happened. Before you ask, no, I didn't sense anything besides Ruth."

Eli made a mental note. "Neither of you saw anything?"

"I didn't say that, Mr. Mothersbaugh," Mary demurred, "I don't know what my mother saw."

Eli thought there was something furtive about her expression that hadn't been there before. He also noticed that she hadn't really answered his question, but before he could say anything, Mary continued: "Mother's looking forward to seeing you again."

Eli resisted the urge to smile. *A bit transparent, Mary. Your mother knew I was alive, but that was about all.*

Eli shut down the sensic. He didn't count himself the sharpest tack in the box, but he knew when he was being distracted. But from what? "I'm looking forward to it, too. It's been a long time. Well then, if you'll finish showing me where I'm staying, I can get started."

Mary led the way and Eli followed. He didn't think too much of it at the time, but in the warm air there was the faintest scent of jasmine.

Supper was in the dining hall, and the management of Water Oaks had gone all out: fine bone china, crystal, silverware. Other legacy items abounded: A shoo-fly fan hung over the table with its cord leading to an empty corner, as if waiting for the young slave who operated it in the old days. There was an authentic flytrap on the sideboard, a contraption that looked like an inverted glass bowl with honey in a dish at the base and small holes for the flies to get in but not quite figure their way out, assuming they didn't drown in the honey. Eli looked at the abundance of forks and felt a little trapped himself.

The guests were a motley lot. Three older couples from Pennsylvania, apparently traveling together, a pair of painfully young newlyweds, a small group of Civil War reenactors from Jackson, and one well-dressed portly man with immaculate hair. It took Eli a moment, but there was no mistaking the man: Malachi Hollingsworth, senior Senator for the State of Mississippi, Minority Whip, and major reactionary, even by local standards.

Water Oaks is definitely attracting some interesting clients.

Hollingsworth gave him an icy smile that made Eli wonder if he had inadvertently offended the man. Eli looked for his own place and found himself at a position of honor near the head of the table. Mary appeared and sat opposite to Eli. Soon after that, Elizabeth Dunstan née Stockard finally arrived.

"Arrived" was actually a bit off the mark. It was closer to the truth to say that Elizabeth made an *entrance*. She wasn't so impractical as to wear a full hoopskirt in proper belle fashion, but the dress was full and red and would have been more appropriate for a night at the opera in the 1920s than at a modern dinner gathering. Still, Eli had to admit that as a bit of showmanship, it was very effective; there was even a burst of applause, which Eli joined in.

In her mid-forties, Elizabeth Dunstan still rated a round of applause in Eli's view. He could still see in her the girl he had known, though whether this was due to her good genes or his own expectations, Eli wasn't sure. He did know that her smile was every bit as dazzling as he remembered. Almost as one, all the men in the room rose from their chairs. Even, looking a bit mystified, the gentlemen from Pennsylvania.

"I see proper manners haven't *entirely* deserted this new millennium," Elizabeth said.

In a very short time, Elizabeth had greeted each of her guests by name, set them at ease, turned on the Southern charm, and fired up conversation to such a degree that Eli was having trouble remembering that they were simply having supper at a bed-and-breakfast, and not attending a dinner party at Water Oaks at the height of its glory. Eli studied the other guests, and was certain they were in a similar mood. Easy enough for the Civil War buffs, that was part of the appeal; but the rest seemed just as enamored.

The years since high school hadn't bought Eli the detachment he'd hoped for, but he found himself wondering about Elizabeth's obvious glamour and presence in more analytical terms. Was it some sort of energy field, related to the bio-remnant signatures that remained after death? Perhaps it could be measured. . . .

"Hello, Eli."

Eli blinked. For a moment he didn't realize who had spoken to him. Later, he would realize that he hadn't wanted to know. He'd both looked forward to and dreaded this moment. Elizabeth was smiling at him. Eli, to his chagrin, felt a little giddy.

"Hello, Elizabeth."

She smiled wider. "Is that all you have to say?"

Off-balance from the beginning, and Eli didn't like it. His annoyance went a great way toward relieving his giddiness. "Nice to see you?" he offered.

Elizabeth laughed softly then, hiding her mouth with her hand. "You haven't changed. Not two words for anyone if one would do." She leaned closer and lowered her voice. "I gather Mary has briefed you on our problem?"

"Somewhat, but I wanted to ask you a few questions."

"Of course."

"Was the stairwell incident the first time you were attacked?"

Elizabeth hesitated. "No."

Mary frowned. "Mother, you didn't tell me about this."

"I didn't want to worry you. Assuming you would."

Mary just glared at her. Eli glanced down the table, but, so far as he could tell, all of the other guests were deep in their own conversations and taking little notice of them. The one exception was Hollingsworth, who gave the impression that he wanted to hear them, whether he could or not. After a moment, Elizabeth went on. "There were two prior incidents. Nothing severe. More like a stinging slap than a blow. Once in my office, once when I was in the kitchen. Frankly, until the stairwell, I thought my mind was playing tricks on me. Apparently not."

"Do you think Ruth Benning is responsible?" Mary asked Eli.

"She's not even aware of us, as I said. It couldn't have been her."

"Then who?" Elizabeth asked.

"I don't know," Eli said, "but I promise you that I *will* find out."

* * *

Later, after the guests had repaired to the ballroom for coffee and more conversation, Eli took a discretionary retreat to the second-floor verandah. His last sight of the guests as he went up the stairs was Senator Hollingsworth in earnest and intent conversation with Elizabeth Stockard Dunstan. To Eli, he looked a little like a love-smitten boar hog courting a doe.

There was a warm breeze out on the verandah, but there was a cool edge to it that Eli appreciated. Frogs were singing from a small pond in back of the mansion near the old kitchen building. The moon was rising, and bats were soaring and swooping at the moths attracted to a pole light near the parking lot.

"There it is again."

Mary stood just inside the French doors that led to the verandah. She walked out and stood beside him at the railing. Eli started to tell her to call him Eli instead of "Mr. Mothersbaugh," but he didn't. Eli felt better with a little reserve and distance from Elizabeth and her daughter both.

Eli nodded. "Jasmine. I smelled it earlier. Curious. . . . So. Why aren't you with the rest of your guests?"

Mary looked grim. "Mother's guests, not mine."

"I gather that you and your mother don't always get along."

Mary laughed. "Rather like saying General Sherman didn't get on with General Lee. After my father died, I ran away from home on three separate occasions, Mr. Mothersbaugh. I assume all this is in your files."

"Most of it," Eli admitted. "In most of these situations, the human element is as important as the spectral."

"Nice to know that the living still count. . . . I noticed you watching the senator and my mother. I'm afraid we banished him from his customary seat at the table so Mother and I could talk to you."

"That explains the 'hurry up and die' look I got from him."

"Simple jealousy. He's in love with my mother, you know. That's why he's a regular here."

Eli nodded. "I assumed as much." He also didn't miss the hint of bitterness in Mary's voice when she spoke of her mother.

Mary sighed. "You knew? Well, I suppose it's pretty obvious, even to a man." She turned to look at Eli intently. "Were . . . were you in love with her, too?"

Eli considered. The look on Mary's face spoke volumes: mild interest on the surface and something raging just below. Jealousy? Envy? Perhaps all those things, or something just trying to be itself separate from Elizabeth Stockard Dunstan. *It must have been very hard for Mary.*

Eli looked out over the woodlands surrounding the house. "The truth? Every male in town with a pulse was in love with your mother, in those days," he said, simply. "I'm afraid I was no different."

"What about now?" Mary asked softly. "I realize you don't have to tell me anything, but I would like to know."

Eli thought about it. "In anything like a real relationship, people fall out of love all the time. They really get to know each other—not always a good thing. They change, they grow apart. When only *one* of you is in love, then you don't get those changes. The ideal remains. Love fades, but it never really goes away. It has no reason to."

"Like a ghost?" Mary asked, looking mischievous.

Eli nodded, and sighed. "Sometimes. Yes. Just like that."

"My mother and I have a relationship too, Eli. Always have. Yet it's . . . complicated. I do love my mother, whatever your files say. Part of the reason I agreed to come to Water Oaks and work for her was that I thought there might be a chance to resolve our differences."

Eli nodded. He had the distinct feeling that this wasn't the only reason she'd agreed to come, but he let it go. "I hope you can."

"I appreciate that, and I hope you'll pardon me for asking this: how do you propose to banish the ghosts of Water Oaks Plantation if you can't even rid yourself of the ghost of an old flame?"

Eli laughed. "Fair question. The answer is: I don't know. I'm not an exorcist, whatever you might have heard, and it's not always the ghosts who have the problem. Right now I have no idea what needs to be done, and what needs to be done is really what I do, Ms. Dunstan, and what I'm looking for. Not ghosts as such, though I'll probably need to find those first."

"I can show you where the ghosts are . . . well, some of them, anyway, if that will help. I'd like to help."

Eli had the feeling that Mary wanted to lead him toward something now, just as when they'd first met, she had turned him away from something else. He did want to do his own count, but he wanted Mary around while he did it. Perhaps she could answer some questions. Perhaps, whatever she intended, she could help him see what questions needed to be asked.

"It might be of help, at that," he said. "No time like the present. Too early for bed, so it's either hunt ghosts or rejoin the party, and frankly I'd rather not rejoin the party."

"You needn't worry about my mother and the senator, in case you were. He has his uses, but frankly, she detests the man."

Eli wasn't worried at all. In fact, at that moment, he felt more than a little sympathy for the blowhard senator. The man was out of his depth with Elizabeth, just as Eli was.

"Lead on," was all Eli said, though he had to wonder just where and why Mary was leading him at all, and what she wanted him to find there.

Eli wanted to take some proper readings on the entity near the entrance, but the area was clearly visible from the open doors to the parlor, too close to Elizabeth's social gathering, and Eli wasn't inclined to trigger a lot of questions. He let Mary lead him out the rear doors. The sun was well down now; the trees behind the mansion grounds were one long dark shadow to the north and east.

Eli took out the sensic and brought up the files he'd stored on Water Oaks, including graphics of the layout. Mary moved closer so that she could see.

"Is everything in that computer of yours?"

"Sensic," Eli corrected, "though it's a computer as well, I guess you could say. And no, not everything. Since Water Oaks was never burned, a good deal of the original records survived, such as they are. I haven't downloaded everything, but most of it's on file at the Department of Archives and History."

"Bear in mind I'm new to this, Mr. Mothersbaugh. Up until six months ago, I lived in an apartment in Atlanta. The ancestral home hasn't been back in the family very long. . . . Say, what's that?"

Mary pointed to a group of building outlines on the display that, as they both could clearly see, no longer existed. Eli tapped a few keys. "The slave quarters. Usually they were a bit farther away from the main house, but Water Oaks was a small plantation as they went."

"Oh." Mary looked at the other outline, and the building it referenced. "The kitchen's still here."

Kitchens in the larger homes were detached in those days, partly because no one wanted to bring that much heat into the living areas, partly due to the threat of fire. A regular kitchen had long since been retrofitted into the house proper. The old carriage house was long gone as well, and the original kitchen building had been converted to a garage long since. It had been freshly painted, but the doors were padlocked. Just beyond that was the pond where the frogs were still in chorus. Eli switched the display back to the sensic proper and made a slow sweep of the area.

"What do you see?" Mary asked.

Eli studied the display. He kept it in charting mode deliberately so that Mary couldn't decipher it so easily. "What should I see? I assume you brought me out here for a reason."

"I just assumed you'd need to cover the entire grounds."

Eli smiled inwardly. Mary, bless her heart, wasn't the actress her mother was. Eli wondered idly why Elizabeth had never sought out a career on stage. "There's a ghost here, no question. Or was."

"Was? What do you mean?"

"I mean what I'm seeing is a residual trace, not the entity

itself. Rather like a footprint, bio-emanations tend to coalesce slightly if an entity stays long enough in one spot. This one apparently likes to walk between the old kitchen and house. That's all I can tell at the moment . . . wait." Eli studied the display. "Strike that. It's back."

"Can I see her?"

Her. The slip told Eli what he already knew; Mary was aware of remnant activity here. But how aware, beyond the simple fact? Eli hesitated, but these was no reason not to show Mary what the sensic had found. Besides, he very much wanted to see the entity for himself. He switched the display.

"Oooh."

Mary's sudden intake of breath was understandable. As with the ghost of Ruth on the stairwell, the image was like an old-fashioned photographic negative, but still striking. They were looking at a tall woman in a simple smock dress; she wore a plain headscarf, in contrast to Ruth Benning's elaborate *tignon*. The woman's age was hard to tell, but there was a definite impression of youth. There was nothing in the image proper to tell what color her skin might have been, but Eli let the facial profile algorithms take their best guess against the databases, and they gave the woman a flesh tone the warm light brown of cinnamon.

"She's beautiful," Mary said finally.

Eli just nodded, not looking up from the sensic for a few moments as he looked at the numbers again. He made a link to the state Department of Archives and History and made a request for additional data. It took him a moment to realize that Mary wasn't standing beside him now. He looked up and found her, hand outstretched, reaching for the spot where the ghost was standing.

"Mary, stop!"

Surprised, she drew her hand back. "What's wrong?"

"I'm taking readings here. Most ghosts aren't self-aware, but this one might be. If she is, she may realize she's not alone. That could interfere with the data I'm gathering."

"Is that all she is? Data?"

Eli looked up, a little surprised at the intensity of Mary's reaction. "Do you know who she is?"

Mary shook her head, and Eli was pretty sure she was telling the truth, but there was an expression on Mary's face that Eli found a little disturbing. He wasn't sure what it meant, but it almost seemed as if Mary expected something from the entity, or, more precisely, *wanted* something.

"There's something you're not telling me. Are you sure you don't know who she is?"

Mary shook her head again. "No. . . . Well, I was hoping she was someone I should know, but there's no way to tell, is there?"

"What are you talking about, Mary? Who do you think she might be?"

"My four times great grandmother."

"All right, Mary. Out with it."

They sat at a small breakfast table in a room just off the kitchen hallway. The window panes showed only darkness, though an occasional moth bumped itself against the window trying to reach the light. Mary poured coffee from an old stained enameled pot. "My mother was attacked; I was there and it happened, just as I said. But it's true I had an ulterior motive in bringing you here."

Eli wasn't exactly surprised. "Me specifically?"

Mary shrugged. "Mother mentioned you now and then. I knew who you were, what you did. So when I contacted the bureau, I used your name as well as the senator's. I used everything I thought would help."

"Your mother mentioned me? Why?"

Mary smiled then. "Well, well. You *do* have a normal male ego, Mr. Mothersbaugh. I was beginning to wonder."

Eli smiled faintly. "Just trying to get the context straight. An offhand, casual mention, yes? No more than that?"

"Well . . . yes. Though it happened more than once."

"So. What's the ulterior motive? Anything to do with your suspicions about that ghost we saw?"

Mary didn't say anything for a few moments. She finally sighed and said, "Look at me, Mr. Mothersbaugh. Look at my mother. Contrast that to the portraits of the original

Elizabeth Stockard. Don't you think perhaps there's something about the two of us that speaks more of certain segments of New Orleans than, say, Atlanta?"

Eli got her implication. It was hard to miss. "You suspect that Elizabeth Stockard is not your direct ancestor?"

"You do put it delicately, but it's more than that. If I'm right, then Elizabeth Stockard not only wasn't my direct ancestor, she *murdered* my direct ancestor!"

Eli considered this. "The Water Oaks Massacre? Aren't there a few things you're forgetting?"

"Such as?"

"The fact that the only survivors of the incident were the infant Joshua Stockard, Elizabeth Stockard, and Ruth Benning, and Ruth was an old woman well past child-bearing. So even assuming that John Stockard had fathered a child on one of the other slaves or servants, none survived. How could the ghost we saw possibly be your ancestor?"

Mary shrugged. "I know all that, including the fact that Ruth Benning died soon after and Elizabeth Stockard was so traumatized that she spent her last years in an asylum. There has to be something we're missing."

Eli sighed. "Records are incomplete; doubtless there's a lot we're missing. However, Mary, you may have to accept the fact that you're *wrong*. I'm going to trust that you can do that."

Mary sipped her coffee. "I just want the truth, Mr. Mothersbaugh. Whatever it might be."

"I'll keep that in mind. You do the same."

Eli glanced back at the sensic, noted a blinking green light. The new data he'd requested was coming in. He pushed a button. Eli turned the display so that Mary could see, and she leaned close.

It wasn't a photograph. Some of those had come in, too, specifically one of Captain John Stockard and his wife Elizabeth, but this was different: it was a digital scan of a painted portrait. Mary's eyes got wide. "That's her! The woman we saw out by the kitchens!"

Eli nodded as he took a closer look at the portrait. "Not much doubt. The sensic was very close in its reconstruction, though it appears her skin color was even lighter than we thought. Her name was Jasmine Devereaux, and, according to this, the portrait was commissioned by Captain John Stockard himself."

"But . . . why would John Stockard commission a portrait of a slave?"

Eli called up the rest of the data. "She wasn't a slave. She was 'a free woman of color' as they said in those days. A young Creole, originally from New Orleans. She was hired by the Stockards to help supervise the household and care for the Stockards' children. Why Stockard commissioned the portrait . . . well, that's a good question. Why someone like Jasmine Devereaux would take part in a slave revolt is another." Eli scrolled through the accompanying text and noticed something he hadn't before. "Strange. There was apparently an outbreak of some sort of fever around the time of the Massacre. Locals thought it might have been malaria but that's not certain."

"Do you think there's a connection? Or just coincidence?"

Eli shrugged. "At the moment, I have no idea."

Mary turned her attention back to the portrait. "Jasmine was very beautiful," she said.

"Yes," Eli said. "And so is your mother and so are you. Other than that, what makes you think she's your ancestor, when all the evidence so far is against it?"

Mary blushed, then took a deep breath, let it out. "I admit it's a feeling. Call it a matter of faith, if you want. That's all. I was hoping you could help me prove it, if you let me talk to her. I've read up on the techniques for direct communication with the bio-remnant personality; I know it's possible."

"Not in this case."

"But . . . why? You should talk to her anyway. For all we know, she's the one who attacked my mother!"

Eli shook his head. "Probably the only thing I *do* know for certain at this point is that the ghost of Jasmine Devereaux did not attack your mother. She couldn't have."

Mary's face fell as Eli's words sank in. "You mean . . . ?"

Eli nodded. "I'm sorry, Mary, but I've checked and

rechecked the data and there's no doubt about it—Jasmine Devereaux is a repeater."

Eli skipped breakfast, mainly to skip the company. It was mid-morning before Mary found him, making sensic sweeps of the area around the vanished slave quarters and the old kitchens. It was good timing. He was just about to go look for her.

"Why are you still looking here? I thought Jasmine Devereaux was a dead end, so to speak."

Eli grunted. "I said we couldn't talk to her. That doesn't mean she doesn't have anything to say."

"A little less cryptic, please. What do you mean?"

"I mean a repeater is basically a recording. Bio-remnant energy, yes, but with little or no trace remaining of the original personality. You can't talk to a recording, but you can *listen*. Ruth Benning stares down the stairwell. Jasmine Devereaux hangs out near the old kitchen. In both cases: why? What's so interesting down that stairwell? Why does Jasmine walk out here? She wasn't the cook; Ruth was. So. I've looked at the stairwell. Now I want to see the old kitchen. Do you have a key to that padlock?"

Eli pointed to a large rusty lock hanging from a chain around the retrofitted garage doors on the old kitchen building.

"Sure . . . just a minute." Mary pulled out an old-fashioned key ring with several black iron keys hanging from it. "I'm not sure which one it is . . . and that lock looks like it needs oil. No one's been in there since we bought the place—"

"Mary!"

They looked back toward the house. Elizabeth stood on the second floor verandah, waving. "Can you come here for a few minutes? I need you to explain something about the property taxes."

"All right," Mary shouted back, then whispered, "Great, I've been trying to get her to look at the taxes for weeks. *Now* she gets busy." She handed the ring to Eli. "One of these should do it. I think Mother bought some machine oil for her sewing machine last week; if you need it come find us."

Eli took the keys and Mary hurried off toward the house. There were seven keys. Eli made a quick judgment based on size and narrowed it down to three. The first wouldn't fit at all. The second fit but wouldn't turn, and Eli was beginning to think he might need that machine oil after all. Just for the sake of argument, he tried the third.

The lock clicked open immediately. Eli frowned, then leaned forward and quickly sniffed the keyhole.

Interesting.

He pulled the chains out of the door handles and pulled the rightmost door. The hinges groaned, but turned. Eli went in, looked around. It was obvious that the building hadn't been used as a garage or anything else in some time; there were the remnants of a carriage, badly in need of restoration, but little else except cobwebs and a fine layer of dust. On the far wall was the old brick oven from the building's kitchen days. Its iron chimney had long since been removed and the ceiling patched over, but the oven was more or less intact. Eli wasn't especially surprised; even when need had prompted the kitchen building to be converted back in the 1930s, there had been great interest in matters of "heritage." Any true relic of antebellum times would be preserved if possible, and the oven certainly qualified.

Jasmine comes in here. Where does she go?

Eli pulled out his sensic. The bio-remnant traces were very faint, but Eli didn't need them; he'd had enough time to make a very good estimate of the remnant's cycle. Eli just waited a few moments and Jasmine Devereaux herself appeared on the sensic's screen. Eli looked up, saw nothing. He sighed. Sensitive as he was to the physical presence of a bio-remnant signature, he seldom could see them without the aid of his sensic. There were others in the bureau who barely needed a sensic at all, at least for visual confirmation; however, they tended to be almost blind when it came to sensing a ghost directly and learning anything useful. Eli wouldn't have traded abilities, but now and then he did envy the convenience of it.

Jasmine walked slowly past, Eli tracking every step on the sensic's screen. He couldn't resist stepping into the ghost's path, since he was sure she was not and could not be aware of him. The familiar sensation spread over him: not cold, exactly, but rather numbing. For a moment, Eli looked at the world through a haze. Eli wondered if this was the way ghosts saw their world, at least those with enough of a mind to truly "see" anything. Then Jasmine swept past and, as quickly as it had come, the feeling ebbed. The scent remained, however: jasmine, just like her name. Had she worn the scent in life? There was no way to know. Eli stayed behind and kept tracking her. Inside the door, across the floor. A look left and right. Searching for someone? Or making sure no one was about? There seemed to be a furtiveness to her now that Eli had not noticed before.

Jasmine Devereaux, what are you hiding?

The question turned out to be more literal than Eli had first thought. The image knelt for a moment by the base of the oven, and then it disappeared. Eli checked the sensic carefully, but that was a formality. Eli was certain he'd watched the end of the loop of all that Jasmine Devereaux was now. Somewhere in Water Oaks was the beginning; Eli wasn't sure where that was and he wasn't even sure if it mattered, though he remembered the scent from the verandah the night before and had a pretty good idea. That wasn't what concerned him just then. There was more to it, as the sensic had just told him.

Eli knelt down at the place where Jasmine had knelt and looked more at the oven. It took him a few moments to spot the loose brick on the corner, even with the energy signatures as a guide. He pulled the brick out and found a crevice going deeper into the oven; apparently a few of the bricks inside had been chipped away to make a hole sufficient for what had been placed inside. Eli reached in and pulled out a small unlocked tin box. It was rusted, of course, but well sealed. Inside was a diary. The handwriting on the cover was faded, and the cover itself spotted and brittle with age, but the script was clear and bold and still very readable. Eli read the name written on the cover.

"Jasmine Devereaux."

Eli looked at the hole again, then put the brick back in place and looked at that more closely, too. He finally nodded, satisfied, and turned his attention back to the diary.

Well, Eli. Looks like you have some reading to do.

Two hours later, Mary found him sitting on the bottom step in the grand staircase, his sensic pointed at a patch of nothing beside the entranceway. Two of the guests walked by, stared for a moment, then wandered on, but Eli paid them no heed. Neither did Mary.

"You're looking for the little girl now," Mary said.

Eli just nodded. He adjusted the sensic to its finest setting. "I walked through her first thing after I arrived, as you'll recall. I'm used to ghosts, Mary. Sometimes I don't pay them the attention they deserve."

Mary looked at him intently. "You've found something, haven't you? What is it?"

Eli picked up the diary from the step beside him and handed it to her. "I've found a couple of things. This, for one. You might want to let the experts at the Department of Archives and History look it over when you're done, but I'm certain it's just what it appears to be: Jasmine Devereaux's journal. It was hidden in the old brick oven in the kitchen building."

"You've read it? What does it say?"

Eli smiled then. "Slow down. I haven't read all of it; Jasmine was quite the diarist and there's a lot there. I read from just before she arrived at Water Oaks. Read it yourself, but start with the entry for January 10, 1865. That's the part that concerns you right now."

Mary sat down beside him and read in silence for several moments while Eli tuned his sensic and waited. Mary finally looked up, and her eyes were shining. "She and John Stockard were having an affair! Jasmine was pregnant with his child. . . ." Mary clutched the book to her breast; she was almost bouncing with excitement. "This is the proof I need!"

"No, it isn't."

Mary glared at him. "What do you mean? Are you saying Jasmine was lying?"

"No, I'm saying it doesn't prove anything one way or another. Even if we assume that Jasmine was telling the truth—and I have no doubt of it, frankly—that doesn't explain how Jasmine Devereaux's child became the Stockard heir. There's still the little matter of Elizabeth's son. Remember him? Joshua Stockard. You'll note that the entry for April 20th is the last."

Mary nodded, solemnly. "Just before the Water Oaks Insurrection. The Massacre."

"The last entry," Eli corrected. "And if you'll read more carefully you'll see what I mean. There *was* no massacre."

Mary just stared at him for a moment. Then she swore softly and flipped several pages until she found the entry Eli mentioned. She read for several minutes while Eli waited, patient as a stone.

"Jasmine just talks about how hard things had been for her and Ruth in the past few weeks. What with the Master still gone, her so far along and sick, and no help. . . ." She stopped. "Oh."

Eli nodded. "Exactly. *No help*. The women were alone, except for the child Margaret and the infant Joshua, and it doesn't take a crystal ball to know why. The field hands and the few remaining house slaves had either been released or had run away. There was no massacre because there was no one left *to* massacre."

"But then what really happened?"

"I think I know. If you'll sit quietly for a few minutes, we might have a chance to prove it."

The readings on Eli's sensic changed. He nodded. Right on time. The ghost was periodic, as he'd suspected. Most were. But was she a repeater? Eli didn't think so, and, in a moment, the numbers told him the same. There was someone there, and he was almost certain that he knew who that someone was. He changed the display from charting to mapping to see if he was right.

The image resolved into a little girl about five years old. Eli adjusted the image data to the finest granularity that did not compromise the raw data, then let the sensic make reasoned guesses about the rest, just as he had with Jasmine Devereaux's image. When he was done, the little girl had turned into a remarkably good match to the only picture surviving.

"Margaret Stockard," Mary said, looking over his shoulder. "But what is that she's holding? A doll?"

"If you'll be quiet, as I asked you to, we might find out. I'm going to try to talk to her."

Eli used the sensic's projection capability to create an image of himself, using the same type of energy field that was all that remained of Margaret Stockard. It covered him in a rough outline and gave him a rather sketchy appearance, but it was more than enough. Eli looked straight at the little girl, and the confusion in her eyes told him that she did, indeed, see him, or at least his projection. Eli spoke carefully.

"Hello, Margaret."

She had no voice, strictly speaking. The sensic simply ran the image's lip movements through a pattern-matching algorithm and read them as a deaf person might. The speaker crackled to life. It was a synthesized voice, but it was Margaret Stockard, shyly speaking to the living again after nearly two hundred years. "Hullo."

"You've been sick, I understand. You should be in bed."

"Are you the dok'ur?"

"Doctor. That's right." It wasn't completely a lie, Eli told himself. He had his PhD. But it still made him feel uncomfortable.

"I feel good now. You're tardy," Margaret said. The synthetic voice was expressionless but there was mischief in her eyes. Margaret's was a child's face; every emotion was clearly readable.

Tardy? Poor thing, you don't know the half of it.

It remained to be seen how much she did know. Eli took a deep breath and asked the question. "Is that your doll?"

Margaret held up the bundle she was carrying, and Eli could plainly see that it was not a doll.

But then, he already knew it wasn't a doll. He waited for Margaret Stockard to tell him just what it was.

"My baby brother," she said proudly. "His name's Jos'ua."

It wasn't very long before Margaret Stockard and her brother faded away. That didn't matter; Eli had learned what he needed to learn.

"Well, there's your smoking gun," Eli said. He started to pack up the sensic.

Mary just stared at the place the ghost children had been. "I don't follow," Mary said.

"You heard what Margaret said. She picked up her baby brother because he was crying. Then she went downstairs to find her mother. She's still looking for her mother, still carrying her baby brother. And Ruth Benning is still looking down the stairwell in shock and loss. Think about that for a moment."

Mary obviously did. "The poor child . . . she fell! She fell down the stairs and died . . . along with Joshua Stockard. The original Joshua Stockard, anyway. He was replaced!"

Eli nodded. "It fits."

"Then Elizabeth Stockard murdered Jasmine Devereaux and took Jasmine's baby as her own!"

Eli considered. "Possible."

"Possible? Mr. Mothersbaugh, if you'll pardon my quoting you, 'It fits.' "

"Up to a point. You're forgetting two things: Ruth Benning and the fever. We know from her diary that Jasmine Devereaux was already ill and weak with fever and overwork as her confinement approached. Now, we also know that she and Ruth Benning were friends, and that Jasmine asked her to take care of the baby if anything happened to her. Perhaps it was a premonition, or maybe she was just being realistic. Childbirth is always dangerous and was more so then." Eli shrugged. "I think it equally likely that Jasmine died in childbirth or soon after, and Ruth simply took advantage of the situation."

"Took advantage? How?"

"By seeing that her friend's child was provided for, of course. How better than as Master of Water Oaks? Jasmine was light-skinned to start with, and her child was probably more so. Captain Stockard was away and had never seen his son; Elizabeth Stockard wasn't in her right mind. In any case, I don't doubt that the child's resemblance to his father was unmistakable. Perhaps Ruth thought she could bring Elizabeth back to her senses if she could convince her mistress that Joshua had survived. Perhaps Elizabeth mistook the child for Joshua in her dementia and Ruth was too tender-hearted to correct her. Pick the truth you want, Mary. We'll probably never know for certain."

"Then why the Massacre story? Wouldn't it have made more sense to say that Jasmine and her child had both died? John Stockard would have had to believe any story they told him."

"True, but was Elizabeth in any condition to stick to a consistent account? Personally, I think the whole 'massacre' business was concocted out of her fevered brain to explain why she and Ruth were all alone. The only one who could contradict her story was Ruth, who would have had her own reasons for keeping quiet."

Mary looked at the diary wistfully. "It's a good story, Mr. Mothersbaugh. Except for the part about picking the truth you want. I wanted to know *the* truth. I believe Jasmine Devereaux is my ancestor. Maybe you believe it too, but you're right that proving that the 'real' Joshua Stockard died in 1865 doesn't prove that Jasmine Devereaux's bastard child carried the Stockard name. I'm no better off than I was!"

"Not quite. You have living descendants in the direct line from Jasmine's parents; I've already checked, and, strangely enough, there are likely candidates living in the area. A simple genetic test can determine if you're related. With what we already have, that's more than enough proof."

Mary looked stunned. "You must think I'm an idiot," she said. "Well, I'm not . . . most of the time. I'm not thinking clearly about this and that's the simple truth. Those descendants . . . whoever they are, they're strangers. Why would they help me?"

Eli grinned. "For a chance to prove that one of the finest First Families of the Confederacy is actually descended from Jasmine Devereaux? I don't think you'll have any trouble there." Eli finished packing up his sensic. He snapped the case shut and Mary blinked, apparently only now realizing what he was doing.

"You're leaving?"

Eli nodded. "I'd like to find a way to free Margaret and her brother and I'm going to work on that when I can. But strictly within the guidelines of my responsibility, it's not necessary. They're no threat to your mother or anyone else."

"They're not? But they're the only ghosts I know of besides Ruth and Jasmine, and you've already said they weren't the ones!"

"And they aren't. You haven't met the ghost who attacked your mother. You probably never will. It's rather hard to detect."

"I have a right to know, Mr. Mothersbaugh. My mother and I have had our differences, but if she's still in danger—"

Eli shook his head. "She isn't in any danger. You'll have to trust me on that because, actually, it's your mother who has the right to know this part of the story, and I'm going to go tell her right now. After that, I think you should talk to her."

Mary looked down at the diary in her hands, and she smiled grimly. "Believe me, Mr. Mothersbaugh—I intend to."

Eli made his way up the creaking stairs. He paused for a moment at the spot where Ruth Benning kept her painful vigil on the second floor landing, then kept walking.

It's not always the ghost who has the problem.

Elizabeth, the namesake of the long dead Elizabeth Stockard, was waiting for him in her study. Eli had rather imagined more of a parlor, suitable for receiving gentleman callers—if the senator qualified—and having tea. Instead, he found a library, ledgers, and a large, workman-like desk. Elizabeth sat behind it, dressed in jeans and a comfortable old shirt, reading glasses perched on her nose. Eli could see the years on her a little more clearly now, but in his eyes she was still the most beautiful woman he had ever seen.

Despite which, at the moment, Eli didn't like her very much.

"Mrs. Dunstan, in a little while your daughter is going to march in here and confront you with Jasmine Devereaux's diary. Please do her the courtesy of acting surprised."

Elizabeth didn't say anything for a few moments. Then she shook her head slowly. "You needn't take that tone with me, Eli—I will play my part. It'd be silly to do otherwise at this point."

Eli sighed. "I wondered if you'd deny it."

"Why should I? Though I'll admit that I'm curious as to how you figured it out," she said.

"For a start, nearly all the incidents took place when you were alone. The one time you had a witness, Mary didn't really see anything; she heard a slapping sound and turned just in time to help catch you, though I imagine you'd have used the railing if she wasn't quick enough. She said you'd been pushed because that's what you told her. You'd already mentioned me, oh so casually, and by the time she called the bureau, Mary probably believed it was her idea in the first place."

Elizabeth smiled at him. "That's it?"

Eli shook his head. "Then there was the diary and its hiding place in the old kitchen. The lock had been oiled recently, although supposedly no one had been in the building in months. My instruments showed a distinctive and much too strong bio-remnant signature. The sort left by someone still living. Plus the cobwebs and dust had clearly been disturbed, and the tin had been opened recently. I considered Mary, but, frankly, she's a poor liar and a poorer manipulator. She doesn't have your raw talent for either, I'm afraid."

Elizabeth's smile didn't waver. "I imagine that felt good,

Eli. Get a bit of your own back for having the bad judgment to lust after me like every other horny dog at school? Feeling righteous and superior now, are we?"

Eli took a deep breath. "I just want to know why," he said. "That's all."

"Is it really? Then I'll tell you: For Mary," Elizabeth said simply. "For my daughter."

"I don't understand," Eli said.

"Then let me help: I grew up with a famous name and no money. 'Genteel poverty'? Isn't that what they call it when the old families hit hard times? Well, there isn't a damn thing gentle about it. Half the people around you thinking, 'ain't it a shame,' and the other half thinking 'serves them *right*'? We may have lived in the same town, but you had no idea what it was like to be a Stockard, Eli. Not one damn clue."

Eli knew it was true. They'd gone to the same school, the same church, but they may as well have been living on different planets. "What does that have to do with Mary?"

"Everything, Eli. Early on, I decided that if I had to be a Stockard, then I damn well would *be* a Stockard. I used my looks for all they were worth. I married a well-to-do man, a sweet fool with some money, but when he died, his estate was worth a thousand times more, which was mostly my doing. I worked for the day I would take back Water Oaks; as all the other generations of Stockards since the war had failed to do. I used all the tools I had and didn't pay too much attention to those that couldn't help me."

"One of those being Mary?"

Elizabeth's smile wavered then and went out like a guttering candle. "Yes, Eli. Mary. She feels that I owe her for the mess I made of her childhood and what I put her father through. You know something? She's right."

"You found Jasmine's diary first." It wasn't a question.

"Of course I did. Aren't you going to ask me how?"

Eli shook his head. "Remember the old Carson place, which a bunch of us walked past every day on the way to school? You used to say you saw Noemi Carson sitting on the porch every day, and she had been dead ten years or more by then. It was only much later that I realized you weren't joking. You can see ghosts, can't you? Even I can't do that most of the time without a sensic."

"Not always," Elizabeth confirmed. "But often enough."

"You had the diary. You also saw Margaret and her baby brother."

The smile returned. "It took a while to realize what the poor child was carrying, but, yes, it was easy enough to put together after that. Another descendant of the Devereaux family lives just up the road, an old friend from school, it turned out. It was easy to get the test. Friends help out friends in Canemill, Eli. Maybe you've forgotten that."

"Friends ask. That's all you really had to do, Elizabeth," he said. Elizabeth, stung, said nothing, and, in a moment Eli continued. "So. Now that you've done all this, what have you done?"

Elizabeth shook her head in exasperation. "Weren't you paying attention? I've just given Mary the one thing she's wanted for years: power! The upper hand. Even, if she's so inclined, revenge. She's going to march herself in here and announce that my carefully tended image of myself as a latter-day Scarlett O'Hara is all a sham."

"Then what?"

"Then we'll *talk*, Eli," she said slowly, as if explaining to a child. "Really talk, for the first time in a while. And fight. Probably cry, and almost certainly negotiate, with Mary holding all the cards. Or so she'll believe, which, for my purposes, is the same thing. Mary's looked forward to this day for a long time and I'm going to give it to her. Afterward . . . well, one way or another our relationship changes. Maybe for the better. I hope so, but it's a risk. I've taken them before."

"What makes you think I won't tell her myself?"

"Are you really so angry with me that you'd take this chance away from her?"

Eli thought about it for a moment, but not too long. "I'm not angry, Elizabeth, and what happens between you and Mary is a family matter and none of my concern. I have to ask, though: after all that you've done to regain Water

Oaks, are you saying you really don't care that you're not a Stockard?"

Elizabeth smiled grimly. "Oh, but I *am*, Eli. A true blood daughter of Captain John Stockard, CSA. Nothing that you've found changes a thing."

"Not even in Canemill?" Eli felt a little ashamed of himself, but only a little.

Elizabeth smiled a rueful smile. "You needn't shuffle around the woodpile, Eli. Yes, there are those for whom it will matter. On the other hand, for my guests, it will make an even better story than the one I have now. Good for business."

"What about Senator Hollingsworth? What do you think he'll do?"

Elizabeth's grin was as wicked as anything Eli had ever seen on a living soul. " 'Shit a brick or grow a dick,' " she said. "Frankly, I can't wait to find out which."

Eli smiled despite himself. "I almost hate to miss that. Goodbye, Elizabeth." He hesitated, and added, "Thank you."

Elizabeth frowned, but she didn't ask why Eli had thanked her and Eli didn't explain. There was no need; Elizabeth already had what mattered to her. As he left Eli realized that, oddly enough, so did he. Eli felt as if an old and painful burden had been lifted from his shoulders. What had passed between himself and Elizabeth wasn't anything like the sort of relationship he'd mentioned to Mary, or had once dreamed about, but it was honest enough, and intimate enough, and real enough for the brief time it lasted.

Despite Eli's best efforts, he had released none of the ghosts of Water Oaks Plantation. He had, though, finally, let go of one of his own.

Elvenbrood

~~~~~~

Tanith Lee

Tanith Lee [www.tanithlee.com] lives in the south of England with her husband, John Kaiine, in a house with a name, and its name is Vespertilio. Her fantasy and horror stories have put her in the forefront of both genres in recent decades. She began publishing in 1968, and her first novel, The Birthgrave, *was published in 1975. Among her most famous works is the series of fantasy stories of Flat Earth, collected in* Night's Master *(1978),* Death's Master *(1979),* Delusion's Master *(1981),* Delirium's Mistress *(1986), and* Night's Sorceries *(1987). She has published more than seventy books including nine collections of her stories, and continues to publish a steady stream of impressive short stories. In 2004, she published* Piratica, *a pirate adventure for girls. Her novel* Metallic Love, *a sequel to* The Silver Metal Lover *(1981), is out in 2005.*

"Elvenbrood," which appeared in The Faery Reel, *edited by Ellen Datlow and Terri Windling, another of the finest original anthologies of 2004, is a tale of a shattered family reconstituting itself, making a new start in a new place. Dad left the family, and now mom and the kids are making a new start in a new house. But there are supernatural beings in the nearby woods who have designs on the daughter—they want to abduct her as part of a bargain the estranged father made.*

> *How beautiful they are,*
> *The lordly ones,*
> *Who dwell in the hills,*
> *In the hollow hills.*
> —"THE IMMORTAL HOUR,"
> FIONA MACLEOD (WILLIAM SHARP)

When they moved to Bridestone, Susie had tried to be very positive. That was the key word, apparently. Positive. What you *had* to be. So Jack tried to back her up. She'd been through enough, they all had. Make the best of things.

He was seventeen and a half, and because of that, she said she *preferred* him to call her Susie, though outside the house, at college, he referred to her, when he needed to, by her true title, which was Mum. Luce still had the unchallenged rights to call Susie Mum, but she didn't either. Luce was fourteen, white-blonde, strange in the way girls suddenly got.

"Susie's a *person*," said Luce, seriously, bossily, "she has a right to have a *name*, not just be our Mum."

"She *is* our Mum," Jack pointed out.

Then Susie had come in, all Positive, and they had to start Positively cleaning the new house up, and unpacking.

It was a new house in every way, as several sections of the sprawling village were, part of a block of houses, all joined up, with big flat glass windows and doors. They were all presumably the same inside, too. One largish downstairs room, kitchen, cloakroom, three small bedrooms upstairs, and a bathroom. The house, though, looked out onto fields and hedgerows, woods. It was all right, better than the flat they'd all been crammed into in outer London, when Dad— Michael—was fired.

The firing had been because Dad drank too much alcohol. Or no, it had been because *Michael* drank too much. Jack could remember a few years before, when Luce had been nine and sweet, and Susie had been, not Positive, just happy, and Dad had been Dad, and brilliant. Michael worked too hard, Susie explained as things ran downhill; he was trying to keep them all going; they must support him. Then he got fired anyway, and they lost the house in Chester Road where Jack and Luce had grown up. They went to live in the flat. Once there, Dad—now truly Michael full time—went on drinking too much. He began to tell Susie, Luce, and Jack that he was sick to death of them and the burden they were, and also he started to hit Susie. One night Jack smashed one of Michael's bottles over Michael's head to stop him. Jack had been crying, just as Luce and Susie were. Michael sat there on the floor looking stunned. Then he just got up, with a trickle of blood from his forehead running down his nose, and walked out. He never came back.

That had been a year and a half ago. Now they were here.

Which was the really stupid part, Jack thought. Mum had had a win on the National Lottery. Oh, not millions, but enough for a decent down payment on a small house, and some left over until, as Susie said (positive enough she'd fooled the mortgage people), she found a job. Being Positive, they'd already found a local school for Luce, and Jack's college was only half an hour away on the train.

Jack couldn't help thinking it was a shame they hadn't won the lottery before all hell broke loose in their lives. Susie said that wasn't the way to look at it. It was wonderful luck. And of course it was.

Bridestone, though.

Jack had stared at the place uneasily, even as the train pulled in. Susie's choice. It was one of those Kent-Sussex villages that had been picturesque, and still was in bits—ye olde smithy, ye olde pub, a church that was built just after the Norman Conquest of England in 1066, even the ruins of a Roman fort and Norman castle nearby. But the village had also grown. It had put on weight since the fifties, got too fat with new houses and estates and silly shops that, Jack thought, sold stuff no one in their right minds could afford, or would want to.

There was a Big Divide here too. There were the Rich, who lived in old timbered houses along the hilly narrow streets or in flash mansions just outside, with gardens like parks. The Rich had huge dogs, rode horses, talked like things yapping to each other. They looked way, way down on "That Common Lot" who'd bought the new houses.

Susie had been an actress once. She'd been on TV and everything, only no one remembered. But she wasn't *common*—she was *un*common.

"Look at the lovely view!" she sang as they saw it first, properly, from the upstairs landing window.

Well, it *was* a good view, Jack had to admit. He was going to be studying photography next year; he was just on his foundation course now. He could take excellent pictures of the green-golden fields, the clouds of dark woods, the sweeps of open land beyond . . .

Why didn't he like that view?

He tried, in a funny way, not even to look at it, not to look out of the windows. Nuts.

Luce *loved* it. She loved the tiny garden, too, with the blue, fake wrought-iron chairs and table Susie bought, the untidy rosebushes and lilac tree. She'd be out there for hours in the evenings, when he and Susie watched TV, alone, singing to herself like she had when she was little. Maybe it was good for her. Over the end fence, the fields buzzed smokily with summer.

At night, the moon sailed white across that countryside, owls eerily cried, and Jack found himself going downstairs about one A.M., not for a drink of juice or piece off the cold chicken, but to check the locks, front and back.

"Susie, do you think these locks are strong enough?"

"They're what we've got, Jackie."

"Yeah, but couldn't I fix for someone to put on better ones?"

"What are you expecting to break in—" she chortled. "A *lion*?"

"Those bloody dogs are about lion size. One of those'd be through that glass in two seconds."

"I *like* dogs. Lucy and I might like to get one ourselves. But listen, Jack, thanks honestly, but we're out of London here. It's much safer, you know."

Luce said primly, "Jack never worried about locks in London. Once he left the front door unlocked all night when he came in."

This had been at Chester Road, so Susie changed the subject.

What *was* it that bugged Jack about this place? A couple of Sundays they went for a walk around the lanes. Susie and Luce chatted about birds and wildflowers. Jack kept looking over his shoulder. Once he heard something following them behind the hedgerow—he got ready to thump it till two crows flew up.

But it wasn't just the wildlife, or the view, or the people here—but—*something*—

Something . . .

Perhaps he was just a city boy, or neurotic, like Susie and Luce were now, a bit. Just that.

The fourth week they were there, Luce ran in one afternoon from school, breathlessly excited to tell them, "I met this *weird* man in the High Street."

Jack and Susie looked up, horrified.

"What do you mean, Lucy?" Susie asked, careful, gripping the edge of the kitchen table.

Jack, home early on what the awkward course tutor called "An Assignment," waited.

Luce said, "I don't mean *that*. He's off his head, out of his skull . . ."

"On *drugs*, do you mean?" demanded Jack.

Luce burst out laughing. She still had this laugh, like silver bells . . . Michael had said that. No, *Dad* had said it. "I just mean crazy. Not dangerous. He just came up and said, 'You be careful, little girl'—as if I was a kid—'careful how you go.'"

"Did you speak to him? Lucy, I've told you—"

"*No*. Of *course* not. Why would I? I just walked on. Then he called after me, 'Just go careful with that hair.' And then something about the Romans leaving the stone, and knights leaving the castle—but I was by the bread shop then, and I went in like you asked and bought this loaf—"

"Forget the loaf. What did he look like?"

"Thin, old. His hair was long. He looked like a woolly sheepdog. His clothes were old, too. Sort of like Victorian for a fancy-dress party—only worn and mucky. But people like that stink. They smell like dustbins and garbage, and he didn't. He smelled . . ." Luce considered, "like grass."

"*Grass?*"

"Off a *lawn*—that sort. And he had green eyes, like me."

Susie and Jack exchanged a worried, brown-eyed glance.

"Tomorrow, Lucy," said Susie firmly, "I will take you in to school. I will collect you in the afternoon."

"Oh, *Mum!*" Luce wailed.

Jack went out after tea, which was their early dinner at six o'clock. He walked down the hill from the grassy estate, past the quaint gate where sometimes cows grazed, and which led to a cornfield. He walked through a couple of narrow streets and into the High Street.

There was a village green with a war memorial on it. The church, with its square Norman tower, was across from the green, and, on the other side, nestled among huge oak and beech trees, the pub. This pub had a strange name. . . . Jack peered round the leaves and past the several posh drinkers gathered outside on rustic benches, with their wine and Real Ale.

The pub sign showed a green hill, and some people dancing together on it under a curved crescent moon. THE LORDS AND LADIES said the lettering.

One of the drinkers had noticed Jack and pulled a face. Ah, Jack could see the man thinking, That Common Lot have now produced a yob intent on underage boozing.

Jack turned his back and strolled on, across the green to the church.

He was looking for the man who had spoken to Luce. In such a stuck-up place as Bridestone, anyone like that, surely, would have been run out of town long ago. Unless— did they still keep a village idiot here? Just for the twee charm of it . . .

What had he meant *Go careful with that hair?* A warning? A threat? Jack badly wanted to see the man, ask him which, and why. And if a threat, tell him that Jack didn't like old tramps threatening his sister, all right?

After a while, Jack left the church. He walked on, up and down roads and through the little between-house alleys. Someone was playing Mozart. Dogs barked, richly, in gardens with not one branch out of place.

Returning to the green, he saw the sun was going. It was getting on for 8:30. An hour at most, and it would be full dark, and Susie getting anxious because he'd only said he was going for a walk.

The church, too, bothered Jack. The graveyard was packed with ancient leaning gravestones with dates like 1701 and 1590. Age so thick you could cut it in slices.

And what had the nutter meant when he said that about the Romans leaving the stone, and the Norman knights? Jack had never heard that the Romans—or the Normans, for that matter—had left there at all. The air was cooling and the smell of flowers blew over on a breeze. It was getting dark quicker than he'd expected.

When Jack got to the front door, Susie was already flinging it wide. "Jack, Jack, thank God—"

"What is it? *What*, Mum?"

"Lucy's gone!"

Jack stood there, with all his blood turning to sand. It felt like the flat again, those times when Michael . . . the raised drunken voice rising in the other room, accusing Susie of caring nothing for her family, only for the career she'd given up, and then the sound of a blow.

"Are you sure, Susie?"

"Of course I'm bloody sure, you stupid moron!"

Unlike Michael, she was seldom rude. She must be at her wit's end. He read the signal and said, "Yes, okay. You've checked. When did you realize?"

"She was up in her room playing her CDs, quite loud—one of those thump-thump people you both like so much . . ."

"U2."

"And it just kept on playing the same track, so I went up to say could she turn it down a little . . . Oh God, Jack, she wasn't there. The window was wide open, that was all—she couldn't have climbed out of the *window*, could she? I mean, why would she do that? I mean, she wasn't in the bathroom, and she didn't come downstairs—I was ironing and I had the radio on—but I'd have seen her go by the main room door. . . ."

"Did you check the other rooms? Yes. The garden?"

"I looked *everywhere*. I even—I even looked in the blasted washing machine for God's sake!" Susie cackled weakly. "Am I being daft? It's all right, isn't it? She's probably somehow been up there all the time. . . ." Susie turned abruptly, raced along the hall and up the stairs like a slim stampeding elephant. Jack followed. Upstairs, there was no sign of Luce.

They craned their necks out the open bedroom window, gazing down at the small patio below. It wasn't such a long drop.

The air smelled wonderful now, scented with flowers and hay and clean growing, living things—and *night*.

"Mum, *look*! I think . . ."

"Oh, oh there she is! Oh my God, what's she doing out there? Lucy! Luce!"

Across a couple of fields of ripening corn or wheat, or whatever it was, among the tall stalks, a short slender figure stood quite still, showing up with an almost luminous whiteness that must be because of lights shining out from the house backs. Luce, with her pale blonde hair . . .

Go careful with that hair.

Susie was already running downstairs again, throwing open the back door. He caught up in the garden. By then she was standing by the back fence, nearly crying, like a scared child.

"She vanished."

"The stalks would hide her from down here."

"No. When I got here I could still see her out in the field. And then . . . she just wasn't."

The night felt chilly, or cold. It was moonless, too.

"I'll go and look for her." Jack sprang at the fence and over.

"Be *careful!*"

Jack grunted, and pelted forward into the stinging coarse slap of the wheat or corn. He hated it, smashing it aside with his hands—he'd probably never eat bread or cereal again.

He heard Susie calling when he thought he'd traveled about a quarter mile. By then the dark shadow of the woods was looming through the stalks, sinister in some electric way.

Jack stood, bewildered.

Behind him floated the voice of his mother, vital again with relief: "Jack! It's all right, she's *here* . . ." And then Luce's voice, "Jackieee!"

While in front of him, against the backdrop of woods, motionless as the unshaken grain, a white-skinned, white-blonde creature was looking back at him, smiling—quiet, and amused—with slanting cat-green eyes. Only a second, this. Then it melted away. Into shadow, into night—*into the ground?*

Jack shook himself. Nothing had been there—adrenaline and an optical illusion. He turned and ran back for the house.

"She says she was everywhere I'd just looked, doing something, not realizing I was looking for her. We just kept *missing* each other."

Jack scowled. "That's dumb. We looked everywhere. You can't *miss* someone anyway in a house this tiny."

"It's what she says. She got bolshy and then tearful when

I kept saying it couldn't have been like that. She said she's not a liar. But she is. I took the flashlight. There're scuff marks on the table on the patio. She must have got out on the windowsill, swung onto the shed roof—I can hardly bear to think of it. What if she'd jumped all wrong?"

"Yeah. Do you want me to speak to her?"

"In the morning. We've had enough for now."

He wondered how Luce had got back in. She must have sneaked in again when he was out in the fields and Susie at the fence. Crazy.

Crazy like the green-eyed man.

That night, Jack dreamed he was still running. Something was chasing him—a dog, he thought, a white dog. He woke up sweating, because he'd left his window shut.

He wondered if that other thing—that white figure Susie and he thought they'd seen—was Luce's *decoy*, so she could get back unnoticed.

The woman behind the library desk was pretty tasty, but she was also pretty nasty. "The computer's crashed. I'm sorry." You could see she wasn't.

He told her he needed to research Bridestone. She raised an eyebrow. "You must have heard of it," he said, "one stop up the line."

"I'm from London," she proclaimed loftily.

The promised data hadn't been much anyhow. Just dates on the castle, and a plan of the Roman remains with some altar to a pagan goddess.

As Jack was stalking through the door, a man's voice sounded behind him.

"Were you asking about Bridestone?"

Jack looked around. A young middle-aged man stood there, frowning at him, as if it was forbidden for people like Jack to ask questions. Jack didn't like men of this age anyway. Michael had been one.

"Yes," said Jack shortly.

"Any special reason?"

"I live there. If that's okay."

Jack saw suddenly the man's frown was because he was squinting out into the sun.

"You might try an old guy called Soldyay," said the man. "That's spelled *Soldier*, by the way. He's dotty, but quite harmless. I've known him years, and he knows Bridestone village, the history and so on."

"Soldier? What do you mean, 'dotty'? You mean off his head?"

"Somewhat. But as I say, no danger. Gentle as a lamb. Really, I wouldn't recommend seeing him otherwise. I'm his dentist. He appears before me once a year to show off his truly wonderful teeth. They really *are* wonderful. Like a young tiger's. Not a single cavity."

"Has he got green eyes?"

"That's another thing. His eyes are as clear as a child's. Green? Yes, I think so. Also his clothes are horrible but somehow he's always fresh as a daisy. Anyway, if you want to know about the village, he's your man. Bridstane it used to be. It's in the Domesday Book and all that. Seen the ruins?"

"Not yet."

"Nothing much left. A few crumbling walls. The Roman fort is even less intact, plus it's up a mountain of a hill. I *don't* recommend *that*."

"Was it abandoned—the fort? Or the castle?"

"Sometimes Soldier seems to say so. But then he has times when he just talks in riddles. He's supposed to have a peculiar history himself. My mother used to remember him first turning up. Old then, she said. I don't know his age. He lies and says sixty to my receptionist, but he's well past that. Catch him on a good day, and you'll get some sense."

"When's a good day?"

"Waxing moon. That's today, in fact. You can call at his house, he won't let you in. You'll have to talk to him in the street. Number Seven, Smith's Lane, behind the old—"

"Smithy," said Jack. "Thanks, Mr. . . . ?"

"Tooth," sighed the dentist. "Please *don't* say it."

* * *

On the train going back, Jack thought how he hadn't gone in to college to check. He had considered it—the computers there might work. But then a foundation student had practically to walk over blazing coals to get access to them. He hadn't spoken to Luce, either. She'd slipped off early to school that morning eluding Susie's escort, so Susie felt she had to phone the place to make sure Luce had safely arrived. She had. Then the phone had rung again, someone wanting Susie for an interview that day, some job she'd applied for—she hadn't said doing what. "Jack, I'll have to go out. Would you please pick Lucy up this afternoon from school? She'll like it better anyway, her handsome elder brother, to her Mum."

Before meeting Luce, he had plenty of time to run Mr. Soldier to ground. But first, lunch was on the agenda. Or it was meant to be. As he opened the fridge door, there was a multicolored explosion.

Jack yelled, staggered back against the kitchen table, soaked and gawping, as a double pack of colas, two cartons of orange juice and one of cranberry, and a bottle of fizzy white wine erupted their contents all over the room—and all over Jack.

He hadn't the heart to leave the mess for Susie when she got back. His note about the ruined food would be bad enough. Most of the stocks in the fridge were now spoiled—unless you really fancied soggy bread, wet butter, cold sausages in an orange and cola sauce. The fruit and salad might make it, if washed. Could you wash *bacon* though?

Jack was glaring into the fridge again when the milk carton, somehow slower than the rest, also decided to blow its top, right in his face.

Eyes full of milk, Jack swore. Spilled milk stank, too. So, not only cleaning the kitchen now, but another shower and a change of clothes.

He got out of the house again about three o'clock, and ran through the village to Smith's Lane.

The street was cobbled, the houses—drab, old, narrow oblongs—slotted together like a kind of jigsaw. Most looked uncared for, but Number Seven won the prize for worst. The door-paint peeled in strips, the windows were nearly black with dirt behind yellowed filthy net curtains. No bell. Jack went at the door knocker as if needing to hammer something in.

He thought no one would answer.

Then, silent as the fall of a leaf, the door opened, and Mr. Soldier stepped out to meet Jack in the street.

His eyes *were* green. They didn't slant, though. And, as Tooth the dentist had said, they were incredibly clear, the whites like enamel. The rest of him—he was old and crinkled up, like scrunched paper. His gray hair poured over his shoulders, over his face. His clothing looked more 1970s, Jack thought, than Victorian, but also as if he slept in it, slept too in a refuse sack.

"You spoke to my sister."

"Did I?" He had a good voice, not overeducated and yappy like the Bridestone Rich, more like an actor. So, was he acting now?

"Yeah, you did. Blonde girl, yesterday."

"Ah." Mr. Soldier smiled. His teeth were just as the dentist had said. "That was your sister, then."

"Why did you try to scare her?"

"Did I scare her?"

"No. But . . ."

"I did mean to, in a way. I meant she should be careful. Sometimes . . ." Mr. Soldier hesitated. He seemed apologetic. "Sometimes I'm not very coherent."

"You get *drunk*?"

Mr. Soldier looked surprised at the rage in Jack's tone. "No, not often. I can't afford to. I simply mean I'm not always myself."

"Do the police know about you? Do you have to attend at a hospital for treatment?"

"Not at all. I seldom cause any bother."

"You bothered my sister."

Mr. Soldier said, "I think it isn't *I* that bother her. Perhaps it's already too late. Maybe not."

Jack snarled. His fists rose.

Mr. Soldier did not react. He said quietly, "Something wants her. Something is *interested* in her."

"*Who?* How do you *know?*"

"I was the same. Once they were interested in me."

"*Who are THEY?*"

Mr. Soldier knelt down unexpectedly on the ground. He licked his finger and wrote in his own spit on a large cobble, one word.

Jack stared at it. ELVNBROD.

"Elven—"

"*Don't.*" Mr. Soldier rose. He sounded oddly proud as he said, "Don't name them. They can be called the Lords and Ladies, or the Royalty. In Ireland, you know, they call them the Gentle Folk, or the Little People. Or the Lordly Ones."

Jack goggled. "*Faeries?*"

"Oh, *that* name. Well. Of a kind, maybe. In the faery tales and legends, it's true, faeries do steal human children. And that is what these ones do, the ones we have here."

Jack stood back. "You are out of your tree."

"They stole me. Yes. Though, believe me, I wanted to go with them. They make you want to go, more than you can bear. They're old as the hills, fair as the morning. They look young as children or adolescents, that's why they like the *mortal* young. In their country, you stay young too, and immortal. They live under the hills. It's like paradise there."

"So what's paradise like, then?" Jack demanded.

"Like the best and most wonderful place you can imagine, then better."

The sun beat on Jack's head. The word *Elvnbrod* had faded from the cobble. He felt dizzy. Did he want to shake the old man, or was he starting to believe him? Don't be a fool.

"So, then," Jack said, adult and cool, "these *things* want to take Luce away with them, like they wanted you when you were a kid. Only you didn't go."

"Oh, but I did."

"You—you what?"

"Listen. Something gives them the right to take a child.

Myself, then. Your sister now. There is a stone in the old Roman fort. The Romans put it there, back in the time of Caesars. It was dedicated to the goddess of light, Brid. They left it here too, when the empire ended. This area has always been a center for *Them*. But the Stone keeps the village safe. Unless . . ."

Jack swallowed noisily.

The old man softly said, "There was a Norman warlord in the castle. He sold his youngest daughter and son to the Lordly Ones, in return for riches and luck for himself. He got what he asked, but later his knights learned of it and gave him to the church. He was burned as a witch. The castle was abandoned as cursed. Even the best luck can run out."

"Luck . . ." said Jack, dully. "Money . . ."

"After a long while, one of the warlord's children was returned. The Lordly Ones had to let him go, because the luck had failed. They didn't want to, nor did the boy want to come back. The moment he breathed the air of this world, he became old as the hills himself. Yet he lived on. The power of immortality preserved him, but not his youth. He lives still. Perhaps he always must."

The man's face was like a carved stone. Jack took a step away.

Just then, the church clock struck four. It didn't always strike, but now it did and the chimes filled him with a terror without cause. Then he knew why. *Luce*. He reeled away up the lane and sprinted for the school.

She was gone. The teacher he found in the tree-planted yard told him she'd seen Luce running off. One of her friends had tried to interest Luce in seeing a new foal someone had, but Luce said today she had to be home.

Jack bolted back toward the house.

As he ran, the thoughts drummed in his skull. Normans, Romans, Brid's protective altar stone that gave its name to the village, Luce so mad to reach the fields she jumped out of a window, singing out there all those evenings in the dusk—to herself? Or to *what*? The figure among the grain, amused, patient—*greedy*. And Susie winning the lottery, such good luck.

When he burst into the house, Susie was sitting there with her shoes off, drinking water from a bottle.

"Jack! I didn't get the job, but there's much better news. I met Ken Angel in town—you know, that TV thing I did. He's down here looking for locations. He *said*—now *wait* for it—he'd like me aboard on this production. Oh, just two or three lines but . . . well don't look so astounded. I can still act, you know."

"Is Lucy here?" said Jack.

Susie's flushed face went white. She dropped the water bottle and he watched the water uncoil along the carpet. "*What do you mean?* Of course she's not here—you just met her at school. *Didn't* you?"

Jack explained Luce had been gone, to a mother whose face was now blank with fear.

He thought, even if any of this were possible it couldn't be Susie's fault. She hadn't met *something*, made a bargain. . . .

She was at the phone, rattling it about. "Damn, no line, now of all times. Where's my mobile . . ." the contents of her bag tipped out on the water on the floor. She stabbed at buttons.

"You're calling the police."

"No, a pizza delivery. *What do you think?*"

Something slid into Jack's mind. He thought of foxes in London, on the streets in the early morning, sleeping in gardens—man had taken over so much of the open country, now the foxes had come to live where the people were.

Were *They* like that? Did they in fact like to be close, maybe just in that wood up there—watching their chance, intrigued by cricket on the green, the pub with their name, the trains. Waiting. In case something might become available. . . .

All this was madness.

Jack stood fighting with himself. Then he realized Susie wasn't talking into her mobile. She said, flatly, "I can't get a signal." Then she said, "*Where are you going?*"

What could he tell her? Nothing.

He ran into the kitchen, opened the back door, ran again. Behind him he could hear her shouting in panic and anger. He couldn't let that slow him down.

He was practiced now getting over the back fence. He heard her bare feet beating on the path. The fields were like a wall of dry white fire, into which, like a moth, he flew.

They were there.

Yes, he could feel them all around, unseen but *present.* Some primitive sixth sense had kicked into play inside him, though really, hadn't it done that from the very start?

Jack stopped running. He pushed forward through the grain. There seemed to be eyes behind every group of stalks. *Green* eyes, and hair that blended with the color of the fields. Yet when they *let* you see them, they were luminous.

It was no good now thinking he was mental. He knew this was *real.*

Above the fields, the woods, dark green, with green-gold glitters of sun.

He strode through them, fast, looking everywhere. Birds shrilled warnings, squirrels darted overhead. They were like the heartless servants of what truly lurked here.

The hot, static air seemed full of mocking laughter. Sometimes he called out his sister's name. It had a hollow sound.

This was useless, but somehow it had to be done. A sick weight was gathering in his stomach. He refused to think about Susie. Even though this was no use, he must go on. He wondered vaguely how many times, since people first lived here, someone or other just like Jack had trudged across this hilly landscape, calling someone's name, knowing it was no use at all.

The sun moved west. He would have killed for one of those exploded colas—of course, *They* had done that, too— and messed up the phones? Some sort of electric psi stuff, like a poltergeist.

Jack came to a halt. Suddenly he'd stepped over dark tree

roots, mosses, ferns, and come out on quite a wide road going sunlit through the woods.

The sense of being watched and laughed at lessened. Then he saw there was an ordinary man standing under a tree.

"Thank God, there you are."

"Mr. Tooth the dentist," said Jack, confused.

"Thanks for the inevitable joke. Try Alan, if you wouldn't mind."

"A. Tooth," said Jack idiotically. He burst into childish giggling, appalling himself. Then he leaned over and threw up.

When he'd finished, Alan Tooth handed him an unopened bottle of water. Jack gulped; the water helped. He said, "How the hell did you happen to be waiting?"

"It seems everyone comes this route. They used to call it Lordly Way—there's an old track under the fields and trees. You can still find traces if you know where to look. I'm into amateur archeology. That's how I first met Soldier. As for you—well after we spoke, I worked it out—abruptly, during my tea break. I canceled a couple of non-emergencies and called on Soldier myself, this evening. Then I knew."

"Do you know . . . does it *happen*?"

"Yes, I think so. Not often. This is the first for about half a century. The police scoured the place that time. They said it was child abduction, the usual filthy human thing. It wasn't, though, I don't think. My mother told me about it. A boy that time, twelve years old. Very fair hair. *They* like the ones that look the most like they do, you see."

"He—Soldier—said it had to be a bargain."

"No. A certain kind of *wishing* seems to do it. The mother of the boy that time, she'd made a thing of telling everyone she wished she'd never had him, was sick to death of him, and wanted a better life instead. And the funny thing is, after this child went missing, the police never had her under suspicion. Then she met a man with a load of dosh and married him."

Jack put his hand on the nearest tree to steady the rocking world.

Now he knew who had made the bargain that involved Luce—or formed the *wish* that wrecked the protective magic of Brid's Stone for her. It was *Michael*. Susie had never *ever* wished her family gone. She had been happy. But Michael invented a new personality for Susie—a woman who hated her kids and only wanted her old life back—and this was the Susie he slapped and punched. And all that time Michael told them all how sick of them *he* was. Sick enough to get up and leave forever. And with that thought he must have changed his loser's luck—and they received the edge of it. They had also been dragged toward the nearest place where the payment for Michael's luck must be made. Jack remembered the three of them looking at the estate agent's stuff. Susie and Luce had fixed on Bridestone the moment they saw it.

"Come on," said Alan Tooth. "We'd better get you home. Your mother'll need you."

"Then it's hopeless—searching?"

Alan's face fell. He no longer looked particularly grown-up himself. "Let's hope not. But better leave it to the police."

"You said . . ."

"I know. But going on the records, no one ever got them back. Not even a body."

"Unless they came back themselves centuries after—like Soldier."

Someone spoke out of the wood. Both Jack and Alan jumped violently. "It's waxing moon," said the voice of Soldier. "Go we up that highest hill. Go careful."

He came out of the wood, his face holy as that of a knight carved on a tomb. His speech was altered by time and memory, and *he* was altered—strong, perhaps irresistible.

The climb up the hill was hard work. Stony outcrops, beech and elder trees, interrupted the path. The hill was coated in tangled grass. Far behind, the golden sun was sinking into the land, taking away the light.

"See," said Soldier, "she is risen."

The crescent moon was up the hill, still faint in the sunset.

The remains of the fort above seemed one with the jumble of the hill.

"This is where the entrance lies to their domain," said Soldier.

Alan added, "Yes, it's supposed to be under this hill. That's why the Romans had trouble here and brought in the druids—most unusual. They weren't normally friends. The druids suggested the Stone of Brid. Roman soldiers tended to prefer worshipping Mithras. Not here."

Alan was seeming more scholarly, and Soldier more insane. Defensive? Jack had no defense. He didn't even know why they had come up here—but again, the *compulsion* was intense.

Maybe *They* liked somebody to see what they could do, how beautiful they were, how clever. . . .

The last sun was squashed out just as they made the final stretch. Both Jack and Alan were dripping sweat. Soldier wasn't, though he looked three times Alan's age. The darkening light now became actual darkness. Shadow sprawled from rocks, trees, down from the sky itself. The moon, though, brightened, a white rip in the dusk.

The jagged Roman walls were in front of them. Ruin and nightfall robbed them of any shape or logic. A portion of archway stood ahead, and beyond it a kind of grassy court that looked as if sheep had grazed it recently. Down a topple of slope, Jack saw a formless stone.

"There," panted Alan. "There it is. The altar."

"They will always come here," said Soldier softly, "when they have gotten, to show their triumph to the Stone. God wills. *They are already here.*"

Jack stared, hair rising on arms and neck.

Through liquid shadow, something pale, that shone—

He could see them. The Lordly Ones, the—

Elvenbrood.

He didn't try to count, but he thought there were fourteen—one for every year of his sister's life. Yes, they were beautiful all right. Their skin was pearl, hair moonlit clouds.

Some were male, others female, but their clothes were the same, misty, clinging on slender bodies, but also flowing. There were jewels on them like nothing he'd ever seen or imagined, with great tears of light inside. They had daggers too, and swords of some silvery metal that couldn't be steel. And as he gazed at them, hypnotized, Jack saw Luce, there in the middle of them. Like them, she had flowers in her hair.

He wanted to shout to her. *They* were smiling and laughing, and so was she. Laughter like silver bells and silver daggers—

His mind yelled in the prison of his paralyzed body—but he couldn't move, and neither it seemed could Alan.

The Lordly Ones danced their stately dance along the hill, with Luce dancing with them, and coming to the altar they bowed, and their bowing was full of the most exquisite scorn.

Alan croaked something. "D'you see?"

Another thing had formed, beyond the altar, right there. It was a hole into emptiness, but down the tunnel of it was a pulsing, gorgeous glow.

"It's the *gate*, the way into the underhill . . ."

Trying to move, heart roaring, pinned to the spot . . .

Jack's struggle seemed to dislodge something outside himself.

Soldier.

"Here I am. Here, your child that you loved, who loved you hundred on hundred years. The one you sent into exile, lost in this world that, to your heaven country, is hell . . ." Soldier moved among them, with extraordinary grace. He moved as *They* did. Not like an old man in clothes from the garbage in a dustbin. He spoke in some language Jack had never heard—almost a twisted sort of Germanic French—yet Jack somehow understood every word.

"Don't take that other child," said Soldier to the Lordly Ones, royally scornful as they were. "Do you really want *her*? Ignorant and unformed and knowing nothing of your glory. No, take me again, out of this bitter world. I love you so. And I have learned all there is to know here. I am like a book you will be able to read for a thousand years."

The beings on the hill had ceased to move about. They looked stilly at Soldier.

Luce, petulant suddenly, cried, "It's only that stupid mad old man . . ."

One of the beings struck her lightly across the face. He did not speak, but turning to Soldier, he reached up and breathed into the old man's mouth. Although there were no words, Jack knew what the being had said: *Let us then remind ourselves of how you were. Let us compare and judge.*

You could make no excuses. It happened in front of Jack's eyes. Age and decay fell from Soldier like a discarded shell. He stood there, straight as a spear, a boy of maybe thirteen, golden skinned, unmarked, sun-gold hair to his waist.

Yes, said the voice that *had* no voice, *he is better.*

Laughing, Soldier looked green-eyed over his shoulder at Jack and Alan stuck there to the ground. "Farewell, men of mud. Farewell, world of dust. Know for always you could not have kept her, had They not loved me better than she."

A dazzle hit the hillside. Treetops and walls flared like neon, faded.

They were gone, the beings from the hill, the old man who had become a boy. Only one last pale shape remained, lying on the grass.

Paralysis left Jack. "Luce!"

When he touched her, she opened her eyes and looked at him, annoyed. "Why did you wake me up, Jack? What time is it?" And then, surprised but not alarmed, "Why am I up *here*?"

Jack couldn't speak. It was Alan who had to spin her some yarn that she'd come up here on a dare. Oddly, as she listened she seemed to believe him, to *remember* the dare— and nothing else unusual at all.

Alan and Jack talked later. It was a secret they had to keep always from Susie, and from Luce too. "It wasn't just they loved Soldier more than Lucy, Jack. It was because you and

Susie love her so *much*. That other woman who hated her boy—Soldier could never have made a swap with him—I doubt if he even tried. I think he only warned Lucy to make her more likely to do it—you know how girls can be. Or maybe when he was saner he did try to stop those things. Would she have been happier *there*? Well, yes. But that's not it. We're supposed to live out *here*."

Jack and Alan often had talks now, since Susie had moved the family to the town, and Susie and Alan became an Item. Susie was rehearsing for her part in Ken Angel's TV drama—it had nothing to do with faeries.

It was a year later that police in Gloucester found the burned-out Jeep Cherokee with Michael's body in it. It had gone off a country road into some trees. They said Michael would have been killed at once, the fire had happened afterward. It seemed, from bits of evidence, that Michael had become rich after leaving Susie. No one could find any trace of how, or where. It was a real mystery.

But Jack knew, he and Alan, though *this* they did not discuss: how Michael had come by his sudden money luck, the edge of which had rubbed off on Susie. Knew, too how Michael would not have been dead when his vehicle caught fire. Like Soldier's father, the Norman warlord ten centuries before, Michael had been burned alive.

Beyond the River

～⌒～

Joel Lane

Joel Lane lives in Birmingham, England. He has published horror and fantasy fiction steadily for twenty years; has written a number of essays on horror fiction, including several on Ramsey Campbell; has edited the anthologies Birmingham Noir *(crime and supense stories)*, co-edited with Steve Bishop *(2002)*, and Beneath the Ground *(supernatural horror stories, 2003)*; and has published two novels, From Blue To Black *(2000)* and The Blue Mask *(2003)*, both post-punk-music novels set in England. Some of his stories are collected in The Earth Wire and Other Stories *(1994)*, and in The Lost District and Other Stories *(2005)*.

"Beyond the River" was published in Acquainted with the Night, *a fine collection of fantastic and horror stories, edited and published by Barbara and Christopher Roden's Ash Tree Press, a distinguished small press publisher specializing in ghost stories. A young journalist goes to interview a distinguished older-woman-writer of children's books, and is shown the real truth. Lane says this story was a conscious homage to writer-illustrator Tove Jansson and her Moomintroll world. It is also a quite nasty allegorical commentary on conglomerate publishing's destructive powers. It is a fascinating contrast and comparison to Neil Gaiman's "The Problem of Susan."*

It's a surprisingly long way from London to Devon: a tilted line across the map of England, from the wealthy Southeast to the poorer Southwest. The landscape becomes more stark and elemental the farther you go. It took me three hours to drive to Exeter on a warm September afternoon, the setting sun ahead of me painting the edges of rock that showed through the hillsides. The fires of late summer had left blackened patches on the rusting wheatfields. I drove through run-down little towns too far from the coast to benefit from tourism. At last, the silver gleam of the Dart estuary was in sight. I would smell the rich odors of marine salt and river mud, faintly tinged with the chemical traces of industry.

Beside my road atlas on the passenger seat was a page from an A-Z map, with the road I was looking for circled in red. Underneath both was a hardback copy of a children's book: *The Secret Dance* by Susanne Perry. The front cover was a color version of one of the interior illustrations, showing a forest in twilight. The trees were ancient, their branches twisted into bizarre shapes. Living things were just visible among the trees and in the tangled undergrowth: a few squirrels, two owls, a fox—and many cats, whose eyes glowed a deep undersea green. The copy was a first edition. I'd had it for thirty years; it had been a present from my parents on my fifth birthday.

The Perry house was set back from the road, behind a tall privet hedge. The front garden was full of roses: tangled, overgrown bushes with heavy bloodred flowers. The appearance of neglect surprised me; Susanne had sounded calm and relaxed on the phone, but perhaps the stress of the last year had got to her. I was here to interview her for the *Observer*, and expected she'd have things to say about her former publisher. But I wanted to tell the readers that she'd risen above the corporate nightmare: the world of her imagination couldn't be touched by business. That was what I wanted to see.

Wind chimes rang behind the panelled door. Susanne opened it. She was taller than I'd expected, and was wearing a blue-black dress that made her appear willowy rather than skinny. Her loose dark hair was flecked with gray, rather like Patti Smith's on a recent *Later With Jools Holland*. She looked no more than fifty, but her eyes were older. She grasped my hand with her long narrow fingers. "Hello there. Julie, isn't it? Do come in."

The house was decorated in tasteful shades of dark green and auburn with abstract pictures and carvings that might have come from Italy or Spain. Susanne led me through into the living-room, whose window overlooked the river. You couldn't hear the boats go by, but you could see them. The back garden was mostly long grass and weeds. Susanne made coffee, and we sat on her green couch at the end of the room. Her writing-desk faced the window; there was a small electronic typewriter on it, but no sign of a computer.

"Beautiful house," I said. "How long have you lived here?" As far as I knew, she lived alone. There'd been a marriage in the past, but no children.

"I was born here. It was my parents' house. I inherited it when my mother died, and moved back in. I used to travel quite a lot, but lately this is all I need. I like living close to an estuary. Where the river becomes something else, the movement flowing into what doesn't change." She said this as casually as if she were talking about the availability of parking spaces at the local supermarket.

"Are there any forests nearby?" I asked. "I didn't see one when I was driving here."

She laughed. "You have to know where to look."

I wondered about asking her to sign my battered copy of *The Secret Dance*. Maybe later, at the end. She was probably sick of maudlin fans trying to relive their childhood. I wanted to appreciate the person she was now.

"How do you want to do the interview?" I said. "I can show you the question and let you think about them before we talk, or we can just start chatting and see how that goes. I'd like to get a photograph as well, if you're happy with that."

"Fine. Let's start there. Maybe by the window?" I fished my Nikon digital camera from my bag, then stood back so I could photograph Susanne with the river-boats as background rather than the forsaken garden. She ran her delicate fingers through her hair. Her face took on a lost, haunted expression, as if she were dreaming with her eyes open. I took three shots.

Afterward, it took her a few minutes to come back from whatever thoughts she'd given herself up to. She sipped her coffee quietly, her eyes closed. Then she smiled at me. "Would you like something to eat? I can have some dinner ready in half an hour. Be easier to talk over a glass of wine."

"That'd be lovely," I said. "If you're sure."

"It's nice to have someone here. I haven't felt like company in a while." She led me into the kitchen and prepared a light, elegant meal of grilled salmon with fennel and toasted ciabatta bread. I admired the tapestry that hung on the wall opposite the stove: an undersea scene of fish swimming through tangled weeds, coral, and the drifting hair of mermaids. It reminded me of Susanne's illustrations, though she always drew forest scenes since her books were set in a forest world.

We ate at a small table in the living-room, and shared a bottle of Chablis. I reckoned I could get away with two glasses if I wasn't driving for a couple of hours. And to be honest, I hadn't felt like company in a while either. It was nice, I thought, to share a drink with someone who didn't have an agenda, whether business or personal. The light dimmed in the bay window, and the small oil-lamps on the mantelpiece filled the room with trembling strands of light.

And she told me about the Forest of Scriffle. The imaginary twilight realm Susanne had developed as a background for the dreams, mysteries, and visions that she had wanted to explore as a young writer. The forest tales began as picture-books with text and illustrations on alternate pages, and ended as short novels with a few pages of artwork. Like

Tove Jansson, she had always drawn her own illustrations. The forest had grown over time, becoming more complex and more strangely populated.

"Did you read that interview with Simon Maxwell-Hoare in the *Sunday Times?*" she asked. I nodded. Maxwell-Hoare was the Managing Director of Neotechnic, the edutainment and educommerce publishing company that was trying to sue Susanne for breach of contract. He had asserted that "Susanne Perry is incapable of understanding the needs of her readership." The interviewer might have pointed out that, as the executive publisher of the magazine *Children As a Market*, Maxwell-Hoare viewed the cultural needs of children primarily in terms of their need for Neotechnic's products. But he hadn't.

Susanne drained her glass and refilled it. "The thing that infuriates me most about what he said is that the whole idea of the Forest of Scriffle was always quite commercial. But it gave me a peg on which I could hang my ideas about faith and imagination. Behind the dancing cats and the nervous squirrels and the world-weary owls were themes drawn from Wicca and nature worship, but I expect you know that."

"I think I did even as a child," I said. "The pictures suggested something more than just a bunch of cute little animals. The patterns, the swirling effects. Things going on in the background that you couldn't quite make out."

"In the seventies, some teachers said my books were a bad influence. They'd led people to take drugs." Her eyes widened. "Which I never did, of course." I suspected she was being ironic, but wasn't sure. "But whatever I was putting into the books, Neotechnic didn't want any of it. They wanted the new books to be like papier mâché: the surface repeated all the way through. I was supposed to let Marketing decide on the content. My job was simply to write and draw what they told me."

The grilled fish was rich and crisp. I relaxed, drank some wine, and kept the Dictaphone supplied with miniature tapes as Susanne told me her story. Part of me was still five years old, dreaming with my eyes open, running with the little lost creatures through the ancient shadows of the Forest of Scriffle.

"I started writing those stories when I was a student at Bristol University. My lecture notes were annotated with little silhouettes of cats and distorted trees. I searched the university library for books of folk tales, and wrote a dissertation on archetypal themes in the tales of Hans Christian Andersen. By the end of my final year, I'd written an early draft of *The Secret Dance*. And drawn most of the pictures.

"Then I got a job in a Bristol museum. I kept putting the book away, then taking it out and doing more work on it. Eventually I had a typed draft with a set of pen-and-ink illustrations. I sent it to Dunwich Books because they were my favorite children's publisher. Once I'd sent the book off, I decided to put my youth behind me and never write or draw again. Then I got a letter from their editor, Judith Williams, saying they wanted to publish the book.

"They had a wonderful office building near Scarborough, full of pictures and book covers. Judith and I became good friends. She encouraged me to write more complex stories, aimed at slightly older children, so that my readership could grow into the series. *The Sleepless Forest* took me three years to write and illustrate, while I drifted from one museum or art gallery job to another. Then I met a teacher called Steven who was taking a group of kids round a dinosaur exhibition. We got a flat together, and got married a year later.

"When the third book, *Shadows That Dream*, won a literary award and became a bestseller, I was able to give up my job. By now I had an agent, Roanne Smith, who kept me busy with school visits and readings. Felicity Kendal read *Shadows That Dream* on the BBC's *Jackanory* program. I had an offer from Puffin Books, but I wanted to stay with Dunwich—or at least with Judith. She was the only person who really understood the Forest of Scriffle. I did a painting of her in the forest, surrounded by cats. It stayed on the wall of her office until . . . the end.

"Steven was never comfortable with my success. He

didn't mind me writing my little books and doing my little sketches, but the fact that I was earning more than him made him angry. Things were different then. He wrote a novel for teenagers but couldn't sell it, and things began to sour between us. Maybe if we'd had children it would have been different. Anyway, he met someone else.

"Then my father became ill and died. I was spending a lot of time here, which meant I was reliving things just as they began to slip beyond my reach. Do you know what I mean? The Forest of Scriffle became an escape for me, but also a place where I could try and make sense of things. That's why *The Moon Cats* was a darker book. I was trying to help children see that life can't always be a happy thing. It didn't do as well as the third book, but I was proud of it.

"I wrote three more books in ten years, then decided that was enough. Dunwich Books kept them in print, and I was making enough money to live on. When Roanne retired, I didn't look for another agent. I suppose I didn't feel confident about writing another Forest of Scriffle book. I started working on an adult novel, a historical novel set in this region, but I still haven't finished it. People are harder to understand than cats. I drew some cards for Dunwich to print as merchandise, but that was all. Until the year before last."

By now, we had finished the meal and drained the bottle of Chablis. I thanked Susanne for her hospitality, and changed the tape in the Dictaphone. She disappeared into the kitchen, then returned with blueberries, ice cream, and coffee. The daylight was fading in the window, and I could see the lights on the river boats floating beyond the tangled shadows of the garden. The coffee was strong; its bitterness filtered through me as Susanne resumed her story.

"I'm sure you know most of it. Dunwich Books was bought out by Neotechnic, an American publishing corporation. They had to close their offices and move to the Neotechnic building in Telford. Have you been to Telford?" I shook my head. "It's a new town, all shopping malls and identical streets, nothing built before 1980. Judith hated it. Then, after six months, they announced a 're-structure.' Dunwich Books would cease to exist as an imprint, and its line would be absorbed into the Neotechnic list of children's fiction.

"Judith was called into a meeting to discuss her future. She told me about it a few days later. At that time, Simon Maxwell-Hoare was the Marketing Director, not the MD. But he completely controlled the meeting. It all revolved around him. Judith was asked to explain her publishing program. She got out about three sentences before he said: 'There's no market for fancy books.' Judith tried to talk about the reputation of the Dunwich Books list, its status in the field, and he cut her off again: 'I call a spade a shovel, dear. I don't give a shit about literary awards. This meeting has five objectives: increase profit, increase our market share, increase the visibility of the Neotechnic brand, reduce overheads, and increase profit again. I don't see that you have much to contribute.' The MD sat there like Buddha and said nothing.

"A month later, Judith and two other Dunwich editors were made redundant. Neotechnic put out a press release expressing regret that the extremely tough market had made this measure necessary. If Judith had stayed in children's publishing I would have tried to move with her, but she decided to take early retirement. She and her husband moved to France. Meanwhile, Neotechnic sent me nothing except a royalty statement and a subscription form for their magazine *Children As a Market*.

"Then I got a personal letter from Maxwell-Hoare, introducing himself as the new Managing Director and claiming to be a lifelong fan of children's fiction. He wanted me to come in and discuss the relaunching of the seven Forest of Scriffle novels in a new edition. As I recall, he said: 'The Scriffle series is a key product within the Neotechnic brand, and we look forward to increasing its market share.' He wanted me to write a new book in the series.

"I wrote back asking them to release me from my contract. That provoked a much less friendly letter informing me that Neotechnic would block any attempt by other publishers to reissue my work. It was their way or nothing. Of course, I should have got another agent. Or at least a solicitor. But I lost my nerve. This was just after my mother's death, and I was moving back here. I was very low, and short of money. Somehow I convinced myself that writing a new book would be good for me.

"So we had a lunch meeting at the only restaurant in Telford. There was Maxwell-Hoare, and the new Marketing Director, and the head of the design department. And Sally Black, my new editor, the only woman in the executive management team. Her contribution to the meeting was to smile and agree with everything that Maxwell-Hoare said. I recalled that Judith had mentioned Sally Black, but I can't quote her comments for legal reasons.

"It wasn't a very memorable meeting. Maxwell-Hoare informed me that he called a spade a shovel. Then he spouted some incomprehensible crap about market penetration and brand visibility. One of the phrases he used was 'old wine in new bottles.' I wish I'd paid closer attention, but I'd had a couple of glasses of real wine and wasn't at my sharpest. So when he said that I'd be working with Sally and the design team to make sure the new book did well for Neotechnic, I didn't ask what changes they had in mind.

"The next day, the contract arrived. It looked normal enough. There was a mention of touching up some of the old covers to give them more impact, and I thought that sounded quite reasonable. To be honest, I just wanted to get back into the Forest of Scriffle. I realized that ideas for an eighth book had been creeping around my head for years, waiting for me to notice them. I wrote the first draft of *Trees Never Forget* in about three months, and sent it to Sally Black.

"Then I was sent proofs of the new edition of *The Secret Dance*. That was a shock. They'd broken up paragraphs, replaced longer or less modern words with simpler ones, and introduced a hundred or so typing errors. Every illustration now had a small version of the Neotechnic logo in one corner. You know, that distorted N in a circle. The one on the cover was red on black; the others were gray on black.

"I sent the proofs back to Sally covered with corrections, and said I wasn't happy about the logos. When the new edition came out, hardly any of my corrections had been done and the logos were still there. I phoned Sally, and she said it wasn't cost-effective to make so many changes. 'It won't affect sales.' I said I had never agreed for the earlier books to be re-edited. She said 'You can't expect us to publish them unless they're appropriate for today's market.' I hung up the phone.

"A week later, my manuscript came back with Sally's comments. She started by saying that the language was too difficult for today's young readers. She wanted it 'rationalized' in line with the changes she was already making to my other books. And she insisted that I use American spellings, in line with Neotechnic's house style. Then she started on the story itself. She felt the hints of nature mysticism and Celtic magic were inappropriate for a mostly Christian readership. She wanted the cats to be friendlier and less mysterious, so that children could 'identify' with them. She didn't like the territorial hedgehogs or the sinister grass snakes. And she wanted me to mention a little blue dog, in order to tie into another Neotechnic product.

"A letter from the Marketing Director was attached. He wanted the illustrations simplified, made more 'accessible,' with more cats and fewer animals that the readers might not recognize. He wanted the little tie-in dog added at least three times, and shown in blue on the cover. A scanned image of said pooch was enclosed. Finally, he wanted the Neotechnic logo drawn into the forest background in every illustration.

"What could I do? I wrote to Maxwell-Hoare, saying that these demands were a violation of my rights as an author and a corruption of the relationship I had built up with my readers. I got a letter from the Neotechnic company lawyer, telling me that I had to comply with their demands; otherwise, my contract would be null and void. So I tore up the contract and sent them the pieces. I got another letter from the company lawyer, serving notice of legal action for breach of contract. The story got out, and here we are."

It was dark outside by now. Susanne looked at me as if I had come with the bailiffs. I wanted to hug her, but didn't know whether that was appropriate. I rubbed my forehead nervously. "I'm really sorry," I said. "It sounds like you've been shafted. But that's corporate publishing for you."

Susanne raised her eyebrows in mock surprise, then smiled. Her eyes looked terribly weary. "Julie, would you like some more wine? Or a drop of brandy? It's getting late, and you're welcome to crash out in my spare room. It's a long drive in the middle of the night."

Ordinarily, I would have suspected an attempt at seduction. Especially as I'd put on a nice outfit for the interview. But my spider-senses weren't picking up any such vibes from Susanne. At the same time, her tone was too level for this to be simple helpfulness. She had an agenda, but I didn't think it was sexual.

So I accepted the offer of more wine. Susanne found a bottle of Chianti, and put on a Dr. John CD to murmur darkly in the background. She drew the curtains, but left a window open. We sat and chatted for a while about subjects of mutual interest: modern art, blues, cats, Paris. I complained about the sexism of male journalists. Then she asked me: "Would you like to visit the Forest of Scriffle?"

"Er . . . pardon?" What metaphor was this? Was she offering me a joint, or a folder of her illustrations?

"I mean it literally." She wasn't smiling now. "It's not far away. Like I said, you have to know where to look."

"Where is it?" I asked, still mystified.

"Beyond the river. We can walk there."

The full moon cast delicate shadows from the trees outside Susanne's house. At the end of the road, a footpath led between two tall hedges. She led me through a gap in a steel fence, and down a precarious slope to the river bank. It was the kind of route I imagined a cat might follow.

"I found the way when I was seven," she said. "I've been coming here ever since. But I think it might not be here much longer. I want to share it with someone while I still can." The bank was overgrown, and I could see a factory wall on the other side. Susanne paused.

"Look."

She was pointing down to the water's edge. The river was

a dark skinless muscle with threads of moonlight. Just where the grass ended and the river-mud began, I could see two stone steps. The water smelled brackish. Susanne gripped my hand and pulled me forward. I felt a sudden, overwhelming sense of strangeness, as when you develop a fever or get caught between sleep and waking. I didn't think about my clothes, or my inability to swim. I just followed.

The steps led down under the water. It didn't feel cold, just a little more dense than the night air. Even breathing wasn't difficult: my chest just seemed to fill with air and exhale thin white plumes through the dark water. Fish or eels slid around my ankles. I walked for some time, holding Susanne's thin hand. It was much darker down here. Then she paused, reaching forward. Her drifting hair touched my face. She moved on, and we began to climb another flight of stone steps.

The moon's reflection shimmered on the water surface just above our heads. My foot slipped on river-weed, but Susanne drew me on. The surface broke, then healed below us. We stood dripping on the mossy bank. And there, just a few yards in front of us, was the Forest of Scriffle. The trees were silhouetted in the moonlight, their twigs as intricately patterned as medieval carvings. Drifts of dead leaves rustled in the night breeze.

I stepped forward, open-mouthed with wonder. My nostrils filled with scents of wood and leaf-mold, ferns and decay. But Susanne didn't move. I glanced at her and saw the growing terror in her face. "What's wrong?"

"I don't know. It's not the same. This time of year, the leaves should all be on the trees." She walked slowly forward. I followed her. Close up, I could see that the trunks were streaked with decay. The branches looked gray and brittle. "What's happened to it?" Susanne said. "The trees are all dead. And I can't hear the birds. At night there should be owls hooting, doves calling. It's silent."

Then something came toward us out of the dark undergrowth. It reached a clearing and stood in the moonlight, uncertain. A black cat. It was sniffing the air, but didn't seem to see us. Susanne walked slowly toward it, reaching out a hand. "Hello, little one. How are you? Where are your friends?" Then she stopped. "Oh, no."

The cat was blind. Its eyes were blank sockets. Its fur was patchy, and its ribs were visible through the taut skin. Susanne dropped to her knees and stroked the cat's neck. "My God, what's wrong with you? What's happened here—" Then she screamed. I saw her rise to her feet and beat her hand violently against the trunk of the nearest tree. Some of the dead bark flaked away at her touch.

I went to comfort Susanne, but she backed away from me. The cat was lying on its side, no longer moving. I knelt to examine it. In the moonlight, I could see things moving through its fur. Crawling rounded shapes, like bugs or lice. Each one had a raised marking that glowed faintly with a terrible light of its own. A shape like a twisted letter N, red on black.

Now that I had seen them, I became aware that they were on the trees also. And on the dead leaves beneath my feet. And on a dead owl that was lying within my reach, its beak stretched open to receive the night. They were everywhere in the forest, infesting every living thing, leaving nothing but gray brittle remains and silence. The rustling I could hear was the lice, hunting restlessly through the dead vegetation in search of something further to eat.

Then another sound reached me. A living sound. It was Susanne, weeping. I couldn't see her at first, wondered if the forest had claimed her for its own. Then I found her crouched behind the dead hair of a willow tree. In one hand she was holding the clean-picked skeleton of a leaf. I pulled her to her feet, held her until she stopped shaking. Her tears were cold against my cheek.

"We have to get out of here," I said. She didn't respond. "Come on. There's nothing to stay for."

"There's nothing to go back to either."

"You know that's not true." I gripped her hand and led her back toward the river. Behind us, I could hear the sound of dead trees creaking, breaking, and falling into the mounds of dead leaves. But something was calling to us through the night, from beyond the river. A heron.

Somehow we made it back the way we had come. The

moon was lower in the sky, and it was colder than before. As we reached the house, Susanne began to shiver violently. She was pulling at her sleeves, checking them for signs of infection. I held both her hands, made her look at my face. "Come on. Let's go inside."

As I'd expected, Susanne seemed calmer indoors. She poured us both a large brandy, drank hers in a slow painful gulp. Then she walked up to the bathroom and closed the door behind her. I sat on the couch, drank my brandy, and reflected that I hadn't asked Susanne to sign my copy of *The Secret Dance*. It didn't seem appropriate just now.

To my relief, Susanne emerged after a while. She was wearing a dark green dressing-gown, and her hair was wet. I poured her another brandy. She sat on the couch for a while, lost in thought. Then she said: "I have to go back there."

"What for? You can't save the cats."

"No, but I can burn them. Like a cremation. The wind will scatter the ashes in the river."

I shook my head. "There's no point, Susanne. If you go back, the forest will trap you. You'll die there. Your life is here."

She looked at me then, and her eyes were full of ashes. "What makes you so sure?"

"Because when things die, they don't stay the same. They rot. They become less than they were." I could feel a bitterness in my throat like nausea as I spoke. "You can't go back like that. No one can."

Susanne didn't say anything more. She finished her glass, then pointed to mine. I shook my head. She spread a thin duvet and a few cushions over the couch, then went upstairs. I turned off the light and spent a sleepless night on the couch, imagining that I could feel dead leaves dropping onto my face.

In the morning Susanne was brisk and efficient, making breakfast and filling a flask with coffee to help me get through the long drive home. We didn't talk about the midnight trip. I never did get that book signed.

The feature article came out a week later. I'd glossed over

most of the Neotechnic business, focusing on Susanne's earlier career and the enduring magic of the Forest of Scriffle. She sent me a card at my work address. On the front was an original sketch, showing two cats walking along a river bank by the light of a full moon. Inside was the message: *To Julie, a moon cat who keeps her feet on the ground. With love from Susanne.* Soon after that, Neotechnic dropped the lawsuit and stopped reprinting her books.

We've been in touch occasionally since then—phone calls, an exchange of Christmas cards—but she hasn't invited me to go back. I like to think that she's able to keep the river between herself and the ruin of her dreams. Sometimes I remember her smile, and it warms me. But sometimes I wake up shaking in the night, clawing at my skin, and nothing can take away the image in my head: an army of sleek black and red lice, working efficiently to pick the bones of a cat.

Out of the Woods

Patricia A. McKillip

Patricia A. McKillip (tribute site: www.evan.org/McKillip. html) lives with her husband, David Lunde, in Bend, Oregon. She is one of the most famous living fantasy writers, the author of the classic Riddlemaster of Hed trilogy. She won the first World Fantasy award for best novel for The Forgotten Beasts of Eld. *She is also one of the finest writers of short fiction in the F&SF field, and of them, perhaps the most underrated. Her stories in recent years present the work of a first-rate talent at the height of her powers. Her recent novels include* Ombria in Shadow *(2002),* In the Forests of Serre *(2003),* Something Rich and Strange: A Tale of Brian Froud's Faerielands *(2004), and* Alphabet of Thorn *(2004).* Odd Magic *is her 2005 novel. Her work is often understated yet filled with subdued passion, and with exact and precise observations. A collection of her short stories is seriously overdue.*

"Out of the Woods" appeared in Flights. *Here a good woman goes to work for a sorcerer at the instigation of her husband; magical things happen, but the protagonist is much more receptive to them than either her husband or the sorcerer. It is tempting to read this as a feminist parable, but with a very delicate touch. Perhaps it is about fantasy. It is interesting to compare and contrast it to Bruce McAllister's story, earlier.*

The scholar came to live in the old cottage in the woods one spring. Leta didn't know he was there until Dylan told her of the man's request. Dylan, who worked with wood, cut and sold it, mended it, built with it, whittled it into toothpicks when he had nothing better to do, found the scholar under a bush, digging up henbane. From which, Dylan concluded, the young man was possibly dotty, possibly magical, but, from the look of him, basically harmless.

"He wants a housekeeper," he told Leta. "Someone to look after him during the day. Cook, wash, sew, dust, straighten. Buy his food, talk to peddlers, that sort of thing. You'd go there in the mornings, come back after his supper."

Leta rolled her eyes at her brawny, comely husband over the washtub as she pummeled dirt out of his shirts. She was a tall, wiry young woman with her yellow hair in a braid. Not as pretty or as bright as some, but strong and steady as a good horse, was how her mother had put it when Dylan came courting her.

"Then who's to do it around here?" she asked mildly, being of placid disposition.

Dylan shrugged, wood chips from a stick of kindling curling under his knife edge, for he had no more pressing work. "It'll get done," he said. He sent a couple more feathery chips floating to his feet, then added, "Earn a little money for us. Buy some finery for yourself. Ribbon for your cap. Shoe buckle."

She glanced down at her scuffed, work-worn clogs. Shoes, she thought with sudden longing. And so the next day she went to the river's edge and then took the path downriver to the scholar's cottage.

She'd known the ancient woman who had died there the year before. The cottage needed care; flowers and moss sprouted from its thatch; the old garden was a tangle of vegetables, herbs and weeds. The cottage stood in a little clearing surrounded by great oak and ash, near the river and not far from the road that ran from one end of the wood to the other. The scholar met her at the door as though he expected her.

He was a slight, bony young man with pale thinning hair and gray eyes that seemed to look at her, through her and beyond her, all at the same time. He reminded Leta of something newly hatched, awkward, its down still damp and all askew. He smiled vaguely, opened the door wider, inviting her in even before she explained herself, as though he already knew.

"Dylan sent me," she said, then gazed with astonishment at the pillars and piles of books, scrolls, papers everywhere, even in the rafters. The cauldron hanging over the cold grate was filthy. She could see a half-eaten loaf on a shelf in the open cupboard; a mouse was busily dealing with the other half. There were cobwebs everywhere, and unwashed cups, odd implements she could not name tossed on the colorful, wrinkled puddles of clothes on the floor. As she stood gaping, an old, wizened sausage tumbled out of the rafters, fell at her feet.

She jumped. The scholar picked up the sausage. "I was wondering what to have for breakfast." He put it into his pocket. "You'd be Leta, then?"

"Yes, sir."

"You can call me Ansley. My great-grandmother left me this cottage when she died. Did you know her?"

"Oh, yes. Everyone did."

"I've been away in the city, studying. I decided to bring my studies here, where I can think without distractions. I want to be a great mage."

"Oh?"

"It is an arduous endeavor, which is why I'll have no time for—" He gestured.

She nodded. "I suppose when you've become a mage, all you'll have to do is snap your fingers or something."

His brows rose; clearly, he had never considered the use

of magic for housework. "Or something," he agreed doubt-fully. "You can see for yourself what I need you for."

"Oh, yes."

He indicated the vast, beautifully carved table in a corner under a circular window from which the sunny river could be seen. Or could have been seen, but for the teetering pile of books blocking the view. Ansley must have brought the table with him. She wondered how he had gotten the mas-sive thing through the door. Magic, maybe; it must be good for something.

"You can clear up any clutter in the place but that," he told her. "That must never be disturbed."

"What about the moldy rind of cheese on top of the books?"

He drew breath, held it. "No," he said finally, decisively. "Nothing on the table must be touched. I expect to be there most of the time anyway, learning spells and translating the ancient secrets in manuscripts. When," he asked a trifle anxiously, "can you start?"

She considered the various needs of her own husband and house, then yielded to his pleading eyes. "Now," she said. "I suppose you want some food in the place."

He nodded eagerly, reaching for his purse. "All I ask," he told her, shaking coins into her hand, "is not to be both-ered. I'll pay whatever you ask for that. My father did well with the tavern he owned; I did even better when I sold it after he died. Just come and go and do whatever needs to be done. Can you manage that?"

"Of course," she said stolidly, pocketing the coins for a trip to the market in the village at the edge of the woods. "I do it all the time."

She spent long days at the cottage, for the scholar paid scant attention to time and often kept his nose in his books past sunset despite the wonderful smells coming out of his pots. Dylan grumbled, but the scholar paid very well, and didn't mind Leta taking leave in the late afternoons to fix Dylan's supper and tend for an hour to her own house be-fore she went back to work. She cooked, scrubbed, weeded and washed, got a cat for the mice and fed it too, swept and

mended, and even wiped the grime off the windows, though
the scholar never bothered looking out. Dylan worked hard,
as well, building cupboards and bedsteads for the villagers,
chopping trees into cartloads of wood to sell in the market
for winter. Some days, she heard his ax from dawn to dusk.
On market days, when he lingered in the village tavern, she
rarely saw his face until one or the other of them crawled
wearily into bed late at night.

"We never talk anymore," she murmured once, surpris-
edly, to the dark when the warm, sweaty, grunting shape
that was Dylan pushed under the bedclothes beside her.
"We just work and sleep, work and sleep."

He mumbled something that sounded like "What else is
there?" Then he rolled away from her and began to snore.

One day when Ansley had gone down to the river to
hunt for the details of some spell, Leta made a few furtive
passes with her broom at the dust under his worktable.
Her eye fell upon a spiral of gold on a page in an open
book. She stopped sweeping, studied it. A golden letter, it
looked like, surrounded by swirls of gold in a frame of
crimson. All that richness, she marveled, for a letter. All
that beauty. How could a simple letter, this undistin-
guished one that also began her name, be so cherished,
given such loving attention?

"One little letter," she whispered, and her thoughts
strayed to earlier times, when Dylan gave her wildflowers
and sweets from the market. She sighed. They were always
so tired now, and she was growing thinner from so much
work. They had more money, it was true. But she had no
time to spend it, even on shoes, and Dylan never thought of
bringing her home a ribbon or a bit of lace when he went to
the village. And here was this letter, doing nothing more
than being the first in a line of them, adorned in red and
gold for no other reason than that it was itself—

She touched her eyes, laughed ruefully at herself, thinking, I'm jealous of a letter.

Someone knocked at the door.

She opened it, expecting Dylan, or a neighbor, or a
tinker—anyone except the man who stood there.

She felt herself gaping, but could not stop. She could only think crazily of the letter again: how this man too must have come from some place where people as well as words carried such beauty about them. The young man wore a tunic of shimmering links of pure silver over black leather trousers and a pair of fine, supple boots. His cloak was deep blue black, the color of his eyes. His crisp dark curls shone like blackbirds' wings. He was young, but something, perhaps the long, jeweled sword he wore, made both Dylan and Ansley seem much younger. His lean, grave face hinted of a world beyond the wood that not even the scholar had seen.

"I beg your pardon," he said gently, "for troubling you." Leta closed her mouth. "I'm looking for a certain palace of which I've heard rumors all my life. It is surrounded by a deadly ring of thorns, and many men have lost their lives attempting to break through that ensorceled circle to rescue the sleeping princess within. Have you heard of it?"

"I—," Leta said, and stuck there, slack-jawed again. "I—I—"

Behind the man, his followers, rugged and plainly dressed, glanced at one another. That look, less courteous than the young man's, cleared Leta's head a bit.

"I haven't," she brought out finally. "But the man I work for is a—is trying to be—a mage; he knows a thousand things I don't."

"Then may I speak with him?"

"He's out—" She gestured, saw the broom still in her hand and hid it hastily behind her. "Down by the river, catching toads."

"Toads."

"For his—his magic."

She heard the faint snort. One of the followers pretended to be watching a crow fly; the other breathed, "My lord, perhaps we should ask farther down the road."

"We'll ride to the river," the young lord said, and turned to mount his horse again. He bowed graciously to Leta from his saddle. "Thank you. We are grateful."

Blinking at the light spangling off his harness and jewels,

she watched him ride through the trees and toward the water. Then, slowly, she sat down, stunned and witless with wonder, until she heard Ansley's voice as he walked through the doorway and around her.

"I found five," he announced excitedly, putting a muddy bucket on his table. "One of them is pure white!"

"Did you see—?" Her voice didn't come. She was sitting on the floor, she realized then, with the broom across her knees. "Did you see the—? Them?"

"Who?" he asked absently, picking toads out of the bucket and setting them on his papers.

"The traveler. I sent him to talk to you." She hesitated, finally said the word. "I think he is a prince. He is looking for a palace surrounded by thorns, with a sleeping princess inside."

"Oh, him. No. I mean yes, but no I couldn't help him. I had no idea what he was talking about. Come here and look at this white one. You can do so many things with the white toads."

She had to wait a long time before Dylan came home, but she stayed awake so that she could tell him. As he clambered into bed, breathing a gust of beer at her, she said breathlessly, "I saw a prince today. On his way to rescue a princess."

He laughed and hiccuped at the same time. "And I saw the Queen of the Fairies. Did you happen to spot my knife too? I set it down yesterday when I was whittling, and it must have strolled away."

"Dylan—"

He kissed her temple. "You're dreaming, love. No princes here."

The days lengthened. Hawthorn blossoms blew everywhere like snow, leaving green behind. The massive oaks covered their tangled boughs with leaves. An early summer storm thundered through the woods one afternoon. Leta, who had just spread Ansley's washing to dry on the hawthorn bushes around the cottage, heard the sudden snarl of wind, felt a cold, hard drop of rain on her mouth. She sighed. The clothes were wet anyway; but for the wild wind that might steal them, she could have left them out. She began to gather them back into her basket.

She heard voices.

They sounded like wind at first, one high, pure, one pitched low, rumbling. They didn't seem human, which made Leta duck warily behind a bush. But their words were human enough, which made her strain her ears to listen. It was, she thought bewilderedly, like hearing what the winds had to say for themselves.

"Come into my arms and sleep, my lord," the higher voice crooned. "You have lived a long and adventurous life; you may rest now for a while."

"No," the deeper voice protested, half-laughing, half-longing, Leta thought. "It's not time for me to sleep, yet. There are things I still must teach you."

"What things, my heart?"

"How to understand the language of beetles, how to spin with spindrift, what lies hidden in the deepest place in the ocean and how to bring it up to light."

"Sleep a little. Teach me when you wake again."

"No, not yet."

"Sleep."

Leta crept closer to the voices. The rain pattered down now, great, fat drops the trees could not stop. Through the blur of rain and soughing winds stirring up the bracken, she saw two figures beneath an oak. They seemed completely unaware of the storm, as if they belonged to some enchanted world. The woman's long, fiery, rippling hair did not notice the wind, nor did the man's gray-white beard. He sat cradled in the oak roots, leaning back against the trunk. His face looked as harsh and weathered, as ancient and enduring as the wood. The woman stood over him, close enough for him to touch, which he did now and then, his hand caressing the back of her knee, coaxing it to bend. They were both richly dressed, he in a long, silvery robe flecked with tiny jewels like points of light along the sleeves, the hem. She wore silk the deepest green of summer, the secret green of trees who have taken in all the light they can hold, and feel, somewhere within them, summer's end. His eyes were half-closed. Hers were very wide as she stared down at him: pale amber encircling vivid points of black.

Leta froze. She did not dare move, lest those terrible eyes lift from his and search her out behind the bush with Ansley's trousers flapping on it.

"Sleep," the woman murmured again, her voice like a lightly dancing brook, like the sough of wind in reeds. "Sleep."

His hand dropped from her knee. He made an effort, half lifting his eye-lids. His eyes were silver, metallic like a knife blade.

"Not yet, my sweet Nimue. Not yet."

"Sleep."

He closed his eyes.

There was a crack as though the world had been torn apart. Then came the thunder. Leta screamed as she felt it roll over her, through her, and down beneath her into the earth. The ancient oak, split through its heart, trailing limbs like shattered bone, loosed sudden, dancing streams of fire. Rain fell then in vast sheets as silvery as the sleeper's eyes. Leta couldn't see anything; she was drenched in a moment and sinking rapidly into a puddle. Rising, she glimpsed the light shining from the cottage windows. She stumbled out of the mysterious world toward it; wind blew her back through the scholar's door, then slammed the door behind her.

"I saw—I saw—," she panted.

But she did not know what she saw. Ansley, his attention caught at last by something outside his books—the thunder, maybe, or the lake she was making on his floor—looked a little pale in the gloom.

"You saw what?"

But she had only pieces to give him, nothing whole, nothing coherent. "I saw his eyes close. And then lightning struck the oak."

Ansley moved then. "Oh, I hope it won't topple onto my roof."

"His eyes closed—they were like metal—she put him to sleep with her eyes—"

"Show me the tree."

She led him eagerly through the rain. It had slowed a little; the storm was moving on. Somewhere else in the wood strange things were happening; the magic here had come and gone.

They stood looking at the broken heart of the oak, its wood still smoldering, its snapped boughs sagging, shifting dangerously in the wind. Only a stand of gnarled trunk was left, where the sleeper had been sitting.

"Come away," Ansley said uneasily. "Those limbs may still fall."

"But I saw two people—"

"They had sense enough to run, it seems; there are no bodies here. Just," he added, "a lot of wet clothes among the bushes. What exactly were those two doing?"

"They're your clothes."

"Oh."

She lingered, trying to find some shred of mystery left in the rain, some magic smoldering with the wood. "He closed his eyes," she whispered, "and lightning struck the oak."

"Well, he must have opened them fast enough then," Ansley said. "Come back into the house. Leave the laundry; you can finish all that later." His voice brightened as he wandered back through the dripping trees. "This will send the toads out to sun. . . ."

She did not even try to tell Dylan, for if the young scholar with all his books saw no magic, how could he?

Days passed, one very like the next. She cooked, washed, weeded in the garden. Flowers she had rescued from wild vines bloomed and faded; she picked herbs and beans and summer squashes. The scholar studied. One day the house was full of bats, the next full of crows. Another day he made everything disappear, including himself. Leta stepped, startled, into an empty cottage. Not a thing in it, not even a stray spider. Then she saw the scholar's sheepish smile forming in the air; the rest of his possessions followed slowly. She stared at him, speechless. He cleared his throat.

"I must have mistranslated a word or two in that spell."

"You might have translated some of the clutter out of the door while you were at it," she said. What had reappeared was as chaotic as ever. She could not imagine what he did at nights while she was at home. Invented whirlwinds, or made his pots and clothes dance in midair until they dropped, it looked like.

"Think of magic as an untamed creature," he suggested, opening a book while he rained crumbs on the floor chewing a crust he had found on his table. "I am learning ways to impose my will upon it, while it fights me with all its cunning for its freedom."

"It sounds like your garden," she murmured, tracking down her gardening basket, which was not on the peg where she hung it, but, for some reason, on a shelf, in the frying pan. The scholar made an absent noise, not really hearing her; she had gotten used to that. She went outside to pull up onions for soup. She listened for Dylan's ax while she dug; he had said he was cutting wood that day. But she didn't hear it, just the river and the birds and the breeze among the leaves.

He must have gone deeper than usual into the woods, she thought. But she felt the little frown between her brows growing tighter and tighter at his silence. For no reason her throat grew tight too, hurt her suddenly. Maybe she had misunderstood; maybe he had gone into the village to sell wood instead. That made the ache in her throat sharper. His eyes and voice were absent, those days. He looked at her, but hardly saw her; he kissed her now and then, brief, chuckling kisses that you'd give to a child. He had never gone to the village so often without her before; he had never wanted to go without her, before . . .

She asked him tentatively that night, as he rolled into bed in a cloud of beer fumes and wood smoke, "Will you take me with you, next time?"

He patted her shoulder, his eyes already closed. "You need your rest, working so hard for two houses. Anyway, it's nothing; I just have a quick drink and a listen to the fiddling, then I'm home to you."

"But it's so late."

He gave her another pat. "Is it? Then best get to sleep."
He snored; she stared, wide-eyed, back at the night.

She scarcely noticed when the leaves first began to turn.
Suddenly there were mushrooms and berries and nuts to
gather, and apples all over the little twisty apple tree in her
own garden. The days were growing shorter, even while there
seemed so much more to do. She pulled out winter garments
to mend where the moths had chewed; she replenished supplies of soap and candles. Her hands were always red; her
hair, it seemed, always slightly damp with steam from something. The leaves grew gold, began to fall, crackle underfoot
as she walked from one house to the other and back again.
She scarcely saw the two men: the scholar hunched over a
book with his back to her, her husband always calling good-
bye as he went to chop or sell or build. Well, they scarcely
saw her either, she thought tiredly; that was the way of it.

She stayed into evening at the scholar's one day, darning
his winter cloak while the stew she had made of carrots and
potatoes and leeks bubbled over the fire. He was at his
table, staring into what looked like a glass ball filled with
swirling iridescent fires. He was murmuring to it; if it answered him, she didn't hear.

At least not for some time. When she began to hear the
strange, crazed disturbance beneath the wind rattling at the
door, she thought at first that the sound came from within
the globe. Her needle paused. The noise seemed to be coming closer: a disturbing confusion of dogs barking, horns,
faint bells, shouting, bracken and fallen limbs crackling
under the pounding of many hooves. She stared at the glass
ball, which was hardly bigger than the scholar's fist. Surely
such an uproar couldn't be coming from that?

The wind shrieked suddenly. The door shook on its hinges.
She froze, midstitch. The door sprang open as if someone
had kicked it. All the confusion in the night seemed to be on
the scholar's doorstep and about to roil into his cottage.

She leaped to her feet, terrified, and clung to the door,
trying to force it shut against the wind. A dark current was
passing the house: something huge and nameless, bewilder-
ing until her eyes began to find the shapes in the night.

They appeared at random, lit by fires that seemed to stream from the nostrils of black horses galloping past her. The flames illumined great hounds with eyes like coals, up-raised sword blades like broken pieces of lightning, cowled faces, harnesses strung with madly clamoring bells.

She stared, unable to move. One of the hooded faces turned toward her as his enormous horse, its hooves spark-ing fire, cleared her potato rows. The rider's face was gaunt, bony, his hair in many long braids, their ends secured around clattering bones. He wore a crown of gold; its great jewel reflected fire the color of a splash of blood. White moons in the rider's eye sockets flashed at Leta; he opened his jaws wide like a wolf and laughed.

She could not even scream, her voice was that shriveled with fear. She could only squeak. Then the door was taken firmly out of her hands, closed against the night.

The scholar grumbled, returning to his work, "I couldn't hear a thing with all that racket. Are you still here? Take a lamp with you when you go home."

She went home late, terrified at every step, every whine of wind and crackle of branch. Her cold hands woke Dylan as she hugged him close in their bed for warmth and comfort. He raised his head, breathing something that may have been a name, and maybe not. Then his voice came clear.

"You're late." He did not sound worried or angry, only sleepy. "Your hands are ice."

"Dylan, there was something wicked in the woods to-night."

"What?"

"I don't know—riders, dark riders, on horses with flam-ing breath—I heard horns, as if they were hunting—"

"Nobody hunts in the dark."

"Didn't you hear it?"

"No."

"Were you even here?" she asked incredulously. He turned away from her, settled himself again.

"Of course. You weren't, though, so I went to bed."

"You could have come to fetch me," she whispered. "You could have brought a lamp."

"What?"

"You could have wondered."

"Go to sleep," he murmured. "Sleep."

Winter, she thought as she walked to the scholar's cottage the next morning. There wouldn't be so much work then, with the snow flying. No gardens to tend, no trees to chop, with their wood damp and iron-clad. She and Dylan would see more of one another, then. She'd settle the scholar and come home before dark; they'd have long evenings together beside the fire. Leaves whirled around her. The brightly colored autumn squashes were almost the last things still unpicked in the garden, besides the root vegetables. One breath of frost, and the herbs would be gone, along with most of the green in the world.

"You'll need wood for winter," she reminded the scholar. "I'll have Dylan bring you some."

He grunted absently. She sighed a little, watching him, as she tied on her apron.

I've grown invisible, she thought.

Later, she caught herself longing for winter, and didn't know whether to laugh or cry.

Dylan stacked the scholar's wood under the eaves. The squashes grew fat as the garden withered around them. The air smelled of rain and sweet wood smoke. Now and then the sky turned blue; fish jumped into sunlight; the world cast a glance back at the season it had left. On one of those rare days Leta spread the washing on the bushes to dry. Drawn to the shattered oak, she left her basket and walked through the brush to look at it, search for some sign that she had truly seen—whatever she had seen.

The great, gnarled stump, so thick that two or maybe three of her might have ringed it with her arms, stood just taller than her head. Only this lower, rooted piece of trunk was left intact, though lightning had seared a black stain on it like a scar. It stood dreaming in the sunlight, revealing nothing of its secrets. Just big enough, she thought, to draw a man inside it, if one had fallen asleep against it. In spring, living shoots would rise like his dreams out of the trunk, crown it with leaves, this still-living heart big enough to hide a sleeping mage. . . .

Something moving down the river caught her eyes.

She went through the trees toward it, unable to see clearly what it was. An empty boat, it seemed, caught in the current, but that didn't explain its odd shape, and the hints of color about it, the drift of cloth that was not sail.

She ran down the river path a ways to get ahead of it, so that she could see it clearly as it passed. It seemed a fine, delicate thing, with its upraised prow carved into a spiral and gilded. The rest of it, except for a thin line of gold all around it, was painted black. Some airy fabric caught on the wind, drifted above it, and then fell back into the boat. Now the cloth was blue, now satiny green. Now colors teased at her: intricately embroidered scenes she could not quite make out, on a longer drift of linen. She waited, puzzled, for the boat to reach her.

She saw the face within and caught her breath.

It was a young woman. She lay in the boat as though she slept, her sleeves, her skirt, the tapestry work in her hands picked up by passing breezes, then loosed again. Her hair, the color of the dying leaves, was carefully coiled and pinned with gold. Leta started to call to her. Words stopped before they began. That lovely face, skin white as whitest birch, held nothing now: no words, no expressions, no more movement than a stone. She had nothing left to tell Leta but her silence.

The boat glided past. Golden oak leaves dropped gently down onto the still figure, as though the trees watched with Leta. She felt sorrow grow in her throat like an apple, a toad, a jewel. It would not come out in tears or words or any other shape. It kept growing, growing, while she moved because she still could—walk and speak and tell and even, with a reason, smile—down the river path. She followed the boat, not knowing where it was going, or what she was mourning, beginning to run after a while when the currents quickened and the trees thinned, and the high slender towers of a distant city gleamed in the light of the waning day.

The Man from Shemhaza

Steven Brust

Steven Brust (www.dreamcafe.com) lives in Las Vegas, Nevada. He describes himself as "the author of twenty-one novels and one solo record." His literary hero was Roger Zelazny, and, like him, Brust is a devoted storyteller with a bedrock devotion to entertaining his audience. His chosen mode is adventure fantasy, and his work is therefore often critically underrated. His story "When the Bough Breaks" was a Nebula Award nominee in 1998. His newest book is Sethra Lavode (2004).

"The Man from Shemhaza" appeared in Thieves' World: Enemies of Fortune, *edited by Lynn Abbey. It was written by Steven Brust, but in a very real sense it's a collaboration. It's set in Thieves' World™, a continuity first devised in the late 1970s by writers Robert Lynn Asprin and Lynn Abbey for a series of original "shared-world" anthologies—the first of the form. Among the many who have contributed to Thieves World, enriching and deepening its range of characters, situations, and background details, have been writers as diverse as David Drake, Vonda N. McIntyre, Joe Haldeman, A. E. Van Vogt, John Brunner, and Marion Zimmer Bradley. This kind of playful sharing, a sort of collaborative world-building jazz, is characteristic of modern SF and fantasy writers, and a strength of the field.*

Pegrin wandered over and said, "Hey. How are things?"

"Splendid," I told him. "Couldn't be better."

He grunted. "You about ready?"

"Almost. Just tuning."

"Why?"

I grinned and didn't answer. My cresca was a pretty thing, with a stained maple neck supporting a teak fret-board, a top of maple, and back and sides of reddish-brown prectawood; but there was an extraordinarily thick steel truss rod running all through the neck, so it was far, far stronger than it looked. It held a tune remarkably well. Me, too, I guess. I mean, about holding a tune remarkably well.

I touched it up a little, then gave Pegrin a small nod and a big smile. "Ready," I said.

He gave me a half-hearted glower. "Do you have any idea how annoying it is to be around someone so perpetually cheerful?"

"Can't help it," I said, grinning. "That's the beauty of the cresca; it's a naturally happy instrument." That wasn't strictly true. The cresca can be mournful just by keeping the low drone going and ignoring the high drone; but I rarely play that way. Who wants mournful?

"Uh-huh." He gestured to what passed for a stage in the 'Unicorn—a place under the rear balcony near the front of the room. "Go," he said.

I went. I flipped my orange cloak over my shoulder (yes, orange. Shut up.) and sat down on a hard, ugly chair. My cresca snuggled into my lap. The audience eagerly awaited my first note. Heh. I made that part up. Actually, one old lady who was leaning on the bar like she needed to gave me barely a glance, and a fat little merchant flicked his eye over me with distaste. He'd either heard me before and didn't like it, or else didn't care for my taste in clothing. Kadasah and Kaytin were enjoying another of their spats, Perrez was scanning the room for anyone stupid enough to fall for one of his deals. (I'm not that stupid. Anymore.) To my delight, Rogi was nowhere in sight. Believe me, the only thing worse than no one singing along is Rogi singing along. I started the drones going, thumb and forefinger, then started in the comp for "The Man from Shemhaza," which is a great opening tune. Two gentlemen who looked to be Rankan at the table nearest me (which meant I could have knocked one of their heads with the neck of my cresca) glanced at me, then went back to their conversation.

> *"In the hills of far Shemhaza lived a man both weak*
> *and strong*
> *Who lived in a house both big and small on a road both*
> *short and long*
> *His hair was dark and fair and red, he was both short*
> *and tall*
> *He was skinny, fat, but more than that he was not a*
> *man at all*
>
> *So sing me of Shemhaza and the man who couldn't fail*
> *And I'll keep singing verses until you buy me ale."*

And then back into an instrumental that my fingers carried without me having to think about it, just as my mouth didn't have to think about the verses. The two Rankan noblemen didn't have to think about them either, they continued a conversation in which the rotting leg of our ruler figured prominently. And so into the second verse. No one sang along, but the 'Unicorn isn't a singalong-on-the-chorus sort of place. And so on for about an hour and a half.

The second verse drove away the Rankan nobles, which was almost enough to hurt my feelings, but three drunken dockhands replaced them by the time the third verse started, and dockhands will occasionally tip.

I made a few padpols in tips and was bought a drink, and

got a meal into the bargain—spit-roasted nyafish with pepper. I packed up my cresca, slung the case over my shoulder, and, with a grin and a wave to Pegrin, headed out into the Sanctuary night.

While I was walking through the Maze, I heard, "Tor! Wait up." I turned and smiled, though I have to say I don't enjoy hearing my name abbreviated. My name is Tord'an J'ardin, or Tord'an, which is already shortened from Tordra Na Rhyan or, "One who follows the Old Ways." It is not Tor. But cutting names down until they are meaningless is the custom in Sanctuary, and nothing good can come of bucking custom.

"Tor! How are things?"

"Wonderful, Dinra. As always. How is your evening?"

"Good enough. Where are you going?"

"Land's End."

"Private party?"

I nodded.

"Oh, lucky you!"

I nodded and grinned. Private parties are one of the few chances a songster has to make any real coin. And one can lead to another, if you're both good and lucky.

"Who are you playing for?"

I shrugged. "In the End you're always playing for Lord Serripines, even if someone else is playing, and even if he never shows."

He nodded. "Yep. Among the Ilsigi, you're always playing for the princes and nabobs, even if they never walk into the room."

"But in the palace you make more money."

"Same artistic satisfaction, though," he said. "That is to say, none."

I grinned and nodded. We'd been over this before. He had his connections among the Ilsigi, I among the Rankans.

I smacked him lightly on the back of the head and said, "Where are you off to?"

"I'm going to pay another visit to Pel."

"Your wrist again?"

He nodded.

"You play too fast," I told him.

He chuckled. "I keep telling you, lessons are available."

"I haven't forgotten. How is Mirazia?"

He smiled. "Wonderful, as always. She asks about you."

"Well, why shouldn't she?" I punched him lightly on the shoulder and winked. "So, what else is new?"

He smiled. "You want to know?"

"Oh? Now I'm suddenly intrigued. Tell."

He stopped walking and glanced around to make sure no one was watching us. Fortunately, there was no one on the street, because I can't think of a better way to attract attention. Then he untied his belt pouch of some really ugly off-white fur, opened it up, and dug around in it. What he showed me was a flat, rectangular piece of what looked like dull gray metal, small enough to fit into his palm (and, for a musician, he had rather small hands).

"We need more light," I said. Dinra grunted and led us around until we spotted a streak of light leaking out from a shutter overhead. He showed me the object again, and now I could see various scratches on it, like glyphs, and the glitter of three red jewels set in a triangle.

"It's a pretty thing," I said. "What is it?"

He chuckled. "My fortune, with any luck. And yours as well, my friend."

"Mine?"

"It was something you said that led me to it, and, with all you've done for me, I think you des—"

"I've done nothing for you," I said, laughing. "Though you're welcome to think I have."

"Uh-huh. Right. Teaching me to play is nothing?"

"I didn't teach you. You learned."

"Heh," he said. We'd had that argument before, and neither of us were ever going to win it. He started to say more, but I shook my head and led him away from the light, indicating he ought to put the thing away.

"Tell me," I said, dropping my voice, "what I said that led you to that thing, whatever it is."

He graced me with one of his, "Are you joking?" looks. "You said there are still artifacts around from when the Hand ruled."

"Well, yes."

"And you spoke of one in particular, for which the right people would pay a fortune. You said it was being passed from hand to hand by those who didn't know what it was, and was presently in the cache of a fat little merchant—"

"Kakos!"

"—who kept it somewhere in his back storeroom. Yes, that's right."

"I told you about that? I mean, that's all true, but I don't remember telling you about it. I can't believe I'd have been so stupid."

"You were a little drunk."

"Oh. But—" I frowned and stared at him. "Wait—is that . . . ?"

He nodded. "The Palm of the Hand," he said.

I don't know if I actually turned pale, but it felt that way. "Put it away, for the love of—"

"Relax. No one—"

I screamed a whisper, if you can imagine such a thing. "Put it away. Now!"

He put it away, giving me a sort of hurt look. Our feet carried us past Carzen the wheelwright's, now closed and shuttered and locked, but with some signs of life. I said, "I did not spend four years teaching you to play in order to watch you get your bloody throat cut. That thing—that isn't us. We sing. We play. We entertain people. We drink a lot. We don't mess with—"

"But I have it already."

Light came flooding out from a doorway, a small public house called the Bottomless Well. I don't know much about it because they don't encourage musicians. When we were out of earshot of the place, I said, "Yes, you do. You survived getting it—and no, I don't want to know how, or from where—but how are you going to survive keeping it?"

He started to answer, but I cut him off, because we'd

reached the Processional, and I needed to head east and out the gates to Land's End. "Look," I said. "Keep it out of sight, and stay safe. I'll talk to you later."

I left him there with a puzzled look on his face and went to do what they pay me for. Finding Land's End is easy; finding this particular residence within its walls was a bit of a challenge, but I managed.

> *His home was in the country in the middle of a town*
> *A simple square with three fine walls it was completely*
>   *round.*
> *It rested in a valley, high up on a hill*
> *It burned down many years ago so it must be there still*
>
> *So sing me of Shemhaza and the man who couldn't fail*
> *And I'll keep singing verses until you buy me ale.*

The Enders spent the night not listening to me, and then told me how good I'd been. Enders—at the least the ones that hire musicians—come in three styles: dirges, fugues, and jigs. Dirges just scowl at you as if you were terrible and that's why they aren't tipping you. Fugues beam at you, telling you how wonderful you were, and calculate that you'd rather hear that than receive a tip. Jigs figure that, if they're going to say you were wonderful, they have to back it up with a soldat or two. In no case, as far as I can tell, does it have anything to do with how well you've played. Dinra said that playing for the Ilsigi is similar, but they are a little more willing to listen, now and then, and will occasionally even admit they enjoyed the music.

Lord Serripines had appeared briefly, but so far as I could tell, hadn't spoken more than three words to anyone or spared a glance in my direction. The story was that his hatred of the Dyareelans was deep and abiding. What would he say if he knew that I'd just seen a powerful artifact of theirs in the hand of my best friend? I very much did not want to know.

In any case, the Ender who acted as host that night was a

jig, so in addition to meaningless praise I had a nice pair of soldats warming my pocket as I packed up my cresca and prepared to head for home.

A servant escorted me to the back door, where there were two uniformed guards. Their eyes pounced on me, and they moved forward on the balls of their feet as if ready to start chasing me. I blinked at them.

"Tordin Jardin?" said the skinny one. Well, he was mostly skinny, but he had big shoulders that looked like they had a lot of muscle under them.

I nodded. "Yes, sir. I am Tord'an J'ardin. May I be of service?" I gave them a smile.

The skinny one nodded brusquely. His partner, who was taller and had amazingly thick, shaggy eyebrows, just stood there, looking like he was ready to leap if I took off.

I didn't take off.

Skinny said, "The Sharda has some questions for you. Come along with us."

The Sharda? I'd heard of the Sharda. I tried to remember where, and in what context.

I smiled again. "Sure."

I know being cheerful to the City Watch just makes them suspicious, but I can't help it; it's how I am.

They positioned themselves on each side of me, but didn't hobble me or anything, so there was a limit to how much trouble I might be in. As we walked, I said, "I don't suppose you can tell me what this—"

"No," said Shaggybrows.

I chuckled. "I hadn't really thought you would." They like to have you on their own turf before they start on anything. There was no point in speculating, but I couldn't help it. When they come and get you, it's something more than to ask if you happened to witness a day laborer ducking out on a bill at the 'Unicorn.

I said, "So, how are you gentlemen doing this evening?"

Skinny grunted. Shaggybrows didn't. This completed the conversation until we reached the post.

It was a long walk, made longer by the conversation, of which there was none whatsoever. They brought me to the

Hall of Justice, near the palace, and deposited me in a room full of blank walls with a single chair. Skinny indicated the chair, and I sat down. They left, and when they closed the door I heard a bolt being shot.

The fact that they hadn't taken my cresca, or, indeed, searched me, was a good sign. And more than a good sign, it also gave me something to do while waiting for the dance to begin, so to speak. Of course, I'd have had something to do anyway: If they'd taken my cresca, I'd have whistled. I whistle very well. But I opened up the case, tuned the instrument, and began running through some scales. I also wondered at the evident cooperation between the City Watch and whoever the magistrate was who was investigating this matter.

Sharda. . . .

Right. They work for the magistrate, Elisar. They investigate crime. Crime important enough to warrant attention from those in power. Therefore, this matter involved the nobility of Sanctuary, in some way, for some reason.

This matter.

What matter?

Who or what could I know that could attract the attention of a magistrate, and was so important the magistrate would enlist the City Watch?

I played my cresca and tried not to speculate.

Presently the door opened, and a fellow with muscles on his muscles, a massive gray-brown beard all over his face, and not too many teeth appeared. "Strip, please."

"Excuse me?"

"You are to be searched."

"For what?"

Evidently, he didn't feel it was his job to answer my questions. I won't go into detail, but my clothes and even my cresca case were searched thoroughly. He kept me there while he searched, and every time they started searching something, he glanced at my face. It was a little comical, to tell you the truth. In any case, nothing they found was even worth a question. I asked him if he were with the City Watch, or the Sharda, and he didn't answer. When he was done searching me, he grunted and left me to dress again, after which I did more scales.

It wasn't too long before a pair of officers appeared.

"I am Sayn," said the man. "This is my colleague Ixma. We work for the magistrate." He didn't bother to add a name.

I smiled at them both and said, "A pleasure. How may I be of assistance?"

Neither of them wore any sort of uniform. Sayn was big across the shoulders, with a bull chest, and a neatly trimmed beard. He might have had some Rankan in him. Then again, maybe not. Ixma was more interesting. Short, tiny, with big black eyes that dominated most of her face, and·if she weren't all or partly S'danzo, my eyes were failing me. From my first glance at her, I wondered if she were a liesayer, one of those who can hear a lie the way I can hear a missed note. I'd heard of such among the S'danzo, and been told that sometimes the magistrates employed them. The concept fascinated me.

What is a lie, anyway?

If I sang to them of the man from Shemhaza, would such a person hear it as a lie? How about if I claimed not to remember a song that I *almost* remembered? Would that be a lie? How about an exaggeration? An understatement? I thought about asking if that's what she was, but thought better of it. The oddest thing was that I was filled with the temptation to lie for no reason, to test her. All of my training—control of voice, control of body language, even control of breath, could be a direct challenge to such powers. I wanted to know if I could tell a direct, bald-face lie that she couldn't detect.

And I knew very well that making such a test would be the height of stupidity when dealing with those who have the power of life and death. I sat on the temptation until it whimpered and went away.

Sayn said, "You are Tordin Jardin?"

I smiled. "Tord'an J'ardin," I agreed.

He stood over me and said, without preamble, "You were seen earlier this evening with a certain Dinrabol Festroon."

He seemed to be waiting for a response, so I nodded. He still said nothing, just looked at me in that way those in power have, so I added, "He's a friend of mine."

"A friend."

I nodded.

He glanced at the one called Ixma, then turned back to me. "When and where did you see him last?"

I frowned. "I . . ."

His lips tightened. That's something else they do.

I said, "If he's in trouble, I wouldn't want to be the one—"

"Answer the question, please."

I sighed. "It was a few hours ago, before I headed out to Land's End. I was just headed out of the Maze."

He nodded. "Yes, that's where he was found."

I stared at him. "Found?"

He nodded again, and went back to waiting for me to say something. It's the way they have, where they're looking for you to give something away, and even if you have nothing to give away, you feel like you've confessed.

I said, "What happened to him?"

"He's dead. Stabbed. One thrust from under the chin up into the brain."

I winced. He'd given me a better image than I wanted.

"Robbed?"

"Interesting question," he said. "He had a purse with a few padpols in it, and various personal items. These things weren't taken. Did he have anything else worth stealing?"

"Everyone has things worth stealing, Sayn. May I call you Sayn? In his case, well, I don't know."

"You don't know? How well did you know him?"

"He was my best friend," I said quietly. "I taught him to play, and to perform. I worked with him on his voice and his stage presence. We'd spend hours together, mostly drinking, or walking around. We—"

"I get the idea. If it wasn't robbery, who wanted him dead?"

"No one," I said. "If there was ever someone who didn't make enemies, it was Din."

He frowned, and tilted his head a little, staring at me. I guess it was supposed to make me uncomfortable, and I have to say it did. It doesn't matter how innocent you are when you're interrogated by someone who knows how; you still get nervous, uncomfortable, and start feeling like you ought to confess to something, just to stop the ordeal.

He said, "You were the last one seen with him, you know."

"I know. Well, except for whoever ki—whoever did it."

"And we only have your word for it that there is such a person. Did you kill him?"

I felt myself flushing. "No," I said.

He gave an expressive nod. What it expressed was, *I don't necessarily believe you, but I'm not going to push it now.* He glanced at his partner, I guess for confirmation. She still had not said a word, and her eyes had never left my face.

He studied me a bit, then said, "You weren't born here, were you?"

I shook my head. "A place called Shemhaza, a few hundred miles inland."

"When did you arrive in Sanctuary?"

"About eight years ago."

"Why?"

"If you'd ever seen Shemhaza, you wouldn't ask."

He was polite enough to chuckle, then said, "Seriously. Why here? Why then?"

"I had played all my songs for all six people in Shemhaza. I wanted an audience. I'm not kidding; I need an audience. I need to play for people. It's what I live for."

He nodded as if he was willing to believe me for the moment. "Do you have a wife, or a lover?"

"Not anymore."

"Oh?"

"I had a woman named Mirazia, but she stopped seeing me a few months ago and took up with Din."

He stared at me. "She left you for your best friend?"

I met his stare. "Yes."

"You know, that does nothing to make me less suspicious of you."

"I know. But what if I'd said nothing about it? You'd

have found out anyway, and then you'd be asking me why I didn't say anything."

I was hoping that would get a chuckle and a nod from him. It didn't.

"How did you feel about that?"

"In truth? It hurt a little. But with Mirazia and me, well, it was never one of the great passions of which ballads are made. I got over it pretty quickly. I will say . . ." I bit my lip. "I'm not looking forward to having to tell her."

"You needn't. I already have. Before I spoke to you."

"Then you knew—"

"Yes."

I nodded. "I'll still need to see her."

He shrugged. "That isn't my concern." He gave me a thoughtful look. "I'm not done with you, J'ardin. But for now, you may go. Don't stray too far."

I nodded. Any other response seemed like a bad idea.

He escorted me out of the building. I tried my best to pick up what I could from the bits of conversations, just as I do when I'm playing. One of the guards was having troubles with a girl, another couldn't decide what to eat tonight, and a third wasn't sleeping well of late; then I was outside once more.

I made my way to Mirazia's walk-up, which was in the east side of town—in the 'Tween off the Wideway. No one followed me, but I hadn't expected anyone to. What happened to Din mattered to me, and to Mirazia, and, I'm afraid, it just didn't much matter to anyone else.

Except, of course, if that were true, why was the Sharda interested?

And even as I asked myself that, I had the answer: He had played for the Ilsigi nobility. He had even performed in the palace. Someone liked him, and someone was unhappy that he was dead.

Well, I was unhappy that he was dead, too.

Mirazia let me in, and instantly had her arms around me, her head in my chest. We just stood like that for a while. She made no sounds, no motions.

"Cry if you wish," I told her.

She shook her head against my chest. "I'm all cried out for now," she said very quietly.

A few minutes later she said, "I'm sorry. Do you want something to drink? Are you hungry?"

I almost chuckled. That was so like her. I didn't, but I let her get me some watery wine and some cheese, because she needed to be doing something.

We sat on the couch and I held her. I said, "I'm suspected of doing it, you know."

"You?"

"Yes. Apparently I was jealous, because you and I used to—"

"They're such idiots."

I shook my head. "No. From their perspective, it makes sense. They don't know us."

"That means they won't be looking for who really did it."

I exhaled slowly. "Mirazia, they aren't going to investigate. People like us, like Din, don't matter. If anyone is going to find out what happened to him, it will be me."

She stared at me with reddened eyes. "Torrie, don't!"

I think we stopped seeing each other because I couldn't get her to stop calling me "Torrie" but now wasn't the time to object. I said, "Nothing will happen to me. I'll ask a few questions—"

"Wasn't it just a robbery?"

"Not just a robbery, no."

"What do you mean?"

I sighed. "Din did something foolish," I said.

"What do you mean?" She sounded like she wanted to get angry, which perhaps would have been good for her.

"He stole something. I don't know how he got it, I didn't want to ask, but—"

She glared. "He'd nev—"

She stopped in mid-outraged denial, stared into space for a bit, then looked down.

I said, "What?"

"I knew something was up. He's been acting funny for the last week."

"Funny, how?"

"Excited. I asked him about it and he'd, well, you know how he'd get when he had a surprise planned, like when he wrote that song about you and sprang it on you at the 'Unicorn."

I nodded. "For the last week?"

"Yes. What did he steal?"

"The Palm of the Hand."

She frowned. "What is that?"

"I'm not sure exactly. Perhaps it is magical, perhaps it has some other significance, but it's important to those who worship Dyareela."

She looked at me like I'd just turned green and grown wings. "The Hand?" she said at last. "Are you sure?"

I nodded.

"How can you know that?"

"Mirazia, think who you're talking to. I'm a musician. I sing in taverns. I listen to gossip. I know songs and stories from everywhere about everything. That thing he showed me is an artifact of the Bloody Hand."

"Did he know that?"

"He knew."

She started crying again.

A little later, she said, "What are you going to do?"

"Find his killer."

"The guards—"

"Will arrest him, if they see proof, and they feel like it's worth their time. They're half-convinced I did it, and they didn't even hold me."

"But—"

"I'll be careful," I said.

She rested her head on my shoulder. Her hair was wavy, and that color that looks red in some light, and almost black in other light. I put an arm around her, but did nothing else; didn't even think of doing anything else.

"How will you find his killer?"

"I don't know," I lied. "I'll think of something."

I held her, and a little later she said, "Tor, tell me a story?" When we'd been together, she had often said that after we made love. I'd tell her old stories, or funny stories, or ballads taken out of verse until she fell asleep. I wasn't about to make love to her tonight.

"All right," I said. "One day a man set out from Lirt to find Shemhaza. He had a mule, enough food for a year, and just kept walking inland. Every night, he'd stop and build a fire and eat his dinner and sleep and get up early the next morning and continue walking. One night he stopped in the middle of a forest, but when he woke, it was raining. He was too wet and cold to continue, so he built up the fire thinking to stay as warm as he could until the rain stopped. The rain didn't stop that night, so he found a dead tree, cut it up, and added it to the fire. The rain continued the next day, so he took branches that he hadn't burned, and his spare clothing, and built a shelter. The rain continued, day after day, and he was determined not to leave until he was dry. One day a pair of travelers came along on their way to Shemhaza and asked to share his fire. He agreed, and they made a good meal together.

"As the rain continued, one of them went out to hunt, and was able to snare a coney, out of which they made stew. They constructed a better shelter together, and cut down trees for firewood and shelter, and the rain continued.

"Soon more travelers arrived and joined them. When the rain finally stopped, winter had begun, and so they remained. When spring came, some of them planted corn and rye, and others hunted. By this time they had made a large clearing in the forest, with a dozen homes made of wood. There were a husband and wife there, and by the time the roads were good for travel, she was great with child, so they all stayed to help her and to care for the child. By the time she and the child could travel, the rains had begun again, and the crops were ready to be harvested, and so they stayed another year, and more joined them.

"One day, a stranger arrived and asked the man if he could stay to get out of the rain. The man said of course he could. The stranger said, 'What is the name of your village?' 'Shemhaza,' said the man. And it is there still."

I stopped talking. She was asleep. I half carried her to her bed, undressed her, and covered her up. Then I went back into the other room and fell asleep on the chair.

The next morning, I puttered around her pantry long enough to eat some of her bread and cheese, and left some out for her. I felt stiff from sleeping in the chair and rather unclean from sleeping in my clothes. I put both feelings behind me and went out into the bright Sanctuary morning.

Somewhere in or around the city were those who still followed the way of Dyareela—probably several groups, in fact, none of whom agreed with each other about what exactly the Mother Goddess wanted. All of them happy to cut each others' throats, in a city happy to cut all their throats. I had to find one of those groups. I glanced down at my unstained hands, thinking about dying my nails red, but I rejected the idea as soon as I thought of it; getting myself killed by some outraged citizen would do no good, and a musician cannot hide his hands for very long.

I took myself back to the 'Unicorn. It wasn't especially busy—just a few of the hardcore drunks—but that was okay. Pegrin wasn't working. The man behind the counter was a fellow called the Stick, whose permanent bad temper matched my permanent good mood. The Stick didn't mind if I played a little; I told him I felt like practicing in front of an audience. He muttered something in which I caught the word "audience" and pointed to the stage.

It was funny, because it remains one of the longest shows I've ever done: I just sat there, mostly running through instrumentals, and tried to pick up pieces of conversation around me. I'm pretty good at that—at least, when there's something to listen to. It is the hardest thing there is . . . playing, and at the same time trying to put together scattered bits of overheard conversation into the one piece of information you need.

His third son was short and tall, the second thin and fat
And ten years after he was dead his first son was begat

> *He grew to fine young manhood, till at midnight one*
> *bright morn*
> *He came to Shemhaza before his father had been born.*
>
> *So sing me of Shemhaza and the man who couldn't fail*
> *And I'll keep singing verses until you buy me ale.*

But it is, after all, what I'd been trained to do. It took me three days.

Outside the western walls of Sanctuary, you'll find the Street of Red Lanterns, which is where the brothels grow, among other things. Between two of the older buildings there is a place where you can duck between them, slide through an alleyway, climb over a low fence, and look behind a moderately heavy barrel to find a rusted grating. You move the grating aside, climb down, and go through a sort of hatchway. You'll find yourself in an old sewer system, that is no longer used except by a curious species of rodent that doesn't bear describing. You can walk upright in it, and if you don't mind the smell it isn't too difficult. You may want to bring a rope, in case the iron ladder down to the lower level has finally rusted away. Better still, don't go.

But I went there, cresca case slung over my back, following bits of footprints in the slime and bits of half-heard conversation, until I came to a place where there was a sort of niche. I went through it, and waited.

Presently they appeared, in just the way they were supposed to—they remembered that much at least. A weak, rather pitiful man from the front looked as if he wanted to talk, and a larger and stronger man (judging by his hand) from behind. Both of their nails were dyed red. The one from behind went for the grip, but I'd been expecting it and caught his hand the way I'd been taught, pressing my thumb into the weak spot on the back of his hand. He went down to his knees. Yes, he was a big man indeed, full of lank black hair and pale skin. He didn't look so big as he knelt, whimpering, however. The wall was close, so I could put a finger into each of the little man's nostril's and pin him against the wall without losing my grip on the other's hand. The little man held perfectly still, his arms off to the sides, which is about all you can do when someone is holding you that way. The big man whimpered.

I addressed the little man. *"Tr'kethra ircastra'n cor leftra, stin!"* I told him.

He swallowed. "I . . . do not speak the Mother Tongue," he said.

I grunted. "You recognize it, at least. Take me to the leader of this *ircastra,* at once."

"Ircastra?"

I rolled my eyes. "This group. This enclave. Do it, or I'll rip your face off your skull."

He whimpered like his friend. I applied a little pressure, and he yelped. "All right!"

I loosened my hold on the big man long enough to get the grip on him he'd been trying to get on me. When he was sleeping, I relaxed my hold on the other, switched to his elbow, and hurt him just enough to let him know how much more I could hurt him if I chose.

"Go."

It was ugly and damp and smelled like mold and the droppings of small animals.

The *ircastra'n* was a man, which I had been warned to expect. He was in his late thirties, with sunken cheeks, wisps of brownish hair, and pale, watery blue eyes. He was sitting in a sort of parlor full of badly made wooden chairs at a makeshift desk. He stared at us and his mouth fell open. I could see him recognizing the grip I had, so his first words were, "Who are you?"

"I am Tord'an J'ardin of Devrith."

"Devrith!"

"Yes." I didn't ask his name. I didn't yet know if it mattered. "The good news is, you have not been forgotten by the Mother Temple. The bad news is, you have not been forgotten by the Mother Temple."

"I don't believe you!"

"From now on, I will be taking charge here. First this *ircastra,* then the others. You may assist me, or join the Mother."

"You lie! Who are you?"

"Shut up and listen, *nief'kri*." He knew enough of the Mother Tongue to recognize the insult—he blanched, bit his lip, started to get angry—and listened.

I said, "You and those like you held Sanctuary, a place the Council of Priestesses badly wished, and then you gave it back."

"Priestesses? But—"

"Priestesses. Things have changed. You might say that the feminine side of the Mother has emerged. Things are different now. And the Priestesses are not pleased with what has happened in Sanctuary. You have lost it for us for at least a generation, with your bickering and squabbling, with your blindness, and with your stupidity. Neither the Council nor the Mother has any wish for rivers of blood to be spilled for no purpose. We are here to cleanse the world. Not to satisfy the bloodlust of fools. The power we crave is to serve the Mother, not to gratify the egos of little men. You will spend the rest of your life trying to get us back to where we were fifteen years ago in this pus hole of a city. Or you may die now. I don't care. But from this day forward, it will be Priestesses who rule. Through me, until another arrives."

"You can't have come from—"

"You need convincing?"

There was fear in his eyes, but stubbornness in the set of jaw. He nodded.

I let go my grip on the little man, who stepped quickly away from me, rubbing his arm.

I unslung my instrument case, set it on the desk, and opened it. Then I took out my cresca, raised it, and brought it smashing down on the desk, leaving me holding the fretboard, with a bit of the truss rod sticking out the end. Some of the splinters hit the *ircastra'n*, which pleased me though I hadn't planned on it. I searched among the remains of my instrument, and found it. I held it in the proper way and showed it to him.

"You recognize this?"

He turned yet another shade of pale. "The Palm! You have the Palm!"

I touched the Palm with the fingers of my left hand, letting them tickle the gems as I'd been taught. Lights flickered among them.

"Any questions?" I asked him.

He stared, his mouth hanging open. "Who *are* you?"

"I gave you my name. I was trained from childhood in the main temple of Devrith."

"Trained . . ."

"I'm a Conversant, of course."

He stared. He was, it seemed, not so far removed that he didn't know at least something of what that meant—the hundreds of hours in memory training, in knowledge of the history and lore of the Temple, learning to listen to four conversations at once and being able to recite every tone and nuance of each one, and then mastery in singing, composition, and musical instruments thrown on top of it almost as an afterthought, because tongues are never looser than in a good inn with loud music. He was impressed, and that was good. But none of that really mattered, because, after years of work, I had the Palm. Without it, he had no reason to listen to me. With it—

He stood up from his desk, stood before me, knelt, and bowed his head. "Your orders, *ircastra'n?*"

I studied the flickering gems and thought to them, "*It is Tord'an, and the work is begun.*" The gems flickered more in answer, and the warmth I felt from it filled my soul. I put the Palm inside my shirt, against my skin, until I could find a thong to hang it from my neck.

Then I nodded to the man who knelt in front of me. "For starters, you'll fill me in on what you know of the other *ircastra'i.* Then we'll make plans. To begin, you'll all wipe that silly paint off your fingernails. We'll move slowly, this time. There is a healer named Pel who may be able to help Arizak. If so, the person who brings the healer will have a nice entry to the ear of those who rule. That will save us a few years. What is your name?"

"Rynith."

I nodded. "We have a lot of work to do," I told him. "Let's be about it. Oh, and as soon as someone has cleaned off his nails, have him go buy me another cresca." I chuckled. "Killing my best friend was easy, but I hated to lose the instrument."

The Smile on the Face

Nalo Hopkinson

*Nalo Hopkinson (www.sff.net/people/nalo/writing/whome.
html) was born in Jamaica and grew up in Guyana,
Trinidad, Jamaica, and Canada, and lives now in Toronto.
She studied with Judith Merril in Canada and attended the
Clarion writing workshop in 1995. After publishing a few
short stories, her first novel,* Brown Girl in the Ring *(1998),
won the Warner Aspect First Novel Contest and established
her reputation as an important new fantasy writer. Her
second novel,* Midnight Robber, *followed in 2000, and a
collection,* Skin Folk, *in 2001. Her third novel,* The Salt
Roads, *was published in 2003. She is also the editor of two
mythic anthologies:* Whispers from the Cotton Tree Root:
Caribbean Fabulist Fiction *(2000) and* Mojo: Conjure Stories *(2003). In 2004 she published the SF anthology* So
Long Been Dreaming: Postcolonial Visions of the Future,
co-edited with Uppinder Mehan.

"The Smile on the Face" was published in Girls Who Bite
Back, *an edgy anthology edited by Emily Pohl-Weary,
Judith Merril's (and Frederik Pohl's) granddaughter, in
Toronto. The title refers of course to the Young lady from
Niger / who smiled as she rode on a tiger (Hopkinson uses
her own variation). Hopkinson has a narrative voice that
immediately sets her apart from other fantasy writers and
rivets the attention, and an acute eye for detail. This story is
about a young girl, a tree that disturbs her, and a series of
difficult social situations that confront her at a teen party.*

There was a young lady . . .

"Geez, who gives a shit what a . . . what? What a laidly worm is, anyway?"

Gilla muttered. She was curled up on the couch, school library book on her knees.

"Mm?" said her mother, peering at the computer monitor. She made a noise of impatience and hit a key on the keyboard a few times.

"Nothing, Mum. Just I don't know what this book's talking about." Boring old school assignment. Gilla wanted to go and get ready for Patricia's party, but Mum had said she should finish her reading first.

"Did you say, 'laidly worm'?" her mother asked. Her fingers were clicking away at the keyboard again now. Gilla wished she could type that quickly. But that would mean practicing, and she wasn't about to do any more of that than she had to.

"Yeah." Damn. If Mum had heard that, she'd probably heard her say, "shit," too.

"It's a type of dragon."

Looks like she wasn't going to pay attention to the other word that Gilla had used. This time, anyway. "So why don't they just call it that?" Gilla asked her.

"It's a special type. It doesn't have wings, so it just crawls along the ground. Its skin oozes all the time. Guess that protects it when it crawls, like a slug's slime."

"Yuck, Mum!"

Gilla's mother smiled, even as she was writing. "Well, you wanted to know."

"No, I didn't. I just have to know, for school."

"A laidly worm's always ravenous and it makes a noise like a cow in gastric distress."

Gilla giggled. Her mother stopped typing and finally looked at her. "You know, I guess you could think of it as a larval dragon. Maybe it eats and eats so it'll have enough energy to molt into the flying kind. What a cool idea. I'll have to look into it." She turned back to her work. "Why do you have to know about it? What're you reading?"

"This lady in the story? Some guy wanted to marry her, but she didn't like him, so he put her in his dungeon . . ."

". . . and came after her one night in the form of a laidly worm to eat her," Gilla's mother finished. "You're learning about Margaret of Antioch?"

Gilla boggled at her. "Saint Margaret, yeah. How'd you know?"

"How?" Her mother swiveled the rickety steno chair round to face Gilla and grinned, brushing a tangle of dreadlocks back from her face. "Sweet, this is your mother, remember? The professor of African and Middle Eastern Studies?"

"Oh." And her point? Gilla could tell that her face had that "huh?" look. Mum probably could see it too, 'cause she said:

"Gilla, Antioch was in ancient Turkey. In the Middle East?"

"Oh yeah, right. Mum, can I get micro-braids?"

Now it was her mum looking like, "huh?" "What in the world are those, Gilla?"

Well, at least she was interested. It wasn't a "no" straight off the bat. "These tiny braid extensions, right? Maybe only four or five strands per braid. And they're straight, not like . . . Anyway, Kashy says that the hairdressing salon across from school does them. They braid the extensions right into your own hair, any color you want, as long as you want them to be, and they can style them just like that. Kashy says it only takes a few hours, and you can wear them in for six weeks."

Her mum came over, put her warm palms gently on either side of Gilla's face and looked seriously into her eyes. Gilla hated when she did that, like she was still a little kid. "You want to tame your hair," her mother said. Self-consciously, Gilla pulled away from her mum's hands, smoothed back the cloudy mass that she'd tied out of the way with a bandana so that she could do her homework without getting hair in her eyes, in her mouth, up her nose. Her mum continued, "You want hair that lies down and plays dead, and you want to pay a lot of money for it, and you want to do it every six weeks."

Gilla pulled her face away. The book slid off her knee to the floor. "Mum, why do you always have to make everything sound so horrible?" Some of her hair had slipped out of the bandana; it always did. Gilla could see three or four black sprigs of it dancing at the edge of her vision, tickling her forehead. She untied the bandana and furiously retied it, capturing as much of the bushy mess as she could and binding it tightly with the cloth.

Her mother just shook her head at her. "Gilla, stop being such a drama queen. How much do micro-braids cost?"

Gilla was ashamed to tell her now, but she named a figure, a few bucks less than the sign in the salon window had said. Her mother just raised one eyebrow at her.

"That, my girl, is three months of your allowance."

Well, yeah. She'd been hoping that Mum and Dad would pay for the braids. Guess not.

"Tell you what, Gilla; you save up for it, then you can have them."

Gilla grinned.

"But," her mother continued, "you have to continue buying your bus tickets while you're saving."

Gilla stopped grinning.

"Don't look so glum. If you make your own lunch to take every day, it shouldn't be so bad. Now, finish reading the rest of the story."

And Mum was back at her computer again, tap-tap-tap. Gilla pouted at her back but didn't say anything, 'cause really, she was kind of pleased. She was going to get micro-braids! She hated soggy, made-the-night-before sandwiches, but it'd be worth it. She ignored the little voice in her mind that was saying, "every six weeks?" and went back to her reading.

"Euw, gross."

"Now what?" her mother asked.

"This guy? This, like, laidly worm guy thing? It *eats* Saint Margaret, and then she's in his stomach; like, *inside* him! and she prays to Jesus, and she's sooo holy that the wooden cross around her neck turns back into a tree, and it puts its roots into the ground *through* the dragon guy thing, and its branches bust him open and he dies, and out she comes!"

"Presto bingo," her mum laughs, "instant patron saint of childbirth!"

"Why?" But Gilla thought about that one a little bit, and she figured she might know why. "Never mind, don't tell me. So they made her a saint because she killed the dragon guy thing?"

"Well, yes, they sainted her eventually, after a bunch of people tortured and executed her for refusing to marry that man. She was a convert to Christianity, and she said she'd refused him because he wasn't a Christian. But Gilla, some people think that she wasn't a Christian anymore either, at least not by the end."

"Huh?" Gilla wondered when Kashy would show up. It was almost time for the party to start.

"That thing about the wooden cross turning back into a living tree? That's not a very Christian symbol, that sprouting tree. A dead tree made into the shape of a cross, yes. But not a living, magical tree. That's a pagan symbol. Maybe Margaret of Antioch was the one who commanded the piece of wood around her neck to sprout again. Maybe the story is telling us that when Christianity failed her, she claimed her power as a wood witch. Darling, I think that Margaret of Antioch was a hamadryad."

"Geez, Mum, a cobra?" That much they had learned in school. Gilla knew the word "hamadryad."

Her mother laughed. "Yeah, a king cobra is a type of hamadryad, but I'm talking about the original meaning. A hamadryad was a female spirit whose soul resided in a tree. A druid is a man, a tree wizard. A hamadryad is a woman; a tree witch, I guess you could say. But where druids lived

outside of trees and learned everything they could about
them, a hamadryad doesn't need a class to learn about it.
She just *is* a tree."

Creepy. Gilla glanced out the window to where black
branches beckoned, clothed obscenely in tiny spring leaves.
She didn't want to talk about trees.

The doorbell rang. "Oh," said Gilla. "That must be
Kashy!" She sprang up to get the door, throwing her text-
book aside again.

There was a young lady of Niger . . .

"It kind of creaks sometimes, y'know?" Gilla inquired of
Kashy's reflection in the mirror.

In response, Kashy just tugged harder at Gilla's hair.
"Hold still, girl. Lemme see what I can do with this. And
shut up with that weirdness. You're always going on about
that tree. Creeps me out."

Gilla sighed, resigned, and leaned back in the chair.
"Okay. Only don't pull it too tight, okay? Gives me a
headache." When Kashy had a makeover jones on her,
there was nothing to do but submit and hope you could
wash the goop off your face and unstick your hair from the
mousse before you had to go outdoors and risk scaring the
pigeons. That last experiment of Kashy's with the "natural" lipstick had been such a disaster. Gilla had been left
looking as though she'd been eating fried chicken and had
forgotten to wash the grease off her mouth. It had been
months ago, but Foster was still giggling over it.

Gilla crossed her arms. Then, she checked out the mirror
and saw how that looked, how it made her breasts puff out.
She remembered Roger in the school yard, pointing at her
the first day back at school in September and bellowing,
"Boobies!" She put her arms on the rests of the chair instead. She sucked her stomach in and took a quick glance in
the mirror to see if that made her look slimmer. Fat chance.
Really fat. It did make her breasts jut again, though; oh,
goody. She couldn't win. She sighed once more and slumped

a little in the chair, smushing both bust and belly into a lumpy mass.

"And straighten up, okay?" Kashy said. "I can't reach the front of your head with you sitting hunched over like that." Kashy's hands were busy, sectioning Gilla's thick black hair into four and twisting each section into plaits.

"That tree," Gilla replied, "the one in the front yard."

Kashy just rolled her perfectly made-up eyes. "Okay, so tell me again about that wormy old cherry tree."

"I don't like it. I'm trying to sleep at night, and all I can hear is it creaking and groaning and . . . *talking* to itself all night!"

"Talking!" Kashy giggled. "So now it's talking to you?"

"Yes. Swaying. Its branches rubbing against each other. Muttering and whispering at me, night after night. I hate that tree. I've always hated it. I wish Mum or Dad would cut it down." Gilla sighed. Since she'd started ninth grade two years ago, Gilla sighed a lot. That's when her body, already sprouting with puberty, had laid down fat pads on her chest, belly and thighs. When her high, round butt had gotten rounder. When her budding breasts had swelled even bigger than her mother's. And when she'd started hearing the tree at night.

"What's it say?" Kashy asked. Her angular brown face stared curiously at Gilla in the mirror.

Gilla looked at Kashy, how she had every hair in place, how her shoulders were slim and how the contours of the tight sweater showed off her friend's tiny, pointy breasts. Gilla and Kashy used to be able to wear each other's clothes, until two years ago.

"Don't make fun of me, Kashy."

"I'm not." Kashy's voice was serious; the look on her face, too. "I know it's been bothering you. What do you hear the tree saying?"

"It . . . it talks about the itchy places it can't reach, where its bark has gone knotty. It talks about the taste of soil, all gritty and brown. It says it likes the feeling of worms sliding in and amongst its roots in the wet, dark earth."

"Gah! You're making this up, Gilla!"

"I'm not!" Gilla stormed out of her chair, pulling her hair out of Kashy's hands. "If you're not going to believe me, then don't ask, okay?"

"Okay, okay, I believe you!" Kashy shrugged her shoulders, threw her palms skyward in a gesture of defeat. "Slimy old worms feel good, just,"—she reached out and slid her hands briskly up and down Gilla's bare arms— "rubbing up against you!" And she laughed, that perfect Kashy laugh, like tiny, friendly bells.

Gilla found herself laughing too. "Well, that's what it says!"

"All right, girl. What else does it say?"

At first Gilla didn't answer. She was too busy shaking her hair free of the plaits, puffing it up with her hands into a kinky black cloud. "I'm just going to wear it like this to the party, okay? I'll tie it back with my bandana and let it poof out behind me. That's the easiest thing." *I'm never going to look like you, Kashy. Not anymore.* In the upper grades at school, everybody who hung out together looked alike. The skinny glam girls hung with the skinny glam girls. The goth guys and girls hung out in back of the school and shared clove cigarettes and black lipstick. The fat girls clumped together. How long would Kashy stay tight with her? Turning so she couldn't see her own plump, gravid body in the mirror, she dared to look at her friend. Kashy was biting her bottom lip, looking contrite.

"I'm sorry," she said. "I shouldn't have laughed at you."

"It's okay." Gilla took a cotton ball from off the dresser, doused it in cold cream, started scraping the makeup off her face. She figured she'd keep the eyeliner on. At least she had pretty eyes, big and brown and sparkly. She muttered at Kashy, "It says it likes stretching and growing, reaching for the light."

Who went for a ride . . .

"Bye, Mum!" Gilla and Kashy surged out the front door. Gilla closed it behind her, then, standing on her doorstep with her friend, took a deep breath and turned to face the cherry tree. Half its branches were dead. The remaining twisted ones made a mockery of the tree's spring finery of new green leaves. It crouched on the front lawn, gnarling at them. It stood between them and the curb, and the walkway was super long. They'd have to walk under the tree's grasping branches the whole way.

The sun was slowly diving down the sky, casting a soft orange light on everything. Daylean, Dad called it; that time between the two worlds of day and night when anything could happen. Usually Gilla liked this time of day best. Today she scowled at the cherry tree and told Kashy, "Mum says women used to live in the trees."

"What, like, in tree houses? Your mum says the weirdest things, Gilla."

"No. They used to be the spirits of the trees. When the trees died, so did they."

"Well, this one's almost dead, and it can't get you. And you're going to have to walk past it to reach the street, and I know you want to go to that party, so take my hand and come on."

Gilla held tight to her friend's firm, confident hand. She could feel the clammy dampness of her own palm. "Okay," Kashy said, "on three, we're gonna run all the way to the curb, all right? One, two, three!"

And they were off, screeching and giggling, Gilla doing her best to stay upright in her new wedgies, the first thing even close to high heels that her parents had ever let her wear. Gilla risked a glance sideways. Kashy looked graceful and coltish. Her breasts didn't bounce. Gilla put on her broadest smile, screeched extra loud to let the world know how much fun she was having, and galumphed her way to streetside. As she and Kashy drew level with the tree, she felt the tiniest bonk on her head. She couldn't brush whatever it was off right away, 'cause she needed her hands to keep her balance. Laughing desperately from all this funfunfun, she ran. They made it safely to the curb. Kashy bent, panting, to catch her breath. For all that she looked so trim, she had no wind at all. Gilla swam twice a week and was on the volleyball team, and that little run had barely even given her a glow. She started searching with her hands for whatever had fallen in her hair.

It was smooth, roundish. It had a stem. She pulled it out and looked at it. A perfect cherry. So soon? She could have sworn that the tree hadn't even blossomed yet. "Hah!" she yelled at the witchy old tree. She brandished the cherry at it. "A peace offering? So you admit defeat, huh?" In elation at having gotten past the tree, she forgot who in the story had been eater and who eaten. "Well, you can't eat me, 'cause I'm gonna eat YOU!" And she popped the cherry into her mouth, bursting its sweet roundness between her teeth. The first cherry of the season. It tasted wonderful, until a hearty slap on her shoulder made her gulp.

"Hey, girl," Foster's voice said, "You look great! You too, of course, Kashy."

Gilla didn't answer. She put horrified hands to her mouth. Foster, big old goofy Foster with his twinkly eyes and his too-baggy sweatshirt, gently took the shoulder that he'd slapped so carelessly seconds before. "You okay, Gilla?"

Kashy looked on in concern.

Gilla swallowed. Found her voice. "Jesus fuck, Foster! You made me swallow it!"

Seeing that she was all right, Foster grinned his silly grin. "And you know what Roger says about girls who swallow!"

"No, man; you made me swallow the cherry pit!" Oh, God, what was going to happen now?

"Ooh, scary," Foster said. "It's gonna grow into a tree inside you, and then you'll be sooorry!" He made cartoon monster fingers in Gilla's face and mugged at her. Kashy burst out laughing. Gilla too. Lightly, she slapped Foster's hands away. Yeah, it was only an old tree.

"C'mon," she said. "Let's go to this party already."

They went and grabbed their bikes out of her parents' garage. It was a challenge riding in those wedge heels, but at least she was wearing pants, unlike Kashy, who seemed to have perfected how to ride in a tight skirt with her knees decently together, as she perfected everything to do with her appearance. Gilla did her best to look dignified without dumping the bike.

"I can't wait to start driving lessons," Kashy complained. "I'm getting all sweaty. I'm going to have to do my makeup all over again when I get to Patricia's place." She perched on her bike like a princess in her carriage, and neither Gilla nor Foster could persuade her to move any faster than a crawl. Gilla swore that if Kashy could, she would have ridden sidesaddle in her little skirt.

All the way there, Foster, Gilla and Kashy argued over what type of cobra a hamadryad was. Gilla was sure she remembered one thing; hamadryads had inflatable hoods just below their heads. She tried to ignore how the ride was making the back of her neck sticky. The underside of the triangular mass of her hair was glued uncomfortably to her skin.

Who went for a ride on a tiger . . .

They could hear music coming from Patricia's house. The three of them locked their bikes to the fence and headed inside. Gilla surreptitiously tugged the hem of her blouse down over her hips. But Kashy'd known her too long. Her eyes followed the movement of Gilla's hands, and she sighed. "I wish I had a butt like yours," Kashy said.

"What? You crazy?"

"Naw, man. Look how nice your pants fit you. Mine always sag in the behind."

Foster chuckled. "Yeah, sometimes I wish I had a butt like Gilla's too."

Gilla looked at him, baffled. Beneath those baggy pants Foster always wore, he had a fine behind; strong and shapely. She'd seen him in swim trunks.

Foster made grabbing motions at the air. "Wish I had it right here, warm and solid in between these two hands."

Kashy hooted. Gilla reached up and swatted Foster on the back of the head. He ducked, grinning. All three of them were laughing as they stepped into the house.

After the coolness of the spring air outside, the first step into the warmth and artificial lighting of Patricia's place was a shock. "Hey there, folks," said Patricia's dad. "Welcome. Let me just take your jackets, and you head right on in to the living room."

"Jeez," Gilla muttered to Foster once they'd handed off their jackets. "The 'rents aren't going to hang around, are they? That'd be such a total drag."

In the living room were some of their friends from school, lounging on the chairs and the floor, laughing and talking and drinking bright red punch out of plastic glasses. Everybody was on their best behavior, since Patricia's parents were still around. Boring. Gilla elbowed Foster once they were out of Mr. Bright's earshot. "Try not to be too obvious about ogling Tanya, okay? She's been making goo-goo eyes at you all term."

He put a hand to his chest, looked mock innocent. "Who, me?" He gave a wave of his hand and went off to say hi to some of his buddies.

Patricia's mother was serving around mini patties on a tray. She wore stretch pants that made her big butt look bigger than ever when she bent over to offer the tray, and even through her heavy sweatshirt Gilla could make out where her large breasts didn't quite fit into her bra but exploded up over the top of it. Shit. Gilla'd forgotten to check how she looked in her new blouse. She'd have to get to the bathroom soon. Betcha a bunch of the other girls were already lined up outside it, waiting to fix their hair, their makeup, readjust their pantyhose, renew their "natural" lipstick.

Patricia, looking awkward but sweet in a little flowered dress, grinned at them and beckoned them over. Gilla smoothed her hair back, sucked her gut in, and started to head over toward her, picking her way carefully in her wedgies.

She nearly toppled as a hand grabbed her ankle. "Hey, big girl. Mind where you put that foot. Wouldn't want you to step on my leg and break it."

Gilla felt her face heat with embarrassment. She yanked her leg out of Roger's grip and lost her balance. Kashy had to steady her. Roger chuckled. "Getting a little top-heavy there, Gilla?" he said. His buddies Karl and Haywood, lounging near him, snickered.

Karl was obviously trying to look up Kashy's skirt. Kashy smoothed it down over her thighs, glared at him and led the way to where Patricia was sitting. "Come on, girl," she whispered to Gilla. "The best thing is to ignore them."

Cannot ignore them all your days. Gilla smiled her too-bright smile, hugged Patricia and kissed her cheek. "Mum and Dad are going soon," Patricia whispered at them. "They promised me."

"They'd better," Kashy said.

"God, I know," Patricia groaned. "They'd better not embarrass me like this too much longer." She went to greet some new arrivals.

Gilla perched on the couch with Kashy, trying to find a position that didn't make her tummy bulge, trying to keep her mind on the small talk. Where was Foster? Oh, in the corner. Tanya was sitting way close to him, tugging at her necklace and smiling deeply into his eyes. Foster had his I'm-such-a-stud smile on.

Mr. Bright came in with a tray of drinks. He pecked his chubby wife on the lips as she went by. He turned and contemplated her when her back was to him. He was smiling when he turned back. The smile lingered happily on his face long after the kiss was over.

Are you any less than she? Well, she certainly was, thank heaven. With any luck, it'd be a few years before she was as round as Mrs. Bright. And what was this less than she business, anyway? Who talked like that? Gilla took a glass of punch from Mr. Bright's tray and sucked it down, trying to pay attention to Jahanara and Kashy talking about whether 14-karat gold was better for necklaces than 18-karat.

"Mum," said Patricia from over by the door. "Dad?"

Her mother laughed nervously. "Yes, we're going, we're going. You have the phone number at the Hamptons' house?"

"Yesss, Mum," Patricia hissed. "See you later, okay?" She grabbed their coats from the hallway closet, all but bustled them out the door.

"We'll be back by 2:00 a.m.!" her dad yelled over his

shoulder. Everyone sat still until they heard that lovely noise, the sound of the car starting up and driving off down the street.

Foster got up, took the CD out of the stereo player. Thank God. Any more of that kiddie pop, and Gilla'd thought she'd probably barf. Foster grinned around to everyone, produced another CD from his chest pocket and put it into the CD player. A jungle mix started up. People cheered and started dancing. Patricia turned out all the lights but the one in the hallway.

And now Gilla needed to pee. Which meant she had to pass the clot of people stuck all over Roger again. Well, she really needed to check on that blouse, anyway. She'd just make sure she was far from Roger's grasping hands. She stood, tugged at the hem of her blouse so it was covering her bum again. *Reach those shoulders tall too, strong one. Stretch now.* When had she started talking to herself like that? But it was good advice. She fluffed up her hair, drew herself up straight and walked with as much dignity as she could in the direction of the bathroom.

Roger and Gilla had been the first in their class to hit puberty. Roger's voice had deepened into a raspy bass, and his shoulders, chest and arms had broadened with muscle. He'd shot up about a foot in the past few months, it seemed. He sauntered rather than walked and he always seemed to be braying an opinion on everything, the more insulting the better. Gilla flicked a glance at him. In one huge hand he had a paper napkin which he'd piled with three patties, two huge slices of black rum cake and a couple of slices of ham. He was pushing the food into his mouth as he brayed some boasty something at his buddies. He seemed barely aware of his own chewing and swallowing. Probably took a lot of feeding to keep that growing body going. He was handsome, though. Had a broad baby face with nice full lips and the beginnings of a goatee. People were willing to hang with him just in hopes that he would pay attention to them, so why did he need to spend his time making Gilla's life miserable?

Oops, shit. Shouldn't even have thought it, 'cause now

he'd noticed her noticing. He caught and held her gaze and, still looking at her, leaned over and murmured something at the knot of people gathered around him. The group burst out laughing. "No, really?" said Clarissa in a high, witchy voice. Gilla put her head down and surged out of the room, not stopping until she was up the stairs to the second floor and inside the bathroom. She stayed in there for as long as she dared.

When she came out, Clarissa was in the second floor hallway. Gilla said, "Bathroom's free now."

"Did you really let them do that to you?"

"Huh?" In confusion, Gilla met Clarissa's eyes. Clarissa's cheeks were flushed and she had a bright, knowing look on her face.

"Roger told us. How you let him suck on your . . ." Clarissa bit on her bottom lip. Her cheeks got even pinker. "Then you let Haywood do it too. Don't you, like, feel like a total slut now?"

"But I didn't . . ."

"Oh, come on, Gilla. We all saw how you were looking at Roger."

Liar! Can such a liar live? The thought hissed through Gilla, strong as someone whispering in her ear.

"You know," Clarissa said, "you're even kinda pretty. If you just lost some weight, you wouldn't have to throw yourself at all those guys like that."

Gilla felt her face go hot. Her mouth filled with saliva. She was suddenly very aware of little things: the bite of her bra into her skin, where it was trying to contain her fat, swingy breasts; the hard, lumpy memory of the cherry pit slipping down her throat; the bristly triangular hedge of her hair, bobbing at the base of her neck and swelling to cover her ears. Her mouth fell open, but no words came out.

"He doesn't even really like you, you know." Clarissa smirked at her and sauntered past her into the bathroom.

She couldn't, she mustn't still be there when Clarissa got out of the bathroom. In the awkward wedge heels, she clattered her way down the stairs like an elephant, her mind a jumble. Once in the downstairs hallway, she didn't head back toward the happy, warm sound of laughter and music in the living room, but shoved her way out the front door.

It was even darker out there, despite the porch light being on. Foster was out on the porch, leaning against the railing and whispering with someone. Tanya, shivering in the short sundress she was wearing, was staring wide-eyed at Foster and hanging on every word. "And then," Foster said, gesturing with his long arms, "I grabbed the ball from him, and I . . ." He turned, saw Gilla. "Hey girl, what's up?"

Tanya looked at her like she was the insurance salesman who'd interrupted her dinner.

"I, Foster," stammered Gilla, "what's 'calumny' mean?"

"Huh?" He pushed himself upright, looking concerned. " 'Scuse me, Tanya, okay?"

"All right," Tanya said sulkily. She went inside.

Gilla stood in the cold, shivering. *That liar! He has no right!*

Foster asked again, "What's up?"

"Calumny. What's it mean?" she repeated.

"I dunno. Why?"

"I think it means a lie, a really bad one." *He and his toadies. If you find a nest of vipers, should you not root it out?* "It just came to me, you know?" Her thoughts were whipping and thrashing in the storm in her head. *We never gave them our favor!*

Foster came and put a hand on her shoulder, looked into her eyes. "Gilla, who's telling lies? You gonna tell me what's going on?"

The warmth of her friend's palm through the cloth of her blouse brought her back to herself. "Damn, it's cold out here!"

Something funny happened to Foster's face. He hesitated, then opened his arms to her. "Here," he said.

Blinking with surprise, Gilla stepped into the hug. She stopped shivering. They stood there for a few seconds, Gilla wondering what, what? Should she put her arms around him too? Were they still just friends? Was he just warming her up because she was cold? Did he like her? Well, of course, he liked her; he hung out with her and

Kashy during lunch period at school almost every day. Lots of the guys gave him shit for that. But did he like her like *that*? Did she want him to? *By your own choice, never by another's.* What was she supposed to do now? And what was with all these weird things she seemed to be thinking all of a sudden?

"Um, Gilla?"

"Yeah?"

"Could you get off my foot now?"

The laughter that bubbled from her tasted like cherries in the back of her throat. She stepped off poor Foster's abused toes, leaned her head into his shoulder, giggling. "Oh, Foster. Why didn't you just say I was hurting you?"

Foster was giggling too, his voice high with embarrassment. "I didn't know what to say, or what was the right thing to do, or what."

"You and me both."

"I haven't held too many girls like that before. I mean, only when I'm sure they want me to."

Now Gilla backed up so she could look at him better. "Really? What about Tanya?"

He looked sheepish, and kind of sullen. "Yeah, I bet she'd like that. She's nice, you know? Only . . ."

"Only what?" Gilla sat on the rail beside Foster.

"She just kinda sits there, like a sponge. I talk and I talk, and she just soaks it all up. She doesn't say anything interesting back; she doesn't tell me about anything she does, she just wants me to entertain her. Saniya was like that too, and Kristen," he said, naming a couple of his short-lived school romances. "I like girls, you know? A lot. I just want one with a brain in her head. You and Kashy got more going on than that, right? More fun hanging with you guys."

"So?" said Gilla, wondering what she was going to say.

"So what?"

"So what about Kashy?" She stumbled over her friend's name, because what she was really thinking was, *what about me?* Did she even like Foster like that?

"Oh, look," drawled a way too familiar voice. "It's the faggot and the fat girl."

Roger, Karl and Haywood had just come lumbering out of the house. Haywood snickered. Gilla froze.

"Oh, give it up, Roger," Foster drawled back. He lounged against the railing again. "It's so fucking tired. Every time you don't know what to say—which, my friend, is often—you call somebody 'faggot.'"

Haywood and Karl, their grins uncertain, glanced from Roger to Foster and back again. Foster got an evil smile, put a considering finger to his chin. "You ever hear of the pot calling the kettle black?"

At that, Karl and Haywood started to howl with laughter. Roger growled. That was the only way to describe the sound coming out of his mouth. Karl and Foster touched their fists together. "Good one, man. Good one," Karl said. Foster grinned at him.

But Roger elbowed past Karl and stood chest to chest with Foster, his arms crossed in front of him, almost like he was afraid to let his body touch Foster's. Roger glared at Foster, who stayed lounging calmly on the railing with a smirk on his face, looking Roger straight in the face. "And you know both our mothers ugly like duppy too, so you can't come at me with that one either. You know that's true, man; you know it."

Before he had even finished speaking, Haywood and Karl had cracked up laughing. Then, to Gilla's amazement, Roger's lips started to twitch. He grinned, slapped Foster on the back, shook his hand. "A'ight man, a'ight," said Roger. "You got me." Foster grinned, mock-punched Roger on the shoulder.

"We're going out back for a smoke," Haywood said. "You coming, Foster?"

"Yeah man, yeah. Gilla, catch you later, okay?"

The four of them slouched off together, Roger trailing a little. Just before they rounded the corner of the house, Roger looked back at Gilla. He pursed his lips together and smooched at her silently. Then they were gone. Gilla stood there, hugging herself, cold again.

She crept back inside. The lights were all off, except for a couple of candles over by the stereo. Someone had moved the dinner table with the food on it over there too, to clear the floor. A knot of people were dancing right in the center of the living room. There was Clarissa, with Jim. Clarissa was jigging about, trying to look cool. Bet she didn't even know she wasn't on the beat. "Rock on," Gilla whispered.

The television was on, the sound inaudible over the music. A few people huddled on the floor around it, watching a skinny blonde chick drop kick bad guys. The blue light from the TV flickered over their faces like cold flame.

On the couches all around the room, couples were necking. Gilla tried to make out Kashy's form, but it was too dark to really see if she was there. Gilla scouted the room out until she spied an empty lone chair. She went and perched on it, bobbed her head to the music and tapped her foot, pretending to have a good time.

She sighed. Sometimes she hated parties. She wanted to go and get a slice of that black rum cake. It was her favorite. But people would see her eating. She slouched protectively over her belly and stared across the room at the television. The program had changed. Now it was an oldtime movie or some shit, with guys and girls on a beach. Their bathing suits were in this ancient style, and the girls' hair, my God. One of them wore hers in this weird puffy 'do. To Gilla's eye, she looked a little chunky too. How had she gotten a part in this movie? The actors started dancing on the beach, this bizarre kind of shimmy thing. The people watching the television started pointing and laughing. Gilla heard Hussain's voice say, "No, don't change the channel! That's Frankie Avalon and Annette Funicello!" Yeah, Hussain *would* know crap like that.

"Gilla, move your butt over! Make some room!" It was Kashy, shoving her hips onto the same chair that Gilla was on. Gilla giggled and shifted over for her. They each cotched on the chair, not quite fitting. "Guess what?" Kashy said. "Remi just asked me out!"

Remi was *fine,* he was just Kashy's height when she was in heels, lean and broad-shouldered with big brown eyes, strong hands and those smooth East African looks. The knot that had been in Gilla's throat all night got harder. She swallowed around it and made her mouth smile. But she never got to mumble insincere congratulations to her friend, because just then . . .

They came back . . .

Roger strode in with his posse, all laughing so loudly that Gilla could hear them over the music. Foster shot Gilla a grin that made her toes feel all warm. Kashy looked at her funny, a slight smile on her face. Roger went and stood smirking at the television. On the screen, the chunky chick and the funny-looking guy in the old-fashioned bathing suits and haircuts were playing Postman in a phone booth with their friends. Postman! Stupid kid game.

They came back . . .
They came back from the ride . . .

Gilla wondered how she'd gotten herself into this. Roger had grabbed Clarissa, hugged her tight to him, announced that he wanted to play Postman, and in two twos Clarissa and Roger's servile friends had put the lights on and herded everybody into an old-fashioned game of Postman. Girls in the living room, guys stationed in closets all over the house, and Clarissa and Hussain playing . . .

"Postman!" yelled Hussain. "I've got a message for Kashy!" He was enjoying the hell out of this. That was a neat plan Hussain had come up with to avoid kissing any girls. Gilla had a hunch that females weren't his type.

"It's Remi!" Kashy whispered. She sprang to her feet. "I bet it's Remi!" She glowed at Gilla, and followed Hussain off to find her "message" in some closet or bathroom somewhere and neck with him.

Left sitting hunched over on the hard chair, Gilla glared at their departing backs. She thought about how Roger's friends fell over themselves to do anything he said, and tried to figure out where she'd learned the word "servile." The voice no longer seemed like a different voice in her head now, just her own. But it knew words she didn't know, things she'd never experienced, like how it felt to unfurl your leaves to the bright taste of the sun, and the empty screaming space in the air as a sister died, her bark and pith chopped through to make ships or firewood.

"That's some crazy shit," she muttered to herself.

"Postman!" chirped Clarissa. Her eyes sparkled and her color was high. Yeah, bet she'd been off lipping at some "messages" of her own. Lipping. Now there was another weird word. "Postman for Gilla!" said Clarissa.

Gilla's heart started to thunk like an axe chopping through wood. She stood. "What . . . ?"

Clarissa smirked at her. "Postman for you, hot stuff. You coming, or not?" And then she was off up the stairs and into the depths of Mr. and Mrs. Bright's house.

Who could it be? Who wanted to kiss her? Gilla felt tiny dots of clammy sweat spring out under her eyes. Maybe Remi? No, no. He liked Kashy. Maybe, please, maybe Foster?

Clarissa was leading her on a winding route. They passed a hallway closet. Muffled chuckles and thumps came from inside. "No, wait," murmured a male voice. "Let *me* take it off." Then they went by the bathroom. The giggles that wriggled out from under the bathroom door came from two female voices.

"There is no time so sap-sweet as the spring bacchanalia," Gilla heard herself saying.

Clarissa just kept walking. "You are *so* weird," she said over her shoulder.

They passed a closed bedroom door. Then came to another bedroom. Its door was closed, too, but Clarissa just slammed it open. "Postman!" she yelled.

The wriggling on the bed resolved itself into Patricia Bright and Haywood, entwined. Gilla didn't know where to look. At least their clothes were still on, sort of. Patricia looked up from under Haywood's armpit with a self-satisfied smile. "Jeez, I'm having an intimate birthday moment here."

"Sorry," said Clarissa, sounding not the least bit sorry,

"but Gilla's got a date." She pointed toward the closet door.

"Have a goooood time, killa Gilla," Clarissa told her. Haywood snickered.

Gilla felt cold. "In there?" she asked Clarissa.

"Yup," Clarissa chirruped. "Your special treat." She turned on her heel and headed out the bedroom door, yelling, "Who needs the Postman?"

"You gonna be okay, Gilla?" Patricia asked. She looked concerned.

"Yeah, I'll be fine. Who's in there?"

Patricia smiled. "That's half the fun, silly—not knowing."

Haywood just leered at her. Gilla made a face at him.

"Go on and enjoy yourself, Gilla," Patricia said. "If you need help, you can always let us know, okay?"

"Okay." Gilla was rooted where she stood. Patricia and Haywood were kissing again, ignoring her.

She could go back into the living room. She didn't have to do this. But . . . who? Remembering the warm cloak of Foster's arms around her, heavy as a carpet of fall leaves, Gilla found herself walking toward the closet. She pulled the door open, tried to peer in. A hand reached out and yanked her inside.

With the lady inside . . .

Hangers reached like twigs in the dark to catch in Gilla's hair. Clothing tangled her in it. A heavy body pushed her back against a wall. Blind, Gilla reached her arms out, tried to feel who it was. Strong hands pushed hers away, started squeezing her breasts, her belly. "Fat girl . . ." oozed a voice.

Roger. Gilla hissed, fought. He was so strong! His face was on hers now, his lips at her lips. The awful thing was, his breath tasted lovely. Unable to do anything else, she turned her mouth away from his. That put his mouth right at her ear. With warm, damp breath he said, "You know you want it, Gilla. Come on. Just relax." The words crawled into her ears. His laugh was mocking.

And the smile on the face . . .

Gilla's hair bristled at the base of her neck. She pushed at Roger, tried to knee him in the groin, but he just shoved her legs apart and laughed. "Girl, you know this is the only way a thick girl like you is going to get any play. You know it."

She knew it. She was only good for this. Thighs too heavy—*Must not a trunk be strong to bear the weight?*—belly too round—*Should the fruits of the tree be sere and wasted, then?*—hair too nappy—*A well-leafed tree is a healthy tree.* The words, her own words, whirled around and around in her head. What? What?

Simply this: you must fight those who would make free with you. Win or lose, you must fight.

A taste like summer cherries rose in Gilla's mouth again. Kashy envied her shape, her strength.

The back of Gilla's neck tingled. The sensation unfurled down her spine. She gathered power from the core of her, from that muscled, padded belly, and elbowed Roger high in the stomach. "No!" she roared, a fiery breath. The wind whuffed out of Roger. He tumbled back against the opposite wall, slid bonelessly down to the ground. Gilla fell onto her hands and knees, solidly centered on all fours. Her toes, her fingers flexed. She wasn't surprised to feel her limbs flesh themselves into four knotted appendages, backward-crooked and strong as wood. She'd sprouted claws too. She tapped them impatiently.

"Oh, God," moaned Roger. He tried to pull his feet up against his body, farther away from her. "Gilla, what the hell? Is that you?"

Foster had liked holding her. He found her beautiful. With a tickling ripple, the thought clothed Gilla in scales, head to toe. When she looked down at her new dragon feet, she could see the scales twinkling, cherry red. She lashed her new tail, sending clothing and hangers flying. Roger whimpered, "I'm sorry."

Testing out her bunchy, branchy limbs, Gilla took an experimental step closer to Roger. He began to sob.

And you? asked the deep, fruity voice in her mind. *What say you of you?*

Gilla considered, licking her lips. Roger smelled like meat. *I think I'm all those things that Kashy and Foster like about me. I'm a good friend.*

Yes.

I'm pretty. No, I'm beautiful.

Yes.

I'm good to hold.

Yes.

I bike hard.

Yes.

I run like the wind.

Yes.

I use my brain—well, sometimes.

(A smile to the voice this time). *Yes.*

I use my lungs.

Yes!

Gilla inhaled a deep breath of musty closet and Roger's fear-sweat. Her sigh made her chest creak like tall trees in a gentle breeze, and she felt her ribs unfurling into batlike wings. They filled the remaining closet space. "Please," whispered Roger. "Please."

"Hey, Rog?" called Haywood. "You must be having a real good time in there, if you're begging for more."

"Please, what?!" roared Gilla. At the nape of her neck, her hamadryad hood flared open. She exhaled a hot wind. Her breath smelled like cherry pie, which made her giggle. She was having a good time, even if Roger wasn't.

The giggles erupted as small gouts of flame. One of them lit the hem of Roger's sweater. "Please don't!" he yelled, beating out the fire with his hands. "God, Gilla, stop!"

Patricia's voice came from beyond the door. "That doesn't sound too good," she said to Haywood. "Hey, Gil?" she shouted. "You OK in there?"

Roger scrabbled to his feet. "Whaddya mean, is *Gilla* okay? Get me out of here! She's turned into some kind of monster!" He started banging on the inside of the closet door.

A polyester dress was beginning to char. No biggie.

Gilla flapped it out with a wing. But it *was* getting close in the closet, and Haywood and Patricia were yanking on the door. Gilla swung her head toward it. Roger cringed. Gilla ignored him. She nosed the door open and stepped outside. Roger pushed past her. "Fuck, Haywood; get her!"

Haywood's shirt was off, his jeans zipper not done up all the way. His lips looked swollen. He peered suspiciously at Gilla. "Why?" he asked Roger. "What's she doing?"

Patricia was still wriggling her dress down over her hips. Her hair was a mess. "Yeah," she said to Roger, "what's the big problem? You didn't hurt her, did you?" She turned to Gilla, put a hand on her scaly left fore-shoulder. "You okay, girl?"

What in the world was going on? Why weren't they scared? "Uh," replied Gilla. "I dunno. How do I look?"

Patricia frowned. "Same as ever," she said, just as Kashy and Foster burst into the room.

"We heard yelling," Kashy said, panting. "What's up? Roger, you been bugging Gilla again?"

Foster took Gilla's paw. "Did he trick you into the closet with him?"

"What the fuck's the matter with everyone?" Roger was nearly screeching. "Can't you see? She's some kind of dragon, or something!"

That was the last straw. Gilla started to laugh. Great belly laughs that started from her middle and came guffawing through her snout. Good thing there was no fire this time, 'cause Gilla didn't know if she could have stopped it. She laughed so hard that the cherry pit she'd swallowed came back up. "Urp," she said, spitting it into her hand. Her hand. She was back to normal now.

She grinned at Roger. He goggled. "How'd you do that?" he demanded.

Gilla ignored him. Her schoolmates had started coming into the room from all over the house to see what the racket was. "Yeah, he tricked me," Gilla said, so they could all hear. "Roger tricked me into the closet, and then he stuck his hand down my bra."

"What a creep," muttered Clarissa's boyfriend Jim.

Foster stepped up to Roger, glaring. "What is your problem, man?" Roger stuck his chest out and tried to glare back, but he couldn't meet Foster's eyes. He kept sneaking nervous peeks around Foster at Gilla.

Clarissa snickered at Gilla. "So what's the big deal? You do it with him all the time, anyway."

Oh, enough of this ill-favored chit. Weirdly, the voice felt like it was coming from Gilla's palm now. The hand where she held the cherry pit. But it still sounded and felt like her own thoughts. Gilla stalked over to Clarissa. "You don't believe that Roger attacked me?"

Clarissa made a face of disgust. "I believe that you're so fat and ugly that you'll go with anybody, 'cause nobody would have you."

"That's dumb," said Kashy. "How could she go with anybody, if nobody would have her?"

"I'll have her," said Foster. He looked shyly at Gilla. Then his face flushed. "I mean, I'd like, I mean . . ." No one could hear the end of the sentence, because they were laughing so hard. Except Roger, Karl and Haywood.

Gilla put her arms around Foster, afraid still that she'd misunderstood. But he hugged back, hard. Gilla felt all warm. Foster was such a goof. "Clarissa," said Gilla, "if something bad ever happens to you and nobody will believe your side of the story, you can talk to me. Because I know what it's like."

Clarissa reddened. Roger swore and stomped out of the room. Haywood and Karl followed him.

Gilla regarded the cherry pit in the palm of her hand. Considered. Then she put it in her mouth again and swallowed it down.

"Why'd you do that?" Foster asked.

"Just felt like it."

"A tree'll grow inside you," he teased.

Gilla chuckled. "I wish. Hey, I never did get a real Postman message." She nodded toward the closet. "D'you wanna?"

Foster ducked his head, took her hand. "Yeah."
Gilla led the way, grinning.

They came back from the ride
With the lady inside,
And a smile on the face of the tiger.

Death's Door

Terry Bisson

Terry Bisson [www.terrybisson.com] lives in Oakland, California. His website lists a bushel of accomplishments. In the late '60s, after scripting several tales for Creepy and Eerie with writing partner Clark Dimond, Bisson was editor of the short-lived Web of Horror. He created the NO-FRILLS BOOKS TM in 1981. He is the author of several works of non-fiction, co-author of two children's books, and author of six genre fantasy or SF novels—Wyrldmaker (1981); Talking Man (1987), a World Fantasy Award nominee; Fire on the Mountain (1988); Voyage to the Red Planet (1990); Pirates of the Universe (1996); The Pickup Artist (2001); and most recently the novella, Dear Abby (2003)—and a number of movie tie-in books of unusually high quality for that subgenre. His short fiction is collected in Bears Discover Fire (1993), In the Upper Room (2000), and in Greetings (2005). Originally from Kentucky, in 1999 he was inducted into the Owensboro, Kentucky Hall of Fame.

"Death's Door" appeared in Flights. Here Bisson returns to one of his recurring themes, death, perhaps because he started out writing poetry when he was young, and he's as old as Samuel R. Delany now. Anyway, in this story, death ceases. For a period of time nothing and no one dies. Sound like fun? Uh-uh.

Her back was broken. Henry knew it as soon as he saw her trying to crawl out of the street, her hind legs useless.

"Daddy daddy daddy!" screamed Carnelia, often called Carny, but not today; not on this awful day in every child's life when, Henry knew, Death is discovered.

"Come here, Carnelia, honey," he said, scooping his seven-year-old-daughter into his arms. She was light, and seemed even lighter, as if Death's heavy presence had given wings to Life.

But Marge wasn't dead yet. She was still pulling herself toward the curb, her hind legs twisted in a strange shape that made her look less like a dog than a giant squid that was somehow no longer giant and no longer squid.

"Daddy, Daddy!"

"She's been hit by a car, honey," Henry said. As if Carnelia hadn't seen the whole thing.

"They were going too fast," said Carnelia, and for the first time Henry saw the ambulance, pulled up at the curb, the light still flashing; and the young black man in the long white EMS coat running across the street toward him.

Oddly, he ran right past the dog, Marge. I'm already thinking of her as the dog, thought Henry.

"The dog ran out in front of me," the young man said. "I couldn't stop. We are on our way to . . ."

"It's okay," said Henry. "Go. It wasn't your fault, I'm sure."

He set his daughter down and followed the EMS guy to the middle of the street. Marge was still trying to make her way toward the curb, as if hoping that once there she would be restored somehow.

"Go," Henry said again.

Her eyes were open and her tongue was hanging out. Bubbles of blood appeared on her black lips and nose. One was big and it lasted a long time. Henry kept hoping it would disappear before Carnelia got there, but it didn't.

"She's going to die! She's going to die!"

Henry stood up and put his arms around his daughter's shoulders; she felt enormously, alarmingly frail. "Yes, honey," he said, gathering her to him. "Now do this for me, and for her: run into the house and get that big box out of the garage, the one the lawn thing came in."

"What for?"

"She needs a place. Just do it, okay?"

Carnelia ran off. Marge was lying on the strip of grass between the curb and the sidewalk, eyes closed, waiting for the transformation that was about to come over her: Death, the Redeemer. It would make her whole again.

"Is she going to be all right?" Carnelia asked breathlessly. She was towing the box behind her, and had picked up two more of the neighborhood kids.

"No, honey," Henry said, kneeling down. "She is going to die. Marge was hit by the ambulance and it's all over for her. Help me now."

The ambulance was driving off, light spinning. Henry eased the dog into the box. He carried the box into the garage, and placed it on the floor under his tool bench.

"Now get her some water," he said. "Bring her a blanket, from that box by the door. Not that one. She's going to die. It's okay; all things die."

Carnelia began to cry again. "This is the blanket she likes."

"OK, then. Now let's leave her alone. Dogs like to die in private."

"How do you know?"

"I just know." Henry knew because he had done the same thing with his dog, Dallie, thirty-one years before.

"If I leave her she'll die."

"She's going to die, honey. All things die, It's the way things are."

"I don't like things then!"

"All things have to die, honey. Even things we love."

Not exactly true, as it turned out. Not that day. For that was the day that Death's Door closed.

"Damn," said Shaheem, as he drove off. One dog down, but hopefully a human saved.

Then when he saw her on her apartment floor he wondered if it was in fact an even trade. The woman was at least ninety years old. About the size and weight of a wet raincoat.

He and his partner loaded her onto the gurney and were easing her down the stairs, when a familiar face appeared in the door below.

Is this a big story? Shaheem wondered. He recognized the face from TV. But there was no TV crew following. Ted Graeme was here to see about his mother.

"Mother?" Graeme said. He kissed her finely wrinkled face, aware that he was being watched. He was used to being watched. He was, after all, the anchor on the Nightly News.

"Mother?"

No answer. Not a flicker of interest or recognition.

Maybe this will be it, Graeme thought. It would be a blessing. She was his mother but everyone had their time, and she had been miserable since his father had died twelve—was it really twelve?—years before.

Tiny strokes had been chipping away at her, piece by piece. It was a cruel way to go.

"Mother?"

Still no answer.

"You want to ride with her?" asked the EMS guy.

"It's okay," said Graeme. "I'll follow. You're taking her to Midcity, right?"

"Whatever you say, Mr. Graeme."

* * *

"We're running late, sir," said Hippolyte. He was the new producer of the Nightly News. Secretly, Graeme called him Still-Polite.

"I'm having a family crisis," Graeme said. "Did the warden call?"

"It's all set up," said Hipp. That was what his friends called him. He was a white man with dreadlocks, and Graeme had to remember not to smile whenever he looked at him. Times were changing. Times were always changing.

"I need to stay in the city," said Graeme. "I think Karin should go in my place."

Hipp looked surprised. "For real?"

"Definitely for real" said Graeme, picking up the phone. The most controversial execution in years, and he would have to miss it. "I'm calling her now."

"I'll prep her," said Hipp. "Meanwhile we have a big story. A plane went down outside Paris, at Charles De-Gaulle."

"God. Not another Concorde?"

"Worse. A 777."

It was the one thing they weren't prepared for. Survival. As Jean-Claude poked through the wreckage he found bodies and part of bodies. The ones that were whole, or even partly whole, were still alive.

"My wife, my wife!" One man was cut almost in half; his entrails were falling out, all over his cheap suit, but he was still alive, asking about his wife in bad African French.

"We're looking for her," Jean-Claude said, even though it wasn't true. They were looking for parts of her; for parts of all of them.

"Bring her to me, *s'il vous plaît*. Let me see her before I die."

"Oui."

Jean-Claude waited for the man to close his eyes but he didn't. Jean-Claude resisted the impulse to reach out and close them for him. People were screaming all around him.

"They're all burned," said Bruno, his second in command. "They come to pieces when we pull them out, but they won't stop screaming."

"I'll help load them up," said Jean-Claude.

When he got back to the African, he was still alive, still clutching his entrails.

"Load him up," said Jean-Claude. "*Mon Dieu*," he said to Bruno. "This is the worst yet. An air disaster with hundreds of survivors."

Karin had managed to sound concerned on the phone but Graeme knew she was pleased. Covering this execution was her big chance. He didn't mind. He would have felt the same. He had once been young and on the make.

He found his mother in the ICU.

"She's still breathing," the doctor said.

"She has a DNR," said Graeme, squeezing his mother's tiny, fluttering, birdlike hand. "It's on her chart."

"I know," said the doctor. "We haven't got her on life support. We couldn't anyway."

"What do you mean?"

"We have an overload today. Lots of serious injuries."

"A bad day?"

"No more than usual, it's just that everyone is surviving." He hurried off.

"I'll be back," Graeme said, kissing his mother's parchment cheek. He hurried out to the lot, beeping his car on the run. With Karin gone he would have to put together the six o'clock broadcast all by himself.

"She's suffering," Emily said to Henry when they were alone in the kitchen.

"Carnelia or Marge?"

"Both, damn it! Carny can learn about death without watching her dog die."

"Marge has a right to die at home, with dignity, and not in some vet's office," said Henry. "And as far as Carnelia's concerned, it's not just about learning. It's about going through the changes. She was terribly upset this afternoon. She'll grieve tomorrow. Right now she's fascinated. Death is fascinating as well as terrifying."

"I work with death every day, remember?" Emily said. But she was coming around. She told him about her day while he cut up the salad, being careful to avoid his fingertips. Emily worked as a pediatric nurse in a preemie ward. "Today I thought death was on a holiday," she said. "Today not a single baby died."

"Not a one?"

"You get a day like that every once in a while," Emily said. "I suppose it's a reward for the others."

It was dark. She had expected the darkness, but not the light. The light was for the gullible, the light toward which you floated when you were dead. But here she was, floating toward it.

There were others, like herself. They were specks, sparks. So many. *I had not thought that death had undone so many*. Floating toward the light. They were rising together.

Then they were slowing. *So this is what it's like*, she thought. She was surprised. She hadn't thought it would be like anything.

Karin found herself eating too many doughnuts, provided by Krispy Kreme. Tasteless but tasty, she thought. Too tasty. You have to watch your weight when you're on TV. It shows up first in the face.

She put the doughnut away and followed the victim's family into the viewing room. Under the new protocol, the execution was set for sundown. It gave it the appearance of inevitability, almost of a natural death. She wondered if it made it any easier for the condemned.

The guards were already strapping Berry to the gurney. Karin wondered if he would get a cigarette.

Apparently not.

"Do you have any last words," asked the warden.

"You know I do," said Berry. He turned toward the window, which Karin had been assured was one-way. Still, she wanted to hide her face.

"You are murdering an innocent man," he said.

"Can you go on?"

The producer had heard about Graeme's mother.

"Sure," Graeme said, "but thanks for asking." As he sat down at his desk, an intern handed him the stories. Hipp had sorted them well. Start with the light, ease into the dark.

"Good news on the home front," Graeme began. "Billy Crystal came home from the hospital in Palm Springs, apparently recovered from the stroke that many thought spelled the end of the aging comedian's spectacular sixty-year career. Doctors are cautiously optimistic."

He turned the page.

"Rescue attempts are continuing in the Paris air crash. There are 255 casualties, passengers and crew, most with serious injuries but as yet, miraculously, no deaths. In Lahore, India, UN authorities are investigating what appears to be the worst massacre in recent history . . ."

"You have prepared yourself for this," Krishna said.

"I have seen it before," said Paolo.

"No, you haven't," Krishna said.

He led the stocky UN rep through the gate into the temple yard where the worshippers had been surprised. The massacre had been done the old way, with swords. People had been hacked to pieces. Arms and legs were lying on the ground, like spare parts. Bodies lay in heaps, their faces slashed into grim simacularums of red mouths. But that wasn't the horror.

"Jesu!" said Paolo.

The horror was that they were all alive.

* * *

The warden himself pulled the switch. There was no sudden killer voltage, no sprung trap, just a slow IV drip—and a peaceful surrender.

The condemned man closed his eyes, and the small crowd sighed with pleasure. Relatives and colleagues of the man he said he hadn't killed. *Of course they all say that*, Karin thought; and as she did, she realized she had been holding her breath.

Berry kicked: one, twice; then lay still.

There was a long moment of silence, and then they all stood, reaching for their bags and the ID cards that would let them out of the prison.

Then, as one, they all stopped at the door and looked behind them.

The dead man had just opened his eyes.

The next morning Marge was still alive. Henry put his hand on her side, expecting cold, and felt her breathing. He considered for a moment telling Carnelia that the dog had died anyway, but she would insist on seeing the body before going off to school.

And there she was in the garage door. "Maybe she's going to be all right," she said, kneeling to pet the dog. "Don't die."

"She needs to die," said Henry. "She has massive internal injuries, her back is broken. She wants to be alone and die in peace."

"And you have to go to school," said Emily, gently pulling her daughter to her feet and leading her out of the garage.

"It was horrible," said Karin on her cell phone. "They had to administer the stuff twice, and he still wouldn't die. They made us leave. We're outside in the parking lot."

"That means there's no story," said Graeme. "Maybe you should head back."

"Not yet, please," said Karin. "They have to finish it somehow. That's our story. How's your mother?"

"Hanging in there," said Graeme. She had been moved into the ward with twenty others, all terminal; six of them with gunshot wounds.

"Did I tell you that I knew your mother? She was my English prof at Northwestern. She was a wonderful teacher."

"I know; you told me."

"She wouldn't let us call her Dr. Graeme. It had to be just Ruth. She made Milton come alive."

Coming alive is no longer the problem, thought Graeme.

"You may have to start with a hard story," said Hipp. "We have an earthquake in Lima, just coming off the wire. 7.6 on the Richter scale."

"Jesus," said Graeme, already reshuffling his papers.

So many lights. Sparks. They were still rising, but they had stopped up "above."

Above?

She floated into the cloud, a cloud of sparks. What had seemed like light now seemed like darkness.

Now she could see the light. It was a thin line, like a horizon. She had been watching it for what seemed hours, days? Years? If only she could remember her name.

The sparks were clustered around the bright line, like bugs around a light. She was one of them.

"I got this thing from the military," said Carlos in breathless Spanish. "It's like sonar. You can pick up sounds. In case anyone buried under the ruins is still alive."

"Not likely," said Eduardo. All around there was nothing but rubble, and the screaming of sirens. The business district had been leveled. *God knows what it's like in the favelas*. "What about the injured?"

"They're flooding the hospital," said Carlos. "More than we're prepared for. Central sent me to look for those who are buried alive, now that we have a way to locate them."

"Let's go, then," said Eduardo. "I've got two crews, and two backhoes. Just point us to the most likely."

"That's the problem," said Carlos, taking off the earphones.

"What do you mean?"

Instead of answering, Carlos handed Eduardo the earphones and scanned the pickup wand in a circle, around the ruined horizon.

Eduardo didn't even have to put them on. The noise was deafening. Knocks, screams, cries for help or at least mercy. It was as if an entire city had been buried—alive.

"A scooper," muttered Shaheem. He hated scoopers, and what was the rush?

But he was a pro; he turned on the light.

The police were gathered around the bottom of 122 Broadway.

The crowd was still there, held back by yellow tape. He had to push his way through.

"She stood on the ledge and took off her clothes," one of the cops told him. "A sure way to gather a crowd. The guys were trying to talk her down when she just stepped off backward, like this." He stepped back off the curb to illustrate.

Shaheem looked up at the ledge, twenty-two stories up. Two cops were still there: one taking photos, one just looking down.

The scooper had hit head first on the concrete, and blood was spattered around for twenty feet, some of it high on the plate glass of "Broadway Jewelry." Her head was flat on one side, as big as a watermelon, and when Shaheem knelt down beside her to unroll the body bag she whispered, "I'm sorry."

Carnelia had sat up with Marge until nine before going to bed. Henry was sure the dog would be dead by morning, but she was still breathing.

The blanket was stiff with blood that had leaked out of

her mouth and nose and anus. Henry stuffed it into the trash, then went back into the house. He was surprised to find Emily dressed for work.

"I thought you had the day off. I thought you said . . ."

"None of the preemies are dying, but we have another problem," she said. "ER is overflowing."

"Overflowing?"

"Everyone they bring in is hanging on," she said. "The halls are filled with stretchers. Midcity has placed us all on call. It's worse than the stadium collapse."

After she left, Henry took a plastic bag out to the garage. Carnelia would be home from school in a few hours. He pulled the bag over Marge's head and sealed it around her neck with with duct tape. It moved in and out, slowly at first; then more and more slowly.

He didn't want to watch so he went back inside and turned on the TV.

The news was disturbing. .

". . . unprecedented meeting of the Security Council with the International Red Cross," read Graeme, editing Hipp's clumsy copy on the fly. He had rushed in from the hospital where his mother was in a dim hallway with 126 other people, some of them screaming, others as quiet as herself.

". . . confirms that no one has died, anywhere in the world, for the past thirty-six hours."

"He cut to the tape. "It's statistically improbable and medically impossible," said a talking head in a white coat. "People are surviving unsurvivable accidents."

Hipp nodded. Graeme came back on the air.

"And now we take you to Cold Spring State Prison, where our own Karin Glass is waiting for . . ."

Won Lee was taking a picture of Hong Kong harbor with his new digital camera when he felt the deck tip under his feet. Irrationally, it was his camera that he reached for as he began to skid across the deck. He almost caught a stanchion but the crush of falling, flailing bodies pushed him into the water.

It was cold and the camera was gone. It was dark and he held his breath for as long as he could, then gave up and felt the cold water filling his lungs, almost as satisfying as air. Then it wasn't so cold anymore. Drifting down was like flying. He spread his arms, or felt them spread. He felt himself slip into the soft muck at the bottom of the harbor.

He waited to die. He could see sparks, all around. Had the ferry caught fire? The mud was cold, then not so cold. It all seemed to be taking a long time.

Someone settled beside him. Was it his wife? There was no light but he could make out a face, the eyes wide open like his own. Was it a man or a woman?

It didn't seem to matter. Something was picking at his hand, uncovering little white bones. He watched and waited. It all seemed to be taking a long time.

". . . governor promises an investigation," said Karin. Her hands were shaking; she tried to hide it.

She had been allowed to see Berry, but not to speak with him. He was still in critical condition, not breathing.

". . . after the last-minute arrival of the DNA test establishing his innocence," she said. She held up the microphone to pick up the chants from the demonstrators. "Meanwhile, the demonstrators outside the prison are calling for the DA's blood, in a dramatic and ironic role reversal."

My best line, she thought. *I'll bet that fucking Graeme cuts it.*

There were so many sparks. The thin line of light was almost invisible. It was like Milton's blindness, she thought; there was plenty to see in the darkness. More than she had ever dreamed possible.

It had been a surprise, then a disappointment. Now she wanted to see what was on the other side. But there was no other side.

Only a thin line of light.

The sparks formed a cloud around it, like smoke. So many: *I had not thought that death had undone so many.* They were swarming and she was swarming with them, forward and back, filling the darkness so that the darkness was lighter than the thin line of light.

She wished she could remember her name.

"I'll be late," said Emily on the phone. "They're putting us on extra shifts."

"I know. It's on TV."

"Something very very weird is going on. The hospital is filled with people who shouldn't be alive. One man who took a shotgun blast in the mouth."

"It's a big story," said Henry. "It's on the news."

"Hey, I even saw what's-his-name, from the Nightly News. His mother is here. There's a whole hall filled with old people who have been taken off life support, waiting to die. Is Carny home?"

"Soon."

"Is Marge—over?"

"Yes. I'm sure." He told her about the plastic bag.

After he hung up, he went to the garage. He didn't want Carnelia to see the plastic bag.

The bag was no longer going in and out. It had been almost two hours.

He unpeeled the tape and pulled off the bag. He hid it under the blanket in the trash. Marge's eyes were closed. She wasn't stiff yet. He curled her as neatly as possible in the blood-stained box, and changed the blanket.

He was tucking it around her when she licked his hand.

"Berry's just one person," said Graeme. "We need you here."

"Please," said Karin. "This is the biggest story of the year. An innocent man almost executed."

"He's still alive?"

"He's on life support," said Karin, "Unlike all the others, who don't need it. Maybe he doesn't either. But I need to stay here for when he wakes up."

"Well OK, but stay by the phone."

She laughed. "The phone stays by me. How's your mother? Ruth?"

"I haven't heard from the hospital. They said they would call. Meanwhile we just got word from the pound that dogs aren't dying either. Cats, yes."

"Figures," said Karin, who had a dog. "Graeme, what in the world do you think is going on?

The Cedars was almost empty. The sound on the TV was off but the text scrolling across gave the story:

NO DEATHS, WORLDWIDE. NO REPORTED DEATHS IN . . .

"Weird, huh?" said the bartender, setting down a cold Heineken. "Where you been?"

"I've worked three shifts straight," said Shaheem. "Who do you think is hauling all those people into the hospital? They used to wait for the guys from the funeral home."

"My girlfriend's into astrology," said the bartender. "She says it's a collusion or something of the planets, never happened before. Unpresidential."

"Unprecedented," said Shaheem.

"But that's fantasy," said the bartender. "Me, I'm a believer in science."

"Whatever that means."

"Science is numbers." The bartender pulled a magazine up from behind the bar. "Ever read *Discover*? This month is about the population explosion."

"Implosion, you mean," said Shaheem. "Guess I could do another."

The bartender set another Heineken on the bar. "More people means more deaths," he said. "It says here that more people die now every day than during World War II. Just of natural causes, plus all the little wars and disasters and shit."

"Not any more," said Shaheem. He told him about the scooper.

"Maybe death is getting behind," said the bartender. "Temporary overload. No way to process them all. Nowhere to put them."

"Does *Discover* tell you what to do?" asked Shaheem. He was not expecting an answer.

"Just wait," said the bartender. "It'll sort itself out. Things always do."

"You wish," said Shaheem. *I wish, we wish, we all wish.* "Ever thought you'd see the living waiting for death?"

The line of light was getting thicker. It was now a band of light. The sparks were flying through, extinguished by the light. She watched, breathless, bodiless, and saw that she was getting closer.

Or was the band getting wider? It was the same thing. So many sparks, all rising. She wished she could remember her name.

"It's for you," said Hipp. He handed the phone to Graeme as he picked up another.

The phones were all ringing at once.

"When is Karin coming back?" Hipp asked, over his shoulder. "We have to start putting the news together."

"I'll call her," said Graeme. "That was the hospital."

"Oh." Then Hipp saw that he was smiling.

"My mother just died."

Henry had quit smoking six months ago but he knew where half a pack was hidden, in his old coat. He smoked two waiting for Carnelia to get home.

There was something on TV but he kept the sound off. It was too weird. It was a worldwide crisis. But the most important thing was the crisis here at home.

Then he heard wailing and he realized that Carnelia had gone straight to the garage.

He found her wrapping Marge in the blanket. She dried her eyes with a corner. "Marge died, daddy. Can we bury her in the yard?"

Henry unwrapped the dog. Her eyes were open. There was no mistaking that peaceful look.

"Of course I will, honey."

"Will you dig a nice hole? Why are you smiling, daddy?"

"Because, Carny. I'm not."

So much light. There it was, all of a sudden, lots of it. Extinguishing the sparks, one by one, like rain drops in the sea.

Ruth, that was it!

Then it wasn't.

"Thanks for hurrying back," said Graeme, "I'm going to pick up my mother. I want to do it myself."

"I understand," said Karin.

"Lead with your big story," said Graeme. "The man they almost executed."

Karin was taking off her coat and combing her hair at the same time. "It's a bigger story now," she said. She held up her cell phone. "Berry died twelve minutes ago."

"Oh shit."

"I'll try and get a statement from the governor."

"And last words."

"He was in a coma," Karin said. "I'll go with the last words we had from the beginning: 'You are murdering an innocent man.'"

Golden City Far

Gene Wolfe

Gene Wolfe lives in Barrington, Illinois, and is widely considered the most accomplished writer in the fantasy and science fiction genres. His four-volume Book of the New Sun is an acknowledged masterpiece. He has published many fantasy, science fiction, and horror stories over the last thirty years and more. Each year he publishes a few short stories, of which at least one is among the best of the year in one genre or another, sometimes several, with 2004 that kind of year, a vintage Gene Wolfe year. Collections of his short fiction (all in print) include The Island of Dr. Death and Other Stories and Other Stories *(1980),* Storyes from the Old Hotel *(1988),* Castle of Days *(1992),* Endangered Species *(1989),* Strange Travelers *(1999), and* Innocents Aboard *(2004), with a new one,* Starwater Strains, *out in 2005. The big fantasy news for 2004 was the publication of a major fantasy work,* The Wizard Knight *(in two volumes,* The Knight *and* The Wizard*).*

"Golden City Far," the adventures of a high school boy who dreams, complete with school psychologists and administrators, old ghosts, a beautiful girl and a beautiful woman, true love, and a talking dog, was published in Flights. *We chose it to end our book this year. It is the longest story in this book and, perhaps, even, the best. What a fine year when stories of this quality contend for best!*

This is what William Wachter wrote in his spiral notebook during study hall, the first day.

"Funny dream last night. I was standing on a beach. I looked out, shading my eyes, and I could not see a thing. It was like a big fog bank was over the ocean way far away so that everything sort of faded white. A gull flew over me and screeched, and I thought, *well, not that way.*

"So I turned north, and there was a long level stretch and big mountains. I should not have been able to see past them, but I could. It was not like the mountains could be looked through. It was like the thing I was seeing on the other side was higher than they were so that I saw it over the tops. It was really far away and looked small, but it was just beautiful, gold towers, all sizes and shapes with flags on them. Yellow flags, purple, blue, green, and white ones. I thought, *well, there it is.* I had to go there. I cannot explain it, but I knew I had to get to that city and once I did nothing else would matter because I would have done everything I was supposed to do, and everything would be OK forever.

"I started walking, and I was not thinking about how far it was at all, just that it was really nice that I had found out what I was supposed to do. Instead of thrashing around for years I had it. It did not matter how far it was, just that every step got me closer.

"Cool!"

He could not think of anything else to write, but only of the golden towers, and how the flags had stood out stiffly from them so that he had known there was a hard wind blowing where the towers were, and he would like that wind.

Someone passed him a note. He let it fall to the floor unread.

Mrs. Durkin took him by the shoulder, and he jerked.

"Billy?"

It was hard to remember where he was, but he said, "Yes ma'am?"

"The bell rang, Billy. All the other kids have gone. Were you asleep?"

Thinking that she meant when he had seen the towers and the flags, he repeated, "Yes, ma'am."

"Daydreaming. Well, you're at the right age for it, but the period's over."

He stood up. "I should have done my homework in here. I guess I did, some of it. I want to get to bed early."

The sea was to his left, the ground beneath his feet great stones, or shale, or soft sand. The mountains, which had appeared distant the night before, were so remote as to be almost invisible, and often vanished behind dunes covered with sparse sea oats. There was a breeze from the sea, and though the scudding clouds looked threatening, it did not rain or snow. He was neither hungry nor thirsty, and was conscious of being neither hungry nor thirsty. It seemed to him that he had been walking a long while, not hours or days or years, but simply a long while, time as it had been before anyone had thought of such things as years or centuries.

He climbed dunes and rough, low hills, and beyond the last found an inlet blocking his progress; long before he reached the point near which she lay, he had seen the woman on the rock in the water. She was beautiful, and naked save for her hair; and her skin was as white as milk. In one hand she held a shining yellow apple.

He stopped and stood staring at her, and when a hundred breaths had come and gone, he sat down on a different rock and stared some more. Her eyes opened; each time he met her gaze, he felt lost in their depths.

"You may kiss me and eat one bite of my apple," she told him. "One bite, no more."

He was frightened, and shook his head.

"One bite will let you understand everything." Her voice was music. "Two bites would let you understand more than everything, and more than everything is too much."

He backed away.

The sun peeped from between clouds, bathing her with black gold. "What color is my hair?"

Perhaps its black was only shadow. Perhaps its gold was only sunlight. He said, "Nobody has hair like that."

"I do." She smiled, and her lips were as red as corals, and her teeth were sharp and gleaming white. "Men have found themselves in difficulties through biting my apple."

He nodded, certain it was true.

"But kiss me, and you may do anything you wish."

"I wouldn't be able to stop," he told her, and turned and ran.

He woke sweating, threw off the covers and got out of bed. The house was dark and quiet. The alarm clock meant to wake him for school said five minutes past four. He carried his books and notebooks to the dining-room table, turned on the light, and began to study.

In study hall that afternoon, he wrote this in his spiral notebook:

"One time Mr. Bates said how do you know this is real? Maybe what you dream is really real and this is a dream. How can you tell? People argued about it, but I did not because I knew the answer. It is because what you dream is different every night. Waking up you are wherever you went to sleep. Last night it was kind of the same as before, but different because the city was gone. Anyhow I could not see it. I met this girl who tried to get me to say what color her hair was, only I could not. She wanted to kiss me and I ran off."

He made a small round dot for the final period, and read over what he had written. It seemed inadequate, and he added: "I would like to go back."

He stopped upon the summit of a hill higher than most, and turned for a last look. She was standing on her rock now, sparsely robed in hair like fire that cast shadows upon her white flesh that were as black as paint. One hand held up her shining apple. When she saw he was watching her, she raised the other, kissed it, and blew the kiss to him.

For one brief instant he saw it fluttering toward him like a butterfly of cellophane. It touched his lips, soft and throbbing and redolent of the flowers that bloom under the sea. He shook, and could not stop.

A long time after that, when she and her inlet were many hills behind him and he had long since stopped trembling, he saw a black and white dog. It had a long and tangled coat, a long and feathery tail, and ears that would not stand up quite straight. He had never had a dog, but the people next door had a dog very much like that, a dog named Shep. He played with Shep now and then, and he whistled now.

The dog turned to look at him, pricking up the ears that would not quite stand up straight. It was some distance away but came trotting toward him, and he himself trotted to meet it, and stroked its head and rubbed its ears. After that the two of them went on together (the dog trotting at his heels) climbing and descending hills which gradually became less lofty and less rugged, sometimes catching glimpses of the sea to their left, where waves flashed in sunshine like mirrors, or stalked from darkling sea to darkling land like an army of ghosts.

The alarm clock was ringing tinnily. He got up and shut it off, stretched, and looked out the window. There were leaves, mostly brown, on the broken sidewalk in front of the house. He tried to remember whether they had been there the day before, and decided they had not.

Later, as he shuffled through the leaves, Shep joined him and accompanied him to the bus stop. He petted Shep and declared him to be a good dog, and found something strange in the way Shep looked at him, some quality that slipped away no matter how hard he tried to grasp it.

On the bus he told Carl Kilby, "He looked right at me. Usually they don't want to look you in the face. That was weird!" Carl, who had no idea what he was talking about, grunted.

* * *

In study hall . . .

"Last night I found this dog that looked exactly like Shep. Maybe it was him. He was a nice dog and we were way out in a pretty lonely spot. (I did not even see the ocean toward the end.) So I was glad to have the dog. Only what was he doing way out there? He was just walking along like me when I saw him.

"I have never had the same dream three nights. Not even two that I can remember."

"Billy?"

"Well, if it happens tonight too, I hope the dog is still there."

Mrs. Durkin touched his shoulder. "The period's over, Billy."

"Just a minute," he said. "I want to get this down."

"A kiss chased me and landed on my face."

It was inadequate, and he knew it; but with Mrs. Durkin standing beside him it was the best he could do. He shut his notebook and stood up. "I'm sorry, Mrs. Durkin."

She smiled. "The other kids rush out at the bell. It's kind of nice to have one who isn't eager to leave."

He nodded, which seemed safe, backed away, and went to his next class.

The dog was still there, lying down as if waiting for him. The weather the same. The city he had seen had been on the other side of the mountains—he felt certain of that, and he could see the mountains far away, a low blue rampart.

He and the dog walked on together until the dog said, "Chief?"

"God bless you!" he told it, and leaned down a little to pat its head.

"Chief, would you maybe like a drink?"

It seemed entirely natural, but somehow deep underneath it did *not* seem natural. Not surprised but somehow (deep underneath) thrown a little off balance, he said, "Sure, if you would."

"There's a nice spring not far from here," the dog said.

"Cold water, with a sort of drink-me-and-be-lucky flavor. I could show you."

He said, "Sure," but when they had gone some distance he added, "I guess you've been here before."

"Huh-uh," the dog said.

"Okay, then how do you know about this place?"

"I smell it." When they had climbed another hill and the spring was in sight, the dog added, "It might not work for me. Only for you."

The dog drank the water just the same, running ahead of him and lapping fast. There was a pool in the rocks, not too wide to jump over, from which a rill ran. He went to the other side and knelt. I've never drunk out of a dog's bowl, he thought, so this is a first.

It was good water, as the dog had promised it would be, cold and fresh. He had no idea what luck was supposed to taste like, so he tried to analyze the flavor, which was very faint. It was a taste of rocks and pines and chill winds, he decided, with just a little touch of sunshine on snow.

"Does he always follow you like that, Bill?"

Sue Sumner was blond and beautiful, and he knew he was apt to stammer like a retard; he also knew he had to answer. He said, "No, just yesterday and today. He's a nice dog, but I don't know why he comes to the stop with me."

She smiled. "You ought to take him on the bus."

"I'd like to," he said, and realized as he spoke that it was true. "I'd like to take him to school with me."

"Like Mary and her little lamb."

He grinned. "Sure. I've been laughed at before. It didn't hurt much, and it hasn't killed me yet."

It was Friday, which meant assembly instead of study hall. He would save his dream in memory, he decided, and write it down in study hall Monday, with his weekend dreams, if there were any. "Probably won't be," he told himself.

From his notebook . . . "The craziest thing happened yesterday. We got back from church and I went up to change back. I was putting on my jeans, and there was this bird singing outside. Singing lyrics. I thought this is crazy, birds don't sing words, and I tried to remember how they really did sing. I could remember the tune, but it seemed like I could not remember the words. I kept telling myself there were not any. I put on a CD, loud, and pretty soon the bird flew away. Now I cannot remember what the bird sang, and I would like to. Something about him and his wife (it rhymed with life, I remember that) building a house and don't come around because we will not let you in.

"OK, I went outside and right away the Pekar's dog started following me. I thought my gosh it is going to turn into The Dream—the hills, the rocks, the dwarf on the horse and all that, and I am crazy. So I walked about three blocks with Pekar's dog along the whole time.

"We got to the park and I sat down on a bench and petted the dog some, and I said, listen, this is serious, so can you really talk? And he looked right at me the way he does and said yep. What is your name, I said, and he said Shep. I was going to ask if he remembered the naked lady with the hair, only he had not been with me when that happened. So I asked about the lucky water we drank, did he remember that? He said yep. He says he cannot talk to other people at all, only to me and other dogs. The dwarf said all that stuff about the writing on the scabbard and the writing on the blade, and I was not sure I remembered it. I still am not. So I asked him about that and he said he—"

"Billy, will you run an errand for me, please?"

He looked up and shut his notebook. "Sure, Mrs. Durkin."

"Thank you. Wait just a moment while I write this note." She wrote rapidly, not scribbling but small, neat, businesslike script. When she had finished, she folded the paper, put it in an envelope, sealed the envelope, and wrote "Mr. Hoff" on it. "Mr. Hoff is an assistant principal. You know that, I'm sure."

"Yes, ma'am."

"I'd like you take this to him, Billy, and I want you to wait for a reply, written or oral. If the bell rings before you get it, you are not to go to your next class. You are to wait for that reply. Leave your books here. I'll give you a note excusing you when you come back for them."

He explained about waiting to Mr. Hoff when he handed him the envelope; Mr. Hoff looked slightly baffled but told him to wait in the outer office.

Sue Sumner sat with him on the bus going home. Sue got off with him, too, although it was not her regular stop. Shep had been waiting at the stop, and she petted Shep until the other kids had gone. Then she said, "What's bothering you, Bill?"

"You could tell, huh?"

"I talked to you twice, and you didn't hear me. At first I thought you were ditching me—"

"I wouldn't do that!"

"The second time I saw that you were just so deep inside yourself . . ."

He nodded.

"Now you look like you're too big to cry. What is it?"

"First period." He cleared his throat. "I won't be there. I've got to go to the office. Are you going to tell everybody?"

Sue shook her head. She was wearing a guy's shirt, jeans, and very little makeup; and she was so lovely it hurt to look at her.

"I've got to talk to the psychologist. They think I'm crazy."

She put her hand on his shoulder. "You're not. You'll be fine."

He shrugged. "I think I'm crazy, too. I have crazy dreams."

"Everybody has crazy dreams."

"Not like this. Not the same thing, night after night."

"About me?" She smiled.

"Yeah. Kind of. How did you know?"

She smiled again, impishly. "Maybe I'll tell you, and maybe I won't."

They began to walk. He said, "Shep and I will walk you home."

"I kind of thought you would."

"Maybe I could leave the house a little early tomorrow and go over to your stop and wait there with you?"

Her hand found his. "I kind of thought you might do that, too. Tell me about your dreams."

"It's all kinds of stuff, only it's always about this place way far off. The gold towers. They're the color of your hair. Don't get mad."

"I'm not mad."

"Me and Shep are trying to get there. Shep can talk."

She squeezed his hand.

"I've got this sword. It's a beautiful sword, and there's writing on the scabbard and writing on the blade. The writing on the scabbard is important. Really, really important."

"Are you making this up?"

He shook his head. "If I was, it wouldn't be so scary. The writing on the blade is more important than the writing on the scabbard, but you have to read the scabbard, all of it, before you read the blade. It's all very hard to read because the writing's really old-fashioned. Shep can't read it at all, but I can a little. Last night I was able to make out the first three words."

"I bet you couldn't remember them this morning."

"Sure I can." He spoke the words.

There was an old woman in a rocking chair on the porch of a house they were passing. She called, "Hello, Sue. Hello, young man."

Sue stared, then smiled. "Hi, Aunt Dinah." (It seemed to him that there had been some slight obstruction in Sue's throat.)

"Would you and your young man like to come in for some iced tea?"

"Next time, Aunt Dinah. I've got to get home and do my homework."

A middle-aged man with glasses came out of the house and spoke to Aunt Dinah. She smiled at this man, and said, "I live here with you, sir." When she turned back to them, she said, "That's a fine young man you've got there, Sue. Hold onto him."

When they were a block past that house, he said, "We're going across these hills, Sue. Shep and me are. We found this girl, a beautiful girl with long black hair. Something had her foot, and it was pulling her into a hole, and—"

"I don't want to hear any more about your dreams," Sue said softly. "Not right now. Let's just walk for a while. Not talking."

He nodded. This was Spruce Street, and there was a house there where the people had actually planted spruce trees between the street and the sidewalk. He did not know the people; but he had always felt sure he would like them if he ever met them, because of that. Three houses down, a sleek Mercedes sedan was parked at the curb. He had seen it before, although he did not know the owner. He stared at it as they passed, because it looked different—different in a warm and friendly way, as though it knew him and liked him.

They had turned onto Twenty-third and walked another block before he figured it out. The Mercedes had always looked like something that would never be in his reach. Now it looked as if it was, as if it was a car he could own any time he decided he really wanted one.

Sue said, "I'm ready to talk now, Bill. Is that all right?"

He nodded. "I'm ready to listen."

"There were two things I had to say." She paused, small white teeth gnawing at her lower lip. "They are important, both of them, and I knew I ought to say them both. Only I couldn't figure out which one I ought to say first. I think I have, now. Have you ever been like that?"

He nodded again. "I usually get it wrong."

"I don't believe you." She smiled very suddenly, and it was as though the sun had burst from behind a cloud. "Here's the first one. Do you know why high school is so important?"

"I think you'd better tell me."

"It's not because it's where you learn History or Home Ec. It's not even because it's where you get ready for college. It's because it's where some people—the people who aren't going to be left behind—decide what they want to do with their lives."

He said, "My brother decided he was going into the Navy."

"Yes. Exactly. And I've decided. Have you?"

He shook his head.

"What I'm going to do is you, Bill." Her voice was low but intense. "I'm going to stick with you. I think you're going to stick with me, too. I'll see to it. But if you don't, I'm going to stick with you anyway. On the bus I thought maybe you were going to try to ditch me. Remember that?"

"I would never ditch you," he said, and meant it.

"Well, even if you do, I'll still be around. That's the first thing I wanted to say—the thing I decided ought to come first. Now I've said it, and I feel a lot better."

"So do I." He discovered that he was smiling. "You know, I've got this problem, and it felt really, really important. But it isn't. Not anymore."

She smiled. "That's right."

"I was thinking how to tell my parents. That was the part that really had me worried—how could I put part of it off onto them. I didn't think of it like that, but that's what it was. Well, I'm not going to. Why should they worry, when maybe they don't have to? If that school psychologist wants them to know, she can tell them herself. 'Oh, by the way, Mrs. Wachter, your son is crazy.' Let's see how she likes it."

"Here's the other thing I have to tell you," Sue Sumner said; her voice was so low that he could scarcely hear her. "That used to be Aunt Dinah's house, back there. But Aunt Dinah's dead."

The sky had not changed. The sun that was always to their left was to his left still. The racing clouds raced on, with more after them, and more after them, a marathon for clouds in which a hundred thousand were competing.

It must never change here, he thought. Then he realized that all his dreams had taken little time here, no more than a few hours.

The black-haired girl was still sitting on the ground, rubbing a slender white ankle that showed the livid mark of a clawed hand.

Soil wet with blood still clung to the blade of his sword. He wiped it with dry grass, wishing for rags and a can of oil. Reminding himself not to read the blade—not that he could have if he had wanted to.

The girl looked up at him, and her eyes were large and dark, forest pools seen by moonlight. "Not many men would have thought to do that," she said. Her voice was music, dark and low. "And no other man would have dared."

"I'm just glad it worked," he said. "What happened?"

For a moment she smiled. (When she smiled he felt he would have followed her to the end of the world.) "I didn't see the hole, that's all. The grass hid it."

He nodded and sat near her, though not too near. Shep lay down at his feet.

"I wasn't looking. I should have been looking, but I wasn't. It's my own fault. I might as well say that right now, because it's the truth and I'll never be at peace until I admit it. I hate stupid, careless people. But I was stupid and careless. Do you try to tell the truth?"

"Mostly, yes."

"I try constantly, but I lie and lie. It's my nature." She smiled again. "I have to keep fighting it, and though I fight it all the time, I don't fight hard enough."

He recalled something his biology teacher had told him. "DNA is destiny."

"You're a wizard, aren't you." It was more accusation than question.

"No," he told her. "No, I'm not."

"Oh yes, you are." The smile teased her mouth; it was a small mouth, and its perfect lips were very red. "You've cast a spell on me, because I lie and lie but when I said you were a wizard that was the truth. How old are you? Really?"

He could not remember.

"You wizards can make yourselves young again. I know that, but I don't care. You're *my* wizard, and you saved me, and I love you. Now you look modest and say you love me too."

He tried.

She gave her ankle a final rub. "I *wish* this mark would go away. I know it won't, but I wish it would."

Rising, Shep licked it once, shook his head, and backed away.

"Your name is . . . ?"

"Bill."

She cocked her head. "Are you making fun of me, Bill?"

"No," he told her. "I wouldn't make fun of you. Not ever." He meant it.

"My name is Biltis." She rose effortlessly, and he stood up hurriedly. She took his hands in hers. "They'll want to know who my lover is, and I'll say Bill, and they'll laugh at me. Don't you feel sorry for me? Look! I've lost a slipper! Am I not richly deserving of your pity?"

"Maybe it's still down in there," he said, and knelt, and was about to thrust his hand into the hole.

"Don't!" She seized his shoulders, pulling him back. "I was only joking! Y-y-you . . ."

Surprised, he turned to look at her. Her crimson lips were trembling, the great, dark pools moist with tears.

"You mustn't! They're down there. You mustn't reach into holes, or go into caves or—or go down in wells or cisterns. Nothing like that, ever again. They never forget and they never forgive. Oh, Bill!"

She was in his arms. He clasped her trembling body, astonished to find it small and light. He kissed her cheek and neck, and their lips met.

"Come in and sit down, Billy." The woman behind the desk was dark, heavy, and middle-aged, with a warmth in her voice that made him want to like her.

"Are you really the psychologist?"

"Uh-huh. You were expectin' Doctor Gluck, I bet. She left at the end of the last term. I'm Doctor Grimes." Dr. Grimes smiled broadly. "Why don't you sit right there? I don't bite."

He did, on the edge of a chair more comfortable than most school chairs.

"Do you like bein' Billy? Would you rather be William?"

"Bill," he said. "I like people to call me Bill. Is that all right?"

"Sure, Bill. Bill, I'm goin' to start right off tellin' you somethin' I ought not to tell you at all. I like havin' you here. I been counselin' for close to twenty years now. That's what I do, I'm a counselor. And it's almost always drugs or liquor. Or stealin'. Here at this school, it's it's been drugs, up to now. Nothin' else. Let me tell you, Bill, a person gets awfully, awfully tired of drugs. And liquor. And stealin'. So I'm real glad to see you."

He waited.

"I got this notebook they took away from you." She opened the file folder on her desk and held it up. "I read it. Probably you mind, but I had to or else I wouldn't have known what was bein' talked about. You see? I wouldn't have known what kind of things to say, either. Maybe you'd like it back?"

He nodded.

She put it down in front of him. "I'll tell you what I thought when I was readin' it. About that dog and the li'l bird singin' and all. I thought, why, this boy's got a real imagination! I told you about those drug people I got to talk to all the time. And the liquor people, too, and the stealin' people. All them. They haven't got—you know why people steal, Bill?"

He shrugged. "They want the stuff, I guess."

"You guess wrong. You ever see stuff you wanted? In a store or anythin'?"

"Sure."

"Uh-huh. You steal it?"

"No." He shook his head. "No, I didn't."

"They do. They take it. They take it 'cause they can't imagine anythin' will happen. They do that maybe a hundred times, and then they get caught. Only next time they can't imagine they're goin' to get caught *this* time. Why are you smilin'?"

"You reminded me of somebody. Not somebody real."

"On the TV?" She was watching him narrowly.

"No." He sensed that he had been cornered and would

be cornered again. It would be best, surely, to tell the truth to this friendly woman and try to get her on his side. "In a dream I've been having. That's all."

"You like her. You wouldn't have smiled like that if you didn't. Is she pretty?"

He nodded.

" 'Bout how tall?"

"Up to my chin." He touched it.

"That's in real high heels, I bet."

"No, ma'am. Barefoot."

"Uh-huh. Hasn't got no clothes?"

It was going to be complicated. He said slowly, "She wasn't barefoot to start with. She had slippers, like. Really beautiful slippers with jewels on them. Only she lost one, so she took the other one off. She has on a—a dress with a long skirt. It comes down nearly to her feet. It's gold and red, and has jewels on it, all over."

He waved his hands, trying to indicate the patterns. "It's really, really pretty."

Dr. Grimes was nodding. "I bet she smells good, too."

He was glad to confirm it. "You're right, she smells wonderful."

"You smell things in this dream?"

He hesitated. "Well, I smelled her. And I smell the wind sometimes, the freshness of it. Or the ocean, when it was blowing off the ocean."

"You ever kiss this girl?"

"Biltis." He felt himself flushing. "Her name's Biltis. We laughed about it."

He waited for Dr. Grimes to speak, but she did not.

"I didn't really kiss her. She kissed me."

"Uh-huh. What happened after?"

"She whistled. I didn't think a girl could ever whistle that loud, but she did. She whistled, and this big bird came down. It looked like an eagle, kind of, but it was bigger and had a longer neck. It had a bridle and reins. You know? Those long leather things you steer with?"

Dr. Grimes nodded. "Uh-huh, I know what reins are."

"And she got on it and it flew away." He closed his eyes, remembering. "Only it talked to me a little first."

"This big bird did."

"Yeah. It said I better not hurt her. But I wouldn't. Then it flew away, and she waved. Waved to me."

"I see. That was real nice, wasn't it?"

He nodded. "I won't ever forget it."

"Maybe you'll see her again." Dr. Grimes was watching him closely.

"I don't know."

"Do you want to, Bill?"

"I don't know that either. She scared me, a little."

Dr. Grimes nodded. "Sure. You ever see her when you weren't sleepin'?"

"I don't think so."

"Only you're not sure?"

"No," he said. "No, I haven't."

"All right. I want to talk about awake now, Bill. Funny things happen to everybody, sometimes. I know funny things happen to *me*. Like just last Wednesday I saw a li'l boy that looked just like a certain li'l boy I had gone to school with—like he never had grown up, and here he was, just the same. Anythin' like that happen to you?"

He shook his head.

"Oh, I bet. You know there was somethin'. Tell me now."

He cleared his throat. "Well, I had walked over to somebody's house, and I was coming back. Shep and me."

"Shep."

He nodded.

"Can I ask why you walked over to this house, Bill?"

"Well, it seemed like I ought to. She got off at my stop. Off the bus."

"Uh-huh."

"So I had walked her over to her house. We talked. You know?"

Dr. Grimes chuckled. "She likes you, Bill. If she didn't like you, what's she gettin' off at your stop for? And you like her. If you didn't, what you walkin' her home for?"

"Yeah, I guess. Well, I was coming back home, and Sue's—this girl's aunt Dinah came out of her house and stopped me. She's an old lady, and she's not really this one girl's aunt. She was a friend of this girl's grandmother's."

"I got it. What she say, Bill?"

"She said she needed a big, big favor. She said she owed me already, but she needed another favor, a big one. Shep didn't like her."

Dr. Grimes leaned forward, her face serious. "Did she want you to do somethin' bad, Bill?"

"I don't think so. She just said that this girl's family probably has some pictures of her when she was young. Of Aunt Dinah. Now she'd like to have them, and would I see if I could get them for her. As many as I could. I said all right, but Shep says—I mean he doesn't like her. I don't think he likes me being mixed up with her."

"Shep's your dog?"

"No, ma'am."

"But he's a dog. Does he really talk, Bill?"

It was easier because he had just said it. "No, ma'am."

"You goin' to try to get the pictures?"

"Yes, ma'am. I asked this girl, and she said she'd look and bring them to school today, any she found. If she's got any, I'll take them over after school."

"That's not a bad thin' you're doin', tryin' to help out a old woman like that."

"No, ma'am," he said, "but I thought it was pretty weird. Why didn't she just phone Sue's mom?"

When they got off the bus that afternoon, he dropped his books at his house and put on Sue's backpack for the walk over to hers. The pictures, faded black-and-white snapshots, were in a white envelope in the pocket of his shirt, under his sweater.

There were more leaves on the sidewalk today; the maples had turned to scarlet and gold, and a bush in somebody's yard to a deep, rich crimson. "In my dream," he said, "where I've got that sword?"

Sue looked at him sidelong.

"It's beautiful. It's just so beautiful I can't hardly stand it sometimes. But it's just brown hills and purple mountains way, way off. And the blue sky, with the white clouds moving fast across it. What makes it so pretty is the way I feel about it. I see everything, and I see how great it is. The big bird with the girl riding him, and her hair and her scarf blowing out behind her. She waved, like this, and she had a gold bracelet on her wrist. The sun hit it, and it was the most beautiful thing I ever saw in my life."

"I don't think I like her," Sue said.

"Aunt Dinah?"

"This girl in your dream."

"Oh. I'm not sure I do either. But what I started out to say was that I'm getting to see things here the same way as there. That's really, really beautiful, like I said. But here it's beautiful, too. More beautiful than there, really. Biltis is beautiful. She really is, and her dress is really pretty, and her jewelry didn't just cost a lot, it's like looking at stars. But you're more beautiful than Biltis is."

Quickly, Sue turned again to look at him.

"If your dress was as pretty as hers and you had jewelry as nice as hers is, you'd be homecoming queen and she'd be a maid of honor. You know what I mean?"

Sue took his hand, and that was answer enough.

"So I've been thinking. Pretty soon I might be able to do that. Give you a dress that was so beautiful people would just stop and stare, and jewelry."

Shep said, "Good!" though Sue seemed not to hear him.

"I've been thinking about other stuff, too."

"Have you, Bill?"

"Yeah. Lots of things." He took the white envelope from his pocket. "Like I'd like to show her to you. Show you Biltis, if I could. If I was good in art, the way you are, maybe I could draw her. I'm not, but I can show you pretty close, just the same."

He took out a photograph.

"Like this. The sharp chin, and the little mouth. The big eyes, especially."

"That's Aunt Dinah," Sue told him. "Aunt Dinah, when she was about twenty."

"I know," he said.

"Anyway, she can't really be dead, can she?"

Shep growled softly, deep in his throat.

"I figured it out," Sue continued, "while I was looking for those pictures. See, my mother didn't want me going over there, so she told me Aunt Dinah was dead so I wouldn't. We went to some funeral, some old lady's, and when we got home she told me it was Aunt Dinah. I think I was in kindergarten then. Doesn't that make sense, Bill?"

"Sure," he said.

"I mean, you said she came out and stopped you on the street. Ghosts don't do that."

"I guess not."

"She didn't want to talk to me, because she knew my mother was mad. And she couldn't phone the house."

He said, "Right."

"But maybe you could get them for her. See? That's the only way everything fits."

He said, "We've still got to take her the pictures."

Sue nodded. "Yes, we do. That's why I brought them. I don't know what my mother was so mad about, and it was a long time ago anyway. You ought to forgive people after a while, unless it's something really bad. Dogs are good at that. We ought to learn from them."

She leaned down to pet Shep. "What about the big Social Studies test tomorrow? Have you been studying?"

"Yeah," he said, "only I missed class today. I had to talk to the shrink."

"It wasn't bad, we just reviewed Europe. Would you like me to fill you in a little, when we get to my house? I mean, I'll just tell my mother you weren't in class today, so I'm going to tell you what we talked about."

"Sure!" He smiled. "I've been hoping I could get you to do that. Boy! Am I lucky!"

"Okay. Suppose you got to go to Paris. Give me three or four things you'd like to see there."

He was silent for a moment, concentrating. "The big art museum."

"The Louvre. Ms. Fournier will give you a lot better grade if you use the French name. She teaches French, too."

"I know," he said.

They had reached the house. Still holding the snapshots Sue had brought to school, he climbed four steps to the porch and rang the bell.

"Maybe she won't be home," Sue said from the foot of the steps. "You could just leave them in the mailbox, Bill."

"I'm going out for football." He looked back at her, grinning. "Football players don't just leave them in the mailbox."

He rang again, hearing heavy male footsteps from inside the house.

Sue joined him on the porch. Her deliciously rounded chin was up, but she took his left arm and held it tightly.

A rumpled man opened the door and asked what they wanted.

"My mother had these . . ." Sue's voice faded away. "Tell him, Bill."

He nodded, and held them out. "There's an old lady living with you, I think her name's Dinah?"

The rumpled man shook his head. "There's no old lady living here, son. Forget it!" His face was hard and a trifle stupid, the face of a man whom life had defeated, who could not understand why he had been defeated so easily.

Bill said, "But you know who I mean. I promised her I'd bring her these pictures if I could, and—"

"Do you know her? You knew her name, so you've got to. You tell her to get out of my house and quit bothering me and my family."

Sue's grasp tightened. "Bill . . ."

"It's her house," he told the rumpled man, "or anyhow she thinks it is. She thought it was hers, probably, a long time before you were born, Mister. I'll tell her what you said if I ever see her again, but I'm going to give you some advice right now. Take these pictures and don't tear them up or anything. Leave them someplace where they'll be easy for her to find. On the mantel or someplace like that. Let go of my arm for a minute, Sue."

He turned over the white envelope, took a pencil from his pocket, wrote "Dinah/Biltis" on the front, and handed the envelope to the rumpled man in the doorway. "That might help. I don't know, but it might. I'd do it if I were you."

After supper that evening, Ray Wachter asked his son why he was studying so hard, saying, "You've been at those books for a couple of hours now. Is it anything I can help you with?"

"Just Social Studies." He closed the book and looked up. "But I'm going out for football—"

"You are?"

"Yeah. It's sort of too late. Almost too late, but I just decided today. You've got to keep your grades up, or they won't let you play."

Ray Wachter tried to conceal the pride he felt; he was a simple man, but not an unintelligent one. "They might not let you play a lot anyway, Bill. You're not a Junior, you know. Don't get your hopes too high."

"Well, this is the first big test in Social Studies, and I'm not too hot in that." Two words from the scabbard popped into his mind, and he pronounced them almost automatically.

"What the hell was that?" Ray Wachter took off his glasses, as if their lens could somehow block hearing.

"What language, you mean?" Bill tilted his chair back, yawned, and stretched. "No language of this world, sir, nor do I know its proper name. I suppose it's nearer to Chaldean than anything else we have here."

"You're a funny kid, Bill."

He smiled. "Only too often, sir. I fall over my own feet, I know." When his father had gone, he murmured to himself, "I think it must mean, 'Let me be numbered among the learned.'"

He and the dog tramped over the plain, mile upon mile. There seemed to be no convenient way for him to wear the sword. He had tried thrusting its scabbard through his belt, but it slipped and tripped him, and proved to be much less convenient than carrying it, and the long blade it held, over his shoulder.

"Dark," Shep said.

"Pretty dark, yes. Do you mean that night is coming?"

"Yep."

"We ought to have a tent or something." He searched his pockets. "I don't even have anything we could use to start a fire, and there's nothing out here to burn except grass."

Shep said nothing.

"This is a little like a Jack London story. But I don't like that story and have no intention of repeating it. Are you getting tired?"

"Nope."

"Then we should keep walking, for a while at least. Why did she blow her kiss at me, Shep? Who was she, anyway?"

Shep said nothing.

"That's right, you never saw her. I don't mean Biltis, I mean the woman on the rock by the sea. She had an apple, a gold one. She wanted me to bite it, but you can't bite gold."

"Nope?"

"Nope. It's a soft metal, but not soft enough to bite, except for very thin gold leaf. They used to coat costly pills with that."

"Spring."

"This weather? Perhaps you're right, but it seems like fall to me. Very early spring, possibly."

"Water. I smell it. Smells strong."

He smiled. "Then it's probably not good to drink."

"Good water."

"If you say so. I'm learned now, or think I may be, but being learned isn't the same as being wise—I'm wise enough to know that, anyway. Wise enough to trust a dog's judgment of what he smells."

The wolf-wind that had driven the clouds before it like terrified sheep had come down to earth. It ruffled his hair and raced beneath his shirt. He shivered, conscious for the first time of both thirst and cold.

"Talking of water brings us back to the woman on the coast," he told Shep to distract himself from his discomfort. "Let's assume she's someone famous, or anyway someone known. A woman as lovely as she is and as mysterious as she is could hardly stay unknown for long. If we list what we know about her, we may find a clue to her identity."

Shep glanced up at him. "If you say so, Chief."

"Prima." He shivered again, and strove to walk a trifle faster. "She was on a rock in the sea. I'm tempted to say by the sea; but it was actually in the sea, although not very far out."

"Okay," Shep said.

"Secunda, she was nude. Both these seem to indicate that she had come up out of the sea. People on land wear clothing to keep off the sun and to keep warm." (At that moment he dearly wished his own would keep him warmer.) "People in the sea have no need to keep off the sun and cannot be warmed by ordinary clothing.

"Tertia, she was strikingly beautiful.

"And quarta, she held the golden apple I have already mentioned. That covers it, I think."

Shep made a small noise that might, or might not, have been of assent.

"You're quite right. There is more. Quinta, she had extraordinary hair. It seemed black and blond together. Not black in places and blond in others, but both at once. Sexta—a suggestive ordinal, Shep—wishing to give a blessing or something of the kind, she kissed."

"Did she, Chief?"

"Yes. Yes, indeed, she did. And if it was not her kiss that made me aware of the speech of animals, what did?"

They walked on in silence for a time. At length he said, "Do we know of any famous female who would appear to fit our description of her? It seems to me we do. We can call her Venus, or Aphrodite, or even Ishtar. She was born of the sea. Paris awarded her the golden prize called the Apple of Discord. She is the goddess of love, and we cannot understand any animal until we love it. Furthermore—"

"Over there!" Shep raced away.

The spring, when they found it, was wide and deep, and its water was clearer than any diamond. Shep drank, and he drank too, and marveled, by the sun's dying light, to see the cold, crystalline water welling from deep in the earth. It raced away as a noisy brook, narrow but by no stretch of the word feeble.

"Neither am I," he told Shep. "That water made me feel much stronger. I suppose I was becoming weak from thirst, and perhaps from hunger too."

He drank again, and the strength he knew was a strength he had never known before.

From his notebook . . . "Dr. Grimes has returned this to me. She wants me to record my dreams as I did earlier, and to show it to her at our next session. I will comply.

"Last night Shep steered me to a spring of strength. We drank from it. I felt much stronger and tested my strength by throwing stones, some so large I was astonished to find I could lift them. Shep ran as fast as my stones flew, which I think remarkable. (This morning he ran alongside our bus, following Sue and me to school. I believe he is out on the athletic field.)

"When I grew bored we sat beside the spring, I laboring to puzzle out the inscriptions on the scabbard by the dying light. The days must be longer there, or perhaps it is only that we move faster. I read each group of symbols again and again, if it can be called reading. Slowly, terribly slowly, the meanings of a few words creep into my mind. There are some I could pronounce if I dared, though I have no notion (or little) of what they may mean. There are others that I understand, or believe I may understand somewhat, although I have little or no idea of their pronunciation. It is a slow process, and one that may never bear fruit.

"And yet these spells are only a distraction, however hermetic they may be. What has happened to me? That is the question. Why do I find myself in that barren land each night? What land is it in which thaumaturgic springs rise from barren ground?"

* * *

"I want you to stay for a minute or two after the bell, Billy. Will you do that?"

His heart sank, but he nodded. "Yes, Ms. Fournier."

The bell rang even as he spoke. As the rest of the class trouped out, she smiled and motioned for him to join her at her desk.

"That essay of yours on the Louvre—I would have been amazed to see it from an undergraduate at Yale or Princeton, and delighted to receive it from a grad student. To get it here . . . Well, there simply are no words. I'm overjoyed. Flabbergasted. *Être noyé. Muet comme un poison.* Was it really a lodge in the dark ages? A place where they hunted wolves?"

"Que, Madame," he said, *"c'était comme les jours du Roi Dagobert."* Seeing her expression he reverted to English, and remained there.

"I shouldn't let you sign up this late," the coach told him. "I wouldn't, if we weren't short. What position do you play?"

"Whatever position or positions you want me to play, sir."

The coach grunted. "Damn right. Where do you think you might be good?"

"Nowhere, probably. But I'll try."

"Okay, we'll try you on the line. I want you to get down like this, see? One hand on the ground. That's good. When I count three, come straight at me as hard as you can. Don't use you hands but try to go through me. Try to knock me over. One—two—THREE!"

It was as though the coach were not in truth a man at all, but a sort of inflated figure, a man-shaped balloon to be shouldered aside.

Sue Sumner was sitting in the living room chatting with his mother when he came home. "I knew you'd be late because of football practice," she said, "but I didn't want to miss our walk. Is that all right?"

He nodded, speechless.

His mother said, "You're going to have supper at Sue's house, Billy. She phoned home, and then I talked with Mrs. Sumner myself. She'll be very glad to have you—she's looking forward to getting to know you. Pot roast. Are you hungry?"

He nodded again, suddenly aware that he was ravenous.

"Your father's so proud of you! What position will you play? I want to be able to tell him when he gets home."

"Linebacker."

"Well, try to catch a lot of passes."

Outside, they petted Shep. "Your mom has no idea what a linebacker does, Bill."

He grinned. "Yes, I know."

"Do you want me to tell her? You know, just girl-to-girl when I get a chance?"

He looked down at Shep, who said quite distinctly, "Yep."

"Yes, I do. She may actually be interested now that I'm playing."

"Do you think they'll really let you? Play? I know a lot of guys just scrimmage with the team for the first year."

It was a good question, and he considered it for a block or more. "Yes," he said. "I'm going to have a tough time of it because I'm so new. Young men who have been on the team for what they consider a long while are not going to like my playing, and they'll like it even less if I start. But I believe I'll play, and even that I'll start."

"Don't count on starting," Sue said. "I wouldn't want you to be disappointed."

"Thank you. 'What if the rose-streak of morning pale and depart in a passion of tears? Once to have hoped is no matter for scorning. Love once, even love's disappointment endears. A minute's success pays the failure of years.'"

"Why, Bill! That's beautiful!"

He nodded. "It should be—it's Robert Browning. Can I tell you what I've been thinking?"

"I wish you would."

"I was thinking that football might just be a letdown. For me, for my parents, and for you. But it wouldn't matter, because you were here waiting for me when I got home from practice. What difference could football make after that? You were here, and it meant I had won. Practice and games are just bother. Busyness."

"Oh, Bill!" She took his hand.

"So after that, I thought what if you hadn't been here. And it hit me—it hit me very hard—that millions of other men will come home, and can't even hope that you might be there, waiting, the way you were for me. That even if you hadn't been there I would be privileged like nobody else on earth, because I could hope—really hope, not deluding myself—that you might be. That love's disappointments are better than success in other things."

He cleared his throat. "I realize I haven't expressed myself very well. But that's how my mind was running, and naturally I thought of Browning then, as anybody would."

"Can I tell you what I'm thinking now?"

He nodded. "Of course."

"I'm thinking what a jerk I was. I rode that bus for three solid weeks before I realized what was on it with me. That my whole future was sitting across the aisle, or three seats in back. What a jerk!"

He sighed, and could find no more words.

"Look sharp," Shep whined.

They were approaching the house at which he had left the snapshots, when a breathtaking brunette threw open its door. She was carrying a blue-and-silver jacket, and she held it up for their inspection before running across the porch and down the steps to meet them. "Remember me?"

He nodded. "Certainly."

Smiling, she held out her hand to Sue. "I'm Dinah— Dinah Biltis. I just want to give Bill this. It's cold, and he'll need it." She turned to him, holding the jacket open. "Here, take off that backpack and put your arm in."

He did.

"It's too big for him," Sue said, "and besides—"

"Bill's bigger than you know. Do you like it, Bill?"

"Yes," he said. "Very much." It was loose, but not excessively so. He lifted his arms to admire the sleeves: blue leather with silver slashes.

Without warning Dinah kissed him. At the next moment, she was fleeing back up the steps and into the house. He got out a handkerchief and wiped his mouth thoughtfully.

"Wow!" Shep barked. "Wow, Chief!"

Sue sighed. "I'm supposed to fly into a jealous rage, I think. Isn't that how it's supposed to go?"

He was snapping the jacket closed. "I have no idea."

"I think it is. Are you going to keep the jacket?"

"For the time being anyway."

"Suppose I asked you to give it back?"

He considered. "I'd want to know why. If you had a good reason, I'd do it."

"Suppose I didn't have any reason at all?"

Shouldering her backpack again, he began to walk. "I wouldn't do it. You told me what you had been thinking, a minute ago. Can I tell you what I'm thinking now?"

For an instant her eyes found his face, although she did not turn her head. She nodded without speaking.

"I've already got a mother. She's a good mother, and I love her. I need you, not another mother."

"If I say one more thing, will you get mad?"

"Nope," Shep told her.

"That's a letter jacket. You're not supposed to wear one unless you've lettered."

"There's no letter on it."

"Guys who've lettered are going to take it away just the same, Bill."

He grinned. "Then you'll have won. What's wrong with that?"

"Do you remember grandma's friend Dinah?" Sue asked her mother over pot roast.

"Oh my goodness! Yes indeed—Auntie Dinah. I haven't thought about her in years and years."

Chick said, "Was she the one that collected shawls? You used to talk about her, Mom." Chick was Sue's brother.

Sue's mother nodded. "That's right. I don't believe you ever knew her, though."

"You will," Sue told her brother. "She's back."

Sue's mother picked up the green beans. "Won't you have some more, Bill?"

He thanked her and took a second helping.

Sue said, "You probably didn't notice how old-fashioned her clothes were, Bill. That dark dress and those black stockings. Jet beads. They didn't really shout it, but they were the kind of clothes people wore—I don't know. A long time ago."

He chewed and swallowed, and sipped milk. No one spoke, and at last he said, "They were in one of the pictures. She will have new ones next time, I think."

"Can she do that?"

He shrugged. "My jacket wasn't in those pictures."

"Take it off!" Seth Thompkins demanded, and Doug Douglas grabbed him from behind.

"Sure," he said. "If you want it, I'll let you have it."

Doug relaxed somewhat. He slipped out of the jacket, kicked Doug, and hit the back of Doug's neck when Doug doubled up.

Seth's right knocked him off balance, and Seth's left caught him under the cheek bone. He hit Seth in the pit of the stomach, knocking him sprawling.

Martha Novick had stopped to watch.

"People on television talk a lot when they fight." He picked up his letter jacket and dusted it with his hand. "I don't think it's ever really like that. You're too busy."

"I guess I ought to tell Mr. Hoff," Martha said, "only I'm not going to."

He thanked her.

"Did you hurt them bad, Bill?"

"I don't think so," he told her. "They'll get up when I'm gone."

Dr. Grimes closed the notebook and smiled at him. "This is interesting stuff, Bill. Did you really dream it?"

He nodded.

"Armor that looked like your school jacket?"

"Somewhat like it," he said. "Not exactly. Do you care?"

Dr. Grimes nodded.

"All right. My school jacket's blue and silver. You must have seen them."

She nodded again.

"This is a short black leather coat. It's not blue or silver at all—the leather isn't, I mean. But it has steel rings sewn on it, and steel plates across the chest. Some of the steel plates and rings have been blued. Heat blued, I suppose. Do you know how to blue steel?"

"I couldn't do it," Dr. Grimes said, "but I've seen it. Sure, Bill."

"The rest have been polished bright. They'll rust, I'm sure, unless I keep them shined and oiled. So will the blue ones. But I'm going to do the best I can to take care of them. I'll put a little can of oil and a rag in my jacket pockets tonight before I go to bed."

She cocked her head. "Will that work?"

"I don't know. I believe it may."

"Uh-huh. You tell me, if it does. You been fightin'?"

He smiled. "You get around, don't you?"

"You goin' to law school when you get out of here?"

"Why do you ask?"

"'Cause you answer a question with a question when you don't want to talk. That's a lawyer trick, and lawyers make real good money if they're good. I don't get around a-tall, Bill. I just sit here in my office, talkin' and writin' down and answerin' the phone. But people come and tell me stuff. Got a li'l bruise on that sweet face, too. You really kick that one boy?"

He nodded. "Are you goin' to report me?"

"Huh-uh. Maybe somebody will. I don't know, Bill. But not me."

"I kicked him, and they would have kicked me if they'd gotten a chance. We weren't boxing, we were fighting. How can you play fair, when you're not playing?"

"You're on the football team now."

He nodded.

"Goin' to start against Pershing. That's what I heard."

"The coach hasn't said that to me. I can play halfback and linebacker—or at least he says I can—and I've been practicing those positions. I just hope I get in the game."

"Uh-huh." She smiled. "I was married to a football player, one time. Dee-troit Lions. I used to go to all the games back then, and I still watch a lot. On the TV, you know. You know what they tell me about you, Bill?"

He shook his head.

"They say you always catch a pass. Two men coverin' you. Three. It don't matter. You always catch it."

"I've been lucky."

"Uh-huh. Ms. Fournier, she says you're a genius. You been lucky there, too, I guess."

"I don't think so."

Dr. Grimes sat in silence for half a minute regarding him. At last she said, "If a boy's too smart, the other boys don't like that, do they? Maybe he was just lucky, but if he'd been luckier he would have missed a question. Maybe two. I ever tell you I like you?"

He nodded.

"I do, Bill. First time I talked to you, you seem like such a nice kid, and you got a good imagination. Now you seem like a nice man with a real good education and a kid's face. That first one was interestin'. This one here, this is real interestin'."

"You're wrong," he said.

"I get up in the mornin', and I want to come to work. That's because of you. How am I wrong, Bill? Tell me."

He rose, sensing that the period was nearly over. "You think I've grown up, somehow, inside. I haven't. I know a lot more than I did, because I've been trying to decipher the runes on the scabbard. But I'm still Bill Wachter, and I'm still young. Inside. 'When all the world is young, lad, and all the trees are green, and every goose a swan, lad, and every lass a queen. Then hey for boot and horse, lad, and round the world away. Young blood must have its course, lad, and every dog his day.'"

Dr. Grimes only watched him with thoughtful eyes; so

when a second, and two, had ticked past, he turned and went out into the hall.

She said nothing to stop him, and he was ten paces from her door when the bell rang.

Sue and a tall, smiling man in a checked sport coat were waiting for him when he left the locker room after the game. "This is Mister Archer," Sue said. "He's going to take us to Perry's for a bite, if that's all right with you, Bill. Is it?"

He smiled. "Do you want to go?"

"Not if you don't."

"Then I do," he said, and her hand slipped into his.

Mr. Archer's car was a red Park Avenue Ultra with tinted windows. "You two sit in back," he told them. "It'll take twenty minutes or so, and I can't talk worth a damn when I'm driving."

Mr. Archer got in and tilted the rearview mirror up; and Bill opened the door for Sue, and got in himself on the other side. By the time that they had left Veterans Avenue behind, and with it the last traffic of the game, his hand had slid beneath her sweater and under the waistband of her skirt.

She was prim and ladylike when Archer opened the door of the car for her; but she left as soon as Perry's headwaiter had seated them, to repair her makeup in the restroom.

"Beautiful girl," Mr. Archer said appreciatively. "You know her long, Bill?"

"Yes and no." Although he had held the restaurant's door for them both like a gentleman, and had pulled out Sue's chair for her (beating the headwaiter to it by one tenth of one second), his mind was still whirling. "We rode the same bus last year, and she was in my home room and some of my classes. It was the fourth week of the school year before we got to be close friends." He cleared his throat. "September twenty-second."

Archer smiled. "You remember the exact day."

"Certainly."

"You didn't play last year, did you? I don't think freshmen are eligible."

He shook his head, trying to recall his freshman year. Things had been so different then. So very, very different. So very much worse. "No," he said. "You're correct, they aren't, and I wouldn't have gone out anyway."

"She couldn't have known you'd be a star."

"She didn't even know I'd go out. That day—the day we really noticed each other—I hadn't decided to do it. Or even thought about it, really."

"Sue didn't tell you what I do." Mr. Archer took a card folder from a pocket of his sports coat, fished out a card, and laid it on the table between them. "I'm an assistant coach, just like that card says. I coach offense, and I go to high-school games whenever I get the chance, Bill, hoping to spot some real talent. Mostly I don't."

"In that case," he said slowly, "it was very nice of you to take us out like this."

A waiter came; Mr. Archer ordered a John Collins and two Diet Cokes.

"There are fifty players on each team this early in the season," Mr. Archer said, "so a hundred altogether. Why am I being nice to you?"

"I suppose because my parents weren't there. I ought to explain that. They wanted to come, but I begged them not to. I was afraid I wouldn't get to play at all, and that if I did I'd play badly."

Returning, Sue said, "You didn't, Bill. You made the Panthers look like monkeys out there."

Mr. Archer said, "The score was twenty zip. Who scored all three touchdowns?"

"I was lucky, that's all."

"Five times I saw you catch passes that ought to have been incompletions. Three times I saw you catch passes that should have been interceptions."

A waitress brought their drinks.

"You know the three times rule, Bill? Once, that's an accident. Twice, that's a coinkydink. Three times, that's enemy action. You were the—what school was that, Bill? Who were you playing?"

"Pershing." Sue had gripped his leg under the table and was squeezing hard, probably as hard as she could, but he had no idea why.

"You were Pershing's enemy," Mr. Archer said. "An enemy they couldn't handle. You weren't watching their coach, but I was—I used to coach high school myself. He was chewing nails and spitting them at his players."

"Bill," Sue whispered, "for just a minute I have to talk to you."

"So do I," Archer told her. "I need to tell him about some of the scholarships we've got. But all my talking will take quite a while, and maybe you won't. I'll go wash my hands."

Over his shoulder he added, "If you want nachos or anything just order. Steaks. Whatever. On me."

Sue leaned closer, her voice almost inaudible. "Our waitress. Did you look at her, Bill?"

He shook his head.

"It's Dinah."

Back in the Park Avenue Ultra, Mr. Archer asked where they wanted to go. Sue said, "Where Edison and Cottonwood cross. It's a white house, two stories, with a big porch. Okay, Bill?"

"We ought to take you home first."

"No way. You won't tell your folks a thing. Take us to Bill's house, Mister Archer. Where I said. His mom and dad shouldn't find out he's a hero from the paper."

"Sue . . ."

Archer said, "You're afraid I'll go in and buttonhole your parents. You want some time to think it over yourself first. Am I right, Bill?"

He was not, but Bill said he was.

"I understand, and I won't do it. Listen, Bill, I want to tell you something and I want you to remember it. I was all-city quarterback once, back before you were born. Where you are now? I've been there, too. I know what it's like. You keep my card and I'll talk to you again in a few days."

* * *

"Your folks are nice," Sue said as he walked her home. "They let me tell them all that stuff before they told us they'd been listening on the radio. Did you notice?"

He nodded.

"College games get on TV. State's always do, around here, because there are so many grads. Mister Archer didn't say that, so I'll say it now. Just something to think about, Bill."

"I am."

Sue glanced at him, then away. "Here's something else. My mom is a very good mother, but she works really hard. She has to be at work at seven, and when she gets home she has to clean and cook. I help as much as I can, and so does Chick. But she does most of it."

This time it was Shep who said, "Sure."

Sue did not seem to notice. "So she won't have listened to the game, Bill. I'm sorry, but she won't. I mean, I'll tell her tomorrow. But she won't have heard much about it on the radio."

He said, "That's good."

"In fact, she'll be in bed asleep by the time we get there. That's something else to think about, Bill."

Bill thought.

The hills were behind them, the plain ahead of them, flat and featureless, an empty expanse of dry brown grass across which a chill wind moaned. He had given the leather coat with its steel rings to Sue; its shoulders were too big for her and its sleeves too long, but that was good and the leather kept out the wind. "Where are we going?" she said.

He pointed. "See those mountains? There's a city, a golden city, on the other side. We're going there."

"What for?"

"Because it's the only place to go. You can go there, or you can die here. That's all the choices we have." He paused, considering. "I can't make you go there. I'd have to hit you or something, and tie you up when I slept, and I won't do that. Maybe there's something over that way, or over there. I don't know, and if you want to go look, I'll go with you. But—"

"I'm going where you're going, Bill." Sue's voice was firm. "I've already told you that. Only I've got a lot of questions."

"I haven't got any answers," he said.

There was a wild cry high overhead, as lonely and inhuman as the keening of a hawk. They looked up, and saw the great bird that had uttered it sailing through ragged cloud, and watched it circle and descend. "That's Biltis," he said. "Maybe she'll help us."

"She gave Sue a wand with which she can start fires," he wrote in his notebook the next day, "and said we would come to a river, and that there would be a cave in the bank which we were not to enter on any account.

"Sue clasped my arm and said, 'He belongs to me!' but Biltis only laughed and said I belonged to both of them, and that I had from the beginning."

"Come on in, Bill, and shut the door." Dr. Grimes waved toward a chair. "This here is Doctor Hayes. Doctor Hayes was my teacher a long time ago. Over there's Ms. Biltis from the School Board. I told them I wanted to get Doctor Hayes to consult, and they said okay, but they had to have somebody here to see what was goin' on. So that's Ms. Biltis."

Dinah said, "Bill and I have met already. Hi, Bill."

He said hi in return.

Dr. Hayes asked, "Does he always bring the dog, Tacey?"

Dr. Grimes shook her head. "He talks about it, but I never did see it before. Is that Shep, Bill?"

He nodded.

Dinah said, "It's contrary to our regulations to have a dog in the building or on school property unless it's a guide dog for the blind. In this case, the Board's willing to make an exception."

"That's good," Dr. Grimes said.

Dr. Hayes shaped a steeple from his fingers. "Why did you bring your dog today, Bill?"

"He's not really my dog," Bill said, "he's my lawyer."

Dr. Grimes looked surprised. Dinah laughed; she had a pretty laugh, and it made him feel better to hear it.

Dr. Hayes's expression did not change in the least. "I'm not sure I understand. Perhaps you'd better explain."

"I don't mean he's a real lawyer. He hasn't passed the bar. But I felt I needed someone to advise me, and I know Shep's smart and that he's on my side."

"I'm on your side too, Bill."

Dr. Grimes said, "So am I, Bill. I thought you knew that."

Dinah grinned; it was an attractive grin, and full of mischief. "We of the Board are always on the side of the students."

"But you're over there," Bill gestured, "and Shep and I are over here."

"I can fix that." Dinah got up and moved her chair so that she sat on his left and Shep on his right.

Dr. Hayes nodded to her. "Is there a statement you wish to make on behalf of the School Board before I begin?"

Dinah shook her head. "I'll reserve it."

"I would prefer that you not interrupt. Quite frankly, your presence poses a threat to the exploratory examination I wish to undertake. Interruptions may render it futile."

"What about the dog?" Dinah smiled.

Shep said, "Nope."

"If the dog proves to be an impediment, we'll dismiss with it, although I doubt that will be necessary."

Bill said, "I'm missing Social Studies."

Dr. Hayes nodded again. "We're aware of it, and we've discussed it with your teacher. She says you have already earned an A, that you know much more of the subject than her course is designed to teach her students. What day of the week is this, Bill?"

"Monday."

"Correct. And the date?"

"October fifth."

"Also correct. We are in a building of some sort. Do you know what building it is?"

"Kennedy Consolidated."

"And why are you here, Bill?"

He stroked Shep's head, at which Shep said, "Dunno."

"Bill?" Dr. Hayes sounded polite but wary.

"I was thinking, sir. I could offer three or four explanations, but I don't have much confidence in any of them. The truth is that I don't know. Why am I?"

"In order that you can provide those explanations, for one thing. Will you?"

Dr. Grimes said, "You see, Bill, what you say to us is goin' to be a whole lot more help than anythin' we could say to you. You been sittin' in some class with a teacher, day after day, I know. This's kinda like that, only you're the teacher now, and me and Ms. Biltis and Doctor Hayes, we're the class you're teachin'."

Shep said, "Go ahead, Chief."

"All right." He paused to collect his thoughts. "I've been writing down my dreams in study hall. You told me to do that, but I was doing it before you told me, and Mrs. Durkin read my notebook over my shoulder and decided that I was psychotic. She likes me, but she still thinks I'm psychotic. She feels sorry for me."

Dr. Hayes said, "We all do, Bill."

"Not me," Dr. Grimes said. "Bill can take care of himself. I only wish he'd help me understand him more, 'cause I don't. I don't indeed."

Dinah grinned again. "Me neither. I feel sorry—"

The telephone rang. Dr. Grimes picked it up and said, "Counselin'. Oh, hello, Sue. You know I never have met you, but I've heard a sight about you from this nice Bill Wachter. He thinks you got angel wings, you know that?

"Why, no.

"Now don't you worry. I got my 'pointment book right here. Maybe two o'clock tomorrow?

"That's good. No, don't you worry none 'bout Shep. I got him right here. I been talkin' to him my own self." Dr. Grimes laughed. " 'Course he hasn't said much back, Sue. But maybe he will. What he say to you?

"That's good. That Shep's a good sensible dog, Sue. Don't you worry. You come see me tomorrow."

Dr. Grimes' smile faded as she hung up. "Shep's been talkin' to Sue too, Doctor Hayes. Sue's Bill's girlfriend."

Dinah said, "One of them."

"He didn't say nothin' bad, only wantin' to know where

Bill was. So she told him and he went off. She'd like to see me, but the door was closed—just a minute ago, I guess—so she called from the phone in the cafeteria. Yes, Bill? You want to say somethin'?"

He nodded. "I've been pondering the speech of animals. It's not that the kiss that flew to me suddenly made animals talk. It's that the kiss let me understand what they were saying. Love is at the root of it. The more you love anyone or anything, the better you understand it. She kissed me, and I kissed Sue, and that may be the reason Sue understands Shep now."

"I got a cat I call Catcat," Dr. Grimes said. "I don't understand Catcat very good, but that Catcat understands *me* backward and forward too. She likes me more than I like her. That what you're sayin'?"

Shep said, "Yep."

Dinah said, "I'm going to interrupt here. Bill promised us several explanations and has delivered only one, that the Durkin woman thinks he's psychotic. I would like to hear the others. Also I want to say that I understand Shep perfectly—not that he's said much, but what he has said has been in plain Doggish, which is quite different from doggerel. If the student who called understands him too, she's no crazier than I am."

Dr. Hayes and Dr. Grimes stared at her.

"Bill's never kissed me. Is that supposed to make a difference? I've kissed him, though."

Dr. Hayes leaned toward Dr. Grimes. "I seem to be losing control of the situation, Tacey. My apologies."

"I guess you see now why I wanted you?"

Nodding, he turned to Dinah. "I take it you're a friend of Bill's family, Ms. Biltis?"

"Why, no. I don't know Bill's parents at all."

He cleared his throat. "She wants another explanation, and one just occurred to me. Would anyone like to hear it?"

Dinah said, "I would, Bill," and Dr. Grimes nodded.

"I don't credit this one either," Bill said. "I should make that clear. But I find it interesting." He held up his notebook. "Before I met Biltis I met a dwarf on horseback. Perhaps it would be more accurate to say that I was overtaken by him. It's all in here."

He paused, inviting them to read his notebook if they cared to. No one spoke.

"He gave me a sword. I want to call it an enchanted sword, and perhaps it is. Certainly the spells on the scabbard are magical, and doubtless those engraved on the blade are magical as well. I can read the spells on the scabbard somewhat. I read them badly and quite slowly, but eventually I can puzzle them out. Sue and Shep cannot read them at all."

Dr. Hayes said, "Do you feel that these enchantments explain your presence here, Bill? That the casting of a spell has compelled you to come, perhaps?"

He shook his head. "Not exactly. First of all, they are spells, not enchantments. That is to say, they're words of magical import. One merely speaks them, and no chanting is required, although I would think that many chants were required for the sword that was to bear so much magic."

Dinah giggled:

"Of course I have asked myself many times why such a sword should be given to me."

Dr. Grimes said, "It was your dream, Bill. You don't think that's reason a-plenty?"

"That's like saying that all islands are inhabited because all the islands from which we've received reports are." He shrugged. "I've had many dreams in which I wasn't given an enchanted sword, or a sword of any kind. If—"

Dr. Hayes interrupted him. "Do you feel a connection between this sword and your penis, Bill?"

He laughed, and so did Dinah.

Dr. Grimes said, "What *do* you think that sword might be connected to, Bill, 'sides this dwarf? Comin' from a dwarf, I know why Doctor Hayes said what he did, and lots of people think like that. How do you think? What does this sword you got in your dream make you think about?"

"Biltis," he said. As he spoke, Dinah slipped her hand into his.

"Is that the girl in your dream that rides that bird? I told Doctor Hayes about her, and maybe he'd like to read about her too, by and by."

Dr. Hayes said, "Perhaps I would, Tacey. Perhaps I should."

"I think so. Why does this sword make you think 'bout her, Bill?"

He looked from Dr. Grimes to Dinah, and back again. "I think that Biltis must be a princess or a queen. Something of that kind, in any case—a woman with a lot of power. I told you about the fire wand."

Dr. Grimes nodded.

"The wand proves that she has magical possessions, and can afford to give them away almost casually. When Sue and Shep and I went into the cave—she had told us not to, but we went anyway, because Sue wanted to get out of the wind. We were attacked, and Sue's wand was at least as important as my sword and Shep's teeth in beating our attackers back and getting the three of us out alive."

Dr. Grimes nodded again, encouragingly. "It was a good thing you got it, Bill."

"It was a good thing Sue did, or we would probably have been killed. And Biltis gave it to her. Sue is jealous of Biltis, but I don't think Biltis is jealous of Sue."

Dinah said, "Neither do I."

"Sue wants to keep me," he continued, "but Biltis feels she already has me, and I think she may be right. When I made the thing that had her by the foot release her, she told me very seriously that I must beware of underground places. I didn't trust her warning then, not wholly. I should have."

Dr. Grimes leaned toward him. "You think that tells why you're here now, Bill?"

"Indirectly. Why did the dwarf give me the sword?"

Dr. Hayes said, "It's your dream, Bill not ours. Why did he?"

"I don't know, of course. I can only guess. But my guess is that he did it because he had been ordered to—ordered by Biltis. When people talk of kings and queens, princes and princesses these days, it's as stock figures in marchen—pictures in a Nineteenth Century book that everyone is too busy to read. But I think that Biltis is a real queen, and real queens have subjects, hundreds of thousands of them, even in a small kingdom. Tens of millions in one the size of England. If a queen with real power had a sword written over with spells she couldn't read, she would look for someone who could, wouldn't she? And get him to read them for her?"

"Right, Chief," Shep said.

"It's your dream, Bill," Dr. Hayes repeated.

He nodded. "I'm not supposed to be explaining my dream, though, am I? I'm supposed to be explaining this—why you got me here. Very well. Suppose you got me here to tell you about the spells on the sword?"

Dinah said, "You've left something out. Perhaps you didn't think of it. Why didn't Biltis simply bring you the sword and ask you to read it?"

He shrugged. "You should know better than I. Possibly because I couldn't. I can read it only very slowly, and when I try, it's usually when we're going to camp, or rest for a while. To read it, I have to be able to see it, and we didn't have any way to make a fire until you gave Sue the wand. Now we'll have a fire and I may be able to puzzle out the writing by firelight."

He turned to speak to Dr. Hayes and Dr. Grimes. "Tell me something, please, and be just as honest as you can. It will mean nothing to you, but it's important to me. Haven't either of you noticed that Ms. Biltis here and the woman in my dream have the same name?"

"What are you talking about?" Dr. Hayes asked.

Dr. Grimes said gently, "They're not the same, Bill. This lady here's Ms. Biltis from the School Board, and the one in your dreams is," she referred to her notes, "Biltis."

Bill turned back to Dinah. "So that's the way it is."

"Yes." She gave him her impish smile. "Don't worry. It won't hurt them."

"I wasn't worried," he said.

"Careful," Shep muttered.

"I have a sword," Dinah told Dr. Grimes. "It's out in my car. I'd like to bring it in and show it to Bill, if no one objects."

Dr. Grimes looked to Dr. Hayes, who said, "What do you think, Tacey? Is he apt to become violent?"

Dr. Grimes shook her head. "He's always been just as nice as pie, 'cept playin' that football, and he's generally just catchin' passes and runnin' then. You want to cut anybody, Bill?"

"No," he said. "Certainly not."

Dinah had already gone, seeming almost to have melted away.

"Somebody goin' to ask you to read that sword, you think, Bill?"

He nodded.

"Me, too. You goin' to do it?"

"I don't know yet."

Dr. Hayes said, "Do you really think that there may be writing on it, Tacey? An engraved blade? Something of that sort?"

"I guess we'll see. Bill thinks she's the same as the lady in his dream, and I see why. She does act sort of like it. You think she got that mark on her foot, Bill?"

He nodded.

"I been wantin' to ask you 'bout that. The first time you seen her, she had her foot down in that hole?"

"Correct."

"She do that on purpose?"

Shep said, "Yep."

"Bill?"

"I don't know. Shep thinks so. If it was intentional, it may have been to explain a preexisting mark on her ankle."

"A birthmark, like," Dr. Grimes told Dr. Hayes. "You can see it through her nylons if you look close."

He shook his head. "You're being drawn into the patient's delusional system, Tacey."

"Okay, maybe I wasn't seein' nothin'. Maybe it was just a shadow. What you think, Bill? You 'gree with Doctor Hayes?"

Shep said, "Nope."

Dr. Hayes murmured, "You must know, deep inside, that there is no such mark, Bill."

"'I am Sir Oracle. When I ope my mouth, let no dog bark.'" He smiled. "Another possibility is that she wanted to warn me about the underground creatures—the cavernfolk, or demons, or whatever we choose to call them. If she wanted to show me—not merely tell me—that they are real and dangerous, she chose a good way to do it."

"Only you went in that cave anyhow," Dr. Grimes said. "Can I see your book?"

He passed it to her, and she flipped it open.

Dr. Hayes said, "Some of the teachers here don't think your dreams are real dreams, Bill. They don't believe that they are dreams and not daydreams, in other words. Does that surprise you?"

"Yes," he said, "I didn't know they knew about them. Mrs. Durkin has been talking in the teachers' lounge, I suppose."

"Are they real dreams, Bill?"

"I don't believe so. I don't believe they're daydreams either."

Dinah returned, shutting the door behind her. "Here it is." She held up a package loosely wrapped in brown paper. "I got it from a company in Georgia." She unwrapped it, ripping the paper. "I had them send it UPS Overnight. It cost a little more, but it was worth it."

A glittering hilt protruded from a sheath of unadorned black leather.

"Here, Bill. I'll hold this part, and you can pull it out."

He looked to Dr. Grimes for permission. She nodded, and he drew the gleaming double-edged blade clear of the sheath.

Dr. Hayes said, "Is that the sword you've been telling us about, Bill?"

He rose, weighing the sword in his hand.

Dr. Grimes said, "That isn't a magic sword at all, is it, Bill?"

He moved the sword, not thrusting or slashing with it, only testing its weight and balance.

"There's writin' on the blade up close to that handle,"

Dr. Grimes continued. "I been tryin' to read it, only I can't. Not from here."

" 'Made in India,' " Bill said absently.

Dr. Grimes laughed. "It can't be no magic sword if it's made there, can it, Bill?"

Dinah sniffed. "It's my sword, and I think it's a very nice sword."

"It feels well in the hand," Bill said, "and I can't believe that anyone would waste so much good workmanship on poor steel." He seemed to be talking to himself.

Dr. Hayes said, "But not a magic sword. I hope you agree, Bill?"

"I do." He looked up. "It is becoming a magic sword, however."

Shep said, "Good!"

"Because I'm holding it. Magic is flowing from me into the sword. I didn't know that could happen, but it can."

Dr. Hayes looked at Dr. Grimes, who said, "Bill, I know you're just havin' fun, but you're makin' Dr. Hayes here think you got something really wrong with you. It's not nice to fool people that way, and you could get in a lot trouble just doin' it."

"Because I said that?" He smiled. "Why is the Holy Grail holy, Doctor Hayes? Why does it perform miracles? It is the cup used by Christ at the Last Supper."

"Perhaps you can tell me, Bill."

"You don't know. Doctor Grimes?"

She shook her head.

"Because something—not magic, let's call it divinity—flowed from Him into the cup. We know that sort of thing happened, because once, when a sick woman touched Him, He said He had felt the power leave Him. *Dynamin* is the word employed in the Greek gospel—power, might. I might guess at the Aramaic word Christ actually employed, but I won't. Such things should not be guessed at. For me the word is *lygros.*"

A glow like the light from blazing wood wrapped the blade of the sword as he pronounced *lygros.*

"The magical power of death, the power to kill," he whispered.

There was a knock at the door.

"You put that away, Bill," Dr. Grimes told him sharply.

He ignored her.

Dinah called, "Come in!"

The door opened, and Ms. Fournier looked in with a worried smile. "Sue Sumner isn't in here, is she, Doctor Grimes?"

Shep said, "Nope."

"One of the students told me she wanted to talk to you, and I thought—I hoped . . ."

Dr. Grimes said, "I haven't seen her, Ms. Fournier. She's in my book for tomorrow."

"The chem lab supplies are stored in the basement," Ms. Fournier continued, "I suppose you know that. Mister Boggs sent her for some—oh!"

Shep had bounded past her, closely followed by Bill, sword in hand. With a murmured, "Excuse me," Dinah followed him, kicking off her high heels to run before she was three steps down the corridor.

"Me, too, honey." Heavier as well as older, Dr. Grimes required most of the doorway.

"Pardon me," Dr. Hayes said. He was holding his pipe; although it contained no tobacco, he thrust it resolutely into his mouth and clamped it with his jaw before striding away.

"I looked!" Ms. Fournier called after him. "So did Mister Boggs! She's not there!"

They caught up with Bill and Shep in the furnace room, where Hector Fuente turned from his unsuccessful argument with Bill to demand. "What're you doing here, lady?"

"I'm Dinah Biltis from the School Board," Dinah explained. "We're here to rescue Sue Sumner, if there's enough of her left to rescue."

"You got to have a pass."

"And I do. I'll show it to you in a moment. Have you looked in there, Bill? That iron door?"

He had not seen it. He lifted the steel bar and threw it aside.

It burst open, nearly knocking him down. The first hideous thing that rushed past him was not quite a corpse or a bear. The next had four legs and a multitude of arms, with an eye at the end of each. His first cut severed two, and they writhed on the floor like snakes. Others seized him; he broke their grip and drove his blade into the bulky, faintly human body. For perhaps five seconds, its death throes made it more dangerous than it had been in life.

Someone was shooting, the shots loud and fast in the enclosed space of the furnace room. He scrambled to his feet, reclaimed his sword, and saw Shep writhing and snapping in the jaws of a nightmare cat with foot-long fangs. With her back to the furnace, Dinah was firing a small automatic. Her last shot came as he took his first step, and the slide locked back. His blade bit the big cat's neck as though it had rushed into battle of itself, dragging him behind it. He felt it grate on vertebrae and cut free, severing the throat and the jugular veins, saw the great cat's jaws relax and the pitiful thing that dragged itself free of them and was so soon soaked by its own spurting blood.

Laying aside his sword, he embraced the dying dog. "Shep! Oh, my God, Shep!"

Dinah bent over them both, her empty gun still in her hand.

"Can't we heal him somehow, Biltis?"

She said, "You can, if you want to," and he repeated the words he had spoken once before, when he and Sue had walked past a certain house, whispering them into Shep's ear. The light of his blade shone through the clotting blood at that moment, purer than sunshine.

The three of them found Sue two miles underground and killed the things that had been guarding her. He wanted to carry her, but she insisted (her voice shaking and sharp with fear) that she could walk. Walk she did, though she leaned heavily on his arm.

Shep scouted ahead, sniffing the air and whining in his eagerness to be gone. After the first quarter mile, Dinah said, "This little flashlight's just about gone, Bill. See how yellow it is?"

"Yes. Out brief candle, and all that. Can we get back without it?"

"I think so. Remember the light from your sword? Do that again."

"I didn't think you saw that," he said.

"I see a lot. Do it again."

He muttered to himself, and when Sue released his arm, he fingered the blade; and a sapphire light crept up and down that deep central groove some call the blood gutter, and spread to the edges after a minute or two, and trailed, by the time they had gone another quarter mile, from the point. He relaxed a little then, and hugged Sue, and tried to make the hug say that they would make it—that she would see the sky again.

"Don't let them get me, Bill." It was a whisper from her mind, yet clear as speech. "Oh, please! Don't let them get me."

"I won't," he said, and prayed that he could keep the promise. "Are you on our side, Biltis? Really, really on our side?"

"Certainly," she said, and grinned.

Sue said, "You shot them. You wouldn't have, if you weren't on our side, would you?"

Dinah did not bother to reply.

"She wouldn't, would she, Bill?"

"Of course not," he said, "but I don't understand how she did it. Her gun was empty before we came in here."

"I had a spare magazine in my purse, that's all."

"One magazine?"

Dinah nodded. "Just one."

As they walked on (he with an arm about Sue's waist, she weeping and stumbling), he wondered whether Dinah had been telling the truth. She had sounded as though she might be lying, and it inclined him to trust her; she had been careful with her voice when she said she was from the school board.

The iron door it was closed and latched. He lifted the

latch, but the door would not open. He pounded on it with the hilt of his sword, which did no good at all, and the four of them threw their combined weight against it, which did no good either.

When the rest were exhausted he went back down the long tunnel, leaving Shep to protect the two women—or perhaps, Dinah and her little gun to protect Sue and Shep. By the fiery light of his blade he found something huge cowering in a crevice; he persuaded it to come out by telling it (entirely truthfully) that he would kill it if it did not.

When the two of them returned to the door, he called out to Dinah not to shoot, saying that the thing came as a friend. "If you will break this down for us," he told it, "we will leave the underground realm forever and trouble it no more. If you will not—or cannot—I will kill you. You've got my word on our departure, and on that too. Will you try? Or would you rather die here and now?"

The thing lifted the latch as he had, but the door would not open. It threw its weight against it, and it was bigger than any bull.

A crevice of light appeared. He put down his sword and got his fingers into it, and spread it as he might have opened the jaws of a crocodile, with veins bulging in his forehead and sweat dripping from his face, and the huge thing he had found throwing its terrible strength against the door again and again until the steel bar bent, and the boxes and barrels, the desks and chairs and tables that had been piled against it gave way.

They rushed out—Shep, Sue, Dinah, and he, climbing and stumbling over the fallen barricade. And the thing came after them, with Bill's sword in its hand; but Shep severed its wrist, Dinah put a bullet into its single eye, and he drove his reclaimed sword between its ribs until the quillons gouged its scales.

They found Drs. Grimes and Hayes dismembering the cat-like monster that had seized Shep, and feeding the parts to a hulking old coal furnace, assisted by Hector Fuente and his machete. "They lef' this ol' furnace here for standby when they went to gas," Dr. Grimes explained. "They lef' coal, too. Hector here, he tol' us all 'bout it. This ol' coal furnace, it don't need 'lectricity, so when the 'lectric goes off, like in a ice storm, he can run it to keep the pipes from freezin'."

"It is a great loss to science," Dr. Hayes added, "but it is not *my* science. Besides, we would be accused of faking our evidence—the inevitable result of such discoveries."

Dinah said, "They shut the door on us, Bill, and barred it, and piled all that stuff in front of us. Shall we kill them?"

He shook his head.

The four of them went up the stairs and out onto the athletic field, past the volleyball court and the tennis court, and onto the field on which the football team would practice after school.

"It's so g-good to be o-outside." Sue was trembling. "Look! There's good old Juniper Street. It—it d-doesn't look the way it did, not to me. It looks like a toy under somebody's Christmas tree. B-but it's Juniper and I love it. I always will, after—after that. Don't you love it too, B-Bill?" Her eyes had filled with tears.

"I do," he said, though he was not looking at it. "See the hardware store? And Philips Fabrics?"

As Sue nodded, Dinah whistled shrilly; a huge black bird plummeted toward earth at the sound of that whistle, a minute dot that became a hurtling thunderbolt. They watched it land (barked at by Shep), watched Dinah mount, and waved good-bye.

"Who is she, Bill?"

He shrugged. "Who am I? Who are you?"

"Bill's girl," Sue replied.

Repeating those words to himself, he turned to look at her. Her eyes were of the blue light he had seen upon his sword, her disheveled hair the gold of the towers; the tilt of her nose and the curve of her smudged cheek filled him with a longing so intense that he dared not kiss her.

"Are you sure, Sue?" He had struggled to control his voice, and failed.

She nodded without speaking.

"Then I want you to look higher than the hardware store and the fabric store."

He watched her. "No, higher. Off into the distance. What do you see?"

"Mountains!" Her eyes were wide. "Bill, those are mountains! There aren't any mountains around here. There aren't any mountains like those for a thousand miles."

"That's right." He began to walk again.

"You're going?"

"Yes," he said. "I'm going."

"Then I'm going with you."

Once they had left the town behind, the mountains were no longer impossibly distant. "One thing for sure," Sue said, "nothing will ever scare me after what happened today."

Shep wagged his tail in agreement. "Me too! Right, Chief?"

William Wachter shrugged. "I have a feeling that this was the easy part," he said.

Story Copyrights